AT THE EDGE OF DEATH

Rockson rolled down the hill as quick as he could move, oblivious to the sharp-edged rocks gashing his flesh. The ground where he had just been was ripped apart by Russian machinegun fire. He flew down the hill with animal speed, sliding, dodging, a bundle of pure energy. But it didn't help him. Two Red choppers suddenly swooped down on him through the smoke and peppered the hill with a blizzard of slugs, digging trenches in straight, deadly lines. Rockson tore to the side and kept heading for cover—until he heard the whoosh of an air-to-ground missile fired by one of the choppers. He knew that sound well. He had heard it a hundred times before. It meant someone was going to die. . . .

DOOMSDAY WARRIOR

BY RYDER STACY

ZEBRA BOOKS
KENSINGTON PUBLISHING CORP.

ZEBRA BOOKS

are published by

Kensington Publishing Corp.
475 Park Avenue South
New York, N.Y. 10016

First printing: May 1984

Printed in the United States of America

Prologue

2089 A.D. Ted Rockson alias "Rock" is "The Doomsday Warrior." He fights back against the Russian invaders who now control post-World War III America—a land decimated by nuclear missiles from Russia's first strike.

One hundred years after the massive Soviet surprise nuclear attack much of the United States is still radioactive and impassible. The world now has twenty percent less oxygen, strange and constantly shifting weather patterns, freezing nights and scorching days, purple clouds, storms of black snow. In the United States, regions of land have been torn by chasms, landslides and earthquakes. Mutated animals roam the plains and mountains. Killer dogs, weighing up to two hundred pounds, with dagger-sharp teeth, hunt in hungry packs. Bloodthirsty rats, two to three feet long, move in bands of thousands across the terrain at night, devouring all that is in their path.

And there are tales of the mysterious "Glowers," who the Russian occupying troops speak of in frightened whispers—radioactive humans who live only in the hottest zones, who glow like a blue flame and whose touch kills instantly. These and even more terrible dangers await Rock as he makes his way across the new America.

Driving stolen Russian vehicles or riding his hybrid horse, shorter and stronger than horses of the past and more resistant to radiation, Rock, armed with his rapid-fire .12 gauge shotgun pistols and the "Liberator" automatic rifle with infrared scope,

5

helps the "Freefighters" of the free American towns and villages fight the Russian occupiers. Rock's only two goals are to throw the Soviet murderers out of the United States, returning America to its great glory and freedom of the past, and to find and kill the squad of Russian KGB officers who murdered his family, torturing them, raping his mother and sisters when he was a child. Hidden beneath a floorboard he had memorized the faces of all ten of the elite Death Squad who committed the atrocities. One by one he will hunt them down and kill them.

Ted Rockson's trail weaves swiftly across the land, the mountains, the hidden free cities, the vast hot zones, as he conquers all that gets in his way in the strange, terrifying world of America 2089 A.D.

* * *

TIME: It is one hundred years in the future. An all-out nuclear war has killed two-thirds of the world's population. The Russians, who were able to get off many more of their missiles in a first strike, were victorious over the United States. Now, in control of virtually the entire world except for China, they ruthlessly rule the People's World Socialist Republics.

PLACE: Atomic bombs exploded all over the planet, but primarily in the United States. The United States lost one hundred million people within one hour of the attack. Another seventy-five million died within a year. The Russians immediately moved in with massive transports of troops and weapons and quickly took control of much of the country. They built forty fortresses in vital parts of the United States, huge military complexes from which they sent out search-and-destroy units of tanks, helicopters and radiation-suited troops to extinguish the still-burning embers of resistance.

The Russians use the American citizens as slave labor, forcing them to grow crops and work in factories. The Russian high command lives in luxury, the officers having taken the best housing in the remaining cities. The American workers must make do in shabby shanty towns around the fortress complexes. Thirty-five million Americans are directly under the Red rule. Sullen and docile, they carry out their Russian masters' orders, but underneath they hate them. They pray for the day when the legendary Ted Rockson, "The Ultimate American," will come with the Freefighters of the hidden cities and release them from their bondage.

ENVIRONMENT: The great number of bombs set off altered the Earth's axis. The polar caps began melting and the forested regions turned to desert. As the world slowly warmed, the higher amount of CO_2 in the air created a greenhouse effect. Lakes, rivers and streams had dried up in many places. Ecology had been almost dealt a deathblow from the war. Ninety percent of the Earth's species of plants and animals were now extinct.

The East Coast of the United States is still extremely radioactive. Vast, bare plains stretch hundreds of miles in New York, Connecticut, New Jersey and Pennsylvania on which nothing grows. At the edges of these hot zones are forests of mutated bushes and trees covered with thorns and rock-hard bark. Parts of the Midwest were spared as the Russians had plans for eventually using the farmland to grow crops for their own clamoring masses back home. But the soil is nevertheless too radioactive for anything but weeds. American slave labor has been taken out by the

7

truckload to work, turning the soil in the medium hot zones—meaning death within a year from handling the rocks and topsoil still hot enough to send a Geiger counter needle off the edge.

The Far West was hit hard. Colorado was spared mostly because of bad aim but further on, in Utah, Nevada and California, there has been heavy damage. The area is now a misty, unknown land. Nothing is thought to even live there. Volcanos and earthquakes have become common and much of the Northwest has been turned into a nightmare of craters, some miles wide.

The South was hit in a haphazard fashion as if the Russians hadn't quite known what to strike. Some states—New Mexico, Georgia—were almost untouched; others—Florida, Texas—had been blasted to bits. Large parts of Florida are gone. Where Orlando and Tampa once stood is now a great jagged, hydrogen-bomb-created canal, stretching hundreds of miles across the interior, filled with red, muddy water.

Slowly, life tries to force its way back onto the surface of the ripped and savaged land. Many forests have expanded over the last century in areas that weren't hit. Great parts of the United States are now thick with brush and trees, and resemble the country the way it was in the 1800s. In other places the deserts cover the earth for four, five hundred miles in every direction—unrelenting, broiling, snake-filled and cactus-dotted obstacles that stand between other living parts of the country.

THE HIDDEN FREE CITIES: Nearly seventy-five towns have sprung up over the last hundred years, hidden in caves, mountains and deep wooded valleys. Located at the edges of hot zones which the Russian troops are reluctant to enter, these towns, known as Free Cities, are made up of armed resistance fighters. Each city consists of anywhere from a thousand to forty thousand people. They are fiercely democratic, using town meetings to discuss and vote on all issues.

The Free Americans, who have been bred out in the country, away from the Russian-dominated "clean" areas, have, through natural selection, become ten times more resistant to radiation than their ancestors. They are bred tough, with weak children placed out in the twenty-below-zero nights. If the child lives he is allowed to develop. If not, he is just as well put out of his misery now.

Ted Rockson fights out of Century City—one of the more advanced Free Cities, and the manufacturer of the Liberator automatic rifle, used by freefighters everywhere. They attack Russian convoys and blow up bridges. But they plan for the day when they can begin their all-out assault on the enslavers.

THE RUSSIANS: The United Socialist States of America is run by the red-faced, heavy-drinking General Zhabnov, headquartered in the White House, Washington, D.C., now called New Lenin. A bureaucrat, careful but not cunning, and a libertine, Zhabnov spends his days eating and his nights in bed with young American girls rounded up by the KGB. Zhabnov has been appointed supreme president of the United States for a ten-year period, largely because he is the nephew of the Russian premier, Vassily. General Zhabnov rules America as his personal fiefdom. The only rules he must obey are (1) no uprisings and (2) seventy-five percent of the crops grown by the enslaved American workers must be sent to Russia. General Zhabnov believes that the situation in the United States is stable, that there are no American resistance forces to speak of other than a few scattered groups that raid convoys from time to time. He sees his stay here as a happy interlude away from the power struggles back in the Kremlin.

Colonel Killov is the head of the KGB in the United States headquartered in Denver, Colorado. He is a ruthlessly ambitious man whose goal it is to someday be premier of the world. Thin, almost skeletal, with a long face, sunken cheekbones and thin lips that spit words, Killov's operatives are everywhere in the country: in the fortresses, in the Russian officer ranks, and lately he has even managed to infiltrate an American-born agent into the highest levels of the resistance. Colonel Killov believes General Zhabnov to be a fool. Killov knows that the American forces are growing stronger daily and forming a nationwide alliance to fight together. The calm days of the last century are about to end.

From Moscow, Premier Vassily rules the world. Never has one man ruled so much territory. From the bottom of Africa to Siberia, from Paraguay to Canada, Russian armies are everywhere. A constant flow of supplies and medical goods are needed to keep the vast occupying armies alive. Russia herself did not do badly in the war. Only twenty-four American missiles reached the Soviet Union and ten of these were pushed off course or exploded by ground-to-air missiles. The rest of the United States strike was knocked out of the skies by Russian killer satellites that shot down beams of pure energy and picked them off like clay pigeons.

Vassily is besieged on all sides by problems. His great empire is threatening to break up. Everywhere there are rebel attacks on Russian troops. In Europe, in Africa, in India, especially in America. The forces of the resistance troops were growing larger and more sophisticated in their operations. Vassily is a highly intelligent, well-read man. He has devoured history books on other great leaders and the problems they faced. "Great men have problems that no one but another great man could understand," he lectures his underlings. Advisers tell him to send in more forces and quickly crush the insurgents. But Vassily believes that to be a tremendous waste of manpower. If it goes on like this he may use neutron bombs again. Not a big strike, but perhaps in a single night, yes, in one hour, they could target the fifty main trouble spots in the world. Order must be maintained. For Vassily knew his history. One thing that had been true since the dawn of time: wherever there had been a great empire there had come a time when it began to crumble.

One

"Should I blow the charge?" Berger, the explosives man asked, his meaty, weathered hands resting on the detonation plunger. A wire ran from the bottom of the gray metal box, a thousand feet downhill through rocks and trees to a narrow, steel girder bridge way below. The North Colorado River Bridge, as it had once been called, was now wired with two hundred pounds of plastique slapped on in two and three pound mounds to the tops of all the supporting girders. A squad of heavy Russian tanks approached from the other side of the bridge, sending up clouds of dust above the parched, rutted road.

"No, wait!" Ted Rockson, the commander of the twenty-man excursion force of Freefighters said firmly. "We want the bridge filled with their heavy stuff before we blow. Patience, my friend, patience and then . . ." His icy eyes, one violet, one aquamarine, glistened with steel rage. Rockson hoisted his Liberator over his shoulder and walked to a large, flat boulder at the edge of the steep slope that dropped down the mountain to the bridge. With a powerful leap he jumped five feet up to the boulder's edge and, getting a handgrip, pulled himself quickly up. He stayed low, not breaking the horizon for Russian binoculars, took his own glasses out, then elbowed up to the edge of the oval-shaped, yellow boulder. The Free-fighters sat hidden behind him amidst the rocks. They wore gray camouflage outfits, mountain boots with cleats, T-shirts and flak vests already drenched with sweat. The twenty-man

12

attack force rested in the shadows created by the rocks, hiding from the noonday sun which beat down like the searing flames of a blast furnace.

It had been overcast for weeks, but today, when clouds would be a blessing, of course, they had vanished. The sky was clear, with only that strange, purplish tint high in the atmosphere hinting that anything was amiss with the world, that the heavens were radioactive. The Freefighters adjusted their weapons, 9mm Liberator automatic rifles, and made sure no dirt was clogging the barrels. During the four-day journey they had made to get here, anything could have crawled in there. They squirmed uncomfortably in their flak vests, silently blasting the Century City rule that required flaks on all attack missions, and looked up impatiently at Rockson perched on the boulder wondering just when in hell he would signal the attack. The mortarmen stacked rows of shells ten to a pile and calculated the trajectory to the opposite bank. Thirty feet to their left, two machine guns had been mounted, their 50mm muzzles painted brown to avoid any flashes of light that would signal the forward Russian scouts.

Rockson peered motionlessly through his 20x binocs. He watched the tanks moving through a blanket of choking dust onto the ancient girder bridge, built in prewar days. Watched the foot soldiers running alongside the steel killing machines. Watched the entire structure tremble and vibrate in protest as the first of the lumbering K-55s roared on. Rock watched and waited. He was calm, ready for the action that would begin momentarily. He had been doing this for a long time—killing Russians. Since he was a boy. It was nasty work, but not as nasty as the bastards had been to America. The killing would stop when their occupation forces left. It was simple. It was their choice: to stay and die, or leave and live. He focused his binoculars on the command tank which was just approaching the ramp to the bridge, and fine focused the beat-up lenses on the officer who directed the tank from the turret. He was arrogant, with his thin lips, his gold-braided collar, and that look of smug self-confidence that all the Russian officers had. Good, let them think there is no danger, Rock thought, ducking down, as he saw the commander lift his own glasses.

So much the easier for us.

The column of twenty Russian K-55 tanks, almost forty feet long, with their huge turrets and 150mm cannons poking forward like dark arms of death, rumbled down the rusty road, the Fifth Sector Highway the Russians called it. The tanks moved slowly, spaced about fifty feet apart. They were surrounded by combat troops in full battle gear and radiation suits. The troops held onto the sides of the battlewagons, letting themselves be pulled along at about ten mph. Their thick anti-rad protective gear and heavy K-200 rifles weighed them down, making movement difficult. But there was no complaining. Not in the Russian Army.

Colonel Antonovich stood in the hatchway of the lead tank peering nervously around at the surrounding hills and mountains. He looked for the slightest trace of metal glinting, of reflection, of a face disappearing behind a rock. This was the perfect spot for an ambush, when they were all bunched together close to move quickly across the narrow bridge. Below the colonel, in the guts of the foot-thick, steel-plated K-55, the six men of the crew were at their battle stations, ready for anything. The tank—equipped with 150mm cannon, twin 55mm machine guns, flame thrower and anti-tank missiles— could take out just about anything . . . if it could see it. That was the rub. If the Americans would fight like men, the colonel thought bitterly, the battle would soon be over. But they wouldn't. It was always hit and run. Kill one soldier here, take out one tank there. They were like mosquitos, stinging, biting. But mosquitos drew blood. He felt a shiver run down his spine, even as his flesh sweated in the thick, rubberized canvas anti-rad suit.

There! What was that? Antonovich swung his field glasses quickly up. A flash on a peak about eight hundred feet away. He licked his lips nervously, preparing to shout out the command to fire. No, there, it was just a quartz formation reflecting the brilliant yellow-orange sun. Damn, he was getting too nervous. If they had fired up there, it could have caused an avalanche of rock to fall on the other end of the bridge. His superiors would love that. Blocking the only crossing for a hundred miles that would safely hold a tank or a

14

supply truck.

These Americans were a ragged bunch. Why should he feel afraid? The Russian forces were so overwhelming in comparison to the feeble resistance. It was a joke. A pitiful joke on the Americans. Nonetheless, he felt his heart beat faster and couldn't help but think of his wife and children back in Vladivostok. He tried to create their images in his mind. The pictures quickly faded as a cloud of dust shot up into his face. Damn, it was hard to wear these face masks and be able to use binoculars, Antonovich thought, opting for the mask. He pulled the visor down over his face and began breathing the pure oxygen that filled the mask, from a small pack on his back. I've got to use this thing more, he berated himself. The dust out here was still radioactive. *He* wasn't going to die in this Godforsaken land. Not him! That was for foot soldiers not officers.

Two of their columns had been attacked in this area in the past month. Though the damage had been minimal, the rebels had to be shown who was the power, the strength. This well-equipped force had twenty tanks, nearly five hundred infantry, and a surprise package of three heavily armed helicopters which flew several miles south waiting for any attack, at which they would swoop in for the kill and wipe out whatever ragged forces these Americans had been able to assemble this time. The secondary attack force was Antonovich's idea. If it succeeded it would be a promotion for him. "We'll see who will be surprised by who," the colonel thought to himself, wondering just when and where the attack would occur. His tank ground onto the gravel embankment to the bridge, and then began the three hundred-foot crossing. The steel-webbed roadway groaned beneath the weight of the tank as Antonovich looked at the dark, rushing water some eighty feet below.

From his rocky perch, Ted Rockson watched as the colonel's tank rumbled onto the girder bridge. "Ready, Berger. Get ready," he barked down, his eyes glued to the column below. Soon, the entire span was filled with tanks, over half the force. The first K-55 was just feet away from the end. "After I fire, blow it!" Rock yelled, jumping free of the boulder and landing on his feet, next to the explosives man. He swung the

9mm Liberator rapid fire on its web shoulder harness and made first-target acquisition through the scope—the officer, the one with the braiding. Rock squeezed the trigger. The muzzle jerked up as the officer's head blossomed red and slumped.

Berger smiled, his thick lips curling back into his thick black beard. He leaned forward, putting his full weight on the plunger which slid down into the innards of the generating box, sending out a surge of current. In less than a second, the bridge erupted in fire and smoke. The charges placed at ten-foot intervals along the underside of the metal grid roadway detonated in unison. Instantly Rockson and the twenty Freefighters opened fire from their positions, shooting at the screaming, burning Russian troops some eight hundred feet below.

The explosion literally ripped away the whole central support system for the bridge and as the Freefighters poured down a hail of lead rain, the bridge slowly, as if in a dream, crumbled in pieces and headed for the water below. All the tanks and troops on the North Colorado River Bridge tumbled end over end, a bloody haze of shrapnel and flesh, into the rushing whitecap of the river. Within seconds, every Russian who had been crossing the structure was dead, sucked down into the dark waters, as if the Colorado River were helping its citizens to fight back against the invaders. Pieces of flesh, legs pouring out blood, helmets, leather cushions to pad hard metal tank seats, all bobbed and twisted, a grisly dance of death in the cold, brown water.

"Perfect!" Berger yelled out in glee, looking over at Rockson who had slid between two elephant-sized rock formations and was firing down at the frantic Red troops trying to regroup on the opposite bank. The remaining tanks pulled alongside each other in a small clearing just before the bridge and began opening up with their 50mms though they didn't have the range yet. The American Freefighters could only stay a few more minutes, inflict what damage they could and leave. They fired down, lining up the scampering Russian troops on the far bank, through crosshair sights on the Liberators and squeezed off three-round bursts at heads and chests that ballooned into red sprays of flesh.

The mortarmen, Hoffman and Jones, began their work, aiming dead center at the line of remaining Russian tanks. The first shell whistled through the air and fell about thirty feet to the left of the end tank. The second shot made contact, blowing the turret right off the K-55. Only two Reds emerged, their clothes on fire. They leaped to the parched ground, screaming, and ran madly in circles, blazing torches of sizzling flesh.

But the Russian tanks were closing in. Their sightmen were finding the Freefighters' position. A 150mm shell landed just below the ridge on which the Americans were dug in, sending out a cloud of pulverized rock dust. Then another, even closer. The Americans returned the message with their own greetings of red-hot slugs. The two machine gunmen, Pincer and Croy, opened up with their 50mms, spraying the opposite bank with a continuous curtain of fire. The Red soldiers dove off in all directions as the burning slugs bit into the clearing like teeth searching for human flesh to bite. Rock swung his Liberator around madly, working the selector by feel into auto-mode, holding the trigger. Red shells began falling every few seconds—closer, closer—ripping boulders apart as if they were made of sand. Rockson was in charge. It was his decision when to fight and when to leave. They had already decimated the Russian column, destroyed a good sixty percent of its force, and sent nine tanks to the bottom of the Colorado where fish were now doubtless peering through the machine gun slits at the charred corpses within. Rock hated to leave a battle, but he was the commander of these men and he was more cautious when it came to other men's lives than he was with his own. He slammed another clip into the Liberator.

He whistled twice, a shrill, piercing sound that snapped the men's heads around. "Freefighters, we're moving out!" he yelled above the battle din. "We've done our work, boys." The attack force ripped off a few goodbye rounds and jumped back from their ambush sites, behind the shield of boulders, that continued to send up waves of dust and smoke as the Russian shells tore in closer. The guerrillas formed a semicircle around Rockson, loading their guns on their shoulders, folding up the machine guns and quickly loading their supplies into thick canvas packs.

Rock stood up to his full six foot, three inches of chiseled muscle and looked around at the assembled men. The streak of chalk white that ran down the middle of his head of jet-black hair burned like a flame as the blazing sun beat down. His deeply tanned, rough-hewn, weathered face turned slowly to check out every one of the fighters under his command. He knew their wives, their girlfriends, their children. He knew that he would be the one to bring back the dreaded news if . . .

The Freefighters looked at one another and then down at their own bodies. Everyone was whole! No flesh pierced, no blood pouring like a river, taking a man's life down into the dirt.

"Rock, you've been hit," Detroit Green, a powerfully built black man, and Rockson's right-hand man, said, pointing to a large gash in Rockson's flak vest. The Survivor looked down. Something had reached him, some spinning piece of shrapnel looking for flesh to slash. He pulled the dirt-brown vest open and looked at his chest and stomach, then grinned. Nothing!

"I'm the one always blasting all of you to wear these damn things. I'm glad I listen to my own orders." A shell whistled overhead and slammed into the plateau behind the wall of boulders, some hundred feet away. "All right, let's get the hell out of here!" Rockson said, swinging his own pack and rifle up over his shoulders. "Let the bastards blow up the whole mountain. Waste ten tons of ammo before they realize we're not even here." The mortarmen loaded up their prize howitzers in field packs and, sharing the weight with another Freefighter, hefted the packs into the air and onto their shoulders, carrying the heavy weapons between them, their taut muscles straining.

"McCaughlin, leave them a few surprises when they come to investigate up here," Rockson said with a grin.

"With pleasure, Rock," the jowled Scotsman replied, smirking. He quickly pulled three Claymore Sprayers out of his pack and placed them carefully around the perimeter of the clearing, clicking the arming devices into place and sprinkling grass and twigs over them. "Should be a nice birthday present for another ten or twenty of our Russian guests," the red-haired McCaughlin yelled out to Rockson as the Freefighters

18

began leaving the plateau and heading down the opposite side of the mountain and its loose sliding rocks and pebbles. The thick green woods below beckoned them. Inside was safety, refuge.

"Move men! Move! Expedite!" Rock yelled out, taking up the rear. The Freefighters slid and half-ran down the steeply sloped ridge. It was a hell of a lot easier going down than coming up, although every few hundred feet someone would slip and go tumbling head over heels, slicing open arms and hands on the coal-sized, sharp-edged rocks. Behind them, the Reds had finally found their targets. The plateau erupted with a thunderous roar into thick, black smoke and flame as shell after shell sped in. "Most expensive rock demolition program in the history of the Soviet Empire," Rock thought cynically to himself. They were nearly halfway down the mountain, the men yelling out playful insults to one another as first one, then another of the Freefighters slipped and slid ten or twenty feet. They were in a good mood. Things had gone well. The last Freefighting Attack Force, sent out only a week before, had met with disaster. Attempting to attack a small truck convoy, they had been ambushed from behind by a second army patrol. Twenty men wiped out. But this mission was an unqualified success. If they could destroy this much Russian armament every time they went out, it would only be a few more years before the bastards would run home with their Commie tails between their legs, and leave this land of thin air and violet, glowing skies.

"Move! Don't slow down!" Rock continued to push the men faster, taking up the rear. He suddenly felt apprehensive. Why, he wasn't sure. Years of fighting the invader had sharpened his senses to a razor-honed edge of perception. Then he heard it! The sound that every American dreaded, the Russian MS-18 helicopters, armed to the teeth with machine guns, missiles and napalm. More than one—he could sense that by the thick whine of the rotors. A trap! They had kept the air support in hiding, waiting until the Freefighters had been flushed out into the open.

"Move, goddamn it!" Rock screamed at the scrambling men below him. The forward men of the Attack Force had already reached the line of trees that marked the beginning of the two hundred-mile pine forest. But six men, the mortarmen and McCaughlin, were still scrambling down the bottom of the hill. There was hundreds of feet of open, rocky slope in front of them with no place to hide.

Suddenly three of the Red helicopters flew around the side of the mountain, swooping down like hawks, firing their 7.62mm machine guns and 20mm mini-cannons. The shells tore into the rock covering of the slope, sending out a mist of dust and lethal rock fragments. Rockson leaped through the air, hit the slope and rolled beneath a low rock overhang.

"Down! Down!" he screamed out to the five Freefighters trapped out in the open. They didn't have a chance. Unless . . . Rock pulled out his walkie-talkie and flipped the send switch.

"Detroit! Detroit, this is Rockson. Everyone all right down there?" A squawking, crackling static filled his ear for a moment, then Detroit's husky voice filled the air.

"Yeah, Rock, we're in the woods. Everyone down here is OK." There was a brief crackle, then, "Are you hurt, Rock?"

"Damnit, I'm all right. It's McCaughlin and Carter and some of the other guys—they're like sitting ducks. I want you to stay at the edge of the woods, but set up some fire. Make them think we've got a whole damn army down there. We've got to get those men out."

"Will do, Rock," Detroit's gruff voice squeaked back over the walkie-talkie as Russian helicopter communications interfered with their signal. Guttural Red commands were screamed back and forth from chopper to chopper. Rockson knew what they were saying. He wasn't exactly a linguist but he'd been around enough to pick up the basic ideas of the Russian language. "Kill them!" they were saying. "They're on the lower ridge."

Christ, they had them spotted and pinpointed. There was hardly a chance. Rockson pulled back the automatic firing lever on his Liberator and rolled out from under the overhang, blasting up at the sky as he twisted and ran along the hard terrain. The three choppers were hovering about two hundred feet away, closing in on the trapped men. Rock heard the other Freefighters open up from the woods. Bullets of every caliber ripped through the air, their sharp, burning hot lead noses screaming shrilly as they flew, seeking out Red bull's-eyes.

Rockson took aim at the closest chopper as it poured down a curtain of bullets at the trapped men. Its huge rotors twisted like a single piece of shimmering steel in the hundred degree air. He could see the Russian pilot and machine gunner peering down. They were sighting in on McCaughlin. Rockson aimed round after round into the engine. He was a marksman, one of the best of Century City, but targets were one thing, moving helicopters another. The chopper's bullet path weaved in closer on the prone McCaughlin who tried to hide behind a boulder no larger than he was. And he was as big as a barn door. Desperately Rockson fired at the MS-18. Not the Scotsman! He loved that overgrown whale of a man.

Suddenly, one of Rock's slugs hit paydirt, ripping through the tail rotor control. The back gyro blade sputtered hesitantly to a stop and the chopper began wobbling wildly, out of control. It swerved quickly to the right and flipped over 180 degrees, the pilot's screams lost in the drone of the still-whipping blade. The helicopter dropped like a stone, about a hundred yards up the hill from Rock, and exploded in a ball of oily fire.

Rockson took advantage of the few seconds of confusion as the two other choppers pulled back momentarily to survey the damage. He raced down the hill to McCaughlin, hooking him beneath the arms and lifting the three hundred-pound man to his feet in a single motion.

"Run, man, run!" Rockson yelled at the pale Scot, turning him around with a spin and then pushing him down the hill. McCaughlin stumbled, half falling again, but barely kept his balance by waving his thick arms wildly over his head. He gained his equilibrium and began running, building speed every second. Several hundred feet away, firing up at the choppers from the dark cover of the forest, the other men of the Attack Force urged him on.

Rock now turned his attention to the other men still trapped on the hill. He glanced up and saw the choppers hovering low over their fallen comrade. But even as he looked they began rising and heading back to the slope. Rockson could see two figures lying prone about 150 feet away. He ran, leaping and twisting, changing direction every three steps. He wouldn't make himself a target. If they wanted to take him down they'd have to work hard, real hard. From the trees below he suddenly heard the roaring sound of heavy fire. They must have unwrapped the machine gun. Good! He liked it when the men could think for themselves. Sometimes they relied on him too much. But he wouldn't be here forever. That was for sure.

He ran forward to the two fallen Freefighters, diving through the dusty, smoke-filled air, almost landing on what had been two of his best men just minutes before. He looked them over quickly. They were out of it now. No more battles for two more Free Americans. Carter's head had been nearly severed from his body, the neck still pulsing out a gusher of thick, red blood every few seconds from a heart that didn't even know it was dead. Sanford had caught a stream of 9mm rounds in the chest and stomach. His guts hung out of him like the stuffing of a slashed pillow, covering his legs and face. A puddle of blood gurgled bubbles of CO_2 in the center of what had been his abdomen.

"Damn!" Rockson spat through his teeth. It had been going so good. He felt the line of bullets coming a second before it arrived. As he rolled again down the hill as quick as he could move, oblivious to the sharp-edged rocks gashing his flesh, the ground where he had just been was ripped apart by the claws of a hundred slivers of metal. He flew down the hill with animal speed, sliding, dodging, a bundle of pure energy, the whirlwind that was Ted Rockson. The three other Freefighters still caught in the open were scrambling for their lives a hundred yards over and down the mountain. Two choppers came soaring in from the sky, swimming through the smoke of their fallen comrade. They peppered the slope with a blizzard of slugs, digging trenches in straight, deadly lines. Rockson tore to the side as he heard an air-to-ground missile whistle above him. He hit another, steeper slope and let himself spin somersaults down it, tucking into a tight ball. He knew that whistle, had heard it a hundred times since childhood—napalm.

Behind him, the ground exploded into a ball of blue-orange

fire. The burning, sticky jelly splattered off wildly in every direction, searching for anything solid to stick to and burn. Rockson felt a sharp sting on his shoulder and ripped a piece of the flaming napalm off with his knife, flinging it to the field of rocks. He heard a scream. Oh Christ, now Nord, the Swede, had been hit. Rockson stood for a split second and scanned the hill. Nord ran madly, his hair and back burning with that hideous blue flame. Two of the Freefighters ran from cover and threw the burning man to the ground, slapping out the flaming jelly with their jackets. They quickly carried him off, behind the trees at the very foot of the mountain.

From the cover of thick Aspens, Detroit Green saw Rockson was in big trouble. Rock still had a good two hundred feet to go and the choppers were coming in for the kill. He ripped two grenades from the bandolier he always wore and ran from the trees, screaming, "Dodge them, Rock! Dodge 'em! I'm coming up from the left with some hardballs, lead them to the right." The short, black bulldog of a man, muscles bulging through his old, army-issue blue sweatshirt, ran like a man possessed. His piston legs pumped up and down like a railroad train. He jumped rocks and dodged dark, spiny cactuses that dotted the lower side of the hill. Without being spotted, he pulled to within a hundred feet of the MS-18s. The choppers slowed to a crawl, aiming with every weapon on board, getting a bead on Ted Rockson who fired up at them from the hip as he continued to sprint down, the trees and safety so tantalizingly close.

Detroit Green pulled both pins with his teeth on the army-issue G41 hand grenades, counted to three and threw them, one a split second after the other. Detroit dove forward, as if from a diving board, straight down the slope, as an explosion rocked the air above him. Both choppers veered wildly, first away from each other, their control rudders shattered by the force of the blast, and then toward each other, two pendulums of steel death. They met in a roaring explosion of blood and fire, a hundred feet in the air. The rotors of the two MS-18s met and cut through each other like two swords crossed by invisible swordsmen of death. Locked together in a molten embrace they plummeted to the earth and exploded, sending up a hundred-foot ball of black smoke and cherry-red flames.

Rockson tore down into the woods, stopping only when he felt the cool darkness surround him. He looked back through the trees. He had survived. The hill was a charnel ground—a cemetery. The Soviet air attack was wiped out. But nearly a quarter of his own men were dead. Detroit came running from a nearby gully of weeds and small stones. He tore into the forest, laughing and clapping his hands.

"Check me out on that one, Rockson," Detroit said, grinning from ear to ear. He held out his palm for the five sign. Rockson looked at the man who had just saved his life, one of his few close friends. He let a smile cross his sternly set face and slapped the black man on the palm with his own hand.

"Thanks, Detroit. I owe you one," Rock said softly.

"Shit, Rock, you saved my damn ass so many times I had to stop counting," Detroit snickered. "Besides, if we lost you we wouldn't even know how to get home. You're the only one knows these hills."

Rock said a prayer at the edge of the woods as the other Freefighters stood, heads bowed, around him. "We lost six good men today. Six Freefighting Americans. Take them to you, God, or whatever is up there, above this hell. They deserve their paradise. For no finer accolade can be given a man than that he died to make his nation free." Their faces set and drawn, the Freefighters picked up handfuls of dirt from the forest floor and threw them out toward their dead fellow warriors. Then they turned as one and walked away without looking back.

Dark green cumulus clouds gathered at the horizon as the ocher sun set over the snow-capped Rockies. In the thin, flickering violet air, a few hesitant stars had already appeared.

Two

A group of filthy, grime-encrusted men and women, their clothes tattered, dove into the rank pile of garbage that a Russian soldier tossed out the back window of the Stalinville Officer's Commissary. They grabbed handfuls of the slop, meat gristle, stale bread and dark brown slimy leaves of lettuce, fighting one another, growling in guttural screams of need, of hunger. Twenty-five descendants of the American dream, now living in a nightmare of filth, poverty, swollen stomachs and death. Their Russian masters took everything of value and shipped it back to Mother Russia, to feed her great armies, her empire of forty million soldiers.

The Russian kitchen man, Lieutenant Sharovsky, from Tuarsk, a small farming village west of Vladivostok, had been in the occupying Red force here in America for nearly two-and-a-half years. Just six months to go! Shit! He looked out the window with disgust and amusement at the groveling American race. They seemed so primitive, so stupid. The Russian peoples were obviously superior—they had won the Great War. Now these pitiful "humans" were hardly worthy of the once-proud name, Americans. Licking their lips hungrily, they pushed against the low barbed-wire fence some six feet from the commissary door and begged. The commander of the fortress allowed the Americans to be fed the Russian troops' leftovers. "It makes us look good. We help the Americans. We even give them our own food," he had explained with a laugh. Now, every morning the kitchen crews would appear at the rear swing windows at the back of the fort's mess halls, and the American dregs would crowd around, scraping up every scrap.

Sharovsky threw them more food, half a steel container of half-rotten beef stew. It flew through the air, a cloud of noxious, meaty spray, and landed on the clamoring beggars. Filthy faces moaning in the growing darkness. "More, comrade. Please, more."

Around them, the fortress city of Stalinville came slowly to life as the morning sun pierced the strontium green-tinged clouds that flew high above the fort. One of the circling clouds of radioactive dust that now eternally orbited the Earth. It looked like it was dropping down toward the Russian complex. But it would take hours. Life in Stalinville must go on. The narrow dirt-paved back streets of the American sector began bustling with activity as the gray-uniformed occupants of the ghetto made their way off to perform their menial jobs for their Russian masters. Many of them worked in the Red canning factories in the southern part of the fort, the industrial sector. Others headed for the textile mills to make clothes for the Soviet troops. Everything was made for the Russians; the Americans were given the leftovers or the occasional surplus.

Peddlers were opening their small businesses along the winding street that was the main shopping area for the Americans. Shops, hidden, half submerged in doorways and basements, selling everything from old knives and pots and pans to scraps of salvaged material for making clothing. They hawked their wares as the crowds filled the muddy streets. Russian armored vehicles stood every five or six blocks, the crews looking down contemptuously. The workers stumbled from their huts, their crumbling tenements, and filed off to work. Those who didn't meet work quotas or were absent from their jobs were subject to be sent out to the fields to do what was generically called Rehabilitation Work, but meant being trucked out to the surrounding countryside of Fort Stalinville. There, they would be made to rip the topsoil from the ground and pry out the boulders. The radioactive surface had to be removed so that the cleaner, purer soil below could someday be used again for agriculture.

"Cigs here! Get your cigs here!" a legless man, seated on a

wooden pulley yelled out to the glum crowds. "We got cigs of every size." He smiled cheerfully. "Got whole cigs for a ruble, half for a half, a quarter for a two cent, and a nibble for a pen."

An old man with a face as long as a shadow came over, his immense, gray coat hanging nearly to his toes, as if to shield him from the darkness of life.

"You got any Marlboros?" he asked hopefully. He had smoked some years ago, when supplies were more plentiful. Before the new Russian premier, Vassily, had started shipping the tobacco out, lock, stock and barrel. The legless man winked, his white face twisting in a strange leer. He reached inside a torn, white corduroy jacket, one of the arms almost toally stained with blue ink, and glanced around con-spiratorially.

"Don't want no one to see this." He held up a whole Marlboro, perfect, still ripe and pungent. The worker looked at it with a glow of recognition. His face lit up.

"How, how much?" The legless man leaned back on his stumps and folded his arms across his chest.

"For you—and I can tell you're a connoisseur—I'm going to let you slide, my Amerikanski friend. Two rubles and it's yours. And I'll throw in a pack of matches—not full, but still has five left." The worker looked at him, decided and reached a long arm down into a cavern of a pocket in the coat and extracted two sweaty rubles.

"Here," he said, handing it over. The cigarette seller handed the man the crisp Marlboro and the matches.

"Enjoy, my dumkov," the legless peddler said, smirking.

"I will," the worker replied, rejoining the migrating lines of laborers. "I will."

Stalinville was one of the larger Russian forts—stretching ten miles in a roughly circular shape, with an electrified wire fence surrounding the city. The Reds had split the complex into four sectors, their own totally separated and secured from the rest by special barbed-wire walls and defensive systems. There was no mixing between the Americans and the occupying Russian forces. The Reds didn't dare go out into the

27

night. The army had set up whorehouses using American women who were carefully screened, controlled and watched.

Stalinville was responsible for the five hundred square mile area around what had been Omaha, Nebraska. It was a large, modern fort, one that had been built in the last thirty years rather than at the very start of the Russian occupation. Those were hellholes, barely capable of supporting life on an ongoing basis. They were highly vulnerable to radioactive storms, filled with leaks and holes through which the constant, deadly mists of the poisoned country blew with unceasing vigor, as if to fill their very pores with this glowing death.

The Russians, even now, a century after the Great War, had to be on their guard against everything. They were more susceptible to radiation over here, for it was much hotter than Russia. Only a few Red cities had been struck after the sneak attack. That was one of the reasons the Russian troops had to be rotated every three years, before their bodies started to suffer irreversible damage. The Stalinville Soviet sector was fed its own constantly filtered air supply, pumped into every Russian room and office. Outside the Red quarters, within the city, the troops would walk around with handkerchiefs around their mouths. And when out of the fort completely, on missions out in the "hot zones," they wore the full radiation combat gear, including face masks, oxygen packs and heavy quilted suits. Somehow, the American Freefighters seemed almost immune to the rads and the thin air.

Stalinville was important, not only for her military might which kept the local populace bent under, but for her KGB Operations Center. She was the main fort of this section of the country for the dreaded KGB Blackshirts who appeared from out of the night and dispensed death to whomever they deemed worthy.

KGB Maj. Gen. Alexi Dashkov sat staring out the polarized window of his fifth-story office at the cactus-dotted plains beyond the fortress, stretching off to the misted horizon. Now the KGB had a new toy in Stalinville—the Mind Breaker. Just recently perfected by their scientists, it was now ready for

28

use on the American resistance that still fought them in the unclaimed lands away from the fort—the mountains, the fog enshrouded valleys, the thick forests. The fools who still fought on would soon face their most fôrmidable enemy. Thus far, they had even withstood torture using the hypnotic blocks that their scientists had taught them. They would only recite nursery rhymes and gibberish, even when excruciating pain was applied. But the Mind Breaker—that was something different, something that would change things. Once they could break some of these rebels, these bandits, and find out where their secret cities lay hidden, the resistance forces all across America could be destroyed.

Oh, how easy it would be to drop just one little neutron bomb on each Free City and eradicate the diseased area. If we just knew where, Dashkov thought, staring out the thick-glassed window, probing into the far mountains with his eyes as if searching for the rebels. Already the results were good. Three captured Freefighters, as they called themselves, had been captured and taken prisoner before they could kill themselves with those little cyanide capsules they carried. Strapped into the Mind Breaker they had quickly broken and a city had been found by the Soviet forces—Glennville, not a big city, about five thousand men and women. Their sobbing comrades could take no more of the Mind Breaker's laser probes. They had told. The Russian MIGs had swooped down, bats of black death from the purple sky, and dropped a 50 kiloton neutron bomb right on the mile-wide grove of camouflaged trees and tunnels that was Glennville. A second later, in a flash of star fire, they had all been taken out. Vaporized, deatomized, riddled with gamma radiation so intense it fried their eyeballs like overcooked eggs and made black blood trickle from their dead, opened mouths.

Not pretty, Dashkov thought, as he had inspected the dead city. But efficient. Oh, how efficient. What a wonderful weapon. I love this neutron bomb. It is a blessing to mankind. And they do not even suffer—out in a second. It is almost humanitarian. And the radiation evaporates in a few days. I must get Killov to allow me to use more of these. Then, if we could just capture Ted Rockson, The Ultimate American, as these rabble love to scrawl on the walls, that would really break the backs of the rebel forces. That would change, as these Americans used to say, the whole ballgame!

The filthy bagman walked slowly down the long, narrow backstreet of Little USA, filled with garbage, excrement and vermin. He was nearly as dirty as the street, covered with a long, flowing, once-brown tweed coat, now more air than fabric, torn and bitten by fleas and mites, and coated with a layer of grease as thick as bark. The bagman's face was brown, the color of wet mud. His unkempt beard covered the lower part of his face and his neck like some sort of net of filth.

He muttered to himself as he moved, slowly, furtively, like a basement rat. He placed one foot down, then the other, waiting, breathing in, then moving again. And he intoned as he walked:

> They will die
> Not I
> They took my bread
> They be dead
> They took my eye
> They will cry.

The bagman's singsong kept the rhythm of his motion as he slipped around the corner of the street and onto one of the main thoroughfares of the poorest area of the American sector—if one could call a thirty-foot-wide track of dirt with a thin layer of gravel on top a thoroughfare. But the Russians didn't care much about the roads of the American section of the fortress. They never came here. They wouldn't dare come alone. Not here. Not where the slaves, the refuse, the lost ones lived. Like him. The ones with nothing. The Russians kept to their part, the southern sector, with their fortress bunkers, their vast, concrete, barbed-wired sanctuary, filled with kitchens and baths and televisions—things the Americans of Stalinville had never seen. The Reds had their own lives—lives of luxury, especially the officers with their clubs, whorehouses and dancehalls. They lived the good life, above lieutenant that is. Below—even for the Red troops—things were not so great. There was meat and warm bunks, eight in a room, but there were no luxuries. Every Red occupation soldier had been drafted. Plucked from the vast reaches of the Soviet Empire that now spanned the entire world. Soldiers from Soviet Georgia, the Ukraine, Bulgaria, East Germany. Units of men who sometimes could only barely communicate with each other and had to use sign language or English, which for the Reds had become a second language, a trade language, just to get the black market goods, the drugs, the girls they couldn't obtain otherwise. But the Red rulers back in the Kremlin wanted it that way. The less in common their empire troops had, the less chance of a revolt.

With Red forces now controlling three-quarters of the world, they were like sitting ducks for the enslaved populations. Any Russian soldier who left his compound without a tank, an APC, or a full regiment was looking for death. And he would find it! Especially here in the back streets of Stalinville. Death from a knife, an ice pick, flashing in the darkness, a sliver of steel fire slashing into a Russian gut, a Red throat. The Russians were not well liked in a city they had destroyed and then taken as their own.

The wretched bagman turned the corner slowly, an arm, then a leg slithering around the chipped brick edge of one of the many run-down, collapsing tenements in this part of the city. There was danger everywhere. He dove to the ground. Three Red armored vehicles rolled by guns at the ready.

They must be making a sweep of some kind, the wretched man thought in the midst of his stupor. For me? No! They wouldn't worry about a nothing like me. Suckers, the Reds called them, those lowest dregs of humanity who slept in the deserted back streets and alleys of the Russian forts. Too dumb or too weak or mad to fit into the Russian plans, the factories, they roamed the streets eking out a miserable survival from the garbage. He was one! Yes, but he was clever.

The bagman felt for the ice pick that he always carried, wrapped just inside one of his big, flapping sleeves. He had used it already and would again if attacked by one of the other lowlifes who existed in this ghetto jungle. He slid through the stark shadows cast by the rising sun, meshing with the orange clouds buzzing with a high-pitched static electricity as they flew by overhead. The APVs rolled by a half block away, not even noticing him. He grinned instantly at his successful avoidance of the Reds and then let his face drop back into its set, eye-bulging sneer of pure madness.

Bagman searched for food as he walked, looking in doorways, stopping at the sight of anything that might be of value—an old boot, a broken bottle. In the world of 2089 A.D. everything was worth something.

"What? What?" he mumbled to himself, spotting a dull shine in the dirt. He walked quickly over and got down on his knees and dug for the object. He pulled out a round piece of metal about an inch in diameter and rubbed at it furiously with his filthy sleeve. The dirt slid away like sand from an old tired eye and revealed, "United States of America" and "Quarter Dollar." He smiled to himself. He had seen these before. Once they had been the money of America. He knew that! Not during his life but once. The ruble had been the currency since he was a boy. The quarter looked strange to him and yet somehow bizarrely familiar as if he had seen it before in another life, another world. His head hurt. He didn't want to think about it. No, no, it was too painful.

Suddenly he heard a noise. Someone talking. He threw the coin into his "special" inner pocket and moved toward the sound, always looking, darting from shadow to twisted shadow. He moved down a flight of old stone stairs, covered with dust and spider webs at every side, forming a canopy of glistening silk threads. The bagman brushed them aside, watching for the spiders that had bitten him once before. Big they were, and fast. Red and orange striped. But now they were gone. He moved into a basement room using the shadows, the darkness and the broken stumps of furniture as cover. This was his world, the underneath, the behind, the under.

There! In the next dank basement room, a man—a black man in a white shirt—was talking softly to eight seated boys and girls. He read from some kind of book. The bagman hid behind a rusting girder and watched. He had seen books before but had never known what they meant. Americans were forbidden to read or learn anything by the occupying forces.

"And Washington was the founder of our country," the black man said. "In 1776 the United States of America declared itself independent from its mother country, England, and after a war and much bloodshed found its freedom." The black teacher spoke in a deep, reassuring voice. "Just as we shall, my students. Just as we someday will. Now today, we will talk about freedom. What it means, what it was like to be free."

"Teacher, what is free?" one of the older boys, John, spoke out hesitantly. The eight students were part of one of several underground schools in the Russian fort which was holding its daily half-hour class. They could only meet for short periods of time for fear of detection, so the conversations between children and teacher were often strong and emotional.

The ebony-faced teacher looked down with a deep sadness in his eyes. "Free is what you can imagine, my children. Free is beyond what is here around you now. You must look beyond, beyond the destroyed land, beyond this fort, and see the new world that was and will be again."

"Teacher, you show us books with pictures of what life was like," Joshua piped up, the youngest and the brightest of the lot, his red hair dancing beneath a blue cap. "You show us strange trees and birds and fields and waterfalls, but we have never seen these things. They're made of paper. How can we feel them?"

"I know." The teacher shook his head and stood up. "That's the hard part. How to imagine something in the middle of nothing. When I was younger," the teacher said, his eyes opening wide in memory of the discoveries of his harsh youth, "I was taught the books and also could not imagine beyond this fort. Till one day I saw the sky turn a perfect blue. Not with the pink-rad haze or the purplish splotches like sores, but a brilliant, perfect blue. My eyes could hardly look at it, but I did. I made myself see it and I know that this was a blue sky like they had in the old days. It had come back again, just for an hour, to show us. The Earth wants to give us back the life that was here. She is trying. And if we try too, we can build life again and live in its beauty."

The class was silent. All felt the emotions of the teacher's secret vision. "Now, I want to try a little exercise. Sit down. All of you."

The bagman stared from the outer room, unseen by the group. He was fascinated in spite of himself, feeling the stirrings of thoughts and feelings he hadn't known for years. He sat and watched and listened, his jaw wide open.

"Now, students," the teacher went on quickly, "today I want to try an exercise. Lie down and close your eyes." The children lay back on the dusty dirt floor, hardly mindful of the filth they were touching. Their own rags were already nearly as dirty. "Let yourself float," the teacher continued, his voice whispering in joy. "Imagine you are floating higher and higher. And out of the fort. You're like a cloud, just floating over everything. You can see down on the fort and it's just a little nothing now. It can't hold you anymore. You float over the country and beyond the dust and the pink mists and you see green. There, do you see it? Those patches of green? Float closer—those are trees, hills and meadows filled with flowers and fruits. Bright rainbows of color. Let yourself crumble the walls, let yourself fly."

"Stop!" a sharp voice barked out, as harsh lights suddenly lit up the illegal class. Five figures stepped from the shadows. They wore black leather uniforms, neck to ankle, and the terrible Red Skull insignia on their lapels. The dreaded KGB—the Blackshirts.

Their captain stepped forward holding a 9mm Soviet Special Service revolver. He aimed it directly at the head of the teacher.

"What are you doing, blackie?" the KGB officer demanded.

"Nothing, sir," the teacher answered calmly, almost smiling at the officer, absorbing the insult.

"This is nothing?" the captain laughed. "There is no factory here. No clothes machinery, no mills. There is nothing a worker would do here. So I ask you again what were you doing?" He cocked the pistol and held it next to the teacher's temple.

"Sir, we were just talking about how to survive. To get food, to live in this city. I was giving them some advice about using

34

old food and where to sleep in the cold. Just survival. We must survive!"

The black-shirted officer looked the teacher in the eyes for a long time. Then without a flicker of emotion he pulled the trigger. The teacher's head turned into a red spray that splashed back onto the students who gagged and screamed in horror. The body of the teacher fell to the stone floor with a sickening thud, its arms and legs twitching violently.

"You goddamn children," the head Blackshirt screamed in his crude English, "get the hell out of here. If I catch any of you doing this kind of thing again, it will be your death. Let this be your lesson for today, my young ones." He pointed with his pistol to the bloody corpse on the floor. The children fled from the basement classroom, crying and moaning. Back, back to their shanty shacks, their subterranean refuges.

The officer looked around the damp, dirty room and snorted contemptuously. "Teach them! Teach them what? The fool. There is nothing to learn—except obedience." He scooped up several books on American history from the floor and slid them under his arm. He walked toward the crumbling doorway, the four KGB underlings fingering their guns nervously as they walked behind him.

Suddenly a figure leapt from the shadows at the Blackshirt. A flash of light, a sliver of steel, a horrible ripping pain in his throat. The bagman pierced the KGB captain again and again with his ten-inch ice pick. He stabbed the Red in the throat, ripping at it, and he screamed as he flailed with the weapon.

"No, no, you killed him. He was a teacher. He was good. No more, no more, more, more, more." The captain's face turned a ghastly pale as his lifeblood spurted from his severed jugular. He fell to the floor clutching at the filthy bagman, who laughed now, laughed wildly with all the madness of hell itself. "I done it now. I killed one. I got me one. They took my mind, but now . . ." The other Blackshirts frantically pulled out their pistols and fired at the filthy, cackling creature. The bagman gasped and flew backward against the dusty basement wall as five 9mm slugs tore through his flesh. He slid to the ground, lifeless, his eyes aimed at the ceiling—softer now as if he had stopped searching. Freedom was finally his.

The KGB officers ran to their leader. It was over for him. His world had ended here, on this slimy floor. His mouth was wrenched open in a scream of sheer horror, as he had gurgled vainly for air and realized he had only seconds to live. His eyes were open wide as silver dollars, the red veins almost popping out from the sockets.

"Trouble now," the second-in-command, Petrov, said ominously. He stood up from the corpse. "There'll be trouble for all of us now!"

Three

The Freefighters marched for days through the thick forests and valleys of the 150 miles of raw terrain. They could hear the buzzing of the Russian spydrones fly overhead every few hours but didn't need to hide as the canopies of trees and lush leaves protected them from the spying Red eye. They had come the hardest route back, right through the center of the wooded region. It seemed a good idea with Russian patrols searching the entire area for them. Rockson had been through this region once before but it had been years ago. The land was more strangely vegetated now. It seemed healthy enough, in fact, very healthy. Large, sturdy bushes and trees. But they were different than years before. Pinkish tinted leaves, gray-green bark almost scaly, like reptilian skin. It was as if the plants and trees of the forests, after hovering on the edge of life and death for decades, had finally adapted to the changed environment by changing themselves, through genetic mutation of their germ plasm.

A forest of mutations, Rockson thought, walking at the head of the Strike Force. Mutated trees, mutated flowers. This whole world is changing. It was nothing like the picture books he had seen. The color photos of America. America the beautiful. Well, parts of her still seemed beautiful to him, but it sure didn't look like the old forests or trees or flowers.

Nothing stayed the same. Everything was evolving. Even he, Ted Rockson. People had not looked like him in the past. His body of pure steel muscle, his skin hard, almost like leather, impervious to cuts, sun and much of the radiation of the surrounding country. He had spent his life on the radioactive plains of the U.S.A., had wandered across her wide terrain. He *was* different; his eyes, the albino streak of hair down the center of his head—and his toughness. Ted Rockson was as hard as they come.

He had already been through a life of hardships that would have killed most men or left them blithering idiots. He had faced exposure to the elements two nights after he was born as he appeared too weak, too soft to survive. He was placed outside with only his meager wrappings—into the twenty-degrees-below night. He survived. Then the attack on his home by the squad of Blackshirts who killed his father and brothers and sisters after torturing them unmercifully, then raped and mutilated his mother. Rock had watched the horror through a knothole from his hiding place in the floor. He had memorized every one of the Red murderers' faces, and vowed to track them down if it took his entire life. Then, the struggle across a thousand miles of wilderness in the middle of winter to join Century City after his own village was destroyed by artillery fire.

As a teenager, Rock had joined commando units attacking Russian convoys. Quickly he was filling out, turning into the muscled avenger who would come to strike terror into the hearts of the Russian troops as his name and uncanny ability to survive became more and more widely known. As he grew older he spent much of his time alone, learning the countryside and how to survive in it on nothing but his skills. He strayed away from Century City for months at a time, living in the mountains, spying on the Red troops, entering the Russian-controlled cities and memorizing their defense, their gun emplacements, their prisons—and most of all, the headquarters of the KGB. His life was dedicated to one thing and one thing only: the destruction of the Red armies in America.

His mind snapped back to reality as the roar of some beast hidden behind a clump of trees startled him. It was unusual for him to be caught off guard. He shifted the Liberator from his shoulder to his arm, but the forest predator, whatever it was, stayed hidden. They traveled during the day, from early morning to sunset, resting at night beneath tall, green-barked pines with gigantic, resiny cones. The air was sweet with the sap of a hundred thousand trees.

Birds appeared more frequently as they forged deeper into the forests. Birds, what a sweet sound. The men laughed and cooed back when they heard the birds chirp and sing. There were no birds in the fortresses and the hidden cities, or in entire sections of the country. Birds had been highly vulnerable to radiation and with the winds filled with radioactive dust for months after the nuclear war, almost all of the Earth's bird life had died within weeks.

But now, as the Freefighters penetrated deep into no man's land, bluebirds, jays, and redbreasts all dove and competed with one another for attention as if wanting to somehow share their song with these passing Americans. Only Rockson remained fully alert. It was good for the men to unwind and laugh, but he knew that danger was ever present in this new world. It was behind the tree, from the sky. It leapt, charged, spat and clawed—and it was always there. He was at one with the environment—a complex sensory apparatus attuned to the postwar world at every level of its twisted surface. He could feel the vibrations of the life around him, could feel the trouble that bubbled and brewed on every surface. But he did not shy from it. He welcomed it. He welcomed the danger so that he could live, so that he could feel his power, his strength. For Ted Rockson was a man who was defined by his adversaries, who was forged ever stronger by the obstacles and the dangers that he faced.

On the third day, the woods grew thinner. Fields of small, highly misshapen, red and pink poppies took over the terrain. Small field creatures were plentiful here, moles and skunks, mice and chipmunks, darting from cover as the men walked near their holes and hiding places. They entered a field of black wheat—long, thin stalks with purple dandelion-puff seeds on the tips. The Freefighters brushed against the puffs with their clothes as they walked through the waving field and freed the seeds which flew into the air by the millions, floating violet in the evening sun.

They walked on for days, continually encountering meadows of constantly changing plant life. It was as if a different strain of seeds had been planted on every hill. The flowers and vegetation were evolving for some reason in isolated little fields of their own. They passed roses with petals as big as baseball mitts, red and green, beautiful, fragrant and ringed with inch-long poisonous spikes; daisies of black and blue, mixtures of pastel gray and maroon, mauve and ember, dark and beautiful in the white light of the rising moon.

Rockson kept the lead as he always did when on the move, always looking ahead into the darkness, beyond the line of sight. Something ahead! He slowed the Freefighters down with a wave of his right hand, one of many hand signals they used, and crept forward on his toes to investigate. A glow. The ground seemed to be shimmering with a strange, wavering fire. He walked closer now. Whatever it was it didn't feel dangerous. Before him lay a large circle of constantly shifting white light, a good hundred feet in diameter. As Rock walked closer he could scarcely believe his eyes. "Good God, it's alive!" he muttered out loud. The phosphorescent circle of light was moving with rippling energy, alive with motion, spinning, whirling. Millions of tiny glowing larvae, wormlike creatures with one eye as big as a penny and bodies that throbbed like a heart from light bulb dim to flash bulb bright. They pulsed in patterns, sending waves of light and shadow across the living pond.

The rest of the Attack Force gathered behind Rockson who stood about thirty feet away from the living organism.

"What the hell is that?" Detroit asked, moving closer.

"No, no, stay away!" Rockson said quickly. "They're an insect of some sort but I wouldn't get too close. That pack has to feed on *something*."

"Ever seen anything like that?" McCaughlin asked Rock.

"No, never," he replied softly. "Never! It must be a totally new life form." They watched in fascination, hypnotized by the warm patterns, the endless mosaics of curves and stretching lines of magnetic pulsation.

Suddenly a forest animal darted near the edge of the glowing organism opposite from where the Freefighters stood. Too close! A pseudopod of the glowing larvae snapped out from the pond and up to the bank, bringing the deerlike creature down instantly. It was pulled back into the throbbing pool and sucked down within seconds into the glow. The millions of larvae now throbbed as one like a great searchlight flashing on and off. After about ten seconds there was calm. The light seemed to dim suddenly and lose energy. The luminescence calmed to a dull glow.

"It ate and now it's sleeping," Detroit said with a chuckle.

"Just like a human," McCaughlin added.

Four

Gen. Mikael Zhabnov peered at his ruddy, fat face in the mirror held in front of him by a trembling barber. The general's black goatee had been well trimmed, his ruddy cheeks had been smoothed and his thinning wisps of blond hair were combed straight and flat across his nearly bald pate. Oily, the way he liked it. Scented.

The diminutive Afghan barber, who Zhabnov had brought with him all the way from Moscow, grinned as he saw the general obviously pleased with the trimming. Zhabnov smiled somewhere in his jowls and ran his thick, hairy fingers over his chin.

"Your excellency is happy with Abdul's work?" the barber asked nervously.

"Don't be presumptuous, barber," Zhabnov snapped. "Your work is adequate, that is all. If it weren't—" The threat went unspoken: the labor brigades in the hot zones. The little man stuttered out a stream of inane apologies to which Zhabnov merely grunted. He pulled the white wrap sheet from his voluminous body and stood up. The barbar ran to him, sprinkling him with talcum powder with one hand and dusting him off with a whisk broom with the other.

"Enough, enough," Zhabnov, the supreme president of all the Socialist States of America, said, waving his hands in the air. "Why must I be surrounded by fools?" He adjusted his bright olive uniform, pressed sharp as a blade, and the twin golden emblems on his collar, an eagle carrying a hammer and sickle in its huge claws, the symbol of his rank, and strode toward the door stiffly, sucking in his gut, raising his broad shoulders. The guards that were present everywhere in the well-preserved White House saluted and clicked their heels on both sides of the door as he exited the barbershop, located in one of many complexes that ran deep beneath the ancient building. From these offices General Zhabnov ruled America, sending out commands, gathering records and proof-of-shipment of crops to designated ports for transport back to Russia. It was a huge bureaucracy that had existed and grown for nearly a century, until it was as fat and complacent as a slug. And it ran itself—which was just fine with Zhabnov, who didn't want to be bothered with "paper work."

He stepped into his private elevator and sped up to the top level and out into the hallway of the West Wing.

Zhabnov was always slightly awed by all the portraits of the past presidents of the United States—Eisenhower, Lincoln, Kennedy, Reagan, and their Soviet successors—and the huge, haunting portrait of Washington, in gilded frame, always staring at him, eyes burning, accusing. He had asked Premier Vassily once if it were not possible to have that portrait of Washington filled in a bit, just around the eyes. Vassily had screamed, "You fool. That painting is priceless. It's a Stuart. Don't you know anything about history? You touch one paintbrush to it and you're out. You serve at my pleasure and never forget it."

Zhabnov glared back up at the portrait as he stepped by. Damn thing took up the whole wall. He sighed as he walked up to the door of the Oval Office. Another Russian guard snapped to attention, holding his Kalashnikov straight out in front of him, his eyes glued on infinity. Zhabnov walked over to the "presidential" teakwood desk and collapsed into his chair. Aside from the present occupant, the building and grounds were still exactly as they were before the war. Washington hadn't even been targeted except for four neutron bombs strategically dropped around the city. The Reds wanted to rule America from the same headquarters the Americans had. It would make the "transition" that much easier. Besides, the American president had been off in Oregon, cutting a ribbon for a new dam. That whole state was just layer upon layer of overlapping craters. The Soviet generals had gone mad in their fear that somehow the American president would survive to lead the United States in a counterattack. A pity! Zhabnov thought. Oregon was said to have once been the most beautiful of the fifty states.

The supreme commander was too fat for the presidential chair. These damn American presidents, how could they have been so thin. And his Russian antecedents in the office that he now held—Bulganin, Medledov, Orlovsky and the others— were they all so narrow, too? Bah. He picked up the ornate antique phone which instantly crackled to life. A male operator said, "Yes, sir," in an excited voice.

"Give me Killov," Zhabnov demanded.

"Home or office?" the new operator asked nervously.

"Office, office," the supreme commander bellowed out. "Do I ever call my *friend* at home? Do you think I want to talk to his maid, his cook? Idiot—his office, of course."

"Yessir, sorry!" the operator sputtered. The phone began ringing. Zhabnov coughed, preparing his warmest voice. Despite his bluster and sarcasm with the operator, Zhabnov had to admit he was a little afraid of this Killov. If Zhabnov hadn't been the nephew of Premier Vassily he would suspect that Killov was being groomed by the premier to replace him.

"Yes?" an unmistakable voice answered. The cold, crisp diction of the head of KGB-Amerika—the dreaded Blackshirts.

"Killov, it's the president." Zhabnov used his title as often as possible. "We've got to talk!"

"Talk!" Killov replied coolly. Zhabnov burned red. Now, the KGB commander was actually challenging him openly. The general calmed himself. He had no desire to tangle with him.

"Well, it's this little matter I have before me on my desk. I just got it actually and I thought I would call you about it so it could be straightened out—ironed out as the Americans say— before it got into the hands of the premier." In fact, Zhabnov had been staring at the document from Killov for some days now. It was a request to use neutron weapons—*neutron weapons*—against some suspected rebel resistance areas around the country. This man Killov always overestimated the

44

danger from these ragged bands of counterrevolutionaries, hiding in caves in the mountains eating berries and rats.

"Oh," Killov said testily, "you only *just* received my urgent request to stop these scum who have attacked our forces with impunity. The army doesn't seem able to handle it properly."

"My staff downgraded its importance," Zhabnov said curtly, fuming at Killov's second dig at his command of all the occupying military forces. "I have been occupied with important matters for days."

"Downgraded the report on clandestine resistance bases?"

"Downgraded the *speculation* you sent me about these so-called Freefighters."

"I assure you, Mr. President, these Americans are much better armed and equipped than you can imagine. Several patrols have simply vanished without a trace in Colorado and Utah lately—and others are being attacked with increasing frequency."

"And you think this is the result of resistance fighters?" Zhabnov asked, turning his chair and staring out the window at the front lawn, with its omnipresent row of tanks next to the rose garden. "Probably some of our green soldiers made a wrong turn in a magnetic storm or got themselves eaten by those toothy American wolf dogs."

"Mr. President, wolves don't make off with all the ammunition and medical supplies." Zhabnov was such a fool.

"So these patrols fell down some crevasses, or died in one of those sandstorms. Killov, you are too excitable. The premier—I know this for sure, I talked to him in person at his granddaughter's wedding in Minsk, only last month—wants to limit military action. You must get out in the fresh clean air of Mother Russia more. The premier pulls me aside at the reception and tells me, 'Nephew, please'—he is so polite—'Please, don't use any more atomic weapons in America. There is enough radiation in the world.' Now is that not what you are planning to do, Commander Killov? Use those Enhanced Radiation Neutron Devices?"

"Small atomic devices. Flashes of radiation that only destroy life and rapidly diminish in a few days."

"Killov, no more radiation! That's what the premier wants.

45

He is a conservationist, an ecologist, a humanitarian. We can't go dropping atomic bombs on a few ragged—" Killov was silent on the other end. His lips were tight and pale. Finally he spoke.

"Mikael Ivanovich," he said using the familiar, "just do me one favor. Bring it to the attention of the premier that we may not have a United Socialist States of America for the centennial next year if I am not able to discharge my duties."

"Your duties are intelligence. Intelligence, Killov. Intelligence, counterespionage and internal security. You have expanded your function, with my—and the premier's—permission. You have expanded your Blackshirt force to over five hundred thousand, with, I must say, a tremendous budget. Do I not let you send in your Deathhead paratroop commandos to destroy these wretched freedom brigades—which, as I'm sure you know, many of the other generals do not appreciate at all, considering it a usurpation of their authority. And now you want still more. Can't you do the job without pulverizing the country that feeds Mother Russia?"

"Approach the premier," Killov continued firmly, as if he hadn't heard a word of Zhabnov's tirade. "Tell him I need more troops, more weapons if he is against using these neutron weapons. We have a situation here in America, a critical one!"

Zhabnov let the KGB leader sweat for a minute as he admired the bright cherry redness of the roses that surrounded the White House. Why, they almost disguised the barbed-wire fence that ran through their delicate petals. "I'll tell you what, my friend," Zhabnov spoke up briskly. "I'm attending the annual party meeting in Leningrad next month. I will personally intervene with my uncle at that time and persuade him you need more of everything—"

"Including the neutron devices—"

"Including a few, two or three, neutron devices to destroy these annoying American bandits once and for all."

"Thank you Mikael Ivanovich," Killov said. "I will, of course, repay you for this favor." He hung up.

Zhabnov let the phone drop from his fingers and fall onto the receiving hook with a snap. Of course he had no intention of letting the KGB expand its operations in the United States. It was already too large, a threat to the normal military channels and control. Zhabnov pleaded with the premier at every opportunity to reduce Killov's Blackshirt force, but Vassily would only smile in that grandfatherly way and say, "You worry too much, nephew. I only let Killov play with his toy soldiers in America to occupy him. He is not . . . normal, you know. He likes to hurt, to destroy things, people, land. So, we in the Presidium asked ourselves: where can such a person be useful? And the answer: America. Let him destroy these Freefighters. They seem afraid of nothing except such as Killov. And does not Killov keep his part of the bargain— sending over good breeding stock of American females with their fertile bodies and radiation-resistant genes? I think you had best put up with the Blackshirts and just keep the production of wheat and corn in line with the five-year plan. That is your job. I know you can handle it, can't you?"

So it went like that. Vassily wasn't letting either him or Killov get too powerful. He was using them to balance one another, leaving the ultimate control back in Moscow. So be it! This job did have its compensations after all. Indeed.

He pressed the intercom. "Prepare the bedroom." Zhabnov smiled. The last one had been a little Negress. Delightful. Absolutely delightful. Too small for breeding purposes. Not meant for Russia's cold winters. Soft, frightened, the kind he liked most.

Killov paced back and forth in his office—a cold, stark, ultra-modern gray-and-white affair. He wore the tight, black uniform of synleather, emblazoned only on the collar with the insignia of his rank—five red stars and the KGB red death's-head. That fat imbecile Zhabnov was probably raping one of those little American waifs right now instead of attending to business.

Am I the only one, the KGB commander asked himself for the hundredth time, *who understands the real threat these American resistances forces pose and the only one who takes forceful action? Zhabnov and his general staff have all grown fat and complacent. Content to mount an offensive here and there once a year. An offensive, ha!* Killov snickered. *Sending out ten thousand troops*

47

surrounded by cranking vehicles. *Why, the rebels could hear them coming a hundred miles away. So, of course, they never run into opposition. So, of course, there is no resistance.*

And yet even I don't know the full extent of the danger. I only suspect—based on disappearing ammunition, fuel, and medical supplies. Based on whole platoons of my men sent out on search-and-destroy being swallowed up in thin air out here in these mountains. He stared out the window at the mist-shrouded Rockies off in the distance. From the eightieth floor of his KGB command building in Denver he could see a good forty miles— when the day was clear of the duststorms or the mists. *I get report after report hinting of a vast network of underground infestations of rebels armed to the teeth and trained to barely leave a trace. Americans who, until the Mind Breakers, would just recite nursery rhymes when captured, even when tortured. They seemed to have learned some sort of mental process—a hypnotic block that let them literally be murdered slowly by my expert interrogators rather than reveal a shred of information.* That is, if he could even get them before they swallowed one of those damn cyanide capsules they always carried. That was something he found hard to fathom. The way they died, instantly, without hesitation, when his Blackshirts would have some surrounded and close in. And when they broke down the door or poured into some cave, guns blazing—just bodies, already turning cold, faces blue from the cyanide. Would he do that—for Russia? Give his life if captured? But then, of course, he would never be captured. Not with his precautions, his elite guard.

Killov glanced down at the request for the use of atomic weapons he had received back from Premier Vassily in Moscow, a big "NYET" stamped on it in red. The intellectual fool, always reading a book on Napoleon or Caesar or Nixon. Always quoting "what other great men have done before me," to tight-mouthed underlings who had to sit and listen in total silence. Sometimes Killov thought that Vassily wanted the Americans to wipe out the Red forces in America. The premier of all the world was a fanatic about American lore and history. His respect for America and her past was too great for him to sanction effective countermeasures. Vassily and his books, Killov thought, like Nero and his fiddle . . . while

48

Rome burned.

Is that how we won world domination? By waiting to be destroyed by the might of America? No! We acted before they would have the upper hand. Our scientists figured that quite accurately. By 1990 the military situation would start turning back in America's favor. She would have nuclear superiority. It was all there in graphs and charts. There would be a war sooner or later so . . . then-Premier Antonin did it. Did it! Launched a pre-emptive strike—over the vehement objections of the party functionaries. And we had won. The Americans hadn't known of the twenty killer satellites the Russians had managed to slip into space in the early 1980s. When they went to counterattack, the killer sats, using laser sighting and particle beam rays, had been able to knock 93.7 percent of the U.S. nuclear missiles right out of the sky. There was devastation it was true, but history vindicated— posthumously—Premier Antonin's decision.

Now, almost a hundred years later, Premier Vassily was about to let it all slip away and permit these mutant Americans to take over the world. They would. He knew that, unless the one man who saw the peril correctly was made president of the United Socialist States—and when the "benign" Vassily died, premier of all the Russias. Premier Killov. But he'd have to wait, have to hide his ambitions or the other leaders back home would have him destroyed from fear. He knew that. And somehow he had to defend that fool Zhabnov from being overrun by the rebels, so when the time was right, there would still be a White House standing.

Killov stopped pacing. He would win. He would win because he was the stronger. It was nature's way. He looked out at the mountains caught in the sunset's purple rays. Beautiful. America the beautiful. And in those purple mountains majesty—nests of resistance—somewhere up there, he'd give his right arm to know where, was Ted Rockson, "The Ultimate American" the populace called him, scrawling his name on army barracks and alley walls. How many were out there? He tried to pierce the mist with his mind, to see, to know. Ten thousand? A hundred thousand? And at what level of attack capability were they? There were disquieting rumors among the itinerant panhandlers and trappers, passed on to him by his operatives among the masses, that the technology of some of these hidden Americans surpassed the finest in Russia. Then why were they hanging back? Why didn't they attack? Killov knew the reason. They were growing stronger while the Russian Empire was growing weaker, more decadent, more lazy, more off-guard every day.

Five

The Freefighters marched through the night as the terrain was fairly passable and Rockson wanted to try to make up time lost spent in the thicker woods. The men nervously ignored the gallery of eyes that peered at them from behind every tree, every shadow. They could hear the rustlings and growls of the forest creatures—some sounded quite large, but they appeared to find the party of Freefighters a little too big or too unknown to attack and stayed in the darkness. As the morning sun began its weary ascent through pink-clouded skies, Rockson ordered his men to stop. They found a grove of very dense palm-like trees that surrounded a pool of cool, blue water and the men threw their supplies to the ground and collapsed in exhaustion, happy to be resting for a few hours.

Within minutes they had stripped down to their birthday suits and were yelling and splashing in the fresh, cold water. After cooking breakfast and feeding the hybrids, they formed a group around the edge of the bank and told stories. Tall tales, the toughest fight they had ever been in, stories of Russian atrocities, gossip about who was sleeping with who at Century City. It felt so good to relax. Life in 2089 A.D. America did not usually allow moments of complete relaxation, total tranquility. But here in the middle of the chirping, shadow-and-sun-dappled woods, tranquility seemed to be the order of the day. There was a harmony here, a perfection, a wholeness that most of them had never experienced.

McCaughlin made a crude fishing pole from a birch branch

51

and twisted a safety pin he used to hold his constantly splitting pants together into a hook. He probed around in the dirt until he found a big, juicy, black beetle and skewered it with the pin. Using nylon thread, he dropped a line into the pond water and lay back on the sandy bank in a state of ecstasy.

"Fishing, now that's my style," the smiling Scotsman said, looking over at Rockson who sat silently, lost in his own thoughts.

Suddenly, about twenty feet out, the water in the tranquil pond was broken by a great splash. "What the—?" McCaughling began, nearly losing his pole which was being yanked wildly in every direction. He sat up and pulled back on the line as something thrashed violently just under the surface, whipping the blue water into a cauldron of boiling foam.

"Got me a big one, goddamn it," McCaughlin exclaimed and whistled loudly. The other men gathered around to cheer him on. The big Scotsman pulled and yanked but the thing on the other end of the line pulled back just as hard. Suddenly it broke the surface, whipping wildly—a horned, multieyed, ten-legged, green, scaly creature nearly two-and-a-half feet long with a row of spikes running the length of its back. It shook and whipped its head this way and that trying to free itself from the safety pin hook solidly embedded in its snapping jaw.

"Damn, that's ugly," Carter said. "I don't think I've ever seen a fish that ugly."

"That's what your mama said when she first saw you," Detroit snickered.

"I don't care if he's ugly or beautiful," McCaughlin choked out, "I'm going to get the little sucker." The Scotsman stood up and, using all his three hundred pounds of strength, pulled the pole high over his head. The green fish-thing came flying from the water straight up at him, snapping rows of razor-sharp teeth like a cutting machine.

"Look out!" the Freefighters yelled, scattering in all directions as the biting, sixty-pound thing flopped on the sand, twisting its hard body around violently, biting at everything in sight.

"Damn, he's mean," McCaughlin said almost proudly, jumping back himself and letting the pole drop to the sand. The fish saw the motion of the branchpole and pushed itself with a thrust of its powerful tail at the object. It slashed at the wooden object, snapping it in two with a single bite of its toothy jaws.

Rockson walked over until he was about six feet away from the thrashing creature. "Come on, boys, it ain't right to torture living things. That's for Russians." He pulled out his twelve-inch bowie knife, reached down and with a single powerful slash cut off the fish's head. It stopped moving, the tail twitched a few times and then it was still.

The men walked over to examine it, still a little cautious. Up close its teeth looked even more formidable. Five rows going back in its mouth, each row containing nearly thirty hooked, razor-sharp teeth. The front row had a set of fang-like protuberances almost five inches long. Equipped with fins and a tail and ten little feet with small claws, the creature looked somehow peculiar as if it was really made up of several different animals, wrongly sewn together.

"It's a strange one, that's for sure," McCaughlin spoke. "Been fishing this part of the country my whole life, ain't never seen one like this."

"Bet he don't taste too good," Saunders, one of the machine gunmen piped up. "Might as well just throw him back."

"Hell I will!" McCaughlin said. He went to his pack, pulled out one of the smokeless stoves the Freefighters carried and set to cooking his catch. A half hour later, the men were all digging into the fish and asking for more.

"Damn thing's delicious, best I ever ate," Saunders mumbled, stuffing his mouth with his third helping. McCaughlin basked in the glory of his catch and now his cooking.

"Boys, you got the best fisherman this side of the Rockies with you. Don't know how lucky you are." The ten clawed, little feet of the fish were particularly tasty and the Scotsman kept most of them for himself—he was the fisherman.

They had been feasting for about half an hour when Rockson felt the air change. It grew cold suddenly, electric. He looked up at the churning gray sky and saw the green clouds. The clouds that meant death.

"On your feet, men. Double time. There's an acid storm coming. We've got five minutes at most." The Freefighters

53

dropped their meals where they stood and ran for their supplies and the hybrids. They had all experienced these storms before. Everyone alive in America had. The green-clouded storms pulsing with electricity that appeared out of nowhere and swooped low to the Earth, releasing a putrid rain of radioactive acid that meant death for anyone caught in its downpour.

The men had trained for this eventuality. They had to—lack of preparation in this new world meant certain doom. They herded the hybrids together and made a circular barrier with their packs and weapons. They quickly pulled out the aluminized tarps which every man carried. Compact, able to fold up into a compartment in their packs, the tarps could expand to twenty foot square to create a momentary haven of safety. Aluminum was one of the few substances that could resist the dissolving powers of the acid rain. The Attack Force quickly created a little lean-to, zipping four of the tarps together and hoisted it over their group, now bunched together. They tied the ends of the silver tarps to four trees.

Not a moment too soon! They pulled down the shiny flaps on the sides of the tarps so they were completely enclosed in the metallic covering. Bunched tightly together, they could hardly breathe in the instantly sweltering enclosure. The hybrids' foul breath, strong-smelling bodies, neighing and shifting made the space a madhouse of activity. Within seconds they heard the thick drops pelting the tarps and huddled closer together in the center. From the woods around them they could hear the screams, the death cries of animals caught in the hail. It was a horrible sound—for though the acid of the rain would burn the flesh, it would not necessarily mean instant death. Instead it caused a slow eating away of hide and muscle that could take hours depending on how much acid fell. It was not a pleasant way to go.

The storm increased in fury, pounding down on the tarp while the men sat, their hearts pounding and their lips dry, in the near-darkness of the enclosure. Several of the hybrids tried to rise, panicked by the sound, but the man nearest them would poke them in the nose with a fist or pull their ears back until they calmed down. The tarp above their heads sagged, rippled with the acid water of the storm. It was a severe one, with high winds, and the entire structure began shaking. Jesus, if it came loose, every man thought silently.

But suddenly, as quickly as it had appeared, the storm passed. There was silence outside. They waited about ten minutes for the drops to dry and then carefully peeked outside. The area that had been directly hit by the acid drops was in shambles. Trees, vegetation, all wilted, eaten away with brown and black holes as if burned by fire. Several animals lay dead, their bodies lying at strange angles, legs and necks broken and cracked as the tormented creatures had tried to outrun the excruciatingly painful drops, flailing their torsos so powerfully that they literally broke their own bones. A deer lay near the pond, its flesh still smoking, its head burned almost entirely away. Nearby, a skull attached to a charred black body was all that remained of some other luckless forest dweller.

The men shuddered, said a silent prayer of thanks for their own survival, and carefully replaced their supplies. They folded the tarps, first carefully shaking out the few drops of the vile rain that had not evaporated, and packed them. One of the hybrid horses had somehow gotten a few drops of the acid on its shoulder and was howling in pain. Brice, the medical man of the Attack Force, got some ointment from his pack and after gouging out the affected area with a scalpel, salved the raw flesh of the hybrid. It would survive. It just wouldn't have hair in that spot ever again.

They headed off into the brush again. According to Rock's calculations they should be emerging from the main part of the forest by the next day. Then just a quick run across the mountains and home again, in Century City. The men were in a good mood. Things had gone relatively well this trip. Except for the dead. But there were always dead on a strike. They all knew that death lay just around the corner. When it came there was nothing any man on Earth could do to stop it. Death was the one certainty in a constantly changing world.

Rock kept the lead, making enough noise so that any hungry cat or wild boar would know they were coming. His experience had taught him that most animals would rather run than tangle with man. They attacked when cornered or suddenly frightened. Most. So he let those in the dark woods know that guests were present but would just be moving through. He didn't like to kill animals unnecessarily. Russians, that was another story. But then they were animals of a different order.

Behind him the men marched at a brisk pace, the machine gun and mortarmen at the back, keeping their equipment balanced on the backs of the occasionally ornery hybrids. The Freefighters began singing, first one voice softly, then another and another, until all fourteen remaining men of Century City Strike Force #1 team were belting out chorus after chorus of:

> Ninety-nine Blackshirt skulls on the wall,
> Ninety-nine Blackshirt skulls
> If one of those skulls should happen to fall
> Ninety-eight Blackshirt skulls on the wall
> Ninety-eight Blackshirt skulls on the wall,
> Ninety-eight . . ."

It was a dumb, stupid song, but the men sang louder and laughed at the start of each new verse. Rockson grinned to himself at the front, pushing forward through increasingly dense growth and thorns, hacking at it when it became entangled around his khaki pants with his twelve-inch bowie knife. But it should be the other way around, he thought. The numbers should go up not down, because we're killing more of them every year now.

When he was a youth, the resistance forces were still unorganized. An occasional Russian truck would be sniped at, a stray Red soldier knifed in the gut. But that was all changing now. The Free Cities were becoming more and more organized and working toward establishing a unified military council that would coordinate all attacks throughout America so as to cause the most damage. The casualties of the occupying forces were more than doubling every year. The price that the Russians would have to pay to continue their enslavement of the United States would rise—until it was too high. Then the Slavic murderers would pack up their things and head for the steppes of Mother Russia, tails between their legs. How Rockson longed for that day. When America would be free again. All other thoughts paled in comparison to this burning dream.

56

The moon rose full, shining like a ghostly eye in the dark sky, lighting up the harsh land below. The woods were thinning out now and Rock knew they couldn't be too far from the other end. A clearing ahead! Rockson surveyed it swiftly with his eyes and ears. He stepped forward, holding up his right hand and then pointing to the ground—meaning stop. Crouching low, the Ultimate American moved forward through the trees, edging along the shadows, so as not to reveal himself in the bathing rays of the now-purple moon, covered with a thin haze of radioactivity that circled the Earth high in the Van Allen Belt.

Something was out there! He could feel it in his tingling flesh. But what? Whatever it was, it wasn't human. He edged closer, taking out his .12 gauge, rapid-firing shotgun pistol that held six shells and two in the chamber, the blast of which could take out two or three Russians at twenty feet. Rockson moved on his toes, his weight perfectly balanced, his ears perked to the most silent of sounds. He peered around a thorny bush, his pistol held high in his hand. Something, something.

A black shadow flew up at him, growling, teeth slashing at his face. Then another! Rockson flew backwards with the attack. He smashed forward with the butt of his .12 into the face of the furry creature, dark, with dripping jaws. There were more. Many more—all around him, he heard their rustlings and snarls from the darkness. He spun to the side as the second attacker pounced, its fanged jaws slamming shut like a vise on the sleeve of Rock's dark green field jacket. He smashed the animal so hard in the face that bloody teeth fell to the ground. It slunk away, yowling. Wild dogs, a pack of them. He'd been attacked before, but never surprised like this. Never so many. Orange eyes glowed at him from everywhere, burning with the flames of death. Of blood. Of throats ripped out and arms torn off, dragged away into the bushes. Rockson had seen what these packs could do to a man. It wasn't a pretty sight.

Three of them approached out of the darkness, from about ten feet away, moving in slowly, in a half crouch, lips pulled back revealing rows of dagger-sharp teeth. They were huge, almost two hundred pounds apiece, covered with matted, dank hair, and those jaws, big as shovels, foaming, dripping with thick saliva in anticipation of their next meal. Two suddenly shifted to the left as the other approached from the right. Strategy, Rockson thought, going to try and outflank me. He stepped back, raised the shotgun pistol and fired at the two big shepherds as they prepared to launch themselves into his space. The .12-gauge lead load tore from the muzzle of the big gun and spread out in an x-shaped pattern. It caught both of the killer dogs square at the neck and ripped through the heavily muscled hide like butter. Both dropped like dead meat to the bloody ground, their rib cages ripped open like a carcass of butchered beef.

His hand moving back in an arc to take the recoil of the pistol, Rockson let the force swing it up and instantly forward again. The third of the attack group, a mutant Doberman with a jagged red scar along its entire body, leaped at Rockson, its jaws open wide. The pistol spoke death again and the would-be killer fell to the earth, its brains blasted from the top of its head, hanging out in dribbles of pink putty. Rockson moved backwards quickly now. They were closing in from out of the darkness. From behind trees and rocks and shadows, their eyes filled the whole night. Everywhere was death.

He kept his eyes on them, moving continuously backwards at an even, almost unnoticeable pace. If he turned and ran they would be on him in a second. His will must tame theirs. He stared at them and aimed the gun at the pack, showing them the weapon that had taken three of them out. "Back! Stay back or I'll kill. I'll destroy you with this." The approaching killers, snarling and snapping at the air with increasing frenzy, smelled the dead members of their pack and stepped over them toward the retreating creature with the glowing fire in his hand. Somehow they knew the gun was poison. It held them back— for a moment. Almost forty of the dogs closed in on Rockson in a semicircle, growling and growing angrier by the second, frustrated at not making the kill. They wouldn't hold much longer, Rockson could see that.

A large Doberman with canines nearly six inches long suddenly charged him from twenty feet away. Fast—a blur of fur and teeth. But Rockson was faster. He blasted the dog from the air, bloody pieces of black fur floating slowly above the shattered body. The rest approached closer, now completing the circle around him, coming in from behind. He was cut off. There were five shots left and then . . .

A shrill sound filled the air. A blinding blue-white light lit the sky, bathing the rock-strewn field with a daylight brilliance. Rockson and the killer pack were caught frozen for a split second as if by a camera—suddenly the dogs ran. Yelping, tails between their legs, they had had enough. The flare floated slowly down, dangling from a small parachute, burning like a sun, sending out waves of purifying light. Within seconds the dogs had bounded back into the darkness from which they had come.

Rockson turned as the rest of the Freefighters came forward from the woods behind him. Detroit stepped up to him, eyes taking in the ripped carcasses on the hard ground.

"We couldn't see what was happening, Rock," Detroit said, bending over and opening the jaws of one of the killers and whistling. "But we sure could hear the growls and gunshots. We figured a little flash bulb might make 'em shy."

Rock reloaded the four empty chambers of his .12-gauge pistol, taking the thick cartridges from his utility belt.

"It did. I would have been dogfood in another five seconds," Rock said, putting the pistol back into its hip holster. "This is getting to be a habit," Rock said, turning to the other men with an ironic grin. "I've got an image to protect. I'm supposed to be the tough guy here."

Six

The Freefighters kept on the move for two days after they left the vast woodlands. They had to be more careful out here because the Russian spydrones flew regular patterns overhead, searching the dusty, rocky terrain for signs of trouble. But because of their regularity, the drones were easy enough to avoid and the men would just take a break when the next one was due over, hiding behind rocks or under trees.

At last they reached the narrow mountain trail thought impassable by the Reds. They hit the start of the winding path that wove thousands of feet in the air, around two peaks, in the early morning, just as the sun shot out of the darkness, piercing the clouds just above them with orange-purple rays. It took nearly two hours to traverse the crumbling trail that sometimes narrowed to under a foot in width. Even the sure-footed hybrids were nearly stumbling as they rounded the last of the four thousand foot drops, straight down, past sheer rock walls of smooth granite. Then down the long, even slope that ended in a thick-wooded valley.

They came to the three pine trees beside two large, square boulders that was the only sign of the main entrance into Century City. They walked silently past the trees and into a tunnel of brush and thickets nearly twelve feet in diameter. An owl hooted.

"That's the signal this week," Carver whispered to Rockson, cupping his mouth to his hands. He gave out three rapid renderings of a wood thrush. The owl hooted twice rapidly—

too rapidly for an owl—and there was a grating sound. What looked like a twenty ton, black boulder at the end of the little tunnel of brush slid sideways and there appeared a dimly lit ramp of black-painted concrete on the other side, lit by faint green lights overhead. The fourteen Freefighters, pulling their pack hybrids behind them, walked into the cavernous space. After the last man had entered, the boulder slid effortlessly shut behind them.

There was a click and overhead arc lights came flaring on. On all sides, khaki-clad guards, with silencer-equipped Sten guns stood, barrels pointing at the arrivals.

"There is nothing like a . . ." demanded the closest figure, his gun at chest level.

"Dame," Rockson replied clearly. The guns were lowered. Greetings and slaps on the back were exchanged. Someone popped a cork and the city's homemade wine flowed into their beat-up canteen cups as was the tradition for all returning Strike Forces. Dr. Shecter, the leading scientist of Century City and one of its most influential men politically, appeared and shook Rockson's hand.

"Good to see you back safe and sound. There's something that I must talk to you about!" Shecter's fierce brown eyes stared straight into Rockson's. The intensity of the man was immense. The scientific "wonderboy" was responsible for half of Century City's development over the last twenty years. An unparalleled genius in many fields, Shecter merely shrugged off any suggestion that he was a new Michelangelo with an "I don't paint."

Shecter moved on to shake each man's hand. In the absence of Council Leader Evans who was away on urgent business in a nearby Free City, Shecter was the highest ranking official around. Obviously he had been drafted for the rituals for he quickly disappeared back into the vast complex of corridors with his omnipresent guards. Shecter was too valuable to lose.

Intelligence Officer Rath sidled over with his debriefing crew of four good-looking women who, he felt, helped in making the men relaxed and eager to talk after such hazardous forays. They eased the Freefighters into the debriefing room off to the side and began questioning them in groups of three

61

and four—what they saw, how many enemy had been destroyed. Intelligence demanded every scrap of information. The Free Forces were building up the big picture of the Reds and the information, fed into Century City's computer bank, was establishing a clear picture of the actual Soviet strength—and weakness—in the thousand mile square around the hidden city.

Rockson, who would write and file his own detailed report later, was spared what the men referred to as the inquisition. As he headed briskly down the main ramp that led from Security Chamber A, a blond, well-endowed woman ran after him.

"Rock, wait!" Shannon yelled, running up the ramp after him. Rockson stopped a moment and waited for the assistant intelligence chief to catch up and then immediately began walking again.

"Can't wait for the report?" Rockson cracked. "Well, let's see—nine K-55s destroyed; three, possibly four, limping. I'd say a hundred to—"

"No, no," she cut in, ignoring his thin-lipped depreciating grin. "Not this time, Rock. I guess you haven't heard. Trouble! Big trouble." Rockson stuck his right index finger against a sensor hidden in the apparently solid rock wall in front of them and a wall opened, hewn from the living granite of the mountain the city was built into. They entered a medium-sized suite reserved for visiting dignitaries and returning fighters. The subdued lighting was more natural than in the corridors outside. As the door slid shut, soft, lilting music oozed from hidden speakers.

"Off!" Rockson said, and the music faded out. Another one of Shecter's little toys. "Tell me while I decontaminate," Rockson said, walking over to the microwave-shower area. In other suites the other Freefighters would also take procedures to minimize the amount of radiation they carried in their bodies—and into Century City.

Rockson dropped his field clothes into a steel container, to be fully de-radiated later, and stepped into the red circle of the shower. A purplish beam played over his body with a soft hiss as he made shadowboxing motions slowly exposing every part

62

of himself to the decon unit. Outside, over the low humming noise, Shannon was momentarily distracted by his nakedness, then told him the bad news.

"They—the Reds—got Preston—from Westfort. He was one of their top military men. He was doing point on a scouting mission in one of the Dead Zones about two hundred miles from Westfort when apparently the whole sky filled with Blackshirt paratroops. The Freefighters put up a hell of a fight, took out scores of Reds, and most of them got out—all except Preston. Evidently they got his belt off in the fighting and he couldn't swallow the pill."

Rockson frowned. There was a beep, the purple rays died down and he stepped from the circle. Now for a real shower. "Well, he won't talk. I know him and—"

"He might talk, Rock. The Reds have this new machine. It literally cuts right through our cortex programming and gets beyond the babble we can implant. No, this new machine—the Mind Breaker they call it—has two long needles. It's like a headset—big, ugly thing—it sticks these needles in and . . . Never mind the specifications, the fact is, it might break down anyone's resistance. Even yours, Rockson." He saw the way her green eyes followed him toward the shower as the intel expert continued.

"According to our information they plan to use them on recalcitrant labor but have discovered it works wonderfully to get information as well. Believe me, the pain—it heightens pain in addition to probing deep into the brain's memory circuitry."

"And," said Rockson, stepping into the shower stall, "Preston knew everything about Westfort—his home base. Has he ever been here?"

"No, never. Only four people in each Free City are permitted to know the location of other cities. He wasn't, because of his military activities. Still—to lose Westfort!"

Rockson turned on the shower, first hot for several minutes, to get every bit of grime and radioactive dust from his skin and hair, then ice cold. Right now the Red bastards could be probing Preston's mind, torturing, searching through layer after layer of false imprinting, going up the pain threshold until . . . Shannon sat, looking depressed outside the stall.

Westfort was a relatively small city with a population of just under four thousand. It was located somewhere in Colorado. Several times Rockson had rendezvoused with Preston and some of his fighting team from Westfort. All hard-fighting, courageous men. They had done joint missions together. Preston's capture felt like a personal blow to him. He would miss the man. For whatever they did to him, he wasn't coming out of it alive. What hellish device could make a man as tough as Preston talk? Betray his home?

But there was nothing to do but wait and see. Every twenty-four hours, pigeons arrived from the other Free Cities bearing micro messages on a peg pouch. In that way the cities kept in communication without radio—and without anyone but a privileged few knowing where the other cities were. It was better that way. If the carrier pigeon didn't arrive that evening, it would mean that Westfort was gone.

Rockson stepped from the shower and said, "Order a full alert, priority two—and let me know when and if the pigeon arrives."

"Right!" Shannon was out the door. When Rockson said something he was obeyed. As first commander he was the highest-ranking military—as opposed to civilian—officer in the city. Donning a new set of indoor clothing—tan, loose-fitting shirt and pants—Rockson went immediately to the computer room. Saying a brief hello to the operator at one side working on cataloguing orders for the Liberator automatic rifle, which were shipped out to other hidden cities by the thousands, Rock sat in front of the main terminal and pushed the "activate" switch. He punched in the code for sequential screening of each and every section of the vast Century City complex. He was looking for something—a way to tell if the city had been breached. Perhaps the Westfort incident was not just a chance occurrence but part of a big Red crackdown on the underground. Rockson had worked out a program without even Dr. Shecter knowing, a way of mapping human activity in the city. It was based on radiation count. Spies, either Russian or traitorous Americans from one of the fortress enclaves, were invariably less radioactive than Free Americans. It was a

64

very small difference he had noted when studying equations on the buildup of radiation levels after the return of Attack Teams. What it boiled down to was his own particular program—which he now accessed with his code word "Possum"—to search each level for lower-rad humans, and to flash a red dot wherever these personnel existed on the plans now flashing one at a time on the green-tinted screen.

"A-1"—that was main Hydroponics, thirteen hundred meters of underground vault lit by growth lights wherein most of the city of fifty thousand's vegetables were produced, without any soil. It had 1,265 personnel on three levels, and "Possum" gave no indication of anything amiss. Next he hit "A-2," the Central Library—a good place to slip unnoticed into the group. The four-level library was filled with 1,237 people. 1,476,391 discs were on file, and 209 people owed library fines for overdue discs. But no red dot.

Century City, the fabulous creation of a hundred years of guts and ingenuity, had a less than auspicious beginning. It was September 11, 1989, the last day of the old era. It was rush hour. The five mile long, eight-lane tunnel of Interstate 70, coursing out of Denver and reaching into Utah, was filled with rapidly moving vehicles of every type—vans, panel trucks, huge double tractor trailers, small imports, rusty, old Chevys. Eager commuters going back to another night of TV, roast chicken or pot roast, extra helpings, in their own little home. The American Dream.

Then it happened. The strike! Out of the skies they came, hundreds of flaming needles ripping the heavens with their screaming descents all over the United States and Canada. Each needle splitting up into five, six, as many as ten glowing warheads heading down to their own special target. Some went off in the oceans or devastated the wrong areas. But seven hundred of the missiles went off. Hitting Aspen and Cheyenne, Las Vegas and Omaha. Hitting Detroit and Tacoma, Texarkana and Little Rock. Everywhere the same—a retina-burning flash, a towering mushroom-shaped cloud. Millions were incinerated, tens of millions, in the first few minutes. Millions more staggered around, their eyes burnt, their skin charred and peeling, in a shock beyond shock. A world of megadeath.

The lucky ones died straight off. Another fifty million men and women and babies lingered on painfully over the months. Their hair and teeth slowly fell out, their flesh wasted away until it looked like something gangrenous and rotted. And then, mercifully, death. Then the cancers, the malformed babies, the plagues of virulent, mutated diseases that took one man by the throat and let the next live. Then came the bandit gangs—murderous packs of marauders, armed to the teeth, who roamed the country raping and burning out of bloodlustful nihilism.

The hardest hit cities were the ones with the large black populations. The survivors concluded that this had been a deliberate racial policy by the Soviets—to get rid of the minorities of the country—to make occupation easier. They knew well how blacks had fought their way up the ladder from slavery in America. They knew that blacks would not accept a new master—ever. So they "sanitized" the largely black cities of Detroit, New York, Newark, Chicago, with multiple hits. So much for freeing the oppressed peoples of the world.

Century City began as a tomb for the people trapped in the five-mile tunnel when the war began. Avalanches from the surrounding mountains, exploding from nearby hits, covered both ends of the tunnel, sealing it off with nearly a hundred feet of dirt and rock—but it also protected those inside. Realizing the horror that had occurred, those inside used the situation to their advantage. They immediately elected leaders and formed into work groups, stripping their cars to make engines for electricity and rigging up an air purification system through the vent holes in the hillside. Somehow they survived and, soon, even began doing well. Names such as Ostrader, Taggart, Meister and Bonne. Men who took charge and made the tunnel dwellers constantly strive for more. They quelled the panic, made the best of the situation, and kept the democratic tradition alive. They realized the Russians were moving en masse into the nearby, unscathed Denver by the number of giant airlifters coming by each day. For anyone to leave and go his own way would mean death. They voted and it was nearly unanimous. They would gather their strength. There were engineers, scientists, mathematicians, plumbers, teachers, auto mechanics—all had been trapped on Interstate 70. They would pull themselves up by their own bootstraps as their ancestors would have done. And there would come a time when they would hit back—hard—against the bastards who were busy enslaving whatever they hadn't already destroyed of America. The child rapers and the mass murderers would pay back with blood—it would be done if it took a century. Hence the name Century City.

They gradually expanded their small society in the tunnel, hewing out more space under the large mountain that stood above them. First, just extra storage rooms, but over the years elaborate complexes of tunnels and multilevels had been built, containing a now-bustling, industrious city. And they had changed too, or their children had. Certain minor mutations began popping up more and more frequently in babies born after the blast. Signs like white-star patterns on the children's backs or different color eyes, such as Rockson's violet and blue combination. Streaks of white on the head, lack of body hair below the face. But it also became apparent that children with these traits were stronger, more radiation-resistant, better able to survive in the hard new world. These were the children of Free America who would inherit the land, who would retake the U.S.A. from her Red rulers.

Ted Rockson continued to look at the screen, his eyes tied like a hawk searching for rats, as detail after detail of the vast complex came on the viewer. Schools, nurseries, exercise rooms, gardens, research and weapons labs—everything linked by ramps, stairways and elevators, so as to keep the movements of the city's inhabitants free and quick. And it all worked. The best part was the Russians had no idea how big it was and how deadly.

Diagrams of the main power generating chambers flashed on the screen, five seconds per schematic. This was Rockson's favorite area in Century City for it was the future. No longer would man's quest for power sources despoil the environment. For here were ecologically sound energies. In the history of Earth, all industry and power production left traces behind, junk fouling the environment. Here the wastes from industrial production—gas, solid and liquid—were re-used. Some for power; some harnessed to react with carefully developed, chemical-eating bacteria and become inert. The byproducts were mixed with dirt and shipped off to hot zones where they were used to create a thin topsoil for the radioactive desert. This soil would block off the radiation beneath to some degree. Simple experiments had shown that many simple grasses and plants could grow in this environment. The dead zones could someday be green again.

Rockson liked to think of a future green America. Greener than it had ever been, for all Free Americans now understood how precious and delicate the environment that had been nearly destroyed was. We will no longer pollute, we will restore, was the credo of most hidden cities. Over the thirty years that Century City's Industrial Waste Removal Program had been in operation, nearly a million tons of synthetic soil had been produced and stored in giant natural caverns and fissures below the mountain, many created from earthquakes during the war. These tons of soil could be pumped up to the surface when the time came, and shipped to dead zones all over the country—on trains, if trains would ever again roll.

Rockson had been sitting in front of the computer terminal screen for almost an hour and had nearly completed checking every one of the 115 sections of the city complex when the intercom rang. It was Shannon. The Council would meet in G-3 at eleven City Time. Rockson flicked off the console. General knowledge of his little surveillance system would render it useless. It was his ace in the hole.

Rockson nodded to Pierce and Evers, the Council guards, as he entered. Pierce, a broad-boned viking of a man with amber eyes and a nearly platinum beard, asked, "How'd you do, Rock? Kill all those bastards yet?"

"Didn't help them any," Rockson deadpanned. "Maybe ten tanks, a dozen half-tracks, and 150—make that 200—Russians."

Evers, the shorter, swarthy one with a shotgun pistol, similar to Rock's, in a quick-draw holster on his thigh, said in a raspy voice, "I have the last batch you disposed of in the memory on my calc." He extracted a flat, tiny adding machine and punched in the new numbers. "Let's see, at the present rate of elimination it would take—" he pressed the tiny total button—"fifty-one years to kill every Red in America."

"Great," Rockson said, turning and walking down the main aisle toward the podium, around which the expectant Council members were already seated in rows of cushioned, low-slung seats. That was much too long, Rockson thought. That was exactly the rub all the time. They were fighting a giant. Even the loss of whole expeditionary forces scarcely made the Red leadership blink. What were ten, or even twenty thousand troops a year to them? They probably expected that in their troop-strength projections. No, somehow the Freefighters' attack had to be a hundred times more violent and destructive. They had to be hurt!

Rockson walked up the four wood steps to the podium and took a seat to the right of the speaker of the chamber, Willis, who shook his hand warmly and then turned to the Council members and addressed them, officially opening the meeting. He expressed the heartfelt thanks of the Council that Rockson had again been so successful in his mission. But the speaker's smile immediately dropped away as he began the session.

"Let's get to the most serious matter immediately—the capture of Preston. This situation endangers not only Westfort but our own Century City as well."

Truer words were never spoken.

Seven

The eighty-story, circular monolith sat in the center of Denver, a statue of death. Black as night, sheathed in impenetrable, shimmering glass, it reached up to the sky, the highest structure in the KGB fortress of Vostok, the center of KGB operations in America. The monolith, called just "The Center" by its personnel and "The Death House" by the Americans, had been built to terrify, to frighten, to intimidate. And it did. Erected nearly sixty years earlier by Commander Jargov, the fourth of the KGB leaders in the occupied United States, it had been constructed of the finest materials, hardened steel and specially made, triple-polorized, brownish blue-tinted glass to withstand the sun and dust of the Colorado climate. "I want this building to last as long as the empire," Jargov had ordered. And it would be standing well after that.

Still as mysterious and conspicuous as the day it was built, the monolith, some two hundred feet in diameter, was the base of all KGB operations in the U.S.A. Over nine thousand men and women worked here daily, pulling up to work early each morning in their Pushka three-wheel cars or on motorcycle. The monolith was set in the center of the KGB fortress, separate from the military base or its housing. The KGB demanded its own space. It did not want to mix. The meaning of the KGB was fear—to watch over the Soviet military as well as the American workers. Fraternization meant familiarization and friendship. This could not be. Not the Blackshirts. Their black uniforms and red death's-head medallions designated

70

that they were out of the ordinary. An image must be created of immortality, of superhuman strength and violence. And that was how it must be. For fear worked only when it was believed.

Within the walls of the Center, myriad functions were carried out. From information fed in from military operations, informers, spydrones and the KGB's own network of intelligence operatives, a comprehensive picture was drawn of the rebel activity and the trouble spots around the country. The intelligence units occupied twenty-five floors, filled with maps—floor-to-ceiling, contoured maps of the entire country, flashing with different colored lights to designate the trouble spots. Green lights for environmental dangers—from earthquakes to radioactive mists—red lights for rebel attacks, orange lights for possible Free American hidden cities, and blue lights for all other KGB centers in the U.S.A. Messengers constantly ran from floor to floor as their superiors yelled out orders. The sheer enormity of spying on such a vast country as the United States was a constant struggle. There were always problems, always emergencies—breakdowns of equipment, rebellions, sabotage of the factories and the Russian fortresses by the underground. The army were fools, barely capable of going out and capturing a few rebels, let alone understanding the whole picture, the emerging pattern. That work was for the KGB.

On the next fifteen floors were the counterespionage "services"—ruling bureaucracy that sent out the Death Squads to liquidate all those thought to be troublemakers. There were no laws they had to obey—they were the law, the judge, the jury and the executioner. They had free rein over the country like some barbarian war lords of the past.

From the forty-first to the sixty-fourth floor were the communications networks, linking all KGB centers in the country with Mother Russia and their comrades in arms around the world. From Timbuktu to London, from Paris to Tokyo, the KGB ruled supreme. Radio, laser systems and giant radar dishes on the roof, slowly turning their fifty-foot cones to follow their linking satellite ten thousand miles up. Information was sent and received from virtually every corner of the world. The wires literally buzzed with energy as the

71

global Soviet Empire talked to itself.

On the top fifteen floors were the administration offices of top KGB officers. Here the rooms were huge and plush, with Persian rugs and flowing copper waterfalls. The elite of the elite—their death's-heads cast in solid gold—the most feared men in America ruled from here: Killov, Turgenov, Dashkov, Mukstadt.

Below the ground floor, the original designers of the monolith had built an additional ten stories, pushing a good 150 feet below the ground. Here, it was thought, just in case of counterattack, the structure could be used as a fallout shelter, and thus was built with twenty-foot-thick concrete reinforced walls, airlocks, self-contained oxygen supply and provisions for years. But the KGB had quickly found a much better use for these subterranean floors—a use more fitting to their work: torture chambers. The floors beneath the Center were equipped with over five hundred cells, in case large-scale interrogations became necessary. The most advanced—and primitive—torture devices known to man were here, a regular testing laboratory of the implements of pain. From bamboo shoots inserted under finger nails, still effective on many American fortress workers, to sophisticated electrode devices, which when attached to the genitals were capable of producing an exquisite pain.

The torture squad consisted of nearly a hundred men, the most sadistic of the KGB crews, who had been chosen just for their qualities of mercilessness and cruelty. Down below they had their own world. There were no rules, no one to answer to. God help the man or woman or child who set foot through those basement doors. Most were never seen again. The few that were released were mindless vegetables, their bodies ripped, scarred, their brains reduced to functions of stumbling and excreting. Most could hardly talk, or if they could, wouldn't. They sat on stoops, and in glass- and brick-strewn lots in the run-down American sectors of the fortresses and moaned softly, unable to communicate their private hell.

Fortunately for them, most did perish within the walls. If death could be termed fortunate, it was here that such a designation would occur. For the KGB of 2089 were experts in

72

every kind of pain that the human body could experience. They studied the ways of pain, the uses of pressure points and blades and electricity and ice and beatings and stretchings and glass inserted in the rectum and broken. But why go on, only those who give torture or feel it would want to know every detail. When death came it was a blessing.

Still, there was one thing that grated on the torture squads. The Free Americans. Somehow, their own scientists and psychologists had come up with a psychological conditioning that could overcome pain. They felt the torture, but blocks came on in their minds that permitted no access to the secret information that the KGB wanted most desperately—the locations of the American Free Cities. The Americans would scream and then spout nursery rhymes, the name of their girlfriend, or their favorite food. Even in death they had the last laugh on their KGB tormentors, who thus far had been totally incapable of breaking through these mind armors.

Until now, that is. The number-one priority of the KGB scientists for the last twenty years had been to develop some method, some device capable of smashing through these blocks, and now, at last, success was within reach. The Mind Breaker, invented by Dr. Nikolai Chernov, would make the difference. The device used laser beams to actually penetrate the brain tissue and short out the brain block, by slicing certain vital brain connections, producing a pain undreamt of heretofore. As Chernov had said when presenting the first of the devices to Killov, "The demons of hell itself would be happy to have such a machine. The pain produced by them is virtually infinite. We've only used them at the lowest power and the results are . . . extraordinary."

Killov immediately ordered extensive testing of the Mind Breaker. If it was true, the shape of America could be changed forever. The Free Cities would be found one by one and destroyed. The last strongholds of resistance to the Soviet Empire would be crushed and Russia could settle into a thousand years of tranquility. Of course, Killov's future would be assured as well. With the destruction of the rebels he would be next in line for the premiership. Every prisoner brought in from now on was to be hooked up to the Mind Breaker. He wanted every detail of the machine. How it worked, what its limits were, if any. But most of all, he wanted the locations of the Free Cities. Blood would flow.

A Skinord attack helicopter swooped down suddenly from out of the sky like a black hawk zeroing in on a kill. The KGB chopper with the red skull on the side was one of the KGB's fleet of one hundred similar, highly armed helicopters used for reconnaissance, counterinsurgency and whatever. It dropped to within a foot of the Center's landing pad, located several hundred feet to the rear of the towering, black structure. The pilot pulled back on the rotor speed and the chopper dropped softly onto the rubber-padded landing zone. It was immediately surrounded by machine-gun-toting guards who waited impatiently for the side door to open. With a click and a slight whoosh of air from the pressure difference, the steel door slid back and a battered man, face dripping with blood, was thrown out by the two KGB men inside. He landed roughly on the ground, wrenching his shoulder, for his hands had been cuffed behind his back. He was instantly lifted at the elbows by the waiting guards and shuffled off toward the Center.

Lt. Col. Bill Preston, one of the highest ranking officers of Westfort, located some five hundred miles to the east of Denver, had been captured. It was one of the Reds' biggest catches in years. He had been traveling by hybrid with a force of twenty men, investigating the possibility of a recently uncovered machine factory still containing parts in collapsed rooms. They had traveled, as did all Freefighters in this part of the country, only at night to avoid the Russian unmanned spydrones which buzzed constantly overhead, video cameras relaying information to control centers set up in every Russian fort. But the KGB had set a trap on one of the forest trails that they suspected was being used by the underground. Preston and his men had just come into a small clearing when they were attacked from every side by the black-garbed, submachine-gun-firing KGB commando squad. The Americans, of course, fought back with everything. There could be no capture by the Russians. That meant only one thing. Death was far preferable. Though hopelessly outnumbered, they pulled knives when their pistols clicked empty and flung themselves on their attackers, stabbing guts and slashing eyes. Though the force of the KGB numbered over a hundred men, the fight went on for almost ten minutes. When it was over, thirty-five KGB commandos lay sprawled in pools of blood. Every Freefighter had been slaughtered except for Preston and an unconscious Freefighter, thought dead, who later escaped. Seeing he was about to be captured, Preston turned his pistol on himself, but the damn thing jammed. He reached for the cyanide capsule in his utility belt and lifted his hand to swallow. An alert officer leaped at him, knocking his hand away with the stock of his SMG.

"Now we have one," the Red said with a smile, looking down at the fallen Freefighter who stared back up scornfully.

"You have one, but you won't get squat from me, comrade. I'll die before I'll spill a thing." He smirked at the futility of the KGB attempts to make Freefighters talk. Many Americans had already died. And many more would before this war was over. He was ready to die himself. Life had been good to him all things considered. He regretted that his wife and children would be alone now. But they were tough. They would fight on.

A helicopter had been called in within minutes of his capture and Preston, handcuffed, had been thrown on board with four guards. Within minutes the chopper was flying, Priority One to Denver. All other air vehicles gave way as the shiny black chopper flitted through the air, a messenger of doom. The crescent moon flickered fingerlike shadows on the craft as it soared along, just below the cloud line.

Once landed, Preston was immediately pushed toward the back entrance to the Center. Death's-head guards, stiffly at attention, saluted and stepped aside as the door creaked open. The captured Freefighter was hustled inside as the inner airlock door rolled quickly closed behind them. He was led to one of ten gleaming chrome elevators and down. Down into the Earth. Preston had never been in the monolith. But he had heard of it. A courageous man, a man who had faced death square in the eye many times, Bill Preston nevertheless felt a knot in his gut as the elevator descended. He tried to imagine what awaited him. He knew that it would be far worse than anything his mind could picture.

The elevator snapped open and again he was pushed out. They led him down a long corridor filled with countless numbered doors. He could hear blood-curdling wails of pain echoing down the hallway. Even steel couldn't stop the sound of a man screaming for his life. At the end of the corridor they came to yet another large steel door. The guards saluted the officer at Preston's right and buzzed the door open. Preston was pulled into a fairly small room equipped with futuristic equipment, blinking computer lights, diodes, dials, video cameras and a large, gridded screen. All the guards exited quickly except two who stood by him, hands at ease behind them.

Preson looked around furtively. There were no whips or chains here. Somehow he had imagined a more primitive dungeon, with racks and burning pokers. Instead, a simple plastic chair, body-contoured with aluminum arms and straps for the wrists. It was the object that waited on a mobile stand above the chair that looked forbidding: a large helmet covered with wires and meters. In the center, underneath, right where the head would fit in when the helmet was lowered, two six-inch long, syringelike prongs.

"Please, Deity, let me die before I betray," he prayed. Death was his only hope. Escape was impossible. He glanced around the room. The device seemed to be wired to some kind of computer terminal, rows of green and amber lights softly glowing, waiting to flash with life. As he swung his head around, he saw a large piece of glass about ten feet off the floor, and behind it, a number of KGB officers stood, talking and laughing. They stopped when they saw him taking them in, and all stared back down at the prisoner. A voice suddenly came over a speaker to the right of the bulletproof, inch-thick glass partition.

"Welcome, Mr. Preston. Welcome to the Center. I am Director Killov. Perhaps you've heard of me?"

Preston stared up at the hawk-faced man speaking into the microphone. "Yes, I've heard of you, Killov. You're the greatest mass murderer alive in the world today. Any loyal American would give his beating heart to see you dead."

"You flatter me," Killov said with a slight smirk. "To be so

76

notorious a man to you so-called Freefighters just fills me with happiness."

"Murder is nothing to be proud of. Your day will come, that I know," Preston replied, almost shouting now. "Why don't you just kill me and get it over with."

"Kill you?" Killov laughed. "Oh no, Mr. Preston, we have much greater things in store for you than that. How unimaginative of you. Don't you see that device near you? The chair, with the metal hat. Won't you have a seat?" The officers around Killov laughed as Preston tried to struggle with the three hulking guards who grabbed him and strapped him quickly to the chair. From a side door, a man emerged wearing a white smock and surgical gloves. He moved slowly over to Preston, a short, fat man with thinning brown hair and black eyes that were dead. Preston shuddered as the man looked him full in the face. He had never seen eyes like that before. They seemed to have no life behind them at all, total blackness that fell back, like a stone dropping into a deep well, never touching bottom.

"I am Dr. Yurov," the short, smocked man said with the sheerest flicker of a smile. "If you will allow me." He reached above Preston's hand and lowered the helmet, attached to a curved stainless-steel arm, until it was halfway covering Preston's face. The points of the twin surgical probes rested just an inch above the Free American's skull. Yurov pressed a button on the side of the black helmet that resembled a kind of ultramodern diving helmet as it covered the prisoner's head. Two foam pads slowly eased out of each side of the helmet and moved forward until tightly pressed against Preston's temples. He tried to move. God, his head was totally immobilized now. He began trembling in spite of himself. Those hypodermic spikes, what were they going to?

"Ready, sir," Dr. Yurov said softly, looking up at Killov about twenty feet away behind the glass partition. The KGB leader merely nodded once and waited. An orderly carrying a tray of drinks walked around to Killov and the other top officers giving out brandies and scotches and Killov's drink, straight gin.

Yurov stroked the hair away from the center of Preston's

head, looked at the spot of bared scalp and nodded to himself. He lowered the two prongs until they rested right on the flesh at the very top of the skull. "Yes, that's just right," he mumbled absent-mindedly. The KGB "doctor" walked to the large control panel along one wall, covered with flickering video screens, read-outs, computer-drawn graphs of CAT-SCANs of Preston's brain that were being taken by a camera at the top of the helmet every four seconds. Yurov switched the Laser On button, and a row of dark green crystal diodes, stretching along a chrome metal cabinet behind the prisoner's chair, instantly lit up. "Yes, yes, everything's working fine," he muttered again, unaware of his spoken words.

"Now, this is going to hurt," he said to Preston, walking back over to the helmet. "It's going to hurt quite a bit. So the best thing I can say to you is to give in to it. The quicker you surrender your personality, your thoughts, your obedience, the quicker the pain will be over."

"Oh, cut all the goddamn bullshit and torture me, I'm getting bored," Preston snapped, trying to maintain a tough front. He steeled himself inside, steeled his guts and his very soul for what was about to come.

Yurov threw a switch at the top of the metal helmet and two brilliant lights shot out from the ends of the needle-sharp prongs. The lights were of an extraordinary green, like the star fire of a burning gem, incandescent. Yurov slowly began turning a small lever which lowered the probes toward Preston's skull. The heat of the laser beams shooting out from the tips instantly vaporized the flesh and bone at the top of the Freefighter's head. He screamed and kept screaming. The probes continued at a downward angle moving at the prescribed rate of ten millimeters per second. The million-degree, green fire of the laser probe burned and sizzled away at the brain tissue, bubbling it and disintegrating it into putrid smoke that rose from the top of Preston's head.

One of the officers behind the partition turned to Killov. "That's apparently one of the only problems, sir," he said in a whisper. "They say the brains smell quite awful as they burn."

"Really?" the KGB boss asked. "The premier won't like that at all when we demonstrate this for him. Tell them that something will have to be worked out. A miniature ventilation fan to suck in the smoke and the odor. Priority!" Killov's right hand man, Colonel Dobrynin, took out a small, red leather notebook and quickly wrote down Killov's command. Every word of the Blackshirt leader must be obeyed. Every.

Dr. Yurov glanced over at the video monitor on the wall displaying Preston's CATSCAN. Every layer of the brain crossed across the green-tinted screen in waves of imagery. The probes could clearly be seen biting into the central tissue of a human mind.

"We're now reaching the cerebral section, sir," Yurov said. "Now is when the process actually starts. You see, as I burn away the older memory system and also apply excruciating pain, the patient is put into an entirely different consciousness." The doctor of torture moved the lever again, and the burning arc of purest pain bit deep into the prisoner's brain.

Preston screamed and screamed, but he no longer knew that. He no longer knew who he was. The screams were entirely involuntary, his lungs filling, hyperventilating with air and rushing back out through his throat with a ghastly wail. His body attempted to jerk wildly in response to the overwhelming pain. But strapped tightly on both sides, he nearly cracked his bones within their muscle and skin confines. The pain! Teeth, razors, flames, ripping through the center of his very being. White hot pain. Memories of his life, his wife and daughter, his childhood, burned and defiled, ripped out and torn from his mind as if they had never existed. He could feel his mind disintegrating, falling into pieces of dust, exploding in every direction.

The pain! The pain! It was so intense, pushing everything to the side as it gripped him in clawlike vises of sensation. He was being sliced by razor blades of liquid fire, slashed open and cut, his backbone and veins, his guts and his tongue and his boiling eyes, all cut and twisted into knots of flame. At last, all he was was his body, and his body was sheer, infinite, unbearable pain. He suddenly snapped, a shudder coursing through the super taut arms and chest, and fell unconscious, held upright only by his bonds.

"Good, good," Yurov said, muttering to himself again. He

pulled the lever the opposite way and the prongs lifted out of the smoking brain. He pushed the Laser Off switch and the green streaks of hellfire died out. He put smelling salts under Preston's nose and slapped his face as the prisoner groaned.

"Very good. Now that wasn't so bad, was it?" Yurov asked blandly. "Now, just one more question and then you can go to sleep. Where is your city?"

Preston's eyes half opened, bloodshot, dead. It wasn't the same man as it had been five minutes before. His brain was different now. He felt . . . He didn't understand. Where was everything? Where was he? He had no past memory beyond the last few hours. He was afraid, so afraid. These men, they had hurt him. He was an animal—dumb, unaware even of his humanity.

"Your city? Your city?" Yurov continued, slapping him lightly on the right cheek.

His what? Oh, his city. They wanted to know. Yes, his city. But no, he wasn't supposed to tell. But why? He couldn't remember. There was a reason, there was.

"Tsk, tsk," Dr. Yurov said, staring down at the trembling shell of a man. "I'll have to use the probes again." He started to lower the helmet.

"No! No!" Preston screamed, bolting up. "It's just about three hundred miles west of here. Westfort. Just inside three valleys, where the Falls River splits into two. It's hidden in the trees and there's . . ." He trailed off, suddenly looking confused, staring down at the floor.

"Good, very good. That's all for today." He lifted the helmet completely to the side and applied an antiseptic to the two quarter-inch holes at the top of his skull, followed by a gauze pad and bandage. "We'll meet again," Yurov mumbled pleasantly as the guards took the nearly catatonic Free American off to one of the holding cells for future interrogation.

"Excellent, Dr. Yurov, excellent!" Killov said, standing up behind the glass partition and clapping. The other officers quickly joined in. "Your device more than lives up to its reputation. I'm very pleased." The KGB leader allowed as much of a smile as his officers had ever seen to pass for a split

80

second across his stone face. "I want to see more. But first, this city must be disposed of."

Killov exited from the viewing booth with the officers following closely behind. Dr. Yurov tidied up. "Such a good machine, such a good machine," he mumbled absent-mindedly, almost stroking the helmet as he wheeled it on its stand back against the wall.

In his eightieth floor office, Killov began shouting orders over telephones and intercoms. "Immediately, I want an advance reconnaissance plane, two drones, to advance to these coordinates: G-5, T-2 on Western Sector grid map. Transmit only in attack mode code. I want them off the ground in three minutes." He turned to General Yablonski, commander of the KGB air force. "I don't want army or regular air force in on this," he said, his eyes as cold as steel frozen by a Russian winter.

"Of course, your excellency," the suave air commander answered, lowering his head in a slight bow.

"We will use two of the neutron bombs that I have stored away just for this eventuality."

"But, sir," Vice General Sracksin spoke up from out of a group of about twenty assembled officers. "Premier Vassily has given direct orders to all military personnel not to use—"

Killov glared at the offending officer. "You dare tell me what to do?"

"Oh no, not at all, sir," the admonished KGB officer said, his voice cracking slightly.

"The premier doesn't want us to go out hunting with atomic bombs—not go setting them off like madmen," Killov said coolly, addressing the Red brass gathered around his office. "But now we know where these rebels are. This is a surgical operation. Clean. Instantaneous. Believe me, my unthinking comrade, when the premier sees what we have done, he will give us medals."

"Yes, yes, of course. I didn't understand," the vice general whispered, trying to blend back into the group of officers. Killov made a mental note to get rid of the idiot as quickly as possible. The man was probably a plant of Zhabnov's or the premier's.

"Now," the KGB commander continued, "I want you personally—" he addressed Yablonski—"to pilot the bomber that takes these in. You've had experience with this sort of thing. This mission *can't* fail. You know what's at stake, and you're the only man I trust to carry it out flawlessly." Killov looked at the young rising star of the KGB. If he handled this one right, big things were in store for all of them.

"I shall not fail you, leader," Yablonski replied. He saluted and walked out the door, heading for the airstrip a quarter mile away. A Ziv staff car picked him up at the door and quickly whisked the general to the air base where his Sukov swingwing bomber was already fueled and waiting. And loaded with the two neutron weapons, mounted under each wing. He suited up and, five minutes later joined his co-pilot, already seated at the controls. Yablonski took command and let the controls ease into his hand with that cool, familiar feel of cold steel. Within two minutes they were tearing down the runway, quickly reaching air speed. Once up a thousand feet, he hit the transsonic overdrive and nosed the death-dealing bomber toward the target coordinates.

Eight

The day began beautifully in Westfort. The green valley was flooded with the clearest sunlight the Free Americans had seen in years. It always thrilled their hearts to see the sky so clear, so open. The town's mules, hybrids, wagons, all began making their way along the hidden roadways, beneath the overhanging trees and camouflage netting. The sun's rays trickled down through the green and red and golden leaves, creating patterns of dappled light along the dirt roads, and onto the hides of the animals protesting at pulling their loads.

The people of Westfort were in a good mood this morning. Somehow things suddenly seemed all right with the world. Oh, there were plenty of problems. Westfort was a relatively primitive city. Without the scientists at the disposal of Century City and some of the other more developed and technologically advanced Free Cities, and without the equipment or supplies, the city had over the years adopted a laid back, Western style of living, of easygoingness. Farmers, small craftsmen, hunters, the city of about five thousand traded with one another and with neighboring towns to meet their subsistence needs. They lived in wooden cabins, fifty or sixty feet apart, and shared communal bathing facilities. There was a sense of comraderie, of sharing, in Westfort that was worth all the gold or electrical generating equipment in the world.

The farmers and tradespeople on the many winding roads of Westfort waved and stopped to talk to one another as they passed as if the morning could go on forever. Here and there, children ran playing, wrapped in different colored ribbons, Tonight was the celebration of the annual harvest planting. There would be dancing and feasting on wild pig and turkey caught especially for the occasion. The festivities would, of course, be held underground in one of the large mining tunnels that the Westfort citizens had expanded during the eighty years since they had founded a community there.

Many of the Free Cities that now lived a secret life hidden from the eyes of their Russian enslavers had sprung up—just out of nowhere. Two families—the Capstans and the Maldanados—fleeing from the storm of atomic bombs that fell that fateful day, a century earlier, had traveled for weeks in the woods and then come upon these valleys at the foot of some low mountains. They had stopped to camp for the night or two to catch their breath, and had never left. Westfort was populated with their descendants and a few lost stragglers who had wandered in from time to time.

The citizens of Westfort set about their daily tasks—working the fields hidden by ingenious brown netting that let light through but created the illusion of being solid ground to any passing videodrones or choppers. There was much to be done this spring. The earth seemed to be growing more and more fertile every year, now that they had learned the trick of dampening the radiation by burying it deep and constantly adding topsoil from the forests and mulch and organic matter. The last three years' crops had each been better than the one before it. This year they had added string beans, pumpkins and peas to their growing list of vegetables. Maybe someday, all the ancient fruits and vegetables of America would be brought back into cultivation. They saw themselves as more than farmers but as the regenerators of a new United States. The keepers of the flame of agriculture and a way of life. These seeds were in their safekeeping for future generations to have and hold and plant.

In one of the fields, little Jamie Curtis ran squealing behind her father's mules as they pulled a large, double-sided plow that swept the dark earth into two mounts on each side of the blades.

"Watch out, Jamie," Pete Curtis, Jamie's father yelled as he pulled the reins of the two stubborn mules as hard as he could. "Come on now, you get away from there. You could get hurt!"

The little girl ignored her father, playing in the spray of dirt that flew up behind the groaning beasts of burden. Her blond pigtails tossed in the early morning breeze as she jumped and frolicked in her denim coveralls. Pete stopped and looked at his daughter jumping. He had to laugh. She looked so darn cute. What a lucky man he was. A wife like Jenny and a little girl who could laugh at life and play. His hunting dogs. Life suddenly seemed rich and even in this half-destroyed world. With renewed vigor he returned to plowing the field.

"Get on there, you damn mules." They brayed back at him, opening their long jaws and pulling back the lips to reveal white, cavity-mottled teeth. This time they weren't going to move and that was that, they decided. Pete dropped the reins and went behind them to start kicking. "Won't move, here, why—"

Everyone in Westfort heard the sound at the same moment. The city was only two miles from one end to the other. You could almost yell to someone on the opposite side. The sound grew louder. A machine? From the sky. A plane! They tensed. They were well hidden, but still. The Sukav roared in until it was directly overhead, four thousand feet up. Through the air holes of the netting, the spaces between trees, the townspeople stared up apprehensively. Two small, glinting objects detached themselves from the jet which immediately wheeled sharply to the left and accelerated its departure in a trail of blue exhaust. The people watched curiously as two parachutes opened over the falling objects and slowed them to a crawl as they dropped directly toward the center of the valley.

"What is it, Daddy?" Jamie asked, standing next to her father who stared up, shielding his eyes from the sun with an upturned hand.

"Don't know, baby, maybe some kind of leaflet, writing or something." The Russians had, in the past, dropped posters ordering the surrender of all Free Americans. They had dropped thousands of tons over vast sections of the country about ten years earlier. "Surrender and you will not be harmed," the badly typed sheets read. The Freefighters had had a good laugh at that.

The parachutes dropped lower and lower, hovering right over the center of town. Every eye watched, every heart slowed to a crawl. Suddenly there was a ball of fire in the sky. A blast so hot that it burned every eyeball, instantly fusing it to its socket, turning the faces of the watchers into a black leathery substance in less than a millionth of a second. They didn't have time to scream as the heat and gamma rays of a million-degree thermonuclear neutron bomb shot through their living cells. They crumpled to the ground, their cellular structures broken down into a mass of putty and charred carbon. Brains oozed out of black eyeholes and wide open, powdery mouths. Fingers slid off of hands and feet dropped from legs as the tissue, the muscle and the tendons dissolved and fell in boiling puddles to the burning ground. Every living thing in Westfort, every man and woman and child, every goat, and dog and sheep and cow, every bird, every plant and tree and blade of grass was instantly and totally annihilated.

The smoke of the two blasts formed into one violently churning mushroom cloud, glowing orange and yellow and black, that quickly stretched up nearly two thousand feet in the air. But with the western wind strong this morning, that soon blew away. Now the town looked positively peaceful. The houses mostly intact, coffee cups standing where they had been set, a canoe drifting silently in a still pond. Only the shriveled bodies, as black as meat cooked for days in a blast furnace, and the stripped and smoldering trees betrayed the fact that something was wrong. Terribly wrong!

Nine

Century City's main underground thoroughfare was bustling with people and activity as Rockson left the Council chambers and walked slowly through the center of the Lincoln Square, nearly a thousand feet square and a hundred high. Here, the main industrial and assembly work of the Freefighters went on, with large ventilation fans in the raw rock ceiling pulling out smoke and chemical fumes. It had been nearly a month since Rockson had had time enough to slow down and see how things were going. Broad smiles met the appearance of the man who had done so much to free America. The Ultimate American was a legend throughout the continent, to the downtrodden masses who saw in the uncatchable Rock the symbol of all their striving, their anger, their hatred for their Red masters. But in his own city, he was also one of the citizens, who the people knew as a compassionate man. Rock knew many of them by name, always talking with them when he could, helping with problems.

"Howdy, Rock," an elderly, white-bearded gent said, pushing a dolly loaded higher than he was with chemicals for the hydroponics.

"Hey, Keaton," Rock said, smiling, slapping the wiry old codger on the back. They had gone out hunting together years earlier and Rock still remembered things the old-timer, who had prospected for years, had taught him about tracking. "We'll have to hit the plains again," Rock said.

"Goddamn right," Keaton replied with a toothless smile,

pushing his load forward. Rockson moved on, exchanging greetings with scores of Century City citizens who stopped to talk and press the flesh of their war champion.

The jobs of Century City were divided up by a complex process of lottery and skills. Those who were highly trained in such work as computer chip assembly, weapon making and hydroponics worked continuously at these jobs, but even they were expected to put in their share of free time working on the ever-expanding tunnel network of Century City, which had to be continually added to to accommodate the city's growing population, storage and industrial needs. Other workers were chosen by rotating lottery to work at the needed labor— changed every few months so that all citizens shared equally in the hardest and least-favored jobs—sewer maintenance, the manual jobs of transporting goods, working on the camouflage materials above the entrances to the city. The most prestigious job of Century City, and the one that all citizens had their names on waiting lists for the apprenticeships to open up, was the building of the Liberator automatic rifle. The rifle, Century City's main export to other Free Cities for use in the war against the Reds, was the pride of every man and woman of the town. Invented by Dr. Shecter, it was a 9mm rifle that could with a snap of a switch change from single shot to full auto. With a muzzle velocity of twelve hundred meters per second firing fifty-round clips, the non-jamming rifle came with silencer and infrared nightscope. As the Reds had found out, the rifle could rip a man's chest apart at half a mile. The Liberator was one of the Freefighters' most potent weapons against the Red invaders and it was much in demand in the other hidden cities who traded back their own small-scale industrial goods, pelts or produce as payment. The Liberator was produced in a large factory assembly-line layout at the northern section of the cavernous industrial square. Work went on twenty-four hours a day in three shifts of two hundred workers each. The need for such weapons was too great and too important to ever stop. Over four hundred of the weapons were produced a day, then shipped out in small ten-man groups on mule and hybrid.

It was Dr. Shecter's dream, and Rock's, that within the next ten years, assembly lines for the rifle and ammunition could be built in all the Free Cities. Shecter was busy designing much more powerful weapons that he promised to reveal to Rock as soon as the bugs were ironed out. The more firepower the Freefighters could train on the Red armies, the quicker their asses would be kicked all the way back to Red Square.

Rock walked over to the Liberator factory and moved from line to line greeting the workers who looked up but continued to perform their jobs for they knew one stoppage would snag the whole line. Rock hefted a just-completed Liberator from the end of one of the lines and sighted down its three cylindrical scopes—one of Shecter's innovations. Perfect! But of course—the men and women of Century City took their work seriously. A faulty rifle could well mean the life of one of their fighting teams. Could be a brother, a son. The rifles were as perfect as human dexterity could produce. Every one they helped turn out had their spirit in it, their guts and dreams for the future.

Rock continued along the assembly line to where about thirty men and women were filing away at the super-hardened manganese stocks, putting them into final form.

"Hello, Mrs. Greiger," Rockson said, putting his hand on the shoulder of a middle-aged woman with deep purple circular lines under her eyes. "How is he?"

"Oh, you must have been away, Mr. Rockson," she answered in a monotone. "He died four days ago. The fever got so high. His flesh turned dry and flaky. He was in much pain." She looked as if she were about to cry. "But he never complained. The funeral was yesterday." Charles Greiger, her husband, had been bitten on the hand by a small albino spider while on a wood-gathering squad. By evening his hand had swollen to the size of a grapefruit. Within twenty-four hours he had lapsed into a deep fever and a semicomatose state. He had somehow lingered on for nearly a month but death was inevitable.

"I'm sorry," Rock said, looking down at the concrete work floor. "Charles Greiger was a good man. A member of the Council, a good hunter and a brave fighter. I will remember him."

The words seemed to genuinely brighten her disposition. Her mouth relaxed for the first time in days. "Thank you, Mr. Rockson," she said in a whisper.

Rockson took the elevator four levels down to hydroponics to see how things were going. There had been a virulent fungus that had killed nearly a quarter of the city's crops just a week before he left with the Attack Force. He walked to a sliding steel door and held his palm up to a sensor set in the solid rock wall. The door slid open and Rockson walked into a well-lit agricultural paradise, nearly a quarter of a mile long. An entire level had been devoted to farming, not just to provide foodstuffs for the citizens of Century City but to perform experimentation, crossbreeding with different vegetables and fruits—more radiation resistant, disease immune—but still maintaining the nutritive value of the crops. Within temperature-controlled walls the biologists who worked these sections had stored and catalogued nearly half of every variety of plant and vegetable from prewar America. They were ecstatic when a member of the community, hunting expedition or Attack Group came back with new varieties of flora. Someday, every one of these seeds would be the beginning of millions, billions, of plants that would cover the decimated continent once again—when it was free.

"Hello, Rockson," chief scientist, head of hydroponics, Kraft said, shaking hands profusely with the warrior. "Good to see you're back safe from another expedition."

"Good for us, not the Russians."

"Of course, of course," the overweight, constantly fidgeting Kraft replied. He was one of the miracle workers, along with Dr. Shecter, of Century City. Kraft seemed able to do absolutely anything with seeds. He had crossbred countless forms of vegetation, making them useful again. Fruits like apricots, pears and strawberries, vegetables such as corn, red onions and asparagus, which had all nearly disappeared from the American continent, being highly vulnerable to radio-activity, he had resurrected and bred back until they were genetically strong enough to withstand the rads and countless new diseases that seemed to mutate and spring up daily.

"How are the plants?" Rockson asked with a concerned

look. "There was some sort of fungus attacking everything just before I left."

"Oh fine, Rock, fine." Kraft smiled, waving his hand in the air as if it had all been nothing. "You know, actually that was quite an interesting case. We were losing about a twentieth of the wheat and barley crops a day and were looking for vegetation fungus—bacteria—as the culprit. The usual—microscopic analysis, then petrie dishes, cultures—would have taken months. Suddenly I had a thought. The way the one fungal sample we had been able to isolate looked reminded me of something from an old textbook. I checked it out. Can you believe it, Rock, it was a mutated form of hoof-and-mouth disease—something that only used to hit animals! We treated it with the drug that had been prescribed and, presto, no more damaged crops. We're working on breeding a resistance into all the grain products now, so there won't be any more such outbreaks."

He and Rockson walked the rows of plantlife that stretched for acres under the luminous heat lights. The hydroponic gardens consisted of long metal troughs, nearly fifty feet in length and three feet wide, filled with a liquid chemical solution. The plants were grown, floating in the mixture, in row after row with specially designed ultraviolet heat lamps shining down from above, placed about five feet apart. The entire operation consisted of over twenty acres of vegetation, using every available inch in the chambers, with rows of plants on top of one another. The gardens easily fed the populace their foodstuff needs, but that was only half the hydroponic's goal. It was also the experimentation, the constant strengthening of grains and fruits and newly arrived seedlings, and the production of millions of plantable seeds that were shipped out to other cities, along with Liberator rifles.

"You might want to take a look at this," Rockson said, pulling out a tiny, shriveled body. It was one of the phosphorescent wormlike creatures he and his men had seen in the giant luminous pond as they returned from their Strike Force expedition. Rockson had spotted the dead insect by the side of the pond and carefully placed it in his utility belt. He told Kraft of the creatures and the scientist seemed fascinated as he gingerly took the two-inch-long sea-horse-shaped body from Rock with the pair of tweezers he always carried in his long, white smock pockets.

"From what you describe, Rock, this could well be a successful new life form. We've heard stories of things like this coming in from all over the country, but we rarely get to actually examine them."

"Successful?" Rock asked skeptically.

"Well, there are many mutations these days. We estimate that fifty to seventy-five percent of all animal and fauna reproduction results in mutation. Most die immediately or within days. Nature doesn't hold much with things out of the ordinary. Only the very adaptable can survive. But new species that are suited to the environment *are* growing and taking root. The world will be populated by a vastly different group of creatures over the next few centuries. It could well be that this is one of them."

"Let's just hope it doesn't eat us," Rock cracked, describing how the deer had been sucked down into the living pond.

"Really, how intriguing. A symbiotic life-support colony is very rare—bees, of course, and ants. I do wish we had a live specimen to work with. If you—"

"Sure, Doc, sure," Rockson said with a smile. He left the scientist to play with his newest exotica and headed out of the subterranean gardens, moving into the series of interconnecting tunnels that led to the large gymnasium of Century City, built in the last ten years. If there was any spot on Earth that truly made him feel at home it was in the Century City Gymnasium, where he had spent years working his body and reflexes until they were razor-sharp. He felt a warm feeling in his gut as he held his hand up to the sensor on the stone wall at the end of a long, dimly lit corridor. The door slid quickly open and Rock walked in.

Ten

The large chamber was quite beautiful with muted light
coming from overhanging rocks giving the illusion of being
outdoors and palm trees ringing the sides. It was a large,
circular space, almost two hundred feet in diameter and fifty
feet high, chopped out of the solid rock of the mountain. The
gymnasium was fully equipped with squash courts, a
swimming pool, weight-lifting and gymnastics equipment and
two large mats for sparring and martial arts.

As Rock walked in, he could hear the sharp intake of breath
and the slapping of flesh against flesh that meant that two
people were sparring. He couldn't help but chuckle as he
sauntered over to the biggest of the thick tatami mats and saw
Rona Wallender and Al Chen engaged in an energetic testing of
skills. Rona was probably the toughest woman in Century City
and was also in love with Rock, which he pretended to ignore.
She was a gymnast, acrobat and fighter, a great-great-
granddaughter of the famous Wallendas of prewar days, who
had been world famous for their expertise in tightrope walking.
But as skilled as Rona was in karate and jujitsu—and there was
many a man, friend or foe, she could best within seconds—she
was no match for the martial arts chief instructor of Century
City, Al Chen.

Rock watched from behind a pillar, unnoticed, as the two
circled each other slowly, carefully placing one foot down,
letting the weight drop fully, then slowly shifting the other
foot. They moved like cats. Their hands were held out in front

of them, prepared to attack or parry. Rona held her hands straight out, the fingers curled back in tight, hard fists. Chen's hands were more relaxed, as was his whole fighting style— fluid and loose. Chen wore an amused smile beneath the thin, black mustache which covered his upper lip and hung down the sides of his mouth, Fu Manchu style.

Rona attacked suddenly, leaping forward with five blurred punches, followed by a roundhouse kick to the head of Chen. But where she struck there was only air. The master of five of the fighting arts—Sing I, Goju, Tai Chi, Aikido and Wing Chun—was quicker than the wind. He didn't even need to block but merely turned his body, timing his motions perfectly so that the attacking woman flew by and landed in a heap on the floor. Rona was tall, five-ten, and beautiful. A striking figure with her brilliant red hair and her full-bodied voluptuous figure. Half the men in Century City would have given a month's R&R to sleep with her, but she only wanted Ted Rockson.

"You miserable bastard," she yelled, only half kidding, at Chen who continued to circle around her, making her come after him. She rose from the mat, brushing back her flowing hair which momentarily covered her alabaster-complexioned face. She moved forward again. With a loud "kaii" she shot from the mat in a lightning bolt of power and speed and directed a flying drop kick at Chen's groin. He stepped back and lightly slapped her leg as it flew by. The extra energy of the block took her another six feet through the air where she landed again on the mat, rolling over in a perfect forward somersault and rising instantly to her feet, red-faced and fuming.

"Good kick, but you're too angry, my sweet warrior," Chen said, letting his hands drop to his sides and shaking them to show how to relax. "When force meets force, the stronger force wins. The purpose of martial arts is to use the stronger force against itself. If I were to let you hit me with one of your blows I'd probably be knocked out. But I don't, you see. You could be one of the best, Rona, but you still have too much anger at the world, maybe at men?" he added, mocking her slightly.

94

"Come on, Rona, you can get him," Rockson said from the back of the mat where he had watched unnoticed.

"Rock!" Rona exclaimed, her face suddenly brightening, her mouth opening in a wide grin.

"Hey, Rock," Al Chen smiled. "Good to see you. It's been months since we worked together."

As Chen turned to greet Rockson, Rona saw her opportunity and leaped at the slim but well-muscled Chinese fighter. She grabbed him around the throat with both arms, applying a judo choke hold which could drop a man unconscious in three seconds. But Chen didn't give her three seconds. Even as he felt the hold go on, he slid his chin to the right, creating a space between her forearm and his throat, to keep his breathing open. He quickly grabbed her around the elbow and pulled her up over his shoulder. As they both fell forward, Chen turned his body completely around, so that they faced each other. As they hit the mat he slid his foot into her abdomen at the same time pulling her forward by the arm. She flew from the grip of the martial arts expert, her choke hold instantly broken, and soared almost ten feet through the air, right into the deep end of the six-lane swimming pool. Waves of flickering, green crystalline water splashed in every direction as she broke the surface.

Both Rock and Chen couldn't help but laugh as the beautiful redhead pulled herself from the pool, her hair flat and wet against her long straight back. She sputtered angrily.

"Oh, you bastard, I'll—I'll—"

"Come now, Rona," Rock said, walking over to her and helping her all the way back up onto the rubber-padded walkway around the pool. "That's not the sporting way. If you were just a touch more relaxed about it all, you'd be a one-hundred-times-better fighter."

"Oh, you too, Rockson. Sometimes you men make me so mad. Just trying to show me up." She seemed angry, but was already beginning to smile, realizing that it all did look rather funny. And she *had* attacked Chen when his back was turned. She could hardly blame him for tossing her into the pool. "I'd like to see you try," she said to Rock, suddenly relaxing and pushing against his tall, strong body. "Try me, that is," she added coyly, her lips fleshing slightly.

"I'd love to take you up on the offer, Rona," Rock said, his mouth twisting up at the right-hand corner, a gesture which Rona found fascinating. There was so much about this man that she loved, was drawn to. If only he would give himself to her the way she wanted to give herself to him.

"But first," Rock continued, taking off his white civilian shirt, and bending down to untie his rubber-padded indoor shoes. "Al and I need a good workout. If I'm going to keep my reflexes sharp, I've got to work with the best. And Al," he said, his purple and blue eyes twinkling as he stepped onto the mat and bowed to Chen, "is the best."

"I'm flattered, my friend," Chen replied, bowing back. "But as to who is the best, only the gods know that."

The two men began slowly, circling each other like two jungle cats, graceful, fluid, their motions a perfect mirror for one another. Rona watched in fascination. Chen, in his kung fu shoes and black, loose-fitting Ninja sparring suit, was a good six inches shorter than the muscular, six-three Rockson, whose deeply tanned chest and arms bulged with the steel muscles of a lifetime of sweat and survival. They circled for almost thirty seconds, watching for a moment's advantage. Each was wary. Chen crouched low in his scissor-leg Ba Gua stance, the knees close together, the feet kicking out like levers at every step. Rockson just circled. He had studied countless systems, read books on all the fighting styles, but mostly he had experienced it. He had fought enemies beyond number and had won. Death was his teacher. The death of all the Reds who had attacked him and paid with their lives. He let his muscles untense, let his mind become blank, waiting, waiting for the opponent's motion, watching the eyes for the flicker of energy that meant attack.

Chen suddenly sprang and released a windmill of punches, one after another, ten of them within a second and a half. Rockson stepped back with the motion and deflected them easily, his hands lightly slapping the punches to the side as fast as they came.

"Good, very good!" Chen said, stepping back again and

continuing to circle. He had scarcely gotten the last word out when he attacked again. This time, Chen feinted to the right and at the last second, as Rockson began a counter, the Chinese expert dove to the left and dropped Rock with a scissors leg. Rockson saw the move an instant before it came. It was too late to resist so he went with it, rolling to the mat, snapping his leg free from the hold with the momentum, so that Chen couldn't pin him, and then rolling and rising again, all in one smooth motion. As Chen leaped up to the mat, he found Rockson's powerful leg coming at him with a circular roundhouse kick to the head. Chen blocked with his forearm and gripped Rock's ankle, turning it to the side, trying to throw him to the mat. This time, Rock let the master fighter hold the foot and came up with the other leg, landing solidly on Chen's stomach. At the same time Rock fell backwards to the mat, so that his motion pulled Chen, still holding the ankle, forward and over his head. They both rolled and came up, facing one another. Chen smiled. "Excellent, Rock. You're getting better all the time."

"Thanks for the kudos," Rock replied, laughing. "But none of my blows are connecting."

"Nor mine," Chen said softly. "Mexican standoff."

They continued for a good ten minutes. Neither was really able to get the upper hand. An occasional punch or kick would slide through the other's defense, but their reflexes and speed were so quick that they would merely twist their bodies to go with the blow and take any sting out of it. They had both built up quite a sweat, drops of salty spray flew from their whipping hands and legs.

Suddenly, Chen stopped. "I think we are both at that stage of martial arts development where there is such an equalness of skill that it is like fighting one's own self. We know what the other is thinking even as he strikes. As my own master, Lieu, once said to me, 'When you meet a man you cannot best nor can he best you, that man is your brother in the spirit of Chi.' Rock, you and I have reached that harmony. You, Ted Rockson, are my brother in the Chi life force." He bowed deeply forward, his hands clenched in fists.

97

Rock was touched. Chen was rarely emotional. Yet he could see that there was something deeply in common between the two men—a certain spirit, the energy of the Warrior. Chen showed Rock some of the new weapons' techniques he had been working on. They worked out with nunchukas, knives and staffs for a good hour, Rockson quickly absorbing each move as Chen showed him the exact motion and angle of attack. Chen was a master at a number of weapons and even Rockson would have a hard time against the Chinese with these. But he was learning. And Chen was happy to show him everything he knew.

At last Chen bowed again. "Ah, Rock, I don't know where you get the strength. I'm beginning to feel tired. And, of course, I can't admit that. But I do have a training class coming up in twenty minutes, and I must do my Chi Kung meditation before training. So, if you will excuse me, my friend." Chen walked off to the showers and then to his private meditation chamber, bare, covered in white cloth with only a single silk pillow for sitting in the center.

Rockson walked over to Rona who lay sprawled on her back, relaxing, in the center of the second tatami mat.

"You're something else, Rock," she said, looking seductively up, water glistening on her skin. "Anyone else in Century City would be out cold in about two seconds with Master Chen, yet you stand your ground."

"Oh, he's a better fighter than I am, Rona. He holds back with me so that the sparring can give him a workout," Rock said self-depreciatingly.

"Bull!" Rona spat out. "If anything, you could beat him. Or at least it would be a hell of a fight."

"Such a fight will never occur," Rockson said seriously. "I fight only my enemies to kill. The fighting that Chen and I do is the fighting of friends, of teaching one another."

"Oh, I know, I know," Rona said, chuckling. "No need to be so heavy-handed philosophical all the time." She put her hand around his taut-muscled thigh. "I want you!" she said directly. "I've missed you a lot." She pulled him on top of her, kissing him full on the lips, crushing her body against his with all of her strength. They embraced for several minutes, hands

98

stroking warm flesh. Then Rock lifted her off of him and silently jumped to his feet. Taking her by the hand, he led her to one of the massage rooms at the far end of the gymnasium and locked the door behind him. Soon they were locked in the oldest embrace of man and woman. And the most pleasurable.

Eleven

Commandant Kuzminski got the orders. There had been one too many incidents in Little U.S.A.—the section of Stalinville where the filthy American children ran in packs, where the bagmen and garbage ladies snarled at the Red troops when they passed, where thousands of rat holes were crowded with hostile thieves and work resisters. The place was rampant with secret cells of teachers, Americans who taught the forbidden skills of reading, writing and the grammar of the English language to the waifs who stole everything that wasn't nailed down off of the convoys of trucks that rumbled through. Sometimes trucks would even be ransacked and shipments of foodstuffs, clothing or even weapons would be carted off by the antlike swarms of violent youths. And now the final blow: an elite officer of the KGB brutally murdered by a bagman while carrying out his duties in Little U.S.A. There had to be drastic action.

Kuzminski assembled thirty men and armed them with flamethrowers and tanks filled with the fuel for the dreaded weapons at Depot C. Authorization to go in and burn out the sewer holes, the basements and alleyway homes of the vermin of Little U.S.A. had been granted. There would be no meetings with trustee civilians this time, no asking for ringleaders to be shot as examples, as in the past. No! This time the flames would cleanse the filthy resisters.

Grim determination etched the faces of the tall, black-shirted extermination squad. Their face shields were pushed up over their cold, intense eyes. Eyes of hate and murder beneath black, steel helmets. Batons hung from their belts—the stun batons of the KGB. Laser electrode firing pistols in long, narrow holsters sat on the other hip. They wore acid-resistant jackets and pants; the scum of Little U.S.A. had started making sulphuric acid bombs from canisters of acid stolen from Russian supply trucks. The little bastards would rush from the shadows and splash the burning acid into Red faces. Eight soldiers had been blinded.

The thirty men were from a special KGB counterinsurgency squad trained to kill without mercy, to spread terror through the populace. The damned regular army troops would let the tots get away with valuable property, hesitant to shoot five and six year olds. But this KGB "Special Unit" had been thoroughly indoctrinated into the realities and necessities of occupation in a hostile country. *Children are our enemies too.* Especially children! With their hand grenades hidden in little paper bags, their acid vials, their hurling of garbage cans filled with rocks from rooftops onto passing troops below—they had a million little tricks. And they were without fear.

This "burn out" should have been authorized long ago, Kuzminski thought, as he hefted his flamethrower, checking the nozzle opening. The way the graffiti got out of control! Imagine a Soviet fortress city scrawled with "USA LIVES" and "BETTER DEAD THAN RED" and the inevitable "THE ULTIMATE AMERICAN WAS HERE." Ted Rockson, the legendary mountain brigand that the rebels and the bagpeople all worshipped like some goddamned god. Kuzminski sized up the thirty-man force, making sure every bit of the dangerous equipment was properly sealed. If gas started leaking once flames were thrown . . . Was this Rockson even a real person? the pale-faced commandant wondered. Or just a myth. Supposedly he could slip through any defense, surmount any obstacle—be everywhere at once. Whenever anything went wrong, even when an accident blew up some ammunition, the writings went up on the brick walls, on the sides of parked Red trucks: ROCK WAS HERE! Fantastic that the higher authorities had let the city walls be smeared like this without taking reprisal action long ago. Kuzminski would have. Now they had learned the hard way what he had been telling them for months in his capacity as KGB Special Units commander for the fort. These incidents will build until there is a disaster, he had warned. They had scoffed. Now the third highest ranking KGB officer of Stalinville was dead, stabbed through the throat with a maniac's ice pick. He shuddered, thinking of the major gasping for breath, hands covering the red blood pouring out of his severed neck. But now he was gone. The commandant was glad. He had been a bastard, always putting the lower-ranked Kuzminski in his place. Always commanding him imperiously in front of other officers and troops. Screw him, he thought with a grin. Now there is more room for the ranks below to be promoted. If he could pull this incineration action off without any casualties he would look good. Very good. The dead KGB officer's position beckoned Kuzminski like the very gates of heaven.

He inspected the gauges of all the fuel tanks strapped to the Blackshirts' backs. Full to capacity. The Death Squad snapped their shields down and, single file, smartly exited the supply station.

Sally, a garbage lady, was picking through the rubble at the southern edge of the Little U.S.A. sector. Overhead, split and twisting radioactive clouds crawled along in a deep indigo sky of death. Though no one in the city even noticed, it was a date that once had made Americans jump and scream in joy: Independence Day. July 4, 2089A.D. She systematically poked through the sprawling refuse heap in which the Reds dumped all their waste, content to let the Americans smell it and pick over its rot. She had found many things in these piles. Once a comb, once a piece of flashlight that had matched another piece she had uncovered. And now she had that flashlight to reach her deep cellar home inside a broken oil tank—a good place for the past few years—warmed by her six scraggly dogs, safe. Safe. Sores of puss oozed down her chin and she wiped at them with cramped hands and arthritis-twisted fingers. She ate the plum peels and banana skins. Imagine, they wasted all that. Her dogs scrounged for bones and chewed hungrily at them. Children and an old, bent man in the muted gray stripes of

102

a Russian prison uniform—an escapee?—loomed nearby. Everybody kept an eye on everyone else but let each other be. They were, after all, Americans. Still, there were always fights for little treasures. It was survival. The first priority was to live and Sally was a survivor. She had killed other Americans. Yes, but only to keep her strength up for Resistance Day. The day Ted Rockson's hordes would sweep through the city. Then her strength would be needed. Not the half-strength of the weak ones she had killed to take away their food. They would have died anyway. She needed it.

Suddenly she heard steps—locksteps like she had never heard before. It was the dreaded Death Squad, KGB soldiers in their midnight black uniforms with the red skulls on their sleeves. They marched like robots over the rolling hills of trash. They were coming with . . . what were those tubes on their backs? What were the long tubes in their hands connected by black hoses to the tanks? She fought through her childhood memories. Memories repressed, finally forgotten— for good reason. Then she remembered. She screamed a scream to wake the dead. Screamed out a warning. Screamed in the loudest, shrillest scream that had ever issued forth from her lungs.

"Flamethrowers! Flamethrowers!" She began running, slipping, stumbling. The children didn't know what was coming. They stood on the rubble piles laughing and jeering the oncoming Red troops as they had learned to do. They picked up rocks and began throwing them as the Blackshirts marched closer and closer. Their face plates reflected the random rays of purple-tinged sunlight that reached down through the poison clouds. They came in four phalanxes. The children weren't listening to her screams. They weren't—

Whoosh. The first flames shot nearly a hundred feet out from five roaring flame-throwing nozzles. The flames just reached the most forward children, the ones advancing to throw fist-sized rocks. Instantly they were aflame, burning candles of flesh. Steam poured out of their sweaters and overalls as the moisture of their flesh instantly evaporated and the pink skin turned charcoal black. Flames shot from out of their bubbling eyesockets, and grotesquely ballooned out of their mouths. The other children's voices died out behind them. There was an unearthly silence for a second. Then they dropped the rocks and turned to run.

Whoosh, whoosh, whoosh. Fifty children fell, twisting in shrieking agony; others continued to run, human torches. They ran among the other children, still further back in the rubble piles, grabbing at them, screaming for help, dragging them along in their mad death hysteria. Sharon, Stella, Rita, Maya, Henry, Cal, Mooney, Flatface—all the garbage children Sally knew, dying, dying as she watched in horror, from her hiding place in the ruins of a wrecked building.

The Death Squad didn't lose step. They just kept advancing in lock step—*thrump-thrump*—goose-stepping to the junction in the road ahead. The Blackshirts stepped over the steaming, eyeless bodies, avoided the still-brightly burning corpses. The streets were deserted. Kuzminski led the second unit down the main avenue of Little U.S.A., a potholed dirt road about forty feet wide. No one was in sight—no resistance. He smiled. True force and they ran like dogs. Treat them severely. Make them hear death screams and they disappear. It's easy. He had an erection in his leather pants as he searched the surrounding crumbling buildings with his cold blue eyes.

There! A hidden entrance, a partially opened cellar door—a way down into the tunnel system of the bag people, beneath the streets. Wordlessly he raised his hand; the unit stopped. He directed his men to the doorway and they poured their flames down. Whatever was there will no longer bother us, the commandant thought with deep satisfaction.

Deke, the leader of the Black Dukes, was the meanest, most feared of all the teen gang leaders of Little U.S.A. He had taken on all the other gangs—the Desperados, the Live Skulls, the Minutemen—and beaten them down. He had ruled his turf in the southern sector of the American town for two years, collecting money from the peddlers, ripping off the stragglers. But as tough as he was, Deke could see that his time had come. He looked out from the third-floor window of the abandoned firehouse that served as the Black Dukes' headquarters. The Reds were coming down the streets with weapons that were pouring fire onto everything. Men and women ran screaming before the onslaught. Within a minute they would reach the Duke's hiding place.

Well he had to die sometime. It had almost happened last week—they were fighting with the Minutemen over a gallon jug of wine. He had been stabbed in the groin by an opposing gang member. He had slashed the guy's throat from ear to ear. But he had known that his days were numbered. He kissed the rabbit's foot on his necklace dangling from his neck along with charms of other animals and tiny, gold-colored cowboys. He woke the other gang members quickly. "The Black Dukes die today," he said to each one. They stood in front of him, their knives at the ready in their hands.

"Nothing much to say, my brothers. We've had good times and bad times together. But we were brothers. Now we'll die as brothers." They slapped hands for the final time, gave their gang war cry and, swinging their bolo nunchakas, flew down the rotted board stairs and out through the slopes of rubble that lined the street.

The Death Squad, with Kuzminski in the lead, had just sent a wall of flames down a stairwell and were now heading toward two crumbling, four-story buildings. Suddenly a group of five animallike black youths wearing black leather jackets attacked, leaping from behind a partially standing brick wall. The sharp blades of the Black Dukes dug into Red throats. The Russians stopped resisting. The gang members rose to their feet and charged toward the remaining troops who stepped quickly back. The flames poured forth again. The five Dukes lit up like Roman candles. Their eyes melted, their faces twisted in unspeakable agony as the liquid fire met their black flesh. Their faces were dissolving, their screams issued forth continuously like the shriek of a siren blaring out death. They staggered forward, toward the Reds. The Death Squad looked nervous. Some cut their throwers and ran as the Americans stumbled forward—flaming, insane, faceless monsters with groping, burning hands. The arms of flame caught one Russian and engulfed him in a death hold. A sound that was recognizable as some kind of twisted laughter screamed out from the sizzling vocal cords of the gang member as he and the Blackshirt exploded in flames. A second and third walking, fiery corpse-thing staggered forth as a second Red was caught in a hold by one of them, its charred black flesh spitting orange and red flame as it reached forward with strangling, smoking hands.

Commandant Kuzminski stared in horror from twenty yards away with the third unit. When would these Americans value their wretched lives? He turned to the right as he heard yells of defiance. A horde of pipe-wielding adult men—of all races, their clothes ripped, their shoes falling off their filthy feet—came storming at the Reds. They came in fast, knocking some of the Russians off their feet, before they were hit with a wall of fire from more flamethrowers. Dead men all, they came forward, most dying within two or three steps, falling forward on their sizzling faces. But some kept coming, even as they burned, cursing black oaths, diving onto the Red killers, igniting them. The screaming Russian troops who were chosen for the sacrificial flames ripped at their burning plastic helmets and their thick clothing.

Incredible insanity—surely not bravery—thought Kuzminski as he quickly dropped back to the rear. As they retreated, sending up wall after wall of flame at the still-advancing crowd of ghastly attackers, the fourth squad met them. Six men sent into one of the deep cellars; they had been lucky to get out. One was limping, one had his hands to his eyes, moaning and blubbering until he fell. A soldier gasped, grasping at his profusely bleeding shoulder, a small dagger still protruding from it. "We went in, but the children—they—they had acid and—" He fell forward, his eyes rolling up as a second knife stuck deep in his back, thrown some forty feet from the cellar entrance.

Kuzminski called a halt to the extermination. A planned careful withdrawal. Soon it became a rout. Then it was only Kuzminski and his second-in-command, Lieutenant Lysenko. Then Lysenko was down. Kuzminski ripped his liquid fuel tank from his back and threw it down along with the flamethrower. He ran in a mad dash toward the fence that separated Little U.S.A. from the Stalinville Soviet army sector. He was at the fence, the Americans were far behind. Just a hundred yards to the gate—he would make it. He would. He began sprinting.

The ax came out of nowhere. Sally's hands were holding the handle. The head of the commandant severed cleanly at the base of the neck and rolled backwards, toward Little U.S.A. Kuzminski got a rolling, topsy-turvy view of the sky and buildings and ground. Something had happened—blackness closing in—the head stopped rolling. It was upright, eyes opened but no longer seeing. The Americans gathered around it. A young boy, burned on the leg and arm, his bubbling flesh peeking through the disintegrating material of his clothes, picked the head up and stuck it on a wood spear. He walked over to the garbage piles and found the highest one. He put the head on top, slamming the spear deep into the moldering rot and walked down.

Other filthy American bag and garbage people gathered silently below, slipping out of the surrounding ruins. Sally, standing nearby with her still-bloody ax, did a macabre dance, holding the weapon high over her head. One by one, the Americans joined the impromptu celebration around the garbage pile as dead Red eyes stared down at them uncomprehendingly.

Later, a boy not older than five, his face a mess of scars and oozing sores, found the body of the dead Red Death Squad leader. He dipped his fingers in the still-lightly bubbling blood that rose from the neck and used it to write, "Ted Rockson was here" on the brick wall that the corpse rested against.

So ended July 4, 2089 A.D. A good day for America, a bad day for the Red occupiers of America.

Twelve

In Washington, President Zhabnov lay in his recliner in the
Blue Room, trying to relax. He couldn't. The events of the past
few days seemed to confirm Killov's ravings about a real threat
of overthrow actually existing in America. The rebels *were*
strong. Events were showing that. The hidden city that had
recently been destroyed—what did they call it? Westfort—had
four thousand bodies in it when the radiation cleared enough
for Red troops to go in and check things out. Killov had
overridden his authority by the use of the neutron bombs, but
the success of the action and valuable information that was
uncovered would preclude a reprimand from either Zhabnov
or Premier Vassily. Killov had lucked out this time, the
president had to admit.

When the ruins had been thoroughly probed it was
discovered that Westfort was filled with quite advanced
weaponry and industrial machinery. It was well-equipped with
both stolen and self-made tools. Most frightening of all, several
areas that contained their most important undertakings and
records had been destroyed with preset bombs designed to go
off in case of attack. And Killov had said to Zhabnov over the
phone after the attack, "I believe this Westfort is really one of
the smallest of the American rebel cities."

Smallest? With ground-to-air missiles and machinery
capable of producing tractors? Zhabnov turned nervously on
the blue velvet recliner. Perhaps he should speak to the
premier about letting Killov have his fun with a few dozen

108

neutron bombs. After all, it was nice here in the White House. Much nicer than it had been in Murmansk. He wouldn't want to lose his position in the United Socialist States if he could help it. Besides, he would lose face if the rebels attacked any further. No, let this sadist Killov have his neutron bombs.

The portraits of his Russian predecessors in the presidential office stared down at him. What would *they* do? His eye caught the picture of Abraham Lincoln: stern, penetrating, watching him from across the large, carpeted room. What would he have done? Lincoln had a rebellious area to contend with. He had freed the slaves, the blacks, and sent in armies of blue-coated troops to stop the gray-uniformed slaveholders. Zhabnov let a little smile cross his thick face. There! He knew his history. He had read a book or two when he came over, feeling it only proper to know something about the history of the beaten Americans. Lincoln had burned and destroyed Atlanta and half the South, 230 years ago. He had acted forcefully. I must act! But there are no slaves to free in the rebellious areas. Could I free the slaves in *our* cities to fight the rebel cities? His eyes lit up at the thought. This Mind Breaker device—if it could be used to make the American workers completely docile, or better yet make them fighting soldiers of communism—on *our* side—perhaps we could send them out to do our fighting for us. What a clever idea, President Zhabnov thought, totally taken with his own imagination. That is why Vassily made me president. I am so clever.

He rose, walked across the Blue Room until he came face to face with the portrait of Lincoln. "Ah, Mr. Lincoln, you have given me an idea. Thank you. Like you, I will free the slaves. Free them to fight for Russia. I will call in all my scientists and this expert on the Mind Breaker and tell them to convert half a million of our work-slaves into soldiers. American against American—as in your own time Comrade Lincoln. What do you think of that?"

He stood back, looking at Lincoln's stern face. The president didn't seem pleased. Zhabnov turned away and headed for his office. He would have to start right away on this brilliant plan. This would be something that even Killov would have to admit was a good idea. Not that I need him for help, but he could be useful. Yes, I will invite Killov and his technical people and we will discuss implementation of Plan Lincoln.

Back in the Oval Office, Zhabnov squeezed down into the presidential chair and picked up one of the eight phones on his cluttered desk. Blue for the KGB, green for his own military hierarchy and red for the premier. But Vassily didn't like to be bothered. He had a whole empire to rule. One just sent him boxes of charts for his staff to study. Charts and graphs showing how Zhabnov was meeting—or exceeding—goals of his five-year grain-and-corn exportation plan. That was a little difficult; the crops were subject to such sudden changes of weather here in America—that damned west wind, and the titanic twisters, as the Americans called them.

The operator's eager voice chimed in. "Yessir, Mr. President?"

"Killov!" he said.

When Killov hung up the phone he was—he hated to admit it—impressed with Zhabnov. The fat fool had a good idea for a change and for Killov's help he had offered a commitment to get more neutron bombs. Killov liked the idea of rapidly expanding the use of the Mind Breaker. After all, it could turn out to be the ultimate weapon that would finally give the Russians complete control. Some 120 years ago, America had had a war in Southeast Asia—the Vietnam War. The then-president of the U.S.A., Johnson, had said that in order to win that war, the United States had to win the hearts and minds of those people. They didn't, and the United States lost a war for the first time. Now we are stuck in a war of attrition with these American rebels, Killov thought, only we *have* the means, thanks to the Mind Breaker, to rule the hearts and minds of every American. Send the useless overpopulation of shiftless slaves from the occupied areas out to fight Rockson and his bandits. Give them the will, the fanatical devotion to Mother Russia, to decimate their own countrymen.

The meeting was two days later. The customary tour of the

110

Rose Garden led by Zhabnov, with all the scientists, technicians and military and KGB top hats, infuriated Killov as a waste of time. But once inside the White House meeting room, they quickly got down to business. Zhabnov's top scientists showed charts in front of the long conference table, charts that detailed the ever-growing research and experimentation results of the Mind Breaker machines. Killov proudly stated that a fortress city of the Americans had been decimated by neutron bombs, when one of their Freefighters was captured—his mind had been probed and the information had been obtained instantly. That man, Preston, hadn't survived the ordeal for more than a few hours. However, later prisoners and experimental subjects did survive attempts to make them loyal to their Russian masters. Two months ago, they had only achieved a twenty-four percent success rate, but now American slaves could be programmed with simple loving devotion to Mother Russia—or dogs, bananas, anything—with a forty-seven percent success. The programming was permanent as all memories of being an American were burned out of their cortex with the burning laser needle probes.

A woman captive was paraded before the assembled chamber. A very attractive woman of about thirty. She was told to turn slowly about. She was naked. It was unmistakable that she was one of the star-patterned American Free Women who had defied mental re-education by other means. Yet here she was, obeying every command of the scientist, Melnitsky, who had programmed her. He asked her a few questions.

"Who are you?"

"Georgina Zhukov, proud soldier of the Soviet Occupation Forces." Her full, melon-shaped breasts, with pointed nipples, bounced slightly as she continued to turn. Her strong legs were tan and supple, meeting in a light blond bush at the top of the thighs. There were murmurs of pleasure.

"And what do you think of the American Freefighters?" She looked suddenly angry, her face reddening. "They should be strung up, butchered, fed to dogs."

"What would you do to achieve this?"

"I would give my life for Mother Russia," she replied, giving the clenched-fist salute of the Blackshirts. Killov now stood

111

up and the room hushed. His cold, calculating look as he circled the naked woman brought a chill coursing up Zhabnov's spine. The man was so thin and gaunt, his face so pale, those eyes staring unblinking. Killov's tight black uniform with the red death's-head gleamed in the ceiling chandelier's many lights—a calculated controlling presence.

Killov walked directly in front of the American female and stared at her from about six inches. "Would you kill the Ultimate American? Would you kill Ted Rockson?" The woman began to respond, "Yes," but then she blinked, seemed to jerk, swallowed hard and stared forward, saying nothing. A strange series of expressions marked her face, her lips parted and she vomited all over the charts around her. She grimaced painfully, foaming a green bile at the mouth, whispered, "Never" and collapsed like a stone onto the floor. She was dead.

Zhabnov stood up, enraged. "Killov, what was that about? Why have you disgraced these proceedings?"

"I have merely demonstrated, Mr. President, that the Mind Breaker has its limits at present. Limits that my staff of technicians—" he proffered a palm toward his side of the table—"will remedy. Your scientists are good, of course, Mr. President, but they haven't been able to totally submerge the will of these Free Americans. This obsession they have with Ted Rockson permeates their very being. It requires a KGB approach. We have the resources and the equipment in Denver to go beyond this mere fascination with Mother Russia your scientists have so far accomplished. The test is whether or not these Americans can forget their superstitious belief in this Rockson. He is the key."

Zhabnov looked around the table, saw general acquiescence to Killov's words even from his own forces and decided to seem gracious in his defeat. "Ah, Killov, I see what you mean. By all means I will instruct my staff to cooperate with the KGB in this matter." He turned to his audience, radiating benign rulership. It had done the trick, no one could say that he was not cooperative. They applauded, as a matter of fact. Killov too.

*   *   *

112

Later, Zhabnov sat at his desk almost gnawing his knuckles in anger. He would have to have the scientist that prepared that little embarrassing demonstration executed. Imagine bringing their defective work—that American girl—and then letting Killov ruin their display, making Zhabnov look stupid. It was a humiliating defeat by Killov. They would all talk.

He tapped his finger by the white phone. He really shouldn't execute his top scientist, he really shouldn't. He decided! Politics takes precedence over a man's utility. Order in the ranks must be preserved. People under Zhabnov must know what failure meant, otherwise . . . He picked up the executioner's phone and ordered the arrest of Melnitsky and his family and their immediate execution.

Thirteen

Century City was low on meat. Several hunting expeditions were called together to go out to the wild country to the west and bring back deer, elk, even bear for the freezers of the butchering rooms. Rockson and the toughest woman in the Civilian Brigade didn't have to be in one of the hunting parties, but Rock loved the hunt, as did Rona. Besides, he needed some non-combat time, some R&R. He had fond memories of the wild, craggy land to the west of Century City, from his survival trek at the age of sixteen from Tremain, Utah, the city he had lived in after the murder of his parents by a Red Death Squad. Tremain had been destroyed like Westfort—only with poison gas. As a child he'd had only the legend of Century City to go on when he began his solitary march without food or water, with just a rusting .45 pistol—pre-cataclysm—to find it. The going had been unspeakably harsh the first few weeks out of Tremain. The little water he had found was only through cutting the bases of cactus and sucking out moisture. He had been growing weaker, and then, then he had come to the western portion of the great hunting land of Western Colorado. A low-rad area resplendent with snow-capped peaks, salmon rivers, wild grizzly bears, tall pine trees such as he had never seen before, with flaky red bark—under which was a juicy, edible sap. The forests contained all sorts of edible plants and berries, cattails, wild maize, clover, mutant pegamen-mint. How he had gorged himself, then used a round to bring down an elk that strolled to within forty feet of him. What was that

114

phrase? "Where the deer and the antelope play"—that was it. The Range—that's what the Freefighters called the rich woods, in memory of the song. Here were beaver and caribou and possum and raccoon. Here was life.

Rona and Rock loaded up eight pack hybrids and provisions and sacks to preserve and protect meat and set out along the forested west entrance to Century City. They had two 30-30 superscope rifles and boxes of ammunition, plus their standard side arms and Liberators, just in case. Rona rode ahead of Rock, joyous to be with the man she loved. Pines were abundant, and chipmunks darted about the feet of the horses, playing games of derring-do.

After several miles, the trail passed directly under a waterfall that protected a large ledge, which spray bounced off, giving the riders below a misty shower. Under the waterfall was a cave filled with Indian drawings, scratched into the dark rock with phosphorescent paints that depicted other hunters in other times—glowing reminders that the Freefighters weren't the only survivors out here. There were the Indians. The elusive, seldom-seen Indians. They had always owned the wild. They still did. Occasionally the Freefighters would find one of their dead, wrapped in ceremonial beads, high atop one of their burial platforms in the mountains. Smelling abominable, pecked at by birds, that's the way the Indians wanted their dead—given back to the environment. To the birds of prey went their flesh and blood, to be eaten, to soar up to the Great Spirit. The Great Spirit that helped all men survive told them to wait. To wait until the Russians died as they inevitably would because of their hatred of nature and all things natural.

The Indians occasionally picked off a straggling Red soldier, plunging arrows deep into a Red neck or chest. Indian war cries would echo through the wilderness while the Russians hit the leaves in fear. But they were will-o'-the-wisp, and as swiftly as they came, they were gone again. The Freefighters had great respect for the Indians. The Indians had been defeated but had never surrendered. Rona pointed out the different paintings on the outside rocks as they passed, the echoes of the unshod pack horses making a cacophany of rhythms in the underpass. They came out of that wonderful dark chamber beneath the

115

waterfall cool and damp and headed back into the brilliant sun. A hawk was circling slowly overhead. Perhaps some Indian was "buried in the sky" nearby. Perhaps it was just catching the winds, soaring on rising currents of cool mountain air. The birds in the thick ponderosas started a trilling song of *twit-ooo*. Those would be the high sparrows. He knew their plaintive cries well. They were like a clock always calling an hour and a half before sunset. Some called them the clockbirds. Some said they were the spirits of the dead Indians. Their hollow, throaty calls penetrated one's soul, made one think of profound things like mortality and joy.

Why did the Russians destroy so much of this bounteous world? Were they so fearful, so cowardly that they had to lash out in their fear? Rockson had heard it said that the U.S.A. back before the strike was fearful and materialistic too. Rock could hardly grant that credibility. It was said by some historians that both sides hadn't negotiated fairly. Both had wanted that "edge" over the other. And so it had happened. But the inescapable culpability was with the Reds. For despite the fact that the negotiations had bogged down, the United States hadn't launched. They hadn't plunged the world into a radioactive nightmare that only now, a century later, was beginning to repair itself. Only now were mothers welcoming a new birth—not fearing the hideous, mutated fetuses that had had to be hacked to death in the early years to end their screaming cries upon entering the world. Rockson know of such births from his high-rad childhood. He had seen the faces and bodies of these infants of the atomic age. His own brother had been one—and he had watched as his father lit the funeral pyre that cremated the little two-headed, clawed corpse.

Rock shuddered. Such thoughts were not for sunny days in the mountains with a beautiful woman. But he couldn't forget his childhood, couldn't forget how far mankind had slipped back. The Russians in their respirators, behind their lead-impregnated glass windows in their fortress cities, the mutations, the radiation soot, the acid storms, the dead zones, the brutal occupation—all couldn't be forgotten. His mind must stay aware of the truth at all times, for the next fire fight, and the next—until America was free. And women fighters like

116

Rona. They were not to be wed. The love they shared could only be fleeting, momentary. The next minute might bring loss, separation, horror. Best to live and love day by dangerous day.

The look on Rona's face as her horse pulled alongside Rock's bespoke her concern. "Rock, what are you thinking? Are you all right?"

"Fine," he said, forcing a smile. Then it became natural as her warm eyes softened the hardness around him. He suggested that, as they had made good time, they stop in the cliff overhangs just to the left of the trail up ahead. There would not be such good shelter on the steeper trail an hour ahead. And there were the Russian drones to consider.

"Oh, I agree," she said, winking. "And we can make love all the sooner." Soon they were encamped and watching the green-tinted sunset.

Their lips met, opened. Her lips were soft as petals and full. Tenderly he pulled down her blouse to expose her firm, upturned breasts and cream-colored aureoles—a common mutation in this area. He cupped her smooth globes in his hands, then his fingers searched lower. She helped him, slithering nimbly out of her hiking pants. She pressed her hot nakedness against him, trembling, moaning softly. She reached down and grasped his hardness, so thick and powerful that she gasped. She was ready. He rolled on top of her, spreading her strong, long legs. He probed her lightly with his hardness and then sank in fully. Around them the nightingales sang out their love song and the glowbirds twittered and fluttered amber as the Freefighters' lovemaking intensified.

They slept well and secure that night and awoke to a brilliant sunrise tinted orange. Overhead the stars were still visible in the thin air for a while, then faded as the dark orange sun rose higher, turned pink, then a glaring, brilliant white. They held each other in their sleeping bags, then rose, packed their trail gear and headed on.

The going was rougher after a few hours. The tangle of brush yielded less and less to their machetes and the slope became steeper. Rockson tried to get a compass reading but the needle squiggled around in its casing as if searching madly for true north. Magnetic interference. He squinted in the direction they were going, saw what looked like an impassable butte ahead—a sheer rock wall of perhaps four thousand feet—and took out the Shecter light binoculars. He swung the lenses slowly in a half circle and discovered a huge vertical crack in the apparently-solid facade of the cliff ahead.

"We can keep going this way, for now, anyway. There's a fissure on that rock wall—we can use it to ascend the peak, practically like a ladder." She took the binoculars and looked. She handed them back again, frowning.

"A ladder for a mountain goat—but I'll help you if you stumble." Laughing, she rode ahead, taking the lead. Halfway up the hill at the base of the mountain, there was a roaring stream. He caught up to her as she was forging it, grabbed her belt loops from atop his hybrid and pulled her down into the foaming water. They rolled about, splashing and laughing like children. She looked at him with wide-open eyes. He was so open now. His face more relaxed than she had ever seen it. Oh God, why couldn't they be in a world together where there were no Russians, no death. So the two of them could always be together in happiness. The air in the mountains was so dry that soon their outfits were dry and together they began the ascent up the escarpment, via the jagged fissure.

"This formation has shifted recently," Rock said, looking uneasily at the chipped fresh rock revealed before him. He ran his fingers over it. "Granite with mica—good old American rock. Igneous extrusion."

"I'm impressed, Mr. Geologist," Rona said with a smirk as big as the sky. "Now let's get climbing. Last one to the top buys the beers at the next diner."

Of course there were no diners—or anything else out this way. Diners, they knew, were places the old Americans used to stop their vehicles at along the highways that once connected every part of the U.S.A. Curious metal structures like the old railroad cars. The people would sit on rotating stools or in booths with a big picture window and eat something called hamburger, which was ground meat of buffalo. Perhaps the buffalo were tastier back in the twentieth century, Rock thought, as the hybrids began stumbling slightly as the slope steepened. Nowadays, buffalo were hardly palatable. Rockson had seen the rusted-out carcass of a diner once—on the way to Century City, during his long trek from Tremain. He quickly shifted his thoughts. The day felt too good, Rona looked too beautiful to bring it all up again.

They ascended slowly, carefully. They needed these heights to re-plot their position since the compass was all but useless in these magnetic hills. The view from the top was breath-taking. They were a little to the north of where Rock expected— explaining the unfamiliarity of the place. To the south was the familiar Kennedy Glacier. It was blue-white with streaks of pink running through it like veins. There were billowing clouds of steam where it abruptly ended—hot springs. The Roosevelt Hot Springs they were called. Usually they were controlled, predictably boiling up—with many different temperature pools to soothe weary travelers in mineral-salted baths. But sometimes, in the periods of new and full moons, it was believed, their nature changed violently. They became gushing geysers of deadly boiling rock magma, lighting up the night for miles in a spectacular display of nature's fireworks. Rock hoped for their sakes that the springs would be pleasantly lukewarm.

He saw a way to breach the mountainside to the south—a way for the pack horses to easily move on. And he saw something else, as he peered through the binoculars: grizzlies, the prize they had come for—bear meat, savory bear meat for the kitchens of Century City. And the pelts which would be turned into winter coats capable of withstanding the most frigid temperatures. They were out there, tearing about. Dimly he could hear their roars. A group of ten or twelve, at least, in the next verdant valley. Ten feet tall when they stood up and mean as a sackful of rattlers. Rock watched them frolic through his binoculars—if tearing apart trees was frolicking— looking for honey, no doubt, or tree termites. They clawed away at rotting trunks, literally tearing the wood apart, growling, sticking their long tongues into the cracks in pursuit of a snack. But those bears wouldn't mind a little human meat. And they could smell you a mile away when you were upwind. Fortunately the wind was blowing the opposite direction. Rona reached over and grabbed the binoculars from Rock, and stared out into the next valley.

"Cute," she said. "Is it true that they surround you, and hunt in a group when they get wind of you? Are they that smart?"

"Look for a tall tree," Rock said with mock grimness, "or it's people meat for them this evening. Would you please put an apple in your mouth and lie on a platter?"

"Very funny. Very funny," Rona said, snapping the safety off on her Liberator. "I suppose Mr. Ultimate American will let me be eaten?" He gave her a knowing look, said nothing, but intimated by a look to her thighs what he was thinking.

They moved across the rise into the next valley and their rendezvous with enough bear meat to last weeks. Down the narrow footing the hybrids stumbled. Actually extremely sure-footed creatures, they always gave the impression of being clumsy by all their clomping and shifting of legs. In fact, they were careful because they instinctively understood the subtle movements essential for survival on these steep mountain cliffs. And in fact, they rarely fell. The wind was still with them as they headed down the tree-lined slope into the thickly wooded valley. Bear valley. He'd have to remember the place for future hunts. He knew he would remember the peak towering behind them with its sharp, twin boulders capping the very top.

Rock put up his hand. Silently they tied the horses to some trees, slid their scoped rifles from their mounts and, moccasin clad, moved silently onward to their prey. If the hunt was successful they would bring up the mounts and load the bear meat. If not, the horses would tear loose eventually and roam free. A few might even find their way back to Century City, grim testimony to the death of Rock and Rona at the tearing paws of the giant black grizzlies. Rockson was confident that they would be successful. He had hunted with Rona before, though there had only been two bears to contend with. Now there was a whole slew of them. Well, the wind was holding up, their friend today unlike the last time.

Rockson motioned for Rona to wait on the bank as he waded across a bubbling stream, cold as mountain ice. Safely on the

120

other side, he motioned for her to cross too. It was damned quiet—the birds didn't seem to like this valley much. Rockson wondered if the rads had only died down here recently as much of the vegetation was lush but strange; there were many leaves and flowers with the sharp spikes that characterized mutated plant life in the central portion of the United States. And the bears did seem unusually tall. Two or three of them had looked over twelve feet. Mutants? He checked his mini-counter. It was quiescent. Good. No need absorbing more rads than one had to although Rockson knew that in his thirty-three years of life he had already absorbed enough radiation to kill a hundred men. He knew he had a far higher tolerance for the deadly rays that shot out invisibly from the decaying, hot materials than most men.

Rona walked alongside him silently, about three feet to his left. They moved as quietly as a slow breeze, their safeties off, fingers on the trigger guard. They were careful where they pointed the Liberators for the rifles had hair triggers. They entered the deep, dark forest ahead, a forest fairly easy to walk through, the trees being only lightly vegetated until about ten feet up, where they became a wild tangle of vine branches. Vines like Rockson had never seen before. Vines that grew out of the tall pine trees, vines with needles. Unusual. It was so dark underneath that they didn't see the lumbering black shadows closing in from the maze like thickets of trees.

Suddenly the huge grizzlies were upon them. Towering, furry bodies, standing upright, claws slashing, jaws snarling and coming right for their throats. Rockson swung his Liberator with lightning speed, but the closest monstrous creature whipped its clawed paw across it, slamming the rifle against a tree with such force that the barrel bent in half and the oak stock smashed into little chunks of useless wood.

There were three of them, and their red eyes seemed to glow in the semi-darkness. They roared in anger and hunger. The second grizzly whipped its five-foot-long arm at Rona who ducked barely in time. The clawed hand, as big as a baseball mitt, tore into the tree just above her head, ripping a chunk of thick bark into the air. She rolled to the side and came up firing her Liberator, getting off three shots into the black-furred grizzly. At the same time, Rock jumped backwards giving himself a ten-foot separation between him and the bear and whipped out his shotgun pistol. He fired point-blank into the advancing monster's chest. Rona's and Rock's shots all made target, blowing bloody holes into the thick, black hair. But the targets didn't seem to know—or care. Both bears, and the third, moving from behind an uprooted tree, kept advancing.

Rock saw Rona sprint for cover just as the bear closest to her made a jumping dive—onto thin air. She ran about twenty feet to two large boulders side by side, with an opening at the base just big enough to hide a body. She dove into the opening, pulling her legs quickly in behind her as the bear ran toward the rock, covering the distance in seconds. Rock slammed the rapid-fire shotgun pistol onto auto and cut loose with three quick shots that smashed his hand back like the whiplash of a bucking bronco. Three loads of .12-gauge lead shot smashed into the grizzly's neck and side. Blood poured out as if several of the bear's arteries had been severed. But it didn't stop him. The grizzly slashed at the boulders, reaching frantically under to get to Rona. Its six-inch-long, curved claws dug out trails of stone, sending rock dust flying, leaving a ridge of half-inch cuts that would last ten thousand years embedded in the rock, a fossil of violence. Rona crawled deeper into the eight-foot-deep wedge-shaped opening, looking back with horror at the grizzly's jaws pushing in at the entrance, foaming, snarling, dripping the blood of its own internal injuries.

From forty feet away, Rock watched. Rona was safe, but he had company. The two other grizzlies, one an almost foxlike red with dark black lines and dots, the other as black as the blackest night, closed in on their human prey. They tried to surround him as they broke apart and came up from each side. Slow, deliberate. Not wanting to let him hide as the other one had. He had two shots left in the pistol. No time to reload. Damn! He wished he had a grenade. But he did have a phosphorous bomb. He reached in his utility belt, slung low around his waist, and opened one of the dark-green pockets. He continued to walk slowly backwards, one hand gripping the .12-gauge pistol, the other lifting out the apple-sized grenade. He flicked the trigger with his thumb and released the safety pin, waited four seconds and threw it at them. At the same instant he turned and ran straight to the left. The two grizzlies dropped to all fours and rushed forward at Rock's sudden motion. They got about three feet before the device went off only inches from their red eyes. They let out screams of pain and fear as they continued to lumber forward, moving from the momentum of their two thousand-pound bodies like engines without a driver. The bomb showered them with burning phosphorous, burning into their thick hides. Their eyes were blinded from the light, brilliant as a sun, the retinas blasted into orbit.

Rock rushed forward as the grizzlies slashed wildly away at the air searching for the thing that had hurt them. He held the pistol two feet from the black-furred one and pulled the trigger. The brains of the grizzly blew out the other side in a spray of blood and bone. This time there would be no more hunts. Blood spurting like a fountain from its torn-open head, the bear fell, shaking, to the ground.

Rock spun instantly around, one shot left. The phosphorous bomb had done its job. The other bear was burning, its thick red-and-black-spotted pelt flaring with blue flames. It howled in anger and agony. No longer interested in the fight, it tore off into the woods, an action that only fanned the flames hotter. Soon Rock could hear in the distance the mournful cries of its death throes.

Rock turned and ran over to the boulder Rona had hidden beneath. A car-sized mass of fur and blood lay on the red ground nearly blocking the narrow rock entrance. Rona had filled her unwanted guest with lead from inside her protective crevasse. He saw a hand coming out from under the huge rocks, trying to push at the bear's wide-open, motionless snout.

"Come on, Rock, for God's sake, help me." Rock walked up to the huge black grizzly and grabbed hold of two thick handfuls of hide on the creature's neck. He pulled with all his strength, moving the giant inch by agonizing inch. As strong as Rock was it was like moving a piece of solid rock. Finally, after a minute of pulling at the creature again and again in red-faced bursts of strength, Rock at least cleared the opening enough for Rona to emerge. She dusted herself off and looked up at Rock who couldn't help but smile slightly at her emergence from literally out of the bear's jaws.

She returned the smile. "Do I get to mount him as a trophy?" she asked, bending over and looking at the monster's teeth. She whistled. "Jesus, Rock, look at these." In the front of the grizzly's arm-sized jaw were two curved fangs, a good twelve inches long, with rows of white pointed teeth disappearing in trails down the creature's throat.

"Mutant," Rock said. "These fangs could be a de-evolution taking place." Rock remembered what Dr. Shecter had said to him recently about a theory he was developing that many species were actually going backwards in the evolutionary progression. "A kind of protective adaptation as far as I can see, Rock. When species are threatened they go to a simple state so as to be more adaptable. I wouldn't be surprised to see mastodons, and saber-toothed tigers returning." And now, here before Rockson was just that, a grizzly with fangs. Shecter would go mad with joy when he had this monster's head down on a lab table.

Rock's keen senses scanned the suddenly silent woods. All he could hear was Rona's breathing, and yet—

"Rona, stay here," Rockson said, hitching himself up the branches of a tall pine. He could barely make them out at first through the veils of leaves and branches ahead, but about a hundred yards away was another group of grizzlies. Normally such a set of explosions would have driven the bears away but these black grizzlies seemed to have the opposite instinct. They were mutants and hunters of human flesh. No wonder no one had ever told him about this lush valley—no one had ever returned alive from it.

The bears were almost running now toward the clearing where the three grizzly corpses lay. Rockson reloaded his shotgun pistol with eight shots and told Rona to hand him the 30-08 rifle with exploding shells. "Get back into the crevasse," Rock yelled down to her. "I'll pick them off from here."

"The hell I will," she replied sharply. "*You* go!" She grabbed her fallen Liberator and climbed up the tree, quickly joining Rock about fifteen feet off the ground in the thick lower branches of the towering pine.

"Make every shot count," Rock said, wrapping his thighs around the two-foot-wide branch. "And go for the head only. The eyes, the brain. That's the only thing that will stop them. I got our furry friend over there—" Rock pointed down to the larger of the two grizzlies he had taken out—"with three hits to the side and it didn't even faze him. These things are as tough as they come."

Rona balanced herself on a long, sap-oozing branch, wrapping her legs and arms around it like a blanket. She took her Liberator, set it on single-shot and aimed at the brush about thirty feet away from which a snapping, growling sound was rapidly approaching.

Four grizzlies, each as wide in girth as the trees Rock and Rona hid in, each snarling and running forward, now on their hind legs, claws flailing. Damned fast and smart. But not enough. The two Freefighters opened up from above, one shot after another, every one finding its deadly mark. The skulls of two of the giants shattered in pieces as Rock's explosive cartridges found a home in bear brain. Rona fired methodically away at a third which stretched up to its full height as if daring death to touch it. Her third shot caught it full in the right eye, blasting the right side of its head away. Her fourth caught it just above the ear but it was already falling by then. The last remaining grizzly stopped momentarily as if to take in the carnage around it. It stared up into the tree and, with a roar that shook the forest, ran forward on two legs right for them. It swung a mighty paw up into the air like a sword. The claws, reaching five feet beyond its eleven-foot shoulders, caught the branch on which Rona was hanging, about four feet away. The wood snapped with a crack and slowly began tilting groundward.

"Rock, Rock," Rona screamed, losing her balance and beginning to tumble forwards. The bear turned toward the human that flew down to it, its jaws opening wide for the kill. Rockson had no choice. Throwing the hunting rifle away, he reached for his .12-gauge pistol, grabbed it in his right hand and jumped. He landed full on the immense grizzly's back. He gripped a handful of thick-matted fur and held the muzzle of the pistol at the creature's cranium. He pulled the trigger once, twice, three times, turning his head as the two-inch-thick skull shattered into a storm of razor-sharp bone shrapnel. Yet, somehow, something lived within the grizzly monster. It reached up with its left claw and slashed at Rockson, swiping down his leg, which opened in rivulets of red. The force of the blow pulled Rock forward, and he found himself falling through the air. He twisted over in midflight so as to land on all fours, and let his body collapse with the hit, rolling over several times. He came to a stop and without a moment's hesitation reached down for the bowie knife strapped to his leg. The grizzly took two steps forward, seemed to waver for a moment, took another step and then fell, only half its huge head still remaining.

Rock stood up, putting a hand to his torn leg. It was deep—about an inch and a half, but from the movement he still had it didn't appear that he had severed any vital muscles or tendons. He would survive and heal. He had been hurt before—many times, and much worse than this.

He walked quickly over to Rona who was sitting up, rubbing her shoulder. Her silky red hair fell down over her face and neck almost covering her. She tossed the camouflaging strands aside and looked up at Rockson.

"I landed all right, but then the damn branch came down on my back," she said defensively, as if ashamed she had been hurt.

"Well, we both got our wounds from this one. Our last little teddy bear hugged me a real sweet goodnight before the lights went out on him." He lifted his hand from his thigh, which was now bright red with blood, the khaki field pants torn into five separate pieces where the claws had cut them like tailor's scissors.

"Oh, Rock," Rona said, jumping to her feet. "You're really hurt." She made him sit down and cut away at the top of the pants leg with her knife, revealing the full extent of the wound. The bear's claws had entered at midthigh, on the very outside of the leg and pulled down a good eight inches of flesh before losing contact. Rock pulled out a leather thong from a back pocket of the utility belt and tied a tourniquet at the very top of his leg.

"That'll hold for twenty minutes or so until we get back to the hybrids where I can patch it up." They stood next to each other and looked around at the scene of carnage. All around the clearing were pools of blood and furry flesh. The huge carcasses still twitched in death spasms. Rock walked around and pumped a few more rounds into the still-breathing ones. Grizzlies had been known to play dead for hours, then come suddenly to life as strong as ever and take their revenge. He heard thrashing coming from the woods, but it quickly grew more distant. They had had enough of man for the moment.

That night they lay together in their joined sleeping bags. Overhead, the aurora borealis rippled and crackled with writhing currents of rainbow electricity. Rona held him close to her, covering his body with hers, draping her arms and legs over his hard flesh. She nuzzled in his neck as he slowly stroked her waist-long, soft, red hair.

"The old America, Rock. What was it really like? I know you study the old history tapes. Tell me, was it really great? Really beautiful?" Rockson had a faraway look in his eyes. He didn't answer for a moment but seemed to draw energy from the pulsating magnetic patterns in the sky. It was as if he were communing with the earth, with the forces of nature. Finally he spoke.

"Yes, it was great, Rona. Great and powerful . . . and polluted and corrupt. The pursuit of money took precedence over the founding fathers' idea of freedom. The pursuit of the 'buck' they called it. You should view the tapes some day, Rona. See what they were willing to do to get money. Freedom came to mean license to do as you wished—if it meant money. The citizens of America were mired in the same materialist obsession that the Russians are in now. And like they fell, the Russians will someday fall. The old America died because it became too soft and fat and lost its will to live. Now it is the Russians who live off the land, the slave labor of others and become soft while the Freefighters become tougher and leaner every day."

127

Rona looked upset. "Rock, isn't that heresy? What you say about the old America?"

"The truth is never heresy," Rock said, his eyes still focused on the magnetic storm that raged above. "America was great for two hundred years. Then it abandoned its ideals and it pursued goals that weren't brave, weren't concerned with peace for the world. It didn't keep the torch of freedom burning. And that torch went out with a bang."

"So we're trying to rebuild something that's not worth—"

"No, Rona. We're trying to restore the dream the way the people back there failed to do. The original dream. Someday we'll fight the Russians off our backs, out of our land and then we'll spread freedom to them. We won't occupy Russia permanently like they've done to us. America spreads liberty—it doesn't take prisoners."

Rona pushed closer against him, spellbound by his words. A meteor shot overhead, cutting the night with a sword of sparkling blue. Then another and another. Soon, the whole sky was filled with the zaps of starlight brilliance, hitting the atmosphere of the Earth from untold billions of miles out and burning up their lives in a final blaze of brilliant glory.

Rock continued after a moment. "Rona, once the United States had another great war—World War II they called it. And America and her allies conquered the whole world. But it didn't subjugate its enemies. It helped them rise again and rebuild the ashes of their society into democracies. That is what we must do."

"But we hate the Russians," Rona said, confused.

"We must hate them for now."

Fourteen

Killov inspected himself in the mirror and was pleased with what he saw. His cheekbones loomed ominously high on his face, little knobs of bone, above which two narrow eyes peered inscrutably out. The little party in Washington was over and he had won the round. Respect! He had gained respect from Zhabnov's forces and all the gathered top brass of the occupying Russian forces. They had seen how much cleverer Killov was compared to that fool of a president. He had humiliated Zhabnov, no matter how adeptly the fat man had tried to recover. He had proven who was the more efficient, who had the best staff, who should really run things—from his eighty-story monolith in the center of the new America, Denver, not from some archaic remnant of the past, fading and crumbling into obscurity.

Washington—whorehouses and black servants everywhere waiting on all the bureaucratic big cheeses. The only blacks in the nation just about. They were carefully population-controlled while being treated with special rights such as extra food, clothing and travel. The Red masters of America didn't want their servants to slit their throats one night while they were sleeping, after all. The Blackies, as they were called by their Russian owners, were even allowed travel outside their city. They set an example for the rebellious people of Africa and the yellows of Asia of the benevolence and anti-racism of the Russian forces in America. Bah, Washington was a stinkhole, Killov thought, strolling around his office, his thin hands clasped tightly behind his black, pigskin military jacket. It was a museum. The capital of America, should be—*would be*—here in Denver. The only thing that could control these rebels was force, not these petty propaganda ploys that the social scientists back in Moscow recommended. The social scientists didn't understand: Everything is pleasure and pain. Pleasure is motivation, pain de-motivation. That's what the Roman emperors understood. They had ruled in a Pax Romana for four hundred years, perhaps more. Then they allowed others—the barbarians—to immigrate, to share their wealth, their power. Finally, they were done in. To share is to lose, Killov thought. He wouldn't share much longer with the fool of a president.

In the war room at the eastern side of his eightieth-floor office the supreme commander of the KGB forces watched as immense laser-lit situation screens lowered silently from the high ceiling. The room had been built by Killov to direct his forces now, and, when the time came for his struggle of ascendancy, to direct, if necessary, Killov's growing strategic forces against Washington.

Killov sat dead-center in the most sophisticated technological room in the world except for the Satellite Control Complex in Moscow. That was the state-of-the-art. The absolute refinement of the technology that had defeated America one hundred years ago, kept constantly up to date. But Killov had been successful in having many of the Satellite Complex's technological secrets stolen and copied for his war room. The red active light came on and the screen lit up with a map of the world, forty feet wide. In the dark of the room, little blue dots marked all known air activity, the ground positions of Russian forces, and the locations of all Russian warships and subs in the world. He had tapped into the satellite information being transmitted back to Central Control in Moscow. The premier, if he knew of this, would have Killov executed. But he didn't know. And he wouldn't until the time was right for Killov to make his move.

The KGB commander watched the dots of light shifting slowly about the flat globe of the Earth. So much power! So many weapons of incalculable destruction. He pressed several control buttons on the large, glowing instrument panel built into the arm of his chair. The map shrank until it was just the United States. Again, all Red forces were shown in their occupying positions across the country. He fed some information into the computer that operated the map: the coordinates of his latest guesswork, aided by information supplied by troop patrols on sightings of rebel forces, as to just where Century City was. He pressed keys on the board, wrote out the question, "Where is the most probable location of Century City?"

The computer whirred and buzzed and seemed to have trouble with the question. Then a blue dot appeared in the nearby mountains. Killov leaned forward. Could it be? Then another blue dot lit up, then another and another. He sat back in disgust. The whole Rocky Mountain range was filled with blue dots, flickering as the computer ran a blurring white arrow through the dots again and again and a mechanical voice spoke out from speakers at each side of the huge map, "Probable location of Century City is the following 15 locations. Probable location of Century City is the following 15 locations. Probable location of Century City is . . ."

Mikael Vassily was not a big man. He was old, and that did not bode well for his continued reign over the vast Soviet empire. But he was good at playing one group against another in the Politburo and presenting himself as the perfect compromise between all the warring factions.

He was seventy-one years old, a good age for this new world. His mind was as sharp and precise as ever. It was just his body that was slowly failing—the legs trembling as he walked, the dark spots showing up with increased regularity on his body, precursors of "cancerous conditions," as his doctors politely put it. Still, not many men reached the age of seventy anymore. Not with all the poison in the air and the water and the ground.

He stood at a window in the Presidium building—the highest and newest structure in the crumbling, red-brick fortress walls of the ancient Kremlin. He could look down at Red Square from here and at the endless line of tourists from all over the empire, shivering in the two feet of snow as they waited hours to enter the hallowed halls of the Lenin Tomb. The tomb that contained both the body of the great founder of the Soviet Union and the body of that heinous criminal, Premier Drushkin, who had unleashed the hell of thermonuclear war upon the planet Earth one hundred years ago.

Premier Vassily was one of the very few in Russia, or in the world, who had seen the original, unexpurgated accounts of that wretched war. Those reports on video and in secret files told of the decision to send in the first strike and the resulting consequences as H-bombs went off all over the Earth. An event that had, of course, been built up ever since as a great triumph of the peoples of the Socialist sphere. The accounts he had read told how Russians had launched in a panic, fearing a U.S. strike—which was not in the offing—how their own paranoia had made them push the button. He'd seen what had been done to the world. Reconnaissance photos made by Russian planes showed a world that had been turned into a boiling hell. Nearly two-thirds of the Earth's population destroyed. Vast regions of lands ripped apart as if by the claws of some monstrous demon from hell. And the Russians had not been spared nearly as much as the authorities pretended. Nearly twenty-five of the United States' "big boys"—more than ten megatons—had struck major cities throughout the Soviet Union, killing at least thirty million in the first hour and double that amount over the next few months. And, by luck or accident, four of the American missiles had landed right in the center of the U.S.S.R.'s wheat-growing region, knocking out a good eighty percent of the land for eons. No, it had not been a good war—not at all.

He watched the snow fall—snow and ice in July, the Volga five feet thick, frozen solid. The world was topsy-turvy and getting more so all the time. And his own rule, that too was becoming more problematic all the time. The empire was in trouble. He had gone through the folders of reports on his desk, just before he took off his thick reading glasses and walked to the window. Now, as he stood watching the lines stretching off to the dimness of the distant snow, Vassily remembered nothing about those reports—soybean virus,

132

crops failed, weather difficulties hampering troop movements, rising resistance in Indian subcontinent, the resurgence of Buddhism in Southeast Asia, with a distinctly anti-Red tinge.

Only one of those reports had raised his big, heavy eyebrows—Killov! Killov had, without permission, without even consulting President Zhabnov—not to mention Vassily himself—dropped two neutron bombs on some rebel outpost in the Rocky Mountains. Damn! There was so much radiation in the world already. The one thing he had asked his military commanders around the world was, please, no more atomic weapons. Let the world repair itself at least slightly. We need food to eat. We need to live on the damn planet. Didn't they understand that?

But what was done was done. Vassily was, if nothing else, a pragmatist. The question was: What should he do *now?* Recall Killov? No, the man was too dangerous to have around. He had gathered a large faction of followers around himself in the Politburo. He was ambitious. Very ambitious. Have him executed? No, if he tried, Killov could well send assassins to do in Vassily, setting off a murderous power struggle within the state that could even lead to more war. Perhaps he could have his nephew, Zhabnov, move against Killov in some way to check him. No, Zhabnov had turned out to be a total disappointment to the premier. He had hoped that the president could balance the power of the growing KGB in America. But he was no match for Killov. Even his report about Killov's use of the bombs was like some schoolboy screaming, "See what Killov did, Uncle, see!" Maybe he would have to replace Zhabnov with a much stronger personality. Yet if he did that, the new president of the United States might well conspire against him—even unite with Killov. Damn, he was getting tired of the game. The constant war of wills.

He buzzed his secretary. "Vanya, take a letter. Superconfidential, all that. To Commander Killov, titles, medals—fill it in like you always do. 'Dear friend and comrade-in-arms, I read with interest a report that you have acted against the American resistance forces with a pair of small-yield neutron bombs. I know you did this in the spirit of my directive not to damage the environment, and I trust that the natural damage has been

133

kept to a minimum. I, er, applaud your initiative and keen analysis of my attitude toward the use of nuclears. That policy is to restrain use unless the gravest of provocations has occurred. Please send details of provocation that led to the use of N-weapons.'

"Paragraph. 'Your long-standing request to use N-weapons has been studied and approved in principle. However, any further judicious use of radiation-enhanced devices should be preceded by a statement from you as to the necessity for such measures. Ten,' no make that, 'eight, small-yield neutron bombs can be used at your discretion if you adhere to these guidelines. Hoping you and your comrades are well, I remain.' Finish it up please."

"Yes, sir," Vanya said, closing her steno pad. "Do you wish it sent—"

"Right away. Let me read it again first. Thank you." As the secretary left, Vassily rang a small white button at the underside of his desk. Less than a minute later the door opened quietly and a black servant, ebony face shining, dressed in a white waiter's tuxedo, walked in with a slow, smooth gait carrying a tray with a crystal decanter and brandy glass in the center.

"Ah, Ruwando," the premier said, looking up with pleasure in his wrinkled eyes. "My favorite time of the evening." He smiled pleasantly.

"And mine as well, sir," the African servant said in flawless Russian. He set the tray down on a small drink stand at the right of the premier's desk and slowly, ritualistically removed the top from the decanter and carefully poured out exactly half a shimmering crystal goblet of golden, sweet brandy. The servant watched, a slight smile on his face, as Vassily lifted the drink to his mouth and took the first sip. His face lit up like a Cheshire cat's. He licked his lips and eased back in the big, blue armchair that he rested in every evening.

"Ah, sir, so good to see you relax," the black servant said soothingly. "Really, you must pay more attention to your health."

"Indeed, indeed," Vassily mumbled, taking another sip, already lost in his own reveries. The servant silently exited the room, closing the door without a sound. Vassily took a book down from the shelf, *Notes from Underground*, by Dostoyevsky, and began reading where he had left off:

> It was still night and the snow was coming down in masses and falling almost perpendicularly, blanketing the pavement and the empty streets. There was no one in the street, no sound to be heard. The streetlamps gave a disconsolate and useless glimmer. I ran two hundred paces to the intersection and stopped short. Where had she gone? And why was I running after her? Why? To fall down before her, to sob with remorse.

But before long, the aging ruler of the world dozed off, his head falling back on the shadowed pillow. The snow outside grew more intense; little dunes were forming in Red Square. The radiation level warnings were going up in Murmansk, the Sikhs were rioting in India in 120-degree temperatures. In South China a war lord was preparing his thirteen thousand fanatical horsemen—fanatical Moslem followers of the Mua-bir, the flame of Allah.

In Rangoon, Buddhist monks burned themselves to protest the new religious limitations and the machine-gunning of one hundred of their number just the day before.

And in the Kremlin, in the breasted snow of Russia, the leader of the empire, the supreme premier of all the Russias, a tired old man, slept with his face pressed into the yellowing paper of Dostoyevsky, page 345.

Fifteen

Rona and Rock had to return to Century City by a fairly roundabout route, avoiding the high mountain passes and the waterfall trail which would be both too steep and too narrow for their heavily laden pack hybrids. The horses were tired, bone-tired after four days of carrying an inordinate amount of grizzly meat and pelts on their broad backs. Skinned and salted by Rock, and cut up into manageable chunks and put in the special airtight, plastic meat sacks that they carried, the grizzly meat would last days. They traveled in the mornings and the dark of the night to avoid the heat of the searing sun and the Red drones which were plentiful in the open country that they had to traverse due to the load. Each day they would set up camouflage netting under a thick grove of trees or a field of house-sized boulders spewed by an active volcano, and rest. Each day they made love. Rona had never felt happier in her life. Spending time with the man she loved, though she never said the words. She knew it would push him away like a frightened woods creature. The man was afraid of nothing on this Earth—no beast or soldier or KGB torturer. But he was afraid of women. Rock let himself enjoy her attentions. He knew there wasn't much time for them. That he or she could be blown away in splatters of skin and blood, just like those grizzlies had. Death was near. Always standing behind one's shoulder. Death had gravitated to Ted Rockson many times. Had come knocking on the door to take him away. And each time Rock had kicked it in the nuts and told it to fuck off, that

136

he wasn't ready to die. But even he knew that someday . . . someday. For in the game of death, the cards were stacked. Death won every hand.

At last they reached the southwest entrance to Century City, which was at a higher altitude though flatter terrain than the way they had departed. The hybrids huffed and wheezed with each step through the thin atmosphere. But soon, they were briskly walking down the final slope to the hidden city. Coming upon a grove of dark black spruce trees, Rock gave a sputtering larklike trill. He wasn't as good as Detroit Green with these bird calls but he was getting better. The customary reply had been changed just last week, when it was feared that the captured Preston might betray the city's location. So the lark got a reply from a starling, rather than an owl. A raucous squawk in three descending notes. A ten-by-ten-foot piece of what looked like solid turf suddenly opened up, rising on two metal poles at the end. Rock and Rona and their team of eight hybrids descended down a wooden ramp into an almost dark chamber. Rock knew that hidden eyes and hidden guns were trained on them at this very second, had been for miles. The entrance fell closed behind them and two guards ran over and knocked it perfectly into place, so that from above not a seam of human touch could be seen. The echoing hoofbeats of the skittish pack animals were the only sounds for a few seconds. Then greetings of, "Rock. Rock. Glad you're back" came from all sides. Still the lights didn't brighten. Torch-lit figures approached from the darkness. In the front ranks, his face garishly lit by the orange flames of his hand-held torch, was intelligence chief Rath.

Rockson took his side arm out, thinking trouble. "What's the matter?" he asked, dismounting.

"A power outage, Rock. It's been going on for nearly twenty hours and looks like it could go on for days. We've got no lights, no power at all, other than the emergency generators which are just keeping life-support systems in the hospital and our defensive electronic apparatus functioning. I'm really worried about the hydroponics. They say another twenty-four hours without any juice and it's all over for everything in there."

"What the hell happened?" Rock asked, putting his .12-gauge pistol smoothly back into its bed of dark leather. "A diode generator blew?"

"Nothing like that, Rock. It's crazy. It—it was the Reds, although they don't know they caused the trouble. One of their big Stalagva airlifters lost an engine—the damned thing fell right off and the ramjet nose-dived into our main solar collector on Ice Mountain. The place is a mess up there. All our solar units, our circuitry, step-up transformers, *everything*—gone. We've sent up three teams already to begin replacing destroyed parts and making whatever emergency repairs are possible. But it's hard going. It's storming up there tonight. We set up a fogger to shield all the activity from the damned drones they sent out to look for the airlifter. It must have gone down a few miles down the road. Their stupid inefficiency has dealt us a blow this time. If they find that camouflaged power installation they'll follow the buried cables to Century City itself. So while two teams are installing new solar panels—disguised, like the old ones, as ice formations—the two other teams are cutting up the wreckage and dumping it down crevasses. If the Reds don't see any pieces up there they won't even come down to investigate."

Rockson took it all in while tying up the hybrids to nearby posts. Rath tried to lighten the mood momentarily by admiring their tremendous bounty of bear meat, but Rockson was scarcely listening. It sounded like everything that could be done was being done—but he had to see for himself. Besides, it would be good for the men's morale up there in that freezing hell to have Rock join them. A leader should be with his men in the best and worst of times.

In an hour he was suited up in nylon double-insulated climbing gear, spiked boots and goggles. He and another ten-man team headed across the two sparsely wooded meadows that separated Century City from the midway point up Ice Mountain. Ice Mountain—19,890 feet high, the top several thousand feet sheer rock face. There was a field of glacial ice atop it exposed to the harsh sunlight virtually every day. The very next peak over, about a mile, from the mountain beneath which Century City was built, the Freefighters had realized almost a decade earlier that it was the perfect spot for a solar generating unit. Small at first, consisting of just a few cells, the power unit had been built up over the years until it supplied nearly seventy-five percent of the city's power. A far better situation than when they had to use gas-powered generators which meant raids on Red gasoline-truck convoys weekly and a tremendous loss of life. The solar plant had made them independent for the first time. It had been a milestone in the history of Century City. And there the unit had been humming away until the crash.

Rock and the climbing squad, loaded down with both climbing tools and packs filled with emergency repair equipment, reached the top tree line of Ice Mountain within an hour. Then they climbed up a slowly steepening ridge for a good two hours more. Finally they reached the base of the fifteen hundred feet—a wall of rock towered straight up above them, rising like an impossibility into the clouds.

Rock immediately saw the spikes that the other climbers had left in the sheer rock face. Foot holds, and eye sockets for securing their nylon climbing ropes. The wind howled around their bundled ears. Pockets of snow were already falling on the team, ice forming so rapidly on their equipment and goggles that there was the immediate danger of being weighed down, of losing balance.

Rock went first, tethered to Carruthers, Sanchez, Moore and the rest by thin but ultrastrong thousand-pound test climbing rope. Each man was connected to the next. If one slipped, it was the other's desperate duty to pull him back or perish. That's the way Freefighters were in all endeavors—they would never let a buddy down. Soon they were moving smoothly if slowly up the side of the nuclear-bomb-created mountain. Rock would follow the holds already made, secure himself at the next possible ledge, tie a safety rope on, and head further up. He knew the team, equipped with laser cutting tools, had to reach the peak soon. Without the tools the job would take until daybreak—and in the daytime the repair crews would certainly be spotted by either the drones or Red planes searching for wreckage. And the fogger couldn't be used. Fog never existed naturally that high up during the day. The Russians would notice the aberration and send a massive force to annihilate the repair crews—and trace the cables back to the city. He pushed himself harder.

They climbed and climbed, the icy wind howling louder and louder, screaming like a pack of frost wolves in their ears. Occasionally they rested against the rock wall to hyperventilate, a trick the Freefighters had learned called Swant's Breath. It opened their lungs to full capacity, enabling them to take in more oxygen and go without the cumbersome masks and tanks. At these heights even the toughened American lungs needed some assistance.

Rock was just reaching up for the next handhold when he felt a sudden jerk that nearly pulled him backwards. Carruthers, twelve feet below him, let out a muffled scream as he slipped and fell off the face of the mountain, only to be pulled short after only a five foot drop by the rope connected to Rock and the others. The second man reached out and grabbed hold of a spike and reattached himself, antlike, to the wall of the mountain. They continued on, through the howling wind, ice forming on gloves and goggles. Below Rockson was 5,670 feet of empty air. Above him was the most difficult part of the steep climb. The famed challenge called The Top Face had to be climbed "clean," without driving steel pitons into the cliff wall, because the rock was a basalt-mica formation and the metal wedges would wiggle free in just seconds. For anchors and fall-stoppers, Rockson began using only the aluminum wedges and nuts that he and the team had dangling from their climbing belts. The aluminum jobs could be popped in and out of the numerous—and more sturdy—cracks with the fingers. On such devices, no larger than a finger nail, they were staking their lives and the hopes of Century City.

After nearly a half hour of muscle-numbing climbing, straining every fiber in their bodies, the team was in sight of the fogged summit. But from here on in, it would take every ounce of energy they had left. They stopped momentarily and chewed the cactus extract, a mild stimulant that gave them a carbohydrate boost. They could not afford the luxury of resting for more than a minute. If the wind should pick up or if a Red search plane dropped too low ... The engineer who maintained the solar power units usually came around the mountain via a trail going up a fairly navigable route. But that took almost a full day, another luxury the repair crews didn't have.

Rockson started up again, looking up the rock wall for any little opening for support. He found a winding eighth-of-an-inch crack that meandered along the face for about twenty feet. It was deeper than he could see into. He picked a tiny aluminum wedge from his belt clips and threaded a loop of rope through its eyelet. He threaded the wedge into the crack and tugged hard on it, as hard as he could. Solid. It would have to hold Rock's full weight if he fell, and the others behind him if they should slip after him. Rockson took his pickax and snagged another, wider crack overhead and pulled himself up.

There were, unfortunately, no "chimneys" on this side of the mountain. That meant none of the crack systems led to a crevice wide enough to rest in, or to use to continue the ascent by pressing against the sides with shoulders, back, arms. The team had to use sheer muscle every inch of the way.

Much of a climb is reflective and silent. You can hear the wind, and you can hear grunts and breathing—but usually just of your own straining breath. However if you pause you can hear the others. It is a strange cacophony, those breaths and grunts. All you are aware of is that each moment is a lifetime in itself—or the moment of a death fall.

Rockson never felt so much like an ant dangling on a gossamer string as he did at these dizzying heights. And he had never seen strong men like Carruthers and Sanchez, coming up below him, look so fatigued. They pushed on ever upwards toward the dome of heaven itself. The moon set and pierced rapierlike through quick-flying narrow lines of clouds. It was growing darker by the minute though as bigger cumulus rumblers came pushing in from the west, meaning even greater menace. A slip or a rock fall at this time would mean disaster. Curse the damn Reds for their stupid luck.

Only the sheer tenacity of the American will to live enabled the whole team to reach the top safely. In the dimness of the green lights undetectable to the drones, amidst the rolling waves of fog from the four foggers that had been set up at the

141

corners of the peak, the previous crews were solemnly working. Rock and the climbers stumbled over, almost wheezing as they tried to catch their breath.

"Here, we've got a lot of that fancy stuff you need—laser torches and metal-cutting clips," Rock said to Saunders, the head of the repair crews, who stood supervising the demolition of the main piece of crashed ramjet.

"Thanks, Rock," Saunders said, his body and half his face covered in a thick, green down parka. "Tell your men to take all their equipment over there to Sturges by the tent we've erected. He's handling materials." The rest of the team hustled over as quickly as their freezing legs and cramped muscles would carry them, praying that somehow there was hot coffee inside the dimly lit storage tent.

"Looks like you've actually got things slightly under control," Rock said, glancing around at the frantically working crews. Then he got the bad news.

"Rock, I wanted to give you thirty seconds to catch your breath," Saunders said grimly, "but something terrible has happened. One of the crews, climbing over to the lower glacial peak about a mile over that way to check for more wreckage, was captured by a Blackshirt patrol just an hour ago. Fiden was watching with binoculars and saw it happen. Two choppers just popped out of the sky and surrounded the men. They didn't have a chance without weapons and were taken. The Reds didn't see us—and had no reason to think there was anyone else. Poor bastards. Armstrong, Smith, Gilhooley, Fitz and Scranton. They'll all be tortured to death for sure."

Rockson didn't let on that the situation was far worse than that. With the new Mind Breakers, the five captured Freefighters might, *would*, talk. Century City would be just a smoldering memory like Westfort within twenty-four hours.

"Keep working," Rock said. "Don't let the men slack off or get depressed because of the capture. You've got your job to do, I've got mine."

The situation was critical. They couldn't use flags to contact Century City, as they often did on routine missions up the mountain. With the moon totally hidden behind ever bigger clouds and the beginning of more snow, the flags would be

142

totally invisible, even to ground watchers with binocs. To wait until dawn could mean disaster. Rock had to get the message to Century City—and there had to be a rapid hit on the Stalinville KGB prison, where the men would have been taken, before the Mind Breakers made them spill their city's location. Rock was the inevitable choice to lead such a team. He would have to somehow get back down the mountain fast, deliver the message of doom and assemble the Attack Force. But how the hell could he do it? It would take twice as long to get down as it had to get up. And it was ten times as dangerous on the descent, especially in the dark, when handholds and footholds were always below one in the shadows, instead of upslope at eye level.

There had to be a way, had to. He glanced around the plateau on which the crews worked feverishly. If only he had a parakite or— Wait a minute! The Russian airlifter ramjet's wreckage— the Reds had huge paragliders built into the wing sections of their large craft, so the planes could glide down to earth in case of trouble. This time the thing hadn't worked. Rock went to the main piece of wreckage. There! Red pieces of fabric in the snow, about fifty feet to the side of the hulking engine. A paraglider—slightly damaged but nothing unmendable. Could it be adapted for him?

Rock quickly got several of the repair crew to help him mend the tears in the fabric with an instantly bonding glue that was used in the solar panel installation. Within minutes the contraption was as good as new. Looking much like a hang glider of the days of old, Rock had the men quickly weld a bar across the underside of the kite-shaped nylon wing. He had the men help him carry it to the edge of the peak and strapped himself in, tying his legs to the steel struts beneath. It was as good as it could get.

"All right," Rock said, holding on to the sides of the paraglider, with a wingspan of ten feet. "Give me a push and pray for me, boys." The men around Rock looked at each other and then back at their top fighter. The paraglider dwarfed the man under it.

"You sure, Rock?" Saunders asked. "I mean, this—"

"If the Reds get the wrong info out of our captured men,

we'll all be dead by tomorrow morning. There's nothing to lose, everything to gain. So push me off, boys."

With two men holding each wing and two behind, they maneuvered the paraglider to the very edge of the four thousand foot drop, straight down—and pushed.

Rock was falling. The glider wasn't catching the air, but just dropping like a stone. He had to change the angle of descent. He kicked his legs hard and managed to flip the nose of the nylon glider up. Suddenly the wings filled with freezing air and the craft began gliding. Wobbly at first, Rock quickly figured out how to shift his weight from side to side or kick his legs to make the strange man-sized kite respond. He could see almost immediately that he couldn't make a direct descent, the angle of the trajectory would make the wings lose their currents of air. No, he'd have to circle around, slowly dropping down. The thin, icy air burned his lungs with cold.

The moon suddenly came out, peeking from behind an opening in the clouds and Rock took a quick look at the bright panorama below him. There, he could see Century City's Mount Carson, towering to the right, and all the woods and valleys spreading off in every direction. God, it was beautiful. He felt his mind getting tired. The air. It was too thin, he'd have to dive quickly.

He came to about a thousand feet down, nearly careening into a rock ledge. He must have blacked out for a second. He shifted his weight with a wild lurch and the paraglider banked to the right, only feet from a projecting cliff. But now he was heading in the wrong direction. Where the hell was everything? He dropped lower and lower, in wide concentric circles, until he saw Vulture's Peak, which was just above one of the city's entrances. He maneuvered in that direction, making fine adjustments with his legs and shoulders, zeroing in. At last he was only fifty feet above the ground, having narrowly missed several trees along the ridge. How in blazes do you stop this thing? he suddenly wondered. He tried several maneuvers to slow it down, and finally settled for what he hoped was the right approach—pulling up at the last instant. The snowbanked slope on the southern side of Vulture's Peak was suddenly upon him. He slid his legs from the tubing and

144

kicked down suddenly, pulling the nose of the paraglider straight up. He landed like a drunken pigeon, crashing into an eight foot drift of cushioning snow.

"I'm alive," Rock said, standing up, half disbelieving he had pulled it off. But the Survivor had beaten the odds once again. He walked quickly toward the hidden entrance to the city on shaky legs, frozen, red-eyed, his lungs rasping from the descent. But he had saved time, valuable time that the rescue mission would need.

Sixteen

Rockson stormed into the Council chamber, beside himself with rage at the taking of the prisoners. It could turn into a disaster. The fifty-man Council was in session, debating emergency procedures to deal with the present solar power crisis. The large chamber was lit by flickering light bulbs strung up haphazardly around the walls, powered by a groaning old gasoline generator that had been dug up from supplies.

All eyes turned toward the sweaty, clothes-torn Rock, his eyes blazing with a mad fire as he made his way to the podium of the oval-shaped chamber.

"Members of the Council," he began immediately without waiting to be recognized. "I have just returned from the salvage operations on Ice Mountain and I have terrible news to report. Five of our men, including Armstrong, were captured by Blackshirts and flown to Stalinville. We all know what awaits them there, the poor bastards. We must immediately mount a rescue operation—an attack. It's not just their lives I'm thinking of," Rock continued, scanning the Council members as he spoke, "but with this new Mind Breaker machine the Reds have, these men will talk. We already know they made Preston talk and we saw what the result of that was."

A chorus of loud voices met his words. From "Yes, let's get the bastards" to "No, we must wait." Immediately the Council

146

members began arguing among themselves. Composed of twenty-nine men and twenty-one women, the Council members were fiercely democratic, debating all issues with a vigor and loudness that sometimes appeared to degenerate into a free-for-all. But it worked!

"There isn't time for bullshit," Rock said, his nostrils flaring. "Every minute could mean the difference between life and death for every man, woman and child in Century City."

"Now, just a minute, Rock," an elderly man, Councilman Rostas, spoke out. "This is a democratic council. All decisions must be approved by a vote. No man—even you—can just come in here and dictate what we *must* do!"

"Well then, goddamn it, debate and vote," Rockson shouted back. "But let's get on with it!" He stepped down from the podium and, glaring at the Council, threw himself down in one of the front rows of circular seats that ringed the central, raised platform of the chamber.

Councilman Rostas, as the eldest member of the Council, was given the protocol of speaking first. He rose slowly and walked with a stately dignity that he had cultivated over the years to the redwood podium, coughed several times to get some quiet and addressed the chamber.

"Ladies and gentlemen of the Council, we have all heard Mr. Rockson's request for an attack on Stalinville. Now without belittling The Ultimate American," he said, with the slightest trace of a sneer, "I do believe that his demand is impulsive, reckless and dangerous." The Council members exploded into a series of bellowing shouting matches for and against the line of the councilman. "Now, you all know my position. I have long believed that an accommodation can be worked out with the Russians. After all, our Free Cities are functioning quite smoothly even in the midst of their occupation. They can't get us and we can't get them. I'm sure that were we to try to deal with them rationally, they would be only too willing to settle things. We could both share this land. It's big enough. They're wasting billions of rubles every year fighting us. I believe, therefore, that to attack Stalinville now would be the height of foolishness and would precipitate a violent counterattack, not just against us but perhaps the Free Cities all over America."

Rock could scarcely believe his ears. His face turned red and it took all his self-control to stop from screaming at the "soft-liner" Council member. As was the rule of the Council, the next speaker presented an opposing point of view. George Sheckle, a man Rockson knew and trusted, walked quickly to the podium, dressed in his ever-present tweed sports jacket, threads hanging from the sleeves, arms swinging loosely around his tall, thin body. Sheckle stood almost six foot, ten inches and was easily the tallest man in Century City, but at a weight of just under 165 pounds, he was like a walking scarecrow, all bone and tendon.

He looked around at the Council members slowly, waiting for a modicum of silence, and then began. "You have all listened to Mr. Rostas, who we all respect and who often has presented valuable ideas to this chamber. But tonight, I believe he is making a grave mistake. Number one, those men are ours. They're about to be tortured beyond anything any of us here can even imagine. Secondly, if they do talk, and from what I've heard of this new Mind Breaker machine they will, all of Century City could be lost—smoking ruins like Westfort. We would be cast back out in the wastelands, those of us who even managed to survive, savages again, like our ancestors after the war. But thirdly, and most importantly, I must take serious disagreement with the idea of accommodating the Russians. There is no accommodation possible with murderers. Good Lord, man," the lanky Sheckle said, staring at Rostas in his seat, some forty feet away, "they've already destroyed most of our country, enslaved all the Americans around the Red forts, and just bombed Westfort, our closest neighbor with more atomic weapons. Something they vowed in those leaflets of theirs they'd never use again."

He looked down at the floor, his eyes bright and burning with belief. "No, I don't trust the Russian barbarians. I never have and I never will. We must respond with an attack. Now, I may not agree with Rock's impulse to send out a team tonight. I think it must be a well-organized force of perhaps two hundred men. We could make a plan over the next twenty-four hours

148

and get a well-equipped Attack Force together—with a much greater chance of success." He smiled sincerely at the Council members and left the podium.

The debate raged on for almost two hours with nearly every speaker getting his or her views in. The arguing grew increasingly raucous with members booing each other and yelling out insults. The Council chamber had rarely witnessed such explosions of feeling. But then they were debating the very future of their city, their lives.

As the highest-ranking military officer of Century City, Rockson was given the opportunity to speak last before the vote was taken. He rose from his seat, where he had been taking it all in and stepped to the platform, behind the podium. He looked down at the floor for a moment, gathering his thoughts, knowing that this could well be the most important speech he would ever make, and began.

"You are the democratically elected representatives of the citizens of Century City and I must respect each and every one of you. For the tradition of democracy and debate is the one feature of our society that enables us to be a million times stronger than the Soviets could ever be. But I can scarcely believe the things I'm hearing here tonight. Are those of you who are opposed to saving our men's lives, those who want to deal with the Reds on a rational basis," he spat the words out, "so naive as to think that they would really live up to their word? Or even want to try? Their aim is *total and complete* destruction of all Free Americans. We are antithetical to their very nature—their very essence of being, which is master and slave. They want one thing: a nation of slaves, of mindless vegetables, of backs to carry their loads and feed their society. As a soldier, a fighter who has spent his entire life battling against the Red murderers, I have seen what they are really like. I have seen them wipe out whole villages, have watched them as they lined up women and children and shot them point-blank in the face. I've seen them rape and bayonet and take American lives as if they were so many ants to be stepped on."

He stopped for a moment to catch his breath and let his

149

emotions which had built to the boiling point, calm down. "Believe me, please believe me, there is no way in hell to work out an accommodation with the Russians. The only thing that we must work for, that my whole life has been devoted to, is to drive out the invader. Every last one. Dead or alive!" Again, he paused, his blue and violet eyes narrowing, the white streak of hair down the center of his head reflecting the ceiling lights like a mirror.

"But it is beyond that. You have been debating a lot of philosophical Mumbo Jumbo. The bottom line is this." His voice became cold, sharp. "They have taken five of us prisoner. In the past, with our mind blocks, these men would have been able to stand up to any torture the Red beast would have inflicted on them. If five men were to die? Well, they gave their lives as any of us would do. But the situation has changed. The Reds now have the Mind Breaker. We still don't know a hell of a lot about how it works, but one thing we do know—it does work. They captured Preston and Preston was a good tough man. I knew him, worked with him several times. They had him for just hours and Westfort was reduced to a city of corpses. That's why we can't delay. At this very moment those men could be in one of those hellish devices spilling their guts. It's not a question of courage or betrayal. Whatever the Russians have, works."

He looked at the rows of eyes peering up at him, hanging on his every word. They all knew the importance of tonight's decision. "Ladies and gentlemen," Rock continued, slowly, "Century City is in grave danger. We can't wait even one extra hour. There's no need for a large force. I propose going in there with just eight men. Surprise them. Christ, they're not expecting an attack on their biggest fortress in the region. A two-hundred-man force would just get bogged down in a battle for days—a battle that we would lose. No! It must be a surprise with a small group of the best fighting men of the city. And it must be tonight!" He stopped speaking and surveyed the Council who were still silent, listening to the man who, they knew, knew the enemy better than anyone. Rockson met every eye, made them feel his anger and his burning guts and then

150

walked from the podium.

Council President Arcades rose and quickly called for a vote. "All those for Rockson's plan, please raise your hand." Thirty-nine voted for it, eleven against. "The plan is passed," Arcades said with a thin smile, turning to Rockson. "It's up to you now, Rock, and God help you."

Seventeen

MS-12 and MS-13, two Soviet choppers from the small base of Volgograd Station in Utah, were making their weekly run with rad reports and lists of casualties to Red Army Control in Stalinville. They came through the high mountain pass at Wilkerson, their crews of eight exhausted from the dangerous twists and turns down the narrow, rocky canyons behind them. But now at least it was safe from rebel gunfire. There hadn't been any attacks on the Wilkerson route, if for no other reason than that there was no really good cover for miles. Just mountains, mountains filled with medium-sized boulders heaved there nearly a hundred years ago by an A-blast forty miles south at the SAC headquarters in Garden-of-the-Gods.

They flew on automatic low pilot, the two choppers moving in a line about eight hundred yards apart for safety. There was a slow turn in the pass a mile ahead, a lazy turn that the auto would handle. But there was one thing they hadn't considered. Not flying close to one another, the helicopters would be out of sight of each other for about a minute on that long turn.

Rockson and his eight-man Attack Force were camouflaged, huddled into round shapes like small boulders, their Liberator rifles under them equipped with grenade launchers. Rock would have given his right eye for a pile of chopper-popper missiles. But all of those had been used up in the past ten years even though the supply of the old missiles that had been found by one of the salvage teams at a SAC crater had seemed inexhaustible. The Freefighters had used each one well,

152

making every shot count. But now they were gone. Now they'd have to shoot fast from directly in front and underneath the passing Red choppers in the dawn's early light.

Rockson pulled his watch up in front of his eyes. Any minute now and the regular run from Volgograd would roar by. All eight Freefighters and Rock would jump up when the first one had passed and, he hoped, blast the second one to kingdom come. Then would the first chopper, not realizing what had happened, come back to look for its friend? He hoped so. For everyone's sake.

The helicopters were a few minutes overdue, adding to the strain of each hunched-over fighter. Gnawing seconds of doubt. Had they been detected by the RPV that had passed overhead ten minutes before? Was the copter run cancelled? Were there—worst of all—hordes of Blackshirts coming over the far ridge this very moment? Each man was lost in his own private hell, until faintly, the whirr of the copters started vibrating in the wind. They were coming low and dead-eyed, meaning the autos were on. Good, the crews were probably half-asleep in the back.

One quickly flew over, about a hundred feet above the hidden American warriors, its blade cutting the air in the glare of the quickly rising sun. As its drone died out the men all stood up, cocked their grenade launchers and waited as the drone of the second chopper grew louder and louder.

"Titov, you cheated," snarled Dregnev. "How can you have an ace when I have four?" The two Russian soldiers had been playing the American game of poker stretched out in the cargo section of the MS-13, the second helicopter. Bored by a year of card games and the hellish isolation of the remote outpost, they were edgy. Titov jumped to his feet and pulled out a Tokarev .32, standard—and archaic—issue for the regular Soviet army. The KGB all had the Tokarev .65 clip-loaders, but these soldiers weren't elite forces. They were crass, uneducated Georgians, sons of manure-loaders and plowmen. Life was cheap to them. Especially here in this Godforsaken country.

As Titov went for his gun, Dregnev fired—and the whole chopper burst into flames as four of the eight grenades launched from below made helicopter interception. Titov's head smashed into the curved steel struts inside the chopper and popped open, a ripe grapefruit splattering blood. Dregnev screamed wildly as the chopper tipped upside down and headed for the hard earth.

Rock and his men cheered the orange ball of death as it erupted one hundred yards down the canyon. They ran closer, until they were within thirty feet of the burning wreckage. They pulled the boulderlike camouflage cloths over their bodies again, panting from exertion. They made position just in time. The first of the Red copters now drifted slowly back along the pass, searching for its lost companion ship. The gun turrets were occupied but surely the Reds hadn't seen the trap. They would suppose that the unstable MS copter—only the KGB had the new MK-30s—had gone down of its own accord. At least that was the idea.

The Reds spotted the wreckage and carefully descended almost dead center of the camouflaged Americans. Norton had to roll slightly out of the way to avoid being crushed by the chopper's metal skids. Rockson could scarcely see through the tiny slit in the canvas opening as the four, then five and six Russians climbed down. Their rifles were dangling over their shoulders; evidently they weren't suspicious.

"Freefighters—now," Rockson shouted as the nine messengers of truth stood up and revealed their message in a burst of concentrated lead that cut down the men like bowling pins blasted to splinters. Six dead Red soldiers. Rockson bounded through the open hatch and, as the pilot twisted frantically in his seat with the Tokarev spitting pellets of red death, chopped the seat in half with the Liberator on automatic fire. Sizzling pieces of flesh exploded against the cockpit window.

Rock heard a clicking sound behind him and whirled, blasting a bloody body on the floor that was drawing a bead on Rock. The slugs from his Liberator tore a jagged hole in the Red's chest, throwing him several feet to the side where the lifeless body lay draped sideways, three little fountains of blood pouring gracefully from the wounds. The old "dead Russian" trick didn't work on Rockson. Now it was no trick.

Rock jumped into the co-pilot's seat and put on the

154

earphones, immediately hearing Russian transmissions from planes and helicopters throughout the region, all transmitting information and asking for flight instructions. The rest of the Freefighters piled in, kicking the two dead Reds out into the blood-muddy dirt. Rock set the rotors on full and nuzzled back the control stick. The Red chopper took off sweet as a bird into the rapidly brightening morning sky, faraway green clouds dappling the stratosphere.

The crew of nine sat around the center of the chopper, talking over final plans for the raid. Rock had picked what he considered the eight best all-around fighters in Century City, each one a seasoned Red killer as well as an expert in some area of warfare. Norton and Sanford—explosives; Smith and Jergins—computers; Detroit and McCaughlin—cover, Pasqual—decoder, and a damned good medic just in case the captured Freefighters required immediate medical attention; and Chen—fighter par excellence. Chen had demanded that Rock bring him along. "My honor is at stake, Rock," Chen had said quietly. "Of course," Rock had replied. "Come." All that Chen carried were two steel-tipped nunchakas, his deadliest weapon.

Rock headed the Red helicopter down the mountain canyon that the Russian pilot had been bearing toward before being so rudely interrupted. Once they had built up air speed, he set it back on auto. Now the damn thing would fly them right to the gates of Stalinville and in. And that's where the trouble that Ted Rockson was bringing on a silver platter would be spooned out.

Detroit sat in the tail gunner's position and made sure the barrel was clean—it wasn't. "Sloppy crew," he muttered. He found cleaning implements in a box under the gunner's seat and quickly disassembled and cleaned each part of the 50mm machine gun. He was a master at Russian equipment maintenance—and use. Over the years Century City had built up quite an arsenal of captured Red booty. And nothing was more satisfying than using the stuff back on them.

McCaughlin walked around the inside of the chopper and took inventory of the cargo: computer dumps of stats, reports on agricultural collections, five boxes of steak, one box of vodka and three sacks of turqoise stones—prized back in Russia and probably dug up by the soldiers to make a few extra kopecks for their brief vacation at Danver Spa. Denver Spa, where the less attractive American women, after the KGB had picked out the ripest and juiciest ones, were employed as "hostesses" for horny second-rate Red troops. The hard life in the harsh outpost of Volograd was over for these simpletons, and some American women would be spared their pawings. How Rockson wished that the Freefighters could move en masse against the occupied cities and free the people. But not yet. Secret cells of opposition existed, of course, in the heart of the Russian forts. When the signal was given, they would swing into action, committing mass sabotage behind Red lines as the Freefighters advanced, guns blazing.

Rock stared out as the desert melted away beneath him. In another five minutes they would be picked up by the Red defensive radar screens of Stalinville and they would demand the signal . . . or else. Pasqual was their decoding expert. He frantically tore the Russian code book apart, trying to come up with the complex sequence of codes to prevent their being shot right out of the sky. The city came into view over a ridge, down below in the distance. Static began coming in over Rock's headphones, followed by a bored Russian voice asking for identification. Rock's hand felt sweaty on the stick as he pretended not to hear.

Pasqual ran over, the book flopping wildly in his hands. "Got it," he said triumphantly.

The radio squawked more insistently now. "Identification. I repeat, identification on helicopter coming in on Vector Five East Stalinville!"

Pasqual read off numbers to Rockson from the book. "1-23-23-14," Rock repeated them into the helmet mike, mumbling into the mouthpiece in sharp Russian. There was a wait of about three seconds.

"Acknowledged. Proceed to scheduled landing site, KGB Center."

"It's a good thing the Reds have to write the damned things down for their peasant-brained troops," Pasqual cracked, breaking the tension on the chopper.

Stalinville grew and grew until it loomed below them, the Russian military fortress taking up nearly half the city area. The rest was the run-down American sector, which even from the sky they could see was filthy and crumbling. About a mile off, Rock saw the KGB Rocky Mountain Control building, a thirty-story, brown X-shaped structure without a single window in the place. The landing pad was on the roof; above the helipad, coming from the center of the X, stood a tall, thin control tower. Rock and the other Freefighters had gone over the smuggled plans again and again—the emergency stairs at the far end of each wing. But stolen plans were vague as to what exactly was on each floor. He knew that the interrogation area was on the west arm of the X, on one of the bottom three levels designated A, B and C. And he knew as well that about one hundred yards off the east wing was a low brick bunker, nearly four hundred feet long, that resistance intel had pinpointed as a main armory for both Red army and KGB munitions for the fort. The only other—but potentially most valuable—info was that the computer room which controlled all the functions of the building, plus the sensitive alarm and intercom systems, was on the H-level—the sixth floor—east wing. This much of a picture of the KGB building that ran the operations for the northwest sector of the U.S.A. would have to serve them well. A half dozen cleaning personnel had been killed over the years sneaking it out.

As near as Rock could figure it, Stalinville was on the location of the old American city of Cheyenne, Wyoming. Someday, when they took the land back from the Reds, it would be called Cheyenne again. But for now, the plan was to destroy everything they could, while rescuing the prisoners, and Rock meant to carry out the mandate of the Council even if it meant his death.

The X-shaped roof got larger and larger as the chopper they had stolen circled in on a landing approach. There was tension inside the craft that you could cut with a knife. None of them really looked like the grim-faced KGB or even regular Soviet Red army for that matter—their uniforms didn't fit well and some of them still had holes. The uniforms had been taken from Century City supplies, collected over the years from

157

encounters with the enemy. But it wasn't exactly a tailor shop, and somehow everyone's outfit either draped loosely over their shoulders and shoes, or seemed skin tight. It would have to do; they didn't intend to spend much time on the landing pad anyway. And after that—well, they hadn't come to talk fashion.

Rock let the chopper hover right over the large rubber mat in the center of one of the arms of the X as a Red landing man flagged them down. The helicopter hit the roof with a hard thud and McCaughlin glanced over at Rock, who muttered, "I'm not good on parking." He cut the engines and the big blades sputtered to a stop. McCaughlin rubbed his rabbit's foot in his pants pocket and hefted his equipment over his broad shoulder.

The eight Freefighters and Rock looked silently at one another as they stood by the side door. They knew that this could well be the last time some of them were ever seen again, and with their tense but fierce eyes they quickly looked in each face as if to say, Goodbye, pal. Rock opened the door, and the crew stepped out onto the wind-swept roof. The ground crewman, his work done, had already stepped away. Somebody in a work smock covered with grease came over to Rock and asked in Russian with a thick Afghan accent if he needed any work on the chopper. Rockson just nodded no and the worker checked something off on a clipboard and walked away into the wash of another chopper making a descent.

The nine Attack Force members walked quickly over to the main exit door, not daring to look up at the control tower staff who, in fact, paid them no mind at all. Not having ever had an attack mounted on their citadel of death in the fifty years of its existence, other than an occasional bagman throwing a bottle at the ground-level electrified gate, they were not exactly alert.

Rock swung the thick black door open and they entered a dimly lit stairwell. They couldn't risk going past the main checkpoint to the elevators. At least not now. Rock stared down the central space of the stairway, some forty flights down. They had to move. They sped down the stairs, guns and packs filled with explosives shaking on their backs. Rock took the lead, then Detroit and Chen, his nunchakas now out and

158

ready. McCaughlin was rear guard, his big burly frame lurching from side to side as he raced frantically after the others.

Things went fine until they reached level M where three Blackshirts suddenly opened one of the hall doors and saw the motley crew rushing by. They were rising young professionals of murder, and their sharp eyes instantly took in the unusual appearance of the strange hallway assemblage. The tallest of the KGB officers, with a narrow face like a weasel, grabbed Rock by the shoulder and spun him around.

"Hey, who the hell are you fools? You're regular army—not even allowed in these sections." Rock's right hand, holding his .12-gauge shotgun pistol, came up in a blur of motion. He let the Red death-mechanic have a full barrel inches from his face, splattering brains and blood like a sickening taffy onto the institutional brown walls behind him. The two others reached for their pistols in terror. Detroit's gun butt hit one of the KGB square in the neck, sending him to the concrete floor gurgling blood. The third Blackshirt had barely lifted his pistol from a hip holster when Chen's nunchakas swung through the air with the whooshing sound of a helicopter blade. It caught the cold-eyed Red in the temple. His eyes rolled up and he slumped to the ground in a broken heap.

"Damn, I hope no one heard that bullfrog of yours, Rock," said McCaughlin. They waited for a moment. All seemed still. They stepped over the bodies that now littered the landing and proceeded down the cordite-smelling stairs.

Eighteen

It took them four minutes to reach B-Level. They had to guess—Rock decided to proceed to the lowest level, A. Just outside the exit, he gathered the men together for a final briefing.

"You all know the plan, but let's go over it once more quickly. We free every American still alive. Arm them—with Red weapons if possible—and then we break into three teams. Sanford heads the team that exits out A-Level. He cuts through the barbed wire around the armory and plants the charges. You, McCaughlin, head the second team. You get to the control tower on the roof, secure it, give cover fire to Sanford and keep out any visitors who might show up with your RPGS and the Liberators—long-cartridge loaded. Detroit, Jergins, Chen and I hit the computer room and do our thing to the building. Then all three teams take out as many Death's-Heads as possible and meet on the helipad for home at 0500—that gives us exactly thirty minutes. Good luck, men. We'll need it."

They burst through the door onto the main floor. Damn, the place was decorated nicely. There were scenes of the American West from the "old days" on the wall: cowboys riding their rearing horses, buffalo. Throughout the dining area, "log" tables and benches were standing. Off-duty technicians—men and women in white smocks—and several KGB officers were dining around a pulsing fountain in the center of the room. Overhead, hanging from the high ceiling, the decorators had

160

gone for the traditional trashy look of Soviet chandeliers, all gaudied with candelabras of electric bulbs. The nine blood-smeared, sweating Americans in their half-assed Red uniforms looked incongruous as they stared back at the pack of incredulous faces around the room.

"Everybody freezeski," McCaughlin yelled in the worst Russian Rock had ever heard, "and you won't get hurt." The Red tech and the four officers who were present began diving for cover, reaching for their holsters. The bastards were armed under those white smocks—the men, not the women. Thirty rounds flamed from four Liberators and foolish Reds tumbled to the floor as the thin pops of the silencer-suppressed muzzles echoed softly off the muraled walls.

"Anybody else want to die?" snarled Rockson. A technician ran for the side door toward the other wing. Chen threw one of his two pairs of nunchakas like a bolo and the man fell screaming, his kneecaps shattered beyond repair.

"All of you into this room over here," Rock ordered, holding his shotgun pistol at hip level as the other Freefighters kept their Liberators trained on the group.

He crowded the remaining Reds into a small game room, tabletops filled with chessboards and decks of neatly stacked cards. "Chen, you and Pasqual and Jergins keep this area free of vermin," Rock said, pointing to the main dining area. Chen walked quickly over to the main entrance, took a nunchaka in each hand and stood just behind the door waiting for any soul unfortunate enough to suddenly have a craving for a snack.

Rock and the rest of Attack Force herded the Reds against the wall of the small red-walled room. He noticed a middle-aged technician with thick glasses and eyes that seemed to be trying to hide something. Rockson grabbed the profusely sweating tech by his white lapels and pulled him forward so that their faces were only inches apart.

"Where are the others? The American prisoners," he snarled, feeling mean and not very generous.

"I'll never talk—I'm KGB," the tech said, halfheartedly, trying to work up a wall of bravado.

"You'll never talk now, will you?" Rock asked, amused. He smashed his fist into the Russian tech's face, smashing his nose

161

into a flat, pulpy disk and knocking out three of the man's front teeth. There wasn't time for subtlety. The man fell to the floor from the blow and wiped a palmful of blood from his mouth.

The Russian started babbling immediately. A giver of pain he was—a receiver, no. "The interrogation section is one flight up. Level B, rooms one through thirty. The American prisoners are in B-28, at least they were yesterday." Rock and the Attack Force exited the game room and McCaughlin ripped a leg from a table and thrust it through the outside handles of the doors.

"That should keep 'em playing cards till we're finished," he said smugly.

"Come on," Rock yelled, "we're wasting precious time. We've already used up eight minutes." They ran like bats out of hell, peering around corridors, blasting two Red security guards who were unfortunate enough to meet the kill-hungry Americans on the stairs leading to B-Level. They died without uttering a warning. The pistols and rifles of the Freefighters had silencers so there was only the sound of a cork popping when they fired—strangely innocuous in relation to the effect it produced in its targets, who were thrown backward, faces and chests instantly covered with rivulets of thick, red blood.

"So far, so good, men," Rock said, crouching and peeking around the corner of the stairwell landing on B-Level. Across the hall and about forty feet away was the usual electrically controlled security door that every floor had, stopping access to the entire section. Foot-thick steel, it also served as a blast door, so strong it couldn't be opened with a direct hit from a bazooka. Somehow they had to get past that final obstacle unobserved. Two white-smocked technicians carrying clipboards exited a room almost directly across from the stairwell landing and Rock eased the door shut, leaving a half-inch space to spy through. The Reds walked slowly toward the security door, chatting, laughing at each other's sick jokes of torture and death.

Rock could pull them into the stairwell when they passed, *if* they passed. But the men paused twenty feet away, shook hands and split up. One of them took his security card, hanging from a cord around his neck, and inserted it into a little slot next to the blast door. He punched in a four-number code on a row of dials and the door slid open, closing as he entered. Rock stared through the crack of the landing door, frustrated. He glanced down at his watch: twelve minutes gone.

The other technician began walking at a snail's pace, deep in his own thoughts, back toward the stairwell door. "That's it, you bastard, just a little closer," Rock whispered under his breath. Behind him, Detroit said a silent prayer, staring over Rockson's shoulder at the Red. The clock was ticking away. The technician stopped again and wrote a brief message on the paper attached to his clipboard. Damn! It was only a matter of seconds until one of the KGB building security patrols—four men armed to the teeth—would come down the stairs. Rock knew that from their intel reports. They made the rounds every fifteen minutes, covering every damned part of the building. They would find the dead technicians and the carnage on the floors below any minute now and then . . .

"Come on, you bastard," Rock prayed, as the Red bent over and took a long drink from a water fountain. Behind Rock, the Freefighters were starting to sweat profusely from the maddening tension. Slowly the technician extracted a handkerchief and dabbed at his lips, folded it back into his pocket and suddenly headed in the Freefighters' direction, walking briskly.

Ten feet. Five. Now! With a grunt of exertion, Rock leaned a big hand out and whipped the Red into the stairwell. He ripped the card key from the man's throat—but that wasn't enough. They needed the code, the four number code. McCaughlin, with his huge, toothy grin and steel eyes, stared the trembling man in the face as they leaned him against the concrete-block walls of the landing. Detroit whipped out a silver-plated KGB Tokarev pistol he had snatched from one of the dead Reds and held it to the Russian's forehead.

"One yell from you and no brains," he said in broken Russian. "Comprendez?" The man nodded frantically, his face growing paler by the second.

"Now, I'm going to ask you just once," Rock said with a deadly tone. "The code. What's the code—and don't give me something I can't use. Don't give me a number that sets off an alarm, because you'll be with us and if anything, I mean *anything,* goes wrong—" he lifted his eyes to McCaughlin— "my buddy here likes to kill Russians. Don't you, McCaughlin?"

"That I do, Rock. Only I likes to play with them first. Cut their balls off and sew them into their mouths." He pulled out a razor-sharp hunting knife and turned it slowly before the Red's huge eyes.

The Russian gulped several times and, barely able to speak, said, "OK, OK. Three, twelve, four, two. And once inside the security door just the card will open all the B doors. Are you going to kill me? Please, I've got a wife and children. I—" Chen deftly cut off his protests with a clunk from one stick of the steel-tipped nunchakas.

"That should hold him for at least half an hour," the lean Chinese fighting master said.

"Let's off him," Detroit said, holding a pistol to the Red's head.

"He's just a light bulb changer," Rock said, pushing the gun lightly away. "Let the poor sucker live. His own people will do him in anyway for giving us the card key. Let them take care of each other. Less work for us."

The Freefighters ran, hellbent for leather to the security door. Rock jammed the plastic card in, pressed the code and the thick door swung open easy as pie. They knew that almost all of the doors on each side of the long corridor were torture chambers so Rock stuck the card into the slot of each one and the Attack Force rushed in, guns at the ready. The first eight doors, B-1 through B-8, produced nothing but empty rooms. But on nine they hit pay dirt. Rock, the first one in, could instantly see that the room was filled with KGB and some half-dozen technicians. Behind a glass wall sat someone, strapped into a Mind Breaker. He didn't look in good health. Detroit and McCaughlin rushed in just behind Rockson and, seeing the welcoming committee, put their Liberators on auto and fired in a full arc around the room as the Reds futilely reached for their weapons. The hot muzzles of the American rifles poured out a rain of death, splattering the nice, white antiseptic walls with a Pollock painting of blood madly twisted into abstract shapes.

Rock ran to the door of the glass-partitioned room and shot the lock off. Inside, strapped into a seat, with the huge, black Mind Breaker attached over his swollen head was Armstrong— or what was left of him. Thin needles of light were whirring into his brain, yet he wasn't screaming. Not anymore. The once-proud Freefighter was drooling a green puke as pulpy pieces of gray brain tissue dripped from his sinuses. He had told them what he had told them. Either they knew where Century City was or Armstrong was the greatest hero America had ever known. Rockson looked into the man's zombie eyes and, with tears in his eyes, held his Liberator to the Freefighter's temple. "Goodbye, brave buddy." He squeezed the trigger.

He rushed back into the other room where McCaughlin and Detroit were freeing the four other Century City prisoners, who were all smiles at their liberators' appearance. The big Scot had the Red chief scientist, Letvok, cuffed.

"Thank God," Gilhooley said, rubbing his wrists where manacles had been holding him pinned down for the fourteen hours since their capture. "You're just in time, Rock," he said, as the other men stood up and moved their aching legs and arms. "They did Armstrong in. But we could hear them trying to get anything out of him. Rock, he didn't talk. I don't know how in God's name a man could take the kind of things they did to him. But he didn't give them shit. They were just coming to get us. I was the next one, they kept telling me, trying to cheer me up, I guess. And I just don't know if the rest of us could have gone out so . . . ." He stared at Letvok. "He's the one."

Rock quickly told them of the plans and the freed Americans scooped up some of the Red weapons lying on the floor, wiped off the blood and grouped behind Rockson. "Gilhooley, you and your friends take charge of Letvok, and rip off one of those Mind Breaker machines. Bring it along."

Chen was outside. "Who's the prisoner?" he asked.

"Gilhooley said he's Letvok. The torturer," snarled McCaughlin. "We'll bring him back with us—with his fucking machine."

The men all smiled, scarcely able to believe that someone had the audacity to actually break into one of the biggest Red fortresses in America. They were now numerous enough to implement Plan Two. Rock was glad. Plan Two was one of three possible scenarios that would allow them to do utmost damage to the KGB center and its environs.

"Plan Two is in effect," Rock said. "You all have your maps and know your jobs. Each group take your choice of our freed Freefighters here, and use them as best you can." He turned around to McCaughlin. "You still got your mortar and the shells we loaded onto you?"

"Aye, these are just wee-bit toys to a fellow my size," said the six-foot-five, 220 pound McCaughlin. "Hardly noticed I was carrying them. I picked up a few Kalashnikovs with grenade launchers and a satchel of grenades. Come on, Smith, let's get moving, old buddy—and finish our job."

"Can do," Rock said. "Let's move, men. I don't know what the hell is going to happen in the next fifteen minutes but remember we reconvene on the roof helipad five at 0500. Don't disappoint me now and get shot or something dumb like that."

They gave short salutes and poured into different corridors and stairwells, each leader glancing at the little plastic maps that had been prepared from the underground reports. The Reds really should have done their own cleaning and vacuuming and laundry—especially laundry. For though every scrap that went in and out of the KGB center was checked for messages and *visible* writing, the invisible laundry marks made nifty maps. Some slaving American laundry woman had paid the Reds back in full for the gang rapes they had performed on her—once, when she was young and attractive. Now the Attack Force had all the locations.

Rock's destination had to be penetrated or it could mean a quick and bloody end to the entire mission. The computer room that controlled the entire center's operations. If he could get control, he could keep the Red troop movements inside the building under lock and key, barring movement from floor to floor. He ran up the stairwell headed for Level M with Detroit and Chen right behind him, Jergins, the computer man, taking up the rear. They had just reached Level J when a Red patrol burst through the landing door on routine patrol. The Reds and the Americans both looked surprised for a second, then reached for their guns. But the Americans were faster. Three of the Reds slumped to the concrete floor, bullets tattooing their twitching torsos. Chen stepped forward and took out the remaining pair with two lightning-fast spins of his nunchakas. This time he didn't hold back. The KGB guards flew back against the wall, their skulls split open, a thin fluid pulsing out.

Rock held his fingers to his lips as the men opened the door to Level M. This would be the most securely guarded section of the center so they had to proceed with extreme caution. Rock and Jergins slipped on the jackets and caps of the security patrol and, without looking back, opened the stairwell door and walked right up to the security entrance. Here, there were thick, bulletproof glass panels on each side of the black steel doors. A guard sat nearby, absent-mindedly reading a book. Rock, his head tilted down and away, with his hand to his mouth as if coughing, waved casually with the other at the guard, who glanced up and then looked down again, unconcerned. Rock slipped the card key into the slot and pressed the code. The door clicked and he pushed it open. The guard glanced up, then his eyes widened in alarm as he saw the two men behind Rock come surging forward. Those guns they were carrying—they weren't Russian, they were—

The Red guard reached for his pistol. A big mistake. Rock, using his shotgun pistol for close-in fighting, blasted him right off his seat, three feet through the air, where he slid down a wall, leaving a messy trail of smeared blood behind him. The twelve technicians and six KGB officers in the vast computer room spun around with a start at the gunfire. Two of the Blackshirts went for the Kalashnikovs slung around their shoulders. But Rockson and Detroit, firing simultaneously, turned the Red torsos into so much hamburger. The others didn't move from their frozen positions.

"Anyone else?" Rockson asked, quickly scanning the group.

"No takers, Rock," Detroit snickered, turning over a dead KGB body with his foot. "Ugh, those .12-gauge shells of yours really make a mess." Half the corpse's face was gone, revealing a ghastly smiling skull.

Rock and the Freefighters lined the surviving KGB personnel up against a wall that faced the hundred-odd feet of computer terminals, keyboards and whirling spools of magnetic tape that clicked on and off, sending out automatic commands to the building's light controls, heat and air conditioning, door locks and just about everything else that ran on electricity. Detroit frisked them quickly, but most were unarmed. They had gotten a good haul, several of the Red officers wore stars on the shoulders.

One of them spoke up brusquely. "Whoever you are," he said, looking at Rockson, "we're technical officers—noncombatants." The man had a swarthy, debauched look. One glance at his big lips and deeply creased face and Rock knew that this man had committed countless acts of torture and murder. It showed. The blood of his victims had seeped into the Red officer's very pores.

Rock noticed something familiar about the two-star, silver-haired officer. It had been a long time but he suddenly flashed back to that day when he was a child, watching from below as a KGB Death Squad swept through his family's cabin, torturing and killing everyone but him. The blood rushed into his head. For one of the few times in his life, Ted Rockson felt himself about to totally lose control of his emotions.

"What's your name?" he snapped loudly at the arrogant Red brass.

"Veliky. Major General Veliky." He reached slowly in his jacket pocket and pulled out a wallet. "You can see by my papers that I'm a—"

Rock knocked the wallet to the floor with a swipe of his .12 gauge. "Were you ever a combatant?"

"Of course not," the Red answered, but there was a definite quaver in his voice.

"Ever been in Tremain or anywhere around there?" Rock still wasn't positive. The face seemed so familiar, but it had been nearly twenty-five years ago.

"No! Absolutely not! Who are you men anyway?" He raised his voice, pulling himself up to his full height. "Why are you here, why—"

"Shut up," Jergins said, lifting his Liberator. "You don't ask the questions here." He spat angrily just to the side of the officer's foot.

"Remember a little cabin?" Rock continued, watching the man's eyes with every word he spoke. "A woman and a man named Rockson. A dog? Think back—twenty-four years ago."

Another Russian spoke up. "Spare me and I will—"

"Shut up," snarled the officer, his face growing livid. "I'll have you shot if you—" Jergins smacked the muzzle of his Liberator across Veliky's face, opening a gash several inches long.

"I told you to keep that fucking Red trap of yours shut. Next time you'll eat lead." Jergins stepped back. The other Freefighters—Pasqual and Detroit—kept their rifles trained on the increasingly nervous computer personnel.

"He was a combatant. He was." The Russian lackey spoke out, turning to Rockson, pleading, "Just don't kill me. I never hurt any Americans. I swear. I just handle the maintenance of the computer."

"Maybe I'll let you live," Rock said, turning to the sniveling, thin, white-smocked technician. "What sector did this man patrol twenty years ago?"

"I don't know, I swear," the squealer said. "But I know he did combat duty. I've heard him talk—brag about the women he had and the power he used to have out in the field. They all do. They all love to talk about killing and burning. I'm sick of it. I—"

"No, I never was in that area," the Red general cried out. "It's all a lie." He glared at the betrayer, with blood lust in his narrow eyes.

Rockson's mind flashed back to the man he remembered ripping the flesh off his mother as she lay tied to her bed. Ripping her flesh with a long knife, scalping her pink, pale skin as she screamed. It was this man! Suddenly he knew it.

"I remember your words, scum," Rock said, turning back toward the Red officer, his eyes blazing with the fires of hell. "Ah, you said, 'a pretty mutant woman with thick skin.' Then you raped her and then you peeled her flesh like I'm going to razor your skin to the bone."

"Rock, we haven't got time," shouted Jergins.

Rockson turned to the Russian who had betrayed the Red murderer. "If you want to live, tell us how to override the door controls on every level with the computers."

"Program 45-A. It seals the doors in case of a radiation leak. I won't just show you, I'll do it." He walked slowly over to the terminal under the watchful eyes of his disbelieving comrades. Jergins raised his Liberator but Rock gave him the No sign. The Russian squealer pushed a series of keys and then stepped back. "Done!"

"Good!" Rock looked at the other Freefighters. "Well, we've performed the first part of our job. Take all these bastards into that room and lock 'em in," he said, pointing to the tight-lipped crew of computer personnel. "But not this one." He looked at Veliky. "I want to be alone with this man."

"What about me?" the Red betrayer pleaded, rushing back to Rock, nearly falling on his hands and knees. "I helped you. They'll kill me if I stay. Let me come with you. I could reveal everything I've learned in my two-year stay here. I hate these bastards, I swear to you I do. They drafted me from the Ukraine. They've made me work for them. But they haven't taken my mind—haven't made me a murderer."

The Freefighters looked at the man as if he were mad. None of them had ever seen a Red who didn't seem to love his work. Rock nodded silently. "But tie him up, till we know we can trust him," he muttered to Jergins. He looked back over at the Red officer who could no longer meet his eyes, staring nervously down at the floor. Rock glanced at his watch. "We're two minutes ahead of schedule, man," he said. "I need to do something." He pushed Veliky ahead of him, toward a second room filled with blank magnetic tapes and supplies. "I'll only be a minute," Rock said. "Only a minute." He pushed the Red general ahead of him, holding his knife loose in his hand. They heard the door close—then they heard the screams begin.

Nineteen

McCaughlin and Smith reached the top floor—a pool area for top KGB officers. They burst through the stairwell door into a scene of horror.

"Now, isn't this cozy," McCaughlin said, finding four naked officers standing around a tied and spread-eagled teenage girl. They had been taking turns raping her and pushing their pistols into her sex, which was bleeding and ripped apart. Her breasts and thighs were covered with dark, charred cigarette burns. Tears ran down her young cheeks.

"Please," one of the Reds choked out as the others stood frozen in place, their tools suddenly hanging limp between their pale legs. "Please, you don't understand, she—"

"What's to understand?" McCaughlin sneered and squeezed the trigger. Three-round bursts caught first one, then another Red torturer, slamming them backward, their arms whipping wildly. The two other KGB officers dove toward the pool. McCaughlin hit one with a neat line of shots up the backbone, severing the Red's spine so that he fell to the pool walkway at an odd angle, his body broken like a rag doll. The fourth Red made the water and began swimming along the bottom to the opposite side.

"Shoot him when he comes up for air," McCaughlin said to Smith, as he went over to untie the girl. Before he had untied the last knot, he heard the sound of a body breaking water followed by a burst of fire. Blood slowly filled the pool, spreading out in scarlet ripples.

McCaughlin looked in the girl's mouth—she was trying to say something. He almost gagged. She had no tongue. The bastards had cut it out as part of their sick pleasure. She was in bad shape though she seemed thankful for her rescue. She couldn't walk and they couldn't carry her. He leaned over the teen and whispered in her ear, "You know how to use one of these?" He handed her one of the Reds' revolvers, from a holster hanging by the bottom of the bed. She smiled grimly. "Take a few out for us—and yourself. We have to go. I'm sorry." Her eyes said, Don't be sorry. She pressed her lips to McCaughlin's cheek.

They left her there, her pistol pointing at the door—the door to the sauna from where the next bunch of torturers would soon emerge to have fun with her body. She held the gun up with both hands, waiting. She hadn't expected to die so well. She was grateful to the big man and his companion for the chance to go out this way—instead of the cross, for the pleasure of the bastards. Now, she would have her pleasure as well. The pleasure of their blood.

McCaughlin and Smith strolled out onto the roof, trying to look nonchalant as they walked past the crews of several choppers lazing around, and headed toward the needle-shaped control tower. They were almost halfway across the roof when someone yelled out, "Hey, you two, there's no helicopters over there. Where are you going?"

In crisp Russian, McCaughlin spoke the only words he had ever memorized of the foul language, "Special orders from Commander Killov, Priority One!" They kept walking. They were about fifty yards from the tower and speeded up ever so slightly.

"What special orders?" They broke into a run. "Stop them! Stop them!" voices screamed behind them. Gunfire broke out; Red slugs ricocheted off a thick antenna only a foot from Smith's head.

"Break for it," McCaughlin yelled. The fleet-footed Smith ran like a bastard, even with the heavy EQ in duffel bags around his shoulders. He covered the fifty yards to the tower in seconds, dodging back and forth every few steps. McCaughlin knew he couldn't outrun bullets. He dove to the black tar roof and began firing full auto with a hip-high sweep of the landing pads and the Red crews. Russian knees and thigh bones broke and shattered and chopper tires blew out as McCaughlin's slugs found a home. Shit, he had only two clips left on him, everything else was in his canvas equipment sack. The Reds ran for better cover—but he knew it was only seconds before they opened up again and this time they wouldn't miss. He edged backward and bumped against an aluminum vent, one of several at this part of the roof. He hid behind it and looked in. Some kind of hatch or air vent with just a thin mesh screen over it. He reached out a meaty fist and ripped the partition away. The Red slugs began tearing up the tar top like pairs of scissors cutting a path toward his gut. He had nothing to lose, that was for sure. Moving fast for a man his size, McCaughlin leaped up into the square shaft and immediately felt himself tumbling end over end. Jesus, he was falling! He threw his thick arms out but they just bounced off the sheer, smooth metal walls. He plummeted down, praying that when he hit he would go out fast.

Smith saw his chance as the Reds fired on McCaughlin. The big Scot could handle his end for a minute, at least until Smith could gain control of the tower. He slid in the door and latched it shut behind him. A row of steep, circular stairs led straight up to the tower about fifty feet above him. He pulled out his army-issue, .45, a prewar antique that he always carried, as it had saved his ass on numerous occasions. Above him, he could hear Red voices talking frantically. His Russian wasn't great, but he understood. "Attack on Center. Yes. Reinforcements immediately. And choppers. Good!" So they were going to send in the whole damn Red army from the other side of Stalinville. He'd have to get in and set up fast.

He came around the top of the stairs, trying to sense from their animated conversation just how many there were. Two just to the left of the stairs, one to the right. But there were more listening, in the back. Well, there wasn't time for computer analysis of that. The Freefighter, drenched with sweat and blood, hefting 175 pounds of arms, charged around the top bend of the metal staircase and blasted the .45, pulling the trigger over and over and turning slowly around the room.

Six shots later three unrecognizable Red corpses, leaking vital fluids profusely, fell to the floor and didn't move.

Smith threw his gear down and immediately began setting up. So far, so good, he thought, kicking two of the bodies through the floor-level entrance and down the stairs to make room for himself in the cramped quarters of the needle-nosed structure. He glanced out the 360 degree window at the roof below where the Reds continued to fire away. But where the hell was McCaughlin? Smith got a sinking feeling in his gut as he scanned the roof and couldn't find the Freefighter anywhere. There's no missing that big body, he thought, feeling his throat tighten up. So they'd finally gotten McCaughlin—the men wouldn't believe it. He was alleged to have a charmed life. Shit!

What had been a cold act of professionalism on Smith's part so far in the attack mission suddenly became a raging need to avenge the Reds' killing of one of the best men that he had ever known. He threw the latches on the windows of the tower and pulled them all open to give himself an unrestricted firing range and shoved the muzzle of his RDP machine gun out the opening. 7.62mm shells migrated toward Red flesh at 650 rounds per minute. The Russians who had been firing on McCaughlin suddenly were being hunted. They ran frantically toward the chopper some fifty feet behind them, but were cut down in a hail of smoking death.

Smith looked down at the pile of twisted bodies. He had surprised them. The fools had still been firing at McCaughlin. Score one for you, buddy, he thought. Even when you ain't around you keep fighting. From the control tower he could see down two sides of the building, toward the main entrance, forty stories below. He had a view of the surrounding air lanes, suddenly realizing with a laugh that *he* was now Stalinville Air Control. He glanced around at the radar screens and radio headsets that lay everywhere. Even from across the room he could hear pilots screaming for instructions. The large, green radar monitor was aglow with dots all sweeping inexorably toward each other.

He was at the very top of the needlelike tower and could feel it swaying in the wind. Christ, I hope the Reds don't figure

174

some way to chop this thing down with a rocket. But then he'd see them coming and get them first. He could lay down all kinds of fire from up here—pin everyone down outside the building while Rock and the others sealed the bastards up inside their steel holes downstairs. And now, he had their weapons as well as his pack of rockets and the grenade launchers. The Kalashnikovs and AK-47s on the floor would do when he ran out of clips for his own Liberator.

He opened up on a group of Blackshirts who tore out the roof stairwell door, heading toward the tower. He splattered one brain, then caught two in the groins, their balls dripping down onto their shoes. That would take care of that for the moment. He pulled the RDP out from its ledge cradle and carried it to the other side of the room. Norton and Sanford, the explosives' men, should be making their move right about now toward the armory. He sighted down the 7.62mm machine gun and saw regular Red troops pulling up at the barbed-wire front gate. He let loose with the full belt, sending hot casings spinning to the right. From forty stories up, it looked like a bunch of ants suddenly running from a rainstorm. Only this was a deathstorm and the Red bodies fell in droves to the ground. A screaming round found the gas tank of the big troop transport and it exploded in a yellow halo of fire, blocking the road to any further movement of personnel.

Suddeny Smith saw the two Freefighters weaving their way across the smoke-filled concrete lot to the left of the building. The armory, a long, low, concrete-sided, metal-roofed structure, lay at the other end of the lot. They just needed a few more seconds. A fusillade of shots rang out from far below and one of the running Americans went down but, just as quickly, rose and hobbled on with the other. Smith aimed the RDP across the fence just outside the compound and sent a mailgram of death streaking down to the APV which was sniping at the munitions men. He razed the vehicle twice, sending the occupants flying from their perches in a tornado of blood. The firing stopped. Smith watched with satisfaction as the two Freefighters disappeared into the long storage depot.

*　　*　　*

175

When Smith set up his covering fire, Norton and Sanford, who had been waiting in the security checkpoint room just inside the entrance to the KGB Center, flew out the door toward the armory. They could see troops pulling up across the road, but they'd have to trust the man above. That's the only way an operation like this could work. They'd gotten about halfway across the truck parking lot that separated the Center from the armory when Sanford went down, a ripping pain in his right calf. He stumbled to his feet. He could walk. Hurt like the devil but still functional. That's when he saw the transport truck go up in a snap, crackle and pop. They made it to the corrugated metal door held with only a padlock which Sanford shot off. They rushed inside, throwing themselves to the ground, pistols ready to take blood. But only silence greeted them. The cavernous dump stretched off into gray, lit by rows of ancient, flickering light bulbs in long, even rows. Everywhere were the implements of death. Rockets, mortar shells, grenades, rows after row, stack after stack of shells, case after case of ammunition for every revolver and rifle and machine gun in the Soviet army. Norton whistled.

"Now, this is what you call armaments. Makes our stockpile back in Century City look shit," he said, unloading his plastique.

"Only they ain't gonna have none in about ten minutes," Sanford replied, resting for a second to put a tourniquet around his leg. "Thank God, we didn't have to shoot it out in here." He looked around at the looming supermarket of murder.

The two men did their work efficiently, placing explosives for several hundred feet along the rows of hardware, each globe of explosive with a small radio-controlled firing device stuck in the center.

They finished their work and shot back out the exit, leaving a single small antipersonnel device just inside the door in case anybody poked their face in ahead of schedule. Smith set up a line of cover fire for them and they made it all the way to the KGB Center entrance safely. Norton ran in first and turned to the right against a wall as Red fire was starting to come through the windows. He waited. Where the hell was Sanford? He edged around the wood-framed doorway and looked out. The Freefighter sat motionless as if he were resting. Only his face was gone. Blown away by an exploding 9mm slug.

Shit! Norton stared down at his friend. Only now there was nothing there. The life was gone. The thing that had been Sanford had flown the coop. He stared, hypnotized until he heard a large shell land just outside the window, showering a pile of smoking dirt onto his feet. Time to go. He said a silent goodbye and ran up the stairs, two at a time. There were forty flights to go and he knew Rock would have no choice but to leave once the allotted time was up.

Rock sat at the controls of the KGB commander's private jet helicopter on the roof landing pad that they had found guarded by only three quickly-dead Reds. A fortunate stroke of luck. He looked at his watch. Where the hell were Sanford and Norton. And McCaughlin. Smith had said he saw the big Scot disappear. Nobody. Nothing. Rock let the blade spin at idling speed. They had to go. The increasing numbers of Red troops below were starting to get their range, too, as shells whistled by. Off in the distance, Rock could hear the drone of what sounded like a fleet of choppers. Where the f—

Norton came hobbling out of the stairwell roof door. He ran to the chopper and dove into waiting arms which pulled him briskly aboard. "They got Sanford," he wheezed, his face beet red, his lungs pumping like overheating pistons.

I've got to go, Rock thought, thinking of the dead McCaughlin lying somewhere in this hellhole. He revved up the rotors and the Red chopper began lifting smoothly off the roof landing pad. Suddenly, out of the corner of his eye, he saw the unmistakable barn of a man—McCaughlin—running as fast as his size twelve feet would carry him. Rock let the chopper drop with a thud to the pad as the lumbering Scot dove in. It took five men to pull the heaviest Free American east of the Rockies into the helicopter. Rock took up and off like a bolt, tilting the copter forward for maximum air speed.

The men gathered around McCaughlin and just as quickly backed off. He smelled like a sewer and seemed to be covered with garbage.

"What the hell happened to you?" Detroit asked, fingers over his broad nose.

McCaughlin looked sheepish. "I fell into a fucking garbage pit, can't you tell? But it saved my ass." He laughed with a twinkle in his green eyes.

Twenty

Rockson could see the rows of troop trucks and tanks pulling up around the KGB Center on all sides. Good, all the better to view the fireworks.

"Norton, come here," Rock leaned sideways and yelled into the guts of the chopper. The munitions man made his way forward. "You all set down there?"

"We loaded her up to her tits, Rock."

"From what you told me, all the plastique's on the same frequency to blow. Yours and the stuff I set in the computer room and downstairs."

"Everything will go at once. Guaranteed, Rock."

"Why don't you do the honors," Rockson said softly, handing Norton the cigarette-pack-sized radio detonator.

Norton took the device and stared out the window at the dump below as Rockson flew a fast, wide circle around the complex.

"For you, Sanford," Norton said, flipping a plastic switch on the side of the transmitter. "A thousand dead Russians."

The entire earth shook beneath them as a hundred thousand square feet of explosive power erupted like a volcano. The copter shook violently from the blast, veering at a forty degree angle to the right. Every man in the craft flew against the wall, and then into a cursing struggling pile on the floor. Rock straightened the jet helicopter and swung by for a final look at the damage.

"Sorry about that," he yelled into the back. "The explosion

was a little stronger than I thought." Beneath the chopper, the explosions continued one after another, blasting the armory to pieces, and hurling chunks of flaming metal and boulder-sized concrete segments through the air and onto the nearly one thousand milling Red troops on the outside of the perimeter fence. Rock glanced up at the KGB Center as a secondary explosion ripped through the walls of the fifteenth through twentieth floors. The building shuddered down to its foundation from the blast, glass exploding out from every window and slowly, like a lightning-blasted tree in a stormy forest, collapsed and fell over, its support beams severed like arteries on three sides.

Rockson cut on the twin-booster jets in the tail of the MS-20 and it roared forward, quickly picking up to six hundred kilometers an hour, far faster than any of the regular choppers that might pursue them. He took a final look over his shoulder at the still-unfolding carnage. A ball of flame three hundred feet high burned with the intensity of a death star. The explosions continued one after another, spreading to other parts of the fort. They had really hurt the bastards this time. Half the fort would be gone by the time this thing blew itself out.

It had been a break finding the jet copter on the pad when they blasted their way back to the roof. The power of the machine was incredible. Rock was barely capable of handling the HP of the craft, and had to keep his hands gripped to the controls as it bucked beneath him. The ground sped by below as if he were flying a jet and Rock took the chopper up fast and high at a steep angle that made the men gulp and swallow uncomfortably in the back.

The roar was deafening but it would have been worse had the KGB commander, Polikarpov, not had it doubly insulated so as not to give him headaches. They quickly left the Stalinville fort and headed out toward the canyons and wild country where they could lose themselves if anyone tried to follow. Rock checked the scanning radar and saw something coming in fast on the screen. From behind. By their speed: jets.

"Detroit! Hit the rear gunner position," Rock yelled out to the black Freefighter, still rubbing his shoulder from the spill of a minute before. Detroit strapped himself into the gunner's chair and turned the switch on under the guns. Three rows of dials lit up—air-to-ground, air-to-air, machine gun. Detroit pushed air-to-air, and looked into the eye-level screen built into the wall of the copter. Two blips appeared, closing range at two hundred feet per second. Detroit pressed the number two on a keyboard and then Fire button. Two laser-guided missiles shot out from underneath the chopper and headed straight back to greet the two pursuing hot-eye missiles. They met in a collision of flame two hundred yards behind the MS-20.

"Good shooting, man," Pasqual said, slapping Detroit on the back.

"I wish I could feel prouder, but to be honest with you the Reds built these missile gizmos simple. If they didn't, the Russian crews would be blowing themselves up all over the place. I know how simple they are—I read the fucking manual."

Up front, Rockson listened to the radio scream with various versions of what had happened at the fort. He decided to add his own.

"Red-One to emergency control. Commander Polikarpov's helicopter is in the lead of the chase to capture the enemy. Do not interfere with the commander's flight path." He switched off. That ought to gum things up a little more. The Reds would be trying to figure this whole thing out for months. Several other voices cut in on the frequency, denying that the commander was flying the helicopter, demanding that the valley defenses shoot it down. And they could. If they dared take the chance of making a mistake that would cost them. The big anti-aircraft guns mounted in the hills around the fort didn't go off as they flew directly overhead.

Detroit's voice crackled over the intercom. "Two Mig Skydog jet fighters coming up on us and boy are they hot-dogging it. They might intercept us before we hit the mountains." Once in the thick mountains, which they knew inside out, the jets couldn't match the copter's maneuverability, but out here . . .

Rockson called back, "Detroit, can you get them?"

"Negative. I've only got laser-guided mothers here. They got some kind of electronic countermeasure—it's showing on my defensive systems screen."

Rock glanced at the beeping distance of the nearest mountain on the screen—thirteen miles to go to rugged terrain, nineteen to the pass where he might be able to elude the jets. Too far. "Do the best you can, Detroit," Rock said quietly.

"Aye, aye, Captain." The men's faces were set in deep grimaces as they overheard the conversation. To have come so far.

In a few moments the jets flew alongside! The radio crackled. "Your excellency, because of the confusion, we are escorting your ship on its mission."

"Acknowledged," mumbled Rockson into the radio. So they had a police escort from the big guy's own men—how fitting an end to the most destructive day the Russians had known in a century. The jets stayed until they reached the high canyons and the going became impossible. They peeled off, their afterburners trailing hellfire up and away over the mountains.

Rockson made a series of hair-raising turns down a narrow gorge, as they entered the first of two hundred miles of jagged mountain range. Detroit crawled up into the co-pilot seat and sat down next to Rock giving him an ear-to-ear grin.

"How on earth did you decide not to fire on those Skydogs? You saved our lives, Green. They would have changed their plans to escort us if you'd fired."

"Simple," Detroit said. "Their ceremonial lights were on. Their pinkish wing-tip lights are only on when saluting a high-ranking officer. You couldn't see them from your position."

"But how the hell do you know something like that?" Rock asked, incredulous.

"I read the fucking manuals." Detroit grinned back. His eye caught a motion on the radar screen blinking above Rock's head. "Company!" he said. He watched the object weave and twist in pursuit of the constantly shifting copper. "It ain't no damn jet, not down in these alleyways. Must be some kind of heat-seeking missile. Gonna be hard to shake this one, Rock."

Rockson placed the helicopter in a steep dive, then made a nearly impossible sharp right around a branching canyon's jutting boulders. But the cruise missile stayed with them easily. But it wasn't gaining either and from the depth of color on the radar monitor it was one of the smaller class.

"I'll try to outrun her in open territory," Rockson yelled going for broke toward a barren plateau. The cruise stayed about three hundred yards behind them, just matching speed. Soon they were up over the flatlands and the copter shuddered violently as Rockson pushed it to its limits. As if the speed—678 mph—wasn't enough to do them in, a storm—purple and brown, one of the electrical monster thunderstorms—was looming like the edge of the Earth itself right over the advancing plains.

They were moving just under the sound barrier when suddenly the storm was on them. They were buffeted about like a cork in an ocean squall and Rock nearly lost control as the chopper went into a downward spiral. He pulled back on the controls and gave her even more speed and the black death machine leveled out and they tore forward through the ever-thickening clouds. Lightning crackled all around, shooting by in jagged pitchforks of blinding white. A screaming sound started to come from the overheated engines and a sickening wobbling from the overhead rotor. If this kept up they'd be splattered from here to Century City. Rockson's knuckles were white on the controls.

"That cruise missile still trailing us?" Rock asked, keeping his eyes glued to the rapidly advancing terrain just a few hundred feet below.

"Radar says it's there," Detroit said almost apologetically. "But it's dropped back a little to five hundred yards."

Rockson eased up just a bit on the throttle and the terrible din cut in volume. He glanced at the steaming right engine, then quickly back at the temperature gauges. They were cooling already, slowly, but cooling. Maybe the cruise missile would be having its problems too. Perhaps the hurricane winds and the hail would tear its stubby, little fucking wings off.

Rock's ground radar was picking up more canyons ahead. They would reach them in three minutes. He didn't want to tell the crew that the worst was yet to come. Suddenly he recognized the contours of the computer profile. "Hey, men,

183

it's Carson Canyon ahead. I know that place. It's a piece of cake—and I think I can dump our friend there, too."

The blades seemed to suddenly shake as the storm again hit them with renewed anger. The engines started spilling oil that spattered back along the body of the chopper.

"You've got to go faster, Rock, it's gaining again. Slowly, but coming up," Detroit said hoarsely.

"How're the guns?"

"Haven't you heard them? McCaughlin's been firing for the last few minutes. Nothing."

"Let me know when she gets within a hundred yards."

"150, 140, 130, 140, 150—hey, what's happening?"

Rockson let out a sigh of relief, and eased up on the throttle.

"180, 200—hey, Cap', she's going down, she's falling."

The cheering was loud throughout the chopper and even the normally restrained Rockson joined in as loud as the others.

"How the hell did *you* know what was going to happen?" Detroit asked, puzzled.

Rockson explained that the little bugger was only a short range. "It just ran out of gas before we ran out."

The rest of the journey home was uneventful other than several dozen heart-wrenching turns in a half-shot helicopter down narrow, dark canyons. At last they were climbing toward Century City. Radio silence was maintained, but Rock knew that gun units down on the ground were keeping a wary eye on the descending helicopter. He landed the bird near the camouflaged hangar in which were stored two other helicopters, much smaller ones, and a prop plane. The bird had scarcely touched down when fifty men, their rifles trained on the chopper, approached in a closing circle.

Detroit jumped out first, then McCaughlin and the others. The Century City Defense Crew embraced the returning Attack Force and stared with wonder at the super chopper.

"This is Commander Polikarpov's personal helicopter," Rock said to the waiting guards. "Make sure she's treated with the royalty she deserves. And a wax job."

Twenty-One

The men they had rescued—Bill Fitz, Pete Scranton and Gilhooley—told of their horrifying experiences as guinea pigs for the scientists who were doing the experimental work with the Mind Breaker. Armstrong had been the first subject of the advanced model, MB II. Since the prisoners were all going to be put to death anyway, after the experiments, the scientist in charge, Letvok, explained the function of the Mind Breaker Model II—how it would probe deeper than the cortex with its laser needles uncovering and activating primitive fear mechanisms in the medulla, bringing nightmares into the awakened state, making the mind of the prisoner experience as real the unconscious fears that he had buried under layers of repression all his life.

Gilhooley described in a shaking voice how the expressions on Armstrong's face had contorted and changed. How he kept yelling out, "The rats! Take the rats away, Mother! The rats are in my bed!" And then the Reds would turn down the machine and his eyes would refocus and they would ask him questions, questions that had to be answered if his mother was to keep the rats away. Armstrong had refused—even at point of being left permanently in that hell of primeval rats that only his imagination could call forth. Armstrong. The man Rockson had dispatched with a shot to the temple. Brave till the end.

Next it had been Scranton, Pete Scranton. They—the scientists—were sure that the Model II Mind Breaker would work in the direction of pleasure as well. It was Letvok's brainchild—a Mind Breaker that alternated patterns of pleasure and pain deep within the brain. The machine played its game in Scranton's brain and every ten or fifteen seconds the expressions on his face changed from anguished grimaces to unparalleled ecstasy. Then they began asking him questions.

"Where is Century City?"

Scranton grunted out, "Mary had a l-little—"

Letvok had turned the dial to full capacity on the pleasure scale. Scranton smiled broadly. Apparently, from his rapid eye movements, he was seeing something. Something that wasn't there. His restrained hands tried to reach up to touch it.

"What do you see?" the Russian scientist asked.

"Violet, violet women, soft—they . . . call . . . so . . . beautiful, so beautiful. I understand everything—all—everything —the world is love. Yes, that's it—ecstasy is at the heart of every movement, every—"

Letvok suddenly spun the Mind Breaker's control to full pain. Instantly the laser needles altered course, tapping the depths of ancestral terror. Scranton had groaned a deep spasmodic groan of a man being immersed in the fires of hell.

"My balls," he screamed. "Make the demons stop. Don't let them. Not—*yaaaaa!*" He had screamed for five minutes without cease until Letvok had turned the dial back to neutral.

"I want to hear you tell me the location of Century City. I will reward you." Letvok had turned the dial up slightly toward pleasure. Scranton stirred, smiling though he had defecated in his pants and urine ran down his leg, forming a yellow puddle on the floor.

"See your violet women?" Letvok asked.

"Faintly, faintly—bring them closer, please bring them closer."

"I will as soon as you tell me where Century City is."

Scranton had smiled. "Century City is in heaven."

"Bah," Letvok had yelled, spinning the dial to the pain side and leaving Scranton as he screamed incessantly about demons eating his testicles. The others were led away. They could hear the screams for the next ten minutes. Then it stopped. Scranton had been dragged into their cell and thrown on the floor.

They had slapped him in the face and kept saying his name until he finally came round.

"Porter," Rockson said softly, "see that Scranton gets the best—give him my rehabilitation suite for as long as he wants. He may act confused or withdrawn for a while. But see that he's not disturbed until he wants to be. I have something I have to do."

Rockson exited the debriefing room and walked down the corridor. He pressed his palm against a wall sensor and the detention-room door slid open. Inside, the captured Letvok sat on a wood chair. He turned and smiled. "Ah, Mr. Rockson—come to talk to me?" He had little fear for it was known that Americans didn't torture.

Rockson icily eyed the man up and down. The cigarette dropped from the fingers of the Russian scientist. Fear widened his eyes as Rock rolled up his sleeves to reveal thick, rippling muscles. Rockson approached the Mind Breaker scientist with balled fists. Letvok began whimpering like a baby.

When Rock left ten minutes later, he felt a little guilty. But only a little. He had stopped short—just short—of finishing Letvok. There would be enough time to nurse him back to health. Then Letvok would serve as the subject of the Mind Breaker that they had taken from the Stalinville lab and brought back with them. There was much that had to be learned about this machine. And its operating secrets would be pried out of Letvok with his own device. Poetic justice.

Rock rolled down his sleeves. He wondered what the Russian version of hell was. Rats? Demons? If they didn't believe in God, could they believe in demons? Or were their deepest nightmares about meeting an American Freefighter in a one-to-one struggle to the death? Soon they would find out what Letvok feared. And Armstrong would be avenged. Cruelty was not the American way—but this was cruelty with a purpose: to extract the information they needed about the Mind Breaker and the extent of its modifications.

So they planned to brainwash the occupied people's brains.

A devilish plot to send out the Americans from the occupied areas to fight their own countrymen. And Letvok knew just how far along the project was. He would know if there was any weakness in the plan, any failure to program the slave populace. Any way to bring them back out of the mindless devotion to Killov and their newly adopted country, Mother Russia.

Twenty-Two

It was Rockson's second day of R&R back at Century City. It had been a long time since he had been able to just sit, think, let his body uncoil. He spent hours in the meditation chamber, a small, sparse white room decorated with only a pillow in the center and a sprig of fresh flowers at one end, set on a small black table. Here, citizens of Century City could come to let their minds, bodies and spirits take a rest. It was a place where they could absorb the energies of daily life and digest them in silence and peace. Rock felt it a necessity to spend a day or two in one of the eight rooms, every month or two. Reflection, self-knowledge, harmony of muscle and brain tissue—these things gave him great strength and power. Where others faltered, ran, or became confused and disoriented, Rock was as centered and set as his namesake.

Letvok, meanwhile, at the other end of the city, in one of Shecter's labs, was spilling the beans about the Mind Breaker: its operation, modification program, and the ways in which the Reds were implementing it. Shecter had read the statements of the freed American hostages and was, therefore, totally committed to using the device on Letvok. His normally humanitarian scruples were somewhat dulled by the brutal realities of the Russian torture factory, which had been managed by Letvok.

The buzzer on Rockson's wrist phone, worn only inside Century City where the low-level frequency ⸳ldn't be picked up by the Reds, went off with a humming ep. He put his

189

mouth to the one-inch grid on the face of the wireless phone. "Yes?"

"Rockson, this is Rath. Expedition Five is back—and I think you'll want to hear their report. In fact, you'd better come take a look at what they found." Rath was unusually excited.

"What'd they find, Premier Vassily on a platter with an apple in his mouth?" Rath let out a forced laugh.

"Really, Rock, it's quite . . . We're having the first debriefing in Intelligence Room C."

"I'm coming," Rock said, touching the small Off dial on the side of the transmitter. He rolled a civilian white cotton shirt on over his muscular frame and was off. Expedition Five had been headed by a tough but untested young man, Walt Brady, Rock remembered. It had headed out into the Northwest—unexplored territory. It was their most ambitious expedition so far—a thirteen hundred mile trek into the hot zone. There were rumors about that area: that it was the home of the Glowers, that no man had ever returned from there. But Brady, if he had done nothing else, had accomplished that.

Rockson went up the four levels to the intelligence section and entered the debriefing room. Rath sat in a broad, plastic chair with the five remaining members of the expedition across from him. The five were bearded, though they were also freshly bathed and patched up, and outfitted in crisp, new white clothes. They stood up, as the military commander of Century City entered. Rockson motioned for them to sit, and walked over to Rath's left, sitting down next to O'Shannon, the intel chief's right-hand woman. She gave Rock a warm and melting look with her fathomless green eyes. He responded with a deprecating grin. The direct stares of women were something he still couldn't quite feel comfortable with. And there were many such lingering stares.

Rock snapped his head forward and looked at the five returned Freefighters. "What's out there?" he asked the one with the insignia, Brady. Brady had been an arrogant young upstart before he left. Too sure of himself. Now he had changed. He had the eyes that you get when you see things no man has seen. Eyes like Rock's. Premature wrinkles etched the young man's darkly tanned face. Brady leaned forward toward

190

Rock, unblinking. He had lost any traces of bulk, now muscle and guts lay under those coveralls.

"Rock," he said, "it's—it's incredible out there. The things we've seen. I—I don't quite know where to start."

"Brady," suggested Rath, "why don't you just begin with your departure from Century City. We need every bit of intel from you to add to our central files and particularly the extension of our mapping data. I trust you kept full compass and landmark records," Rath added hopefully.

"Got it all right here, sir," Brady said, pulling out a weather-beaten notebook. He handed the data to Rath and then breathed out a deep sigh, as if in preparation for a long story. "Well, we encountered fairly normal conditions the first two, three days out. The Rockies are much the same for a distance and then we came to some lower terrain that looked fairly easy going. We headed across some really immense fields of weeds and small game. Very rich. In fact, I'd say that heading due west for almost two hundred miles the land has really grown back. It's beautiful, Rock," he said, his face lighting up. "Deer, raccoon, birds, even berries and sassafras tea. Things I'd just read about in the books. It's all out there."

"Bagged us some mighty tasty boar, out in them wilds," Keppler, the oldest member of the expedition, spoke up. "Tuskers, a tribe of them. Mean, too. They attacked us. Had to take out the whole advancing front line to stop 'em. Meat succulent as a sweet woman, Rock." The other men laughed, as O'Shannon's ivory complexion blushed pink.

"Anyway," Brady continued, "after less than a day on the open brush country, we encountered some heavy hit zones. The Reds must've dropped two or three within a thirty-mile radius. The land was wrecked, a sickly gray color, like ash left out in the rain. Nothing grew there—nothing normal. There was some sort of algae growth, big blankets of a greenish-red plant that just lived on top of the radioactive dirt. The radiation grew intense very quickly and we suited up with the anti-rad Dr. Shecter provided. We had to stay sealed for two days, drinking only the water we carried. We didn't dare stop for sleep, but just kept going. It was too far to turn back. We'd either make it to some hospitable spot or—" Rath looked on, adjusting the sound level on his recorder. He was a fanatic on the subject of geographic mapping of America, believing that through a clear picture of how the United States was now altered, they could plan for the future development of the nation.

"Strangely," Brady went on, "we found water in an unexpected place, to say the least. We came upon three immense volcanos—must have been created from the H-blasts. Two were totally dead, craters as big as the moon's, but a third was still active, or had been recently. The ground was hot, and inside lava was still bubbling, sending up clouds of steam. The volcano had also created underground springs around the area, some which fed right out of the side of the crater, hot but drinkable. We camped in one of the dead volcanos and filled the hybrids with water. The hardened lava beds tore the hell out of our boots, and even cut up the 'brid's stone-hard hoofs.

"The next day we headed on, and came out of the dead zone by nightfall. We had fairly clear going again for about a day and a half, mostly savannah-type terrain. Saw some large cats—fangs, odd stripes and patterns—Draper sketched some of them," Brady said, nodding to the youngest member of the expedition, a budding artist, who had drawn nearly two hundred pictures of their encounters. "Took photos, too, but lost them in a 'brid fall.

"Then we came upon a pink mist. It was like a fog, so thick you couldn't see more than three or four feet in front of you. We used the compass and just kept heading exactly 275 degrees. Jefferson fell into a damn quicksand pit," Brady said, smiling at the black member of the expedition who looked down sheepishly, "but we got him out before any permanent damage was done.

"The fog wasn't dangerous—that was our first surprise. As we descended, at probably five hundred feet an hour, the fog lifted from around us—it covers this whole area, Rock, acts as a sort of greenhouse effect. Lets heat and an eerie, pinkish glow come down, then keeps it all contained. We were in temperatures and humidities I never felt except in the steambaths here. It was a veritable sauna and as we went on we came upon something unbelievable: dense jungle as far as the eye could see. Trees, vines, screaming birds and insects everywhere. And most of the inhabitants of the place were big. Write this down in your records, Rath," Brady said, turning to the intel chief. "Giant bees as big as—" he held his hands out until they were about two feet apart—"moths with wings as big as newspapers, velvet-winged dragonflies as big as a man's leg. And vines and ferns everywhere. There were ferns that must have been 100, 150 feet high. If my history's not mistaken— terrain like that is very similar to the prehistoric days on Earth."

"That's right," Rath said. "It's one of Dr. Shecter's theories that the long-term radiation makes some species revert to their primitive genetic programming. A de-evolution if you will."

"Well, I for one believe the venerable doc is right," Brady said. "The whole area looked primeval. As we went in further there were these creepers everywhere—we had to hack our way through. The first night camping in the jungle we noticed that the tips of the vines were moving—and as it got darker the damn things grew right into our encampment. We would have been smothered by morning, if not for taking turns burning the things away and hacking at them with machetes. They're apparently—" he paused—"carnivorous. Grab insects and small mammals. Some sort of walking Venus's-flytrap. I don't know if they have a taste for humanity or not but we didn't give them a chance to find out. They burn pretty good for fresh green pulp—and they make a nerve-wracking noise as they die, a high-pitched squeal like a finger being raked across a chalkboard. Anyway, it went on like that all night and we were exhausted by dawn. The creepers only moved at night however and we got into higher elevations by the next nightfall.

"We moved on for the next few days without incident, making good time until we came to a wide, roaring river. We had to stop for nearly a day to make a raft capable of carrying us and the 'brids across the river. Then, again, it was vast, empty stretches populated only by strange vegetation that kept changing every twenty or thirty miles. We were attacked here by several carnivores: two big cats, a bear and a—I can't really call it anything, because none of us had ever seen one before, but it had horns and . . . The kid has pictures. Finally—

193

Draper, hand me the map, will you?" He was given a wrinkled, folded map which he spread out on a flat coffee table between the Expedition Force and the intel chief. A gnarled finger with a torn nail descended on a spot at the very left edge of the map. There were mountains drawn in and rivers, and a red line showing their progress.

"At this point we found footprints. Small hurried prints of a boot without a heel. We spent a day and a half tracking the prints—the ground was black here, Rock. It was the deadest looking soil I've ever seen. Not a damn thing grew here. We finally caught up with the print maker. Never saw anything like him—it—before. He was about three feet tall and—here're some pics." He produced some faded drawings of the creature and showed them to Rath and Rockson. Rock whistled as he flicked through the prints one by one. They showed a tiny, pale man with bulging forehead, wearing some sort of blue one-piece suit. Then a drawing showed him stripped, obviously dead. Bluish-white skin, shrunken, useless genitals, lesions of unhealing rad burns. It was a pathetic sight. There was a weapon next to it—a strange pistol that Rock figured shot some sort of liquid or gas, not bullets, from its smooth, chamberless design. It was sized just right for the tiny hand beside it.

"Too bad it was dead when you found it," Rockson said. Brady looked him squarely in the eyes.

"It wasn't, Rock. And it spoke English—kind of."

"What did it say?" Rath asked impatiently, leaning forward in his stiff way.

"It was frightened. It had taken a pot shot at us while it was running up a pumice dune. You should see the beam that comes out of that little weapon. It creased my field shirt." Brady rolled up his white coverall sleeve and showed an ugly straight scar about six inches long just below the shoulder. "Hurt like hell—still, I can't blame it. We fired back and missed, but as it ran it slipped and fell a good sixty feet onto some rocks. We ran to it and it was still alive, barely. It was amazed that we spoke English. It said it had never seen the likes of us before and was afraid we were one of the predators that stalks the edges of the dead zone. But get this, it's an American,

194

just like us. It's descended from the original technicians who manned the missile silos in that area. They've stayed there all these years. They call themselves the Technicians. It told us its people were dying. It was called Vorn and was the hunter for its people. It kept saying, 'They'll die without me, without sustenance. I am the hunter.' Then it died.

"We searched for days for its underground silo complex but to no avail. That land is nothing but black soot. No Russian force would ever go out there. It's a blank hot zone on their maps too. Seems the silos were covered with layers of sand and dirt thrown up by three or four big blasts. Hidden from any satellite's prying eyes. Before the little guy died he said he figured us for mutated predators, because—get this, Rock— the Technicians think they're the only ones left of the Americans. Imagine, all these years living underground, inventing new things to keep them alive—like these black-beam pistols, and God knows what else—thinking that blackness around them was all that was left of the entire world. Incredible."

"It is," Rath mumbled.

"We finally had to give up trying to find the silos as our food and water were running low again. We charted some other territories and headed back. This weapon of theirs—we brought it back. It's incredibly powerful. I feel that we should mount a better-equipped larger force to go back. It could mean—"

"Our ace in the hole," Rock said. "A new weapon to fight the Reds with—a force that, from what you say— You have the pistol with you?" Rock asked, looking suddenly around for a bag.

"Down in Dr. Shecter's laboratory. He was enthralled. Started spouting formulas, yelling orders to his assistants. They're performing full-scale tests on it right now. It's apparently some sort of—" Brady hesitated at the unfamiliar words—"particle beam disintegrator. Sir, I'd like permission," Brady said, turning to Rath, "to head the second expedition."

"Not a chance," Rath said bluntly. "You and your men have absorbed too many rads even for Freefighters. You need complete decontamination procedures including a series of iodine and calcium injections to evacuate any radioactive trace elements. Two months minimum. That's Century City policy," Rath said almost apologetically.

"I have more mutant cells than anyone," Rock said drily. "I want that expedition, Rath."

"Impossible, Rock. You've been through a major engagement just days ago. Your wound is still healing, your—"

"*My* expedition," said Rockson. "You can't deny me the right. As military commander, it is I who makes the final determination of expeditionary forces." Rock was pulling rank now.

Rath stared at him coolly. "I've never seen a glutton for punishment like you. You've earned a rest."

"If I've earned anything, it's the right to head the second expedition."

Rath couldn't meet Rock's forceful blue-purple eyes any longer. "Maybe, maybe if you get a complete physical and it all checks out—"

"It will!"

"Then—"

Brady gripped Rockson on the shoulder. "Rock, it's something indescribable—beautiful and horrible—out there. It changed me; it will change you too."

Rockson took the arm of the brave soldier of democracy. "For the better, Brady, just like you. For the better."

Brady took Rockson down to the pistol range of Shecter's experimental level. Shecter had gone over it thoroughly.

"Rock, it's absolutely amazing. The device is as light as plastic but extremely hard. It's molded, one piece, so I can't open it without possible destruction to the inner workings. But from our tests, it's equal to a whole battlefield full of tanks in terms of its power." Shecter handed the small, curved pistol to Rockson.

Rock pointed the diminutive weapon at a red and white bull's-eye some one hundred meters away.

"Now, look through the triangular scope on top," Shecter said from the side. "Press the small red dot on the right side.

That locks a laser sight on target. Thing actually has a mini-memory. Once you lock in the target settings, it hardly matters which way you fire—it's programmed to head for the previously set coordinates. Now just squeeze the trigger. It has almost no pull at all."

Shecter was right. It was like pulling a leaf, so lightly balanced was the trigger. These Technicians must have been as weak as babies to have such a infinitesimal pull. As Rock pulled back, a nearly silent response occurred. He heard the slight scream of superheated air as the black beam shot straight out from the pistol and hit the target dead center. A rough-edged circle six inches wide appeared, burnt through the foot-thick wooden target.

"That's it! Pretty neat, isn't it?" Brady asked, as excited as a schoolboy. All activity on the testing range had ceased and about fifteen men and women who had been testing various modified Liberator rifles and machine guns turned to focus their attention on the grizzled veteran.

Rock hefted the pistol in his hand, throwing it an inch in the air and catching it again. "It's so light," he said to Dr. Shecter, who stood admiring the new weapon. Rock looked closely at it. It almost had the solid texture of metal but was some sort of feather-light plastic. Great to carry long distances. Rockson pressed a lever on the wall behind him that set a target with Colonel Killov's body and face painted on it, bobbing and weaving. He took aim through the weapon's tiny scope, got Killov's head in the three cross hairs for a second and pressed the laser sensor. Then he lowered the pistol and casually let the weapon rest by his leg. He flipped his hand up a split-second later and fired three hundred feet at the two-dimensional Killov. Again, there was no kick, no sound. The black death-beam shot forward and bent slightly to the right aided by the memory set of the laser sight. Killov's face melted away in a puff of bluish smoke, followed by a sharp retort from the imploding air rushing to fill the vacuum of disintegration. The Freefighters along the railing of the range all cheered. The United States had a new weapon.

"Kind of handy," Rock said, handing the pistol back to Shecter. "How long does it have before the charge—or whatever—wears down?"

"Beats me," Dr. Shecter replied. "We're still working on that one. Hasn't been recharged since it's been here and I'd say we've fired it at least two hundred times. It has other features as well, Rock. At least some we can find. And I'm sure we'll uncover much more about this weapon as time goes on. Just take this adjustment here." He pushed a calibrator on the side until it was next to the number one. "There—it's broad-beamed now. Could set a barn on fire at one hundred yards if you held the trigger a few seconds."

"Does this thing have a safety?" Rock asked, staring at the pistol.

Shecter smiled back. "Sure does. Just pull this switch here." He reached around with his thumb to the top of the pear-shaped butt of the pistol. "It's as safe as a Liberator," Dr. Shecter said.

"I'd hate to burn my foot off by accident when I put that thing in a holster," Rock said, looking skeptically at the head scientist.

"It won't be American feet that will be burned by this," Shecter said, putting the pistol carefully back into a gun box specially made for it. "I just pray to God Almighty that we can learn to duplicate them."

Twenty-Three

Twelve hundred miles to the north and west of Century City, a small man, dressed in a stained, gray laboratory smock, ran crouched over through a narrow circular tunnel only inches higher than he was. His large, hairless head, shaped like an egg, and huge brown eyes without eyelashes or brows above them gave him a top-heavy look, as the rest of his three-foot-tall body was shrunken and pale. Thin, splindly arms and long, bony hands with fingers as narrow as pencils trembled as he walked. His legs were hardly more than stalks that carried him shakily along the barely lit tunnel.

"I must relay data," Ullman, the leader of the Technicians mumbed to himself. "The others will be in timesynch, waiting for information reception." They would be sitting, the thirty-two of them who still survived, in the computer room, silent, waiting. And he, the thirty-third, Ullman. Ullman the Quantum. He who computed the trajectory of things and their time relationships. They were waiting for Vorn, the hunter, to bring back food. But Vorn existed no longer. His molecular stasis had been violently interrupted by a large carnivore with a powerful need for sustenance.

Ullman clicked a small transmitter button on an odd plastic device on his thin, synthalum belt and a round, steel hatch at the end of the tunnel slid smoothly open. Ullman stepped through, steadying himself against the wall as he prepared to climb a towering metal ladder above. Dizzy! Again. More and more now the spells came. Food? The disease? Who could

199

calculate for sure. But he knew there wasn't much time left. For he or the others. It was equated already—their fate. Death equals

$$\frac{Food/Health^2}{Rad.\ units \times .3176}$$

The equation was known. These things were simple. Absurdly so. Mathematics showed the truth to the infinite power. Still, they didn't want to die. They were, after all, human. Descended from humans. Even with their super intellects and their mathematical genius, the emotions of survival still stormed inside. What living thing goes willingly? Ullman mused. None—not a thorn tree, not a speck of lichen, neither a snarlizard nor a hydrabeast gave up its atomic essence willingly. Nor would he.

The leader of the last of the Technicians, all three-foot-two-and-a-half inches, sixty-nine pounds of him, looked up the dark cylindrical silo looming overhead like the dark jaws of the radioactive heavens. He wrapped his thin, chalk-white fingers around the third bar of the ladder and began his ascent, letting out a deep sigh. Every step was torture. His body had never been strong, but in his youth he had been able to run sometimes and lift objects as heavy as chairs or video consoles. Now, like all the Technicians, he was as weak as a baby. The mind of an Einstein in the body of an arthritic skeleton.

Ullman pulled himself up, rung by painful rung. He knew just how many steps it was to the fourth level where the people would be waiting, huddled together around the main console accepting data. He would have to tell them. There would be no more sustenance.

He reached the living level after what seemed like an eternity, his body pressed to the limits of its strength. He felt terribly tired, his small lungs were heaving for air, his pale face was splotched with dots of red, a sickly smelling sweat covering his forehead and flesh with a clammy dampness. He pulled himself onto the landing and stared out at the wide concrete expanse, with a single brilliantly lit room at the other end.

Even from here, he could see them, at the window, staring out, with the remaining functioning computer whirring behind them, flashing amber and green signal lights.

He walked slowly across the expanse, his huge eyes able to see clearly into every corner of the football-field-size level. At the far ends of the floor were the stacked chairs, tables, dishes and belongings of the original inhabitants of the silos. The accessories were far too big for the Technicians to use and so the goods had all been dragged off nearly thirty years ago, to make way for a planned scientific complex of factories, a highly ambitious plan to begin manufacturing some of the Technicians' revolutionary inventions. A plan that had never materialized. The last two generations had grown weaker from disease and slow radiation poisoning of the highly hot soil that still covered the silos. Plutonium, strontium, iridium—radmetals with half lives of up to twenty thousand years. They had grown weaker and infertile. Fewer and fewer children had been born—until, in Ullman's generation, not one. They were dying. It seemed ironic somehow. After putting all their power and energy into pure science for the last hundred years, to somehow better mankind, and perhaps someday reclaim America—the Technicians had let their bodies waste away, smaller and smaller, until now they were literally disintegrating into nothingness. And soon they would be nothing, like Vorn.

Ullman reached the living quarters and again pushed a match-head-sized button on his control belt. The door slid open and the leader wearily trod up the three metal steps to the large, open computer room. The people looked at him. All of them stared silently, trying to read his thoughts—Reva, Ret, Karlo, Oeten, Spath, Nasqwar and the others. They looked, their eyes dark as he had ever seen them, dark as midnight without moon or stars.

"No," Ullman whispered softly. "No, there is no sustenance. There is no Vorn. They are negative quantities."

"What was his final equation?" Oeten asked, his toothless mouth moving like a piece of drooping rubber.

"He equated Carnivore × Food Factor = Death for Passing

201

Technician. I have returned from the sighting. I propelled for three cycles through the radlayers. Look at my protective covering."

He held out his spidery arms which had been singed and blistered with red bumps from the sun's rays and the radioactive sands for three days. He had never been above ground for more than two hours in his life, and now he had spent three cycles looking for Vorn. "I survived by $Q = VR^2 \times$ constant .29998/water-heat loss."

".2 return probability," Reva said softly, looking at Ullman with longing. She had prayed to whatever gods there were for his safe return. She felt hidden factors for the leader. Though he had never accepted input on his sexual energy bands.

"I beat the odds," Ullman grinned sarcastically for a moment, then let his face fall back into its usual dead, thin-lipped expression of hopelessness.

"My people," Ullman said, letting his wasting body collapse onto a plastic semi-seat. "We, the Technicians, are at the end of our continuum. We can no longer receive sustenance factors to maintain our physical structure and without carbohydrate and protein fuels we shall soon be energyless.

$$\frac{Physicality = FF^3 \times .78002}{Energy\ Loss \times Age}$$

Anyone wish to equate?"

There was silence. They all knew the answer. Vorn had just kept them functioning at a minimal level for years. His forays into the outer world had brought back elk and deer and buffalo backs. Somehow they had continued to survive. But no longer.

"What is our function now?" Naras the Exponential asked, staring wide-eyed at Ullman.

"Our function is as it has always been—to explore every area of mathematics and physics. To uncover the secrets. The secrets that our ancestors—the Americans—had only just begun to discover before they and the Russians stupidly decided to end it all with energy dispersals to the realm E = 1,000,000 megatons of TNT + rad and heat factor of 7,926,786.30098 Death Quotient."

202

"They were so close to so much," Norad said wistfully. "If the old world had had what we've uncovered—the energy sources, the spectrum control—all Homo sapiens could have lived in comfort and peace."

"Ah, Norad," Ullman said compassionately. "You're mind dreaming again. What is, is. We are here and we are extinction. Extinction within two or three cycles."

"There is the paste," Exeter the Algebraic said, referring to the rancid flour stored for a century. It was edible—barely.

"Yes, the paste," Ullman echoed. "Very well, we will go and get more. I will require an exponent of three. We will have to carry the container three levels. And the last one caused sickness, physicality disruption."

"The paste, the paste," several of the Technicians moaned softly, their hunger taking away all but animal need. Even their minds, their intellects, so used to pure thought, to ideal states and intra-infinitudes. Those Technicians, who had dreamed only of formulas, of new fluid mechanics and laser optics, of particle expansion and light dissection. Even they could only think now of food, as their starving bodies growled aloud, stomach acids eating away at what little flesh and muscle remained on them. Digestive fluids filled their hollow stomachs, churning, boiling.

"Yes, the paste," Ullman replied, almost in tears as he saw the hungry faces of his fellow Technicians and how far and fast they were falling.

Twenty-Four

Willis, the Century City Council president, brought the session to order as the raucous Council members continued to argue and debate this or that issue with high-decibel vigor. Never noted for quiet, the Chamber of decision-making in Century City seemed unusually boisterous as of late, as if the members were anticipating some great, wonderful or disastrous event to befall them and were preparing themselves for the greatest decision of their lives.

"Order, please, ladies and gentlemen of the Council chamber. We have an important issue before us that must be decided posthaste!" He banged his wooden gavel several times and at last the democratic roar of the chamber dulled to an occasional whisper-broken silence. Willis put his right hand across his heart and turned toward the flag that hung on the wall behind him. The American flag. The real American flag— not the Red version with a hammer and sickle where the stars should be. The flag, hurt but not forgotten and still the symbol behind which the Freefighters of Century City and all the hidden cities rallied around.

"We pledge allegiance to the flag of the United States of America and to the past glory and the ideals for which it stands, fifty Free Cities, under God, for liberty and justice for all true Americans."

"Amen," Councilman Chalmer said, the only priest on the council and a staunch supporter of prayer and religious studies both as a link with the past and, of course, God, and as a means of countering the Reds' anti-religious, atheistic babble.

Rockson stood off to one side, a lopsided grin on his dark, rugged face. Willis glanced over at the white-haired mutant, his one aquamarine and one violet eye twinkling with amusement as they always did when he entered the Council chamber. Rock apparently found something humorous in the goings-on of Century City's political apparatus. Willis himself had to admit that the amount of hot air outweighed the true decision making by a hundred to one. Still, when the votes were cast, somehow things came out right. Free Americans exercising their right to choose, to decide for themselves, through their elected representatives. The collective mind. Not the mind in the collective as the Russians liked to implement it. That was the difference and the saving grace.

"As you all know," Willis said, addressing the restless Council reps, "Walt Brady returned recently from Expedition Five to the Northwest and had an amazing story to recount—which those of you who were present two days ago had the pleasure of hearing. His discoveries include the BlackBeam pistol, or Particle Beam as Dr. Shecter calls it, a weapon which could give us a tremendous advantage over the Reds. Now Rockson has volunteered to lead a second expedition back. Rock?"

Rock rose and walked to the Council stage, a place he had grown familiar, if never comfortable, with over the years.

"Thanks, speaker Willis," Rock said, resting his dark-veined hands on the walnut podium. "I'll need nine men and supplies, including ten riding and ten pack hybrids, weapons and ammunition, and food supplies for at least two months."

"That's a lot of material you're asking for, Rockson," McGuire, one of Rock's bitter opponents from way back, said. One of the "soft liners" on the council, McGuire challenged all the military expenditures of the city, saying the money should be plowed back into peaceful activities.

"And," Rock continued, ignoring the dig, "some special supplies that Dr. Shecter has cooked up for us."

"What special supplies might that be?" McGuire cracked from the back of the room. "Your own mobile 150mm cannon?" He looked around as he laughed but no one joined in.

"Supplies that are still experimental," Rock said calmly. He had been through too much to lose his temper at one misguided councilman. "I think Dr. Shecter would have to say anything about them. They're all under his supervision." Shecter sat silently at the far side of the front row of the chamber, taking it all in, remaining cold as a stone, as was his wont.

Willis broke in between the two before a real argument could get going. "Now tell us, Rock, why you think this trip justifies this output of supplies—at a time when supplies are in fact quite low because of the large number of Attack and Expedition Forces over the last six months."

"Chamber members," Rock said, putting on his best political smile. Why wouldn't they just let him get out and do his thing: fighting for and strengthening Century City and America. He was a warrior, not a damn manipulator of the media, currying everyone's favor with all that ass-kissing and kowtowing. Rock just couldn't get into the spirit. "We must go because of the potential power of the weapons that Brady has brought back. As I see it, the only thing that's ever going to make the Reds leave the United States is a confrontation with a force that's more powerful than they are. They sure as hell ain't waiting for any petitions. Force, blood, blasted fortresses, downed planes, tanks filling the plains like rusting cans in a dump—that's what the Red leaders understand."

"Thank you, Rock," Willis said as the Ultimate American stepped back from the podium and down onto the chamber floor. "Now, Dr. Shecter, could you come up here please and describe this new weapon that Rockson has mentioned. Tell us your evaluation of its military potential."

Dr. Shecter rose slowly and walked to the front of the filled semicircular chamber. A hush fell over the members—Dr. Shecter was the most revered man in all Century City. Single-handedly his inventions had transformed the Free City from a primitive village to a bustling modern city with every comfort. Shecter's arctic eyes took in every face, every friendly or malevolent glance, as he walked slowly, his arthritic leg acting up, to the platform and then up the steps to the podium. He faced the Council members. He didn't have to call for quiet. You could hear a pin drop.

"Good day, Council people. I haven't been here for a while but somehow I'm sure I haven't been forgotten." Several members chuckled at the memory of his last visit when he had engaged in an extremely heated argument for hours over the need for increased manufacture of the Liberator rifle so it could be shipped off to other cities. Shecter saw himself and his work as being bigger than just the needs of Century City and therefore often found himself in disagreement with the councilmen who were looking out just for the city's interests.

"My technical team and I have been working feverishly trying to uncover the secrets of the Particle Beam pistol. And frankly, I'll be damned if we've gotten anywhere." The aging scientist, dark spots and moles covering his long, narrow face, looked perplexed. He wasn't used to not being able to decipher scientific mystery. The doors of science and technology had always opened wide for his piercing analytic mind. "But, we do know that it's a particle-beam technology. I've read notes on the experimental work that was being done on them before the Great War. Apparently both the Reds and our own R&D men had been making great strides in the military application of such energies, then the war and— The bitch of it is, gentlemen," Shecter said, looking at his audience with fiery eyes, "we can't get inside the damn thing. It's made of a plastic synthmetal that's virtually impenetrable. I could blast it open with a laser probe but that would surely fuse the insides. No, Council members, whoever made this weapon has a highly advanced technology. I'm impressed."

"And what of the military applications, Dr. Shecter?" Willis asked respectfully from the side. "Are they worth justifying the expedition that Rockson proposes?"

Shecter was quiet for a moment as if trying to suppress great anger. Then he said simply, "Without question! If my intuitions about this weapon are correct it would make all conventional armaments instantly obsolete. The firing tests we've performed so far have produced astounding results. Range—up to five miles. Kill proportion: one hundred percent. Ammunition: none. The damn thing seems to have some sort of infinite energy source. That's what I'd like to figure out." His eyes lit up like shooting stars. "But, yes," he went on impatiently, "give Rock what he wants, for Christ's sake. We've got to get more of these and whatever else is out there and find out what makes them tick. If I had to make some damn fool statement to impress on all of you just what the power or worth of this pistol is, I'd say one Particle Beam Disintegrator is worth about, oh, say ten thousand Liberator rifles." He turned without waiting to answer more questions and made his way on slightly unsteady feet back to his chair at the front of the large chamber.

Willis looked out on the thoughtful Council members, fingering his wispy white goatee absent-mindedly. "Well, I think Dr. Shecter has answered our questions. Now is there any more debate or can we vote?" Several members grumbled, knowing that Shecter's forceful pronouncements meant unquestionable passage of the expedition. Willis called the vote. It was thirty-nine affirmative, eight opposed, three abstentions.

"Well, Rock, you have our full confidence," Willis said, looking over from the podium at Century City's top military commander, who leaned against the parchment-colored wall. "Good luck, Rock, and God be with you."

By midnight, Rockson had already picked his team. The basic Rock Squad, of course—Detroit Green, Al Chen and McCaughlin—and Berger, the explosives man. He had gone through the central files, sitting at the computer for three hours. He wanted this expedition to be thoroughly documented—and he wanted to be prepared for anything. Perkins would come as the city's most knowledgeable archaeologist. Rockson wanted someone who could decipher any of the artifacts they uncovered. Harris was one of the best trackers and climbers around and tough as nails. Slade was a sharpshooter and a linguist, which from Brady's description of the strange man's language might well be needed. And Rock picked Erickson, the Swede. They might be gone for months. And well, Erickson was one of the best cooks in the whole Rocky Mountains. What that man could do with cactus or rat's feet was truly a miracle. And he was a good, battle-hardened fighter. A man Rock wouldn't ever have to wonder about. Finally, he chose Lang, the kid. Tough, brash, somewhat of a troublemaker. He was only nineteen but Rock saw in him the makings of another Ted Rockson. The kid was a mutant like Rock—tall, with the star pattern on his back, dark blue eyes, like the seas in gale, dark skinned and strong as an ox. Someday he would be a leader—if he survived.

That was it. Rock signaled the End Search code and switched his monitor off. The computer fell to a dim hum as it rested its circuitry. Rock had his team. Now for the supplies and weapons.

At 5:00 the next morning, Rock and his nine-man team pulled up with their pack and riding hybrids in front of the back loading platform of Century City, a large concrete-walled warehouse from which Liberators were shipped out all over America. Shecter was standing there impatiently, his arms folded across his chest in that ever-present gesture of disgruntlement. Five of his weapons team had just finished loading the supplies in cartons and out onto one of the raised loading platforms.

"Howdy," Rock said, tying his hybrids to a tethering post. "Hope we're not up too early for you."

"Please, Rockson, I'm always up at the crack of dawn. As you get older you need less and less sleep. At the age of seventy-four I find I must obtain only three to four hours a night to be sufficiently refreshed."

"So what have you got for us this time?" Rock asked, smiling. Dr. Shecter was always coming up with strange new gadgets and weaponry that he wanted the Freefighters to test out for him.

"The usual mountain-climbing equipment, slip-on cleats, thousand-pound nylon test, pulley equipment. I think you'll find them much more efficient now. Acid-rain tarps and this time, Rock, I'm giving you all an alumasynth reflective poncho which should keep both the sun and the high-rad ground soil off you. We've improved the reflective capability of gamma radiation by eighty-three percent and dropped the weight by nearly half."

Rock remembered the old aluminum blankets Shecter had

had them try once. The things were heavy, cumbersome and tended to wrap around arms and legs when riding. The men had just dumped the things without a word. If Shecter had really perfected the shields they would be able to travel through the day even in the desert. The other members of the Expedition Force stood along the landing bay loading the supplies that Shecter's men handed them onto the 'brids. The backpacks were ingeniously devised to allow tremendous amounts of material to be stored in forty different pockets, twenty of them expandable. And the hybrids, at least half again as strong as the horses of old, could easily carry an additional 150 to 200 pounds of field equipment.

Men behind Dr. Shecter began bringing additional wooden boxes filled with exotic devices out from the inner laboratories. "Some things we've been playing with for some time, Rock," he said with that odd grin he wore whenever attempting to get Rock to try his most recent creations. "And this expedition is the perfect time to try them out.

"First," he said, reaching down with that long, bony arm of his into a large wooden crate and pulling out a cylindrical flashlight-sized metal object with air vents at both ends. "A solar-cell-driven condenser that collects humidity from the air and makes water. Depending on the moisture density in the air—anywhere from zero to a quart an hour."

"I'll give it a try first time we run out of water," Rock said, hefting the device and loading it into one of the side pockets on the back of his pack hybrid. He had chosen the palomino for his riding steed, largest of the 'brids that were going on the expedition. Rock had used the strong animal in Bear Valley and it had acted calmly. It seemed a highly intelligent animal. The horse looked at Rock as he swung back around to face Dr. Shecter. Large and broad shouldered, it had the markings of the palominos of the Old West. Stark black spots on a flawless white hide. A trail of reddish hair hung just below the stomach—a trait of all the hybrids, as were its pinkish tipped ears, almost flesh colored. The hybrid moved constantly as if anxious to start the journey while Rock loaded one after another of Shecter's supplies into the various packs he had cross-rigged over the back of both 'brids.

"Here, Rock," Dr. Shecter said, reaching into another crate. "An ultralight rad suit, not much bigger than a pack of cigarettes." In a line, moving from the right of Rockson, the other men of the team were receiving the same supplies and instructions from Shecter's assistants. Dr. Shecter always felt it incumbent upon himself to personally explain details to Rock. "I know you men don't put much faith in rad suits," Shecter continued, "and it's true that most Freefighters have extremely high tolerance for radiation. Still, Rock, there are hot zones out there that would fry any living thing. Even you. So please." He looked at Rockson with concern. The man wasn't exactly foolhardy but he didn't fear death at all. And that made him take few cautions.

"Positively, Doc," Rock said, slipping the small container holding the suit into his saddle pouch for quick usage.

"Now, this is something we're extremely proud of, Rock." Shecter beamed, pulling up another device. "An atomic cell inertial sextant navigation computer." He handed Rock an oddly shaped half-globe with various lenses affixed every few inches. "Just place it on any surface, adjust the small, expandable legs beneath it until these four bubbles on top come together and line up. Easy to use, works off either the sun or the stars. Can be programmed for locations, directions, distance between points. And under a pound." Shecter was positively glowing.

Rockson took the device. "Here, McCaughlin," he yelled out. "You're the sighting man. Here's a toy for you." McCaughlin walked around several hybrids, pushing them rudely out of the way and took the sextant, looked at it bemusedly and walked back to his own riding 'brid and four pack brids. He was responsible for all their larger supplies. Erickson, the cook had to contend with his own four packers, who seemed to be resisting taking on the mini-stoves and cooking supplies that Shecter's men were helping the Swede load up.

"Now, Rock, you like to use one type of shell in your .12-gauge pistol, the X-pattern heavy shot, but I've got something that I think could have numerous uses." He handed Rock a handful of loads. "Gas, Rock. Explode and release an invisible cloud of MR-3 gas. Anything within twenty feet will go out like a light. And it's non-lethal. Might feel sick as a horny dog in August for several days but definitely survivable. Just make sure you're at least thirty feet away. The winds break it down molecularly within seconds. Bio-degradable nerve gas." Shecter chuckled.

"Now this sounds interesting," Rock said, loading the shells into his cartridge belt around his waist. "How many you got of these?"

"Just a dozen for testing, Rock. The damn nozzle on the gas injector broke last week. All we have is these experimental samples. But they work." He handed Rockson the rest of the ammunition."

"I'll be sure to use one on the first killer dog pack that finds me appetizing," Rock said.

"Here's the emergency pack, as always," Dr. Shecter mumbled, handing Rock a small canvas pack about five-by-ten inches and just over an inch thick. "Poison tabs, anti-venoms—with serum in hypo ready to use. These poison things here, by the way, are much more potent than the old ones, Rock," Shecter said ominously. "We're using shellfish toxin. Takes three seconds. Just a jab of the needle and—no pain."

"Sounds wonderful," Rockson said, throwing the emergency pack into his forward saddle pouch. "I'll take a dozen."

"And last but not, as they say, least," Shecter said, picking up a lunchbox-sized container. "The medikit—has spray-bandage, plastisalve, seal-gauze, antizones, a mini-fluoroscope for locating bullets or shrapnel and, oh, etc., etc. You know what's in there, for Christ's sake," Shecter said abruptly, growing suddenly impatient with the whole procedure.

"Indeed I do," Rock grinned. "And have had cause to use all of them." Rockson had been skeptical of Shecter's doohickeys at first. But after they helped him out of numerous tight situations and saved his mutant hide again and again, he was a believer. He mentally memorized the location of everything he had just loaded. Once Rock placed something firmly in his consciousness, it was never forgotten. He glanced around at the other members of the Expeditionary Force Six. They were all loaded up, mounting their 'brids. McCaughlin still struggled with several boxes on his last unloaded 'brid. "Damn box!" he yelled, trying to balance the thing on the hybrid's curved back. Every time he reached for a piece of rope to tie it, it began slipping out of his hands. The others stared on, suppressing belly laughs.

"Well, Doctor, I hope we see you again soon and that we're all still alive."

"And I hope that your mission is a success, Rock. I can't overemphasize the importance of this strange race's weapon. Their technology must be incredible. These kinds of weapons would make mincemeat of Russian armor. Even fortresses could be directly attacked." He shook hands with the warrior. "God and science be with you, Ted Rockson," Shecter said.

Rock swung his booted leg up over the palomino's wide back and pulled the reins ever so slightly to the right. The hybrid responded instantly, giving off with a little snort by way of comment.

"Freefighters, we move," Rockson said, holding his arm in the air and letting it fall slowly until it was pointing straight forward. The horse walked slowly through a long, ten-foot-wide concrete road, its hard hoofs echoing like shots from the flat walls. The other men fell in, single-file behind Rock, talking, joking, looking back at McCaughlin who sat twisted around in his saddle, yelling at the pack 'brids as they juggled the supplies on their writhing backs, moving jerkily along behind him.

The multilayered weaving of netting, branches and leaves was pulled aside at the end of the square tunnel by automatic motors. Rock and his men emerged into the cool night air of the Rocky Mountains in the middle of thick woods. The branches closed behind them. The men ceased their chatter so as to be alert to every movement and sound of the night. Their hybrids picked up speed as they came to sloping fields until they were moving at a brisk trot. The half moon, misted over with the high purple clouds of the stratosphere, peeked from behind openings in the puffy layers from time to time as a billion twinkling stars rayed down from the heavens onto the mounted force.

The night was beautiful, Rock thought, letting his head drift

213

up across the infinite sky. He rocked gently back and forth atop the powerful hybrid, its thick muscles tightening and relaxing as its legs pushed the ground past. Rock let his eyes drop again until they were peering directly ahead into the gray darkness of the hills and woods. What was ahead? Only God knew that. But he, Ted Rockson, would find out.

Twenty-Five

President Zhabnov read the reports of the massacre of the KGB flamethrower squads in the Little U.S.A. sector of Stalinville with mixed emotions. He was glad that the KGB had looked bad, but did it mean that there was a serious problem in the American sections? And what was he to make of the attack on the KGB headquarters there and the blowing up of a major munitions dump? The natives were growing restless. Too restless! There had been a munitions depot blown up before he came but that had been years ago. What the hell was going on?

And the letter from Premier Vassily disturbed him. He had expected that the premier of all the world would at least chastise Killov, give him a slap on the wrist for his unauthorized use of N-bombs on the hidden American city. But the old coward had knuckled under to Killov. The colonel's faction on the Politburo must indeed be powerful. And Killov didn't like him one bit. Put the two together and Zhabnov could see that it all spelled, Goodbye presidency—or worse.

I must make my mark, Zhabnov said to himself after mulling it over for a while. The two Negro waiters who stood next to his desk in the Oval Office remained silent while he paced the room. They poured out new glasses of brandy when he stopped in front of them.

"I need to do something to impress the premier that I am as powerful as Killov, that I can do an even better job in keeping order than he." He spoke at the black servants, immaculate in their white tuxes, but looked at them as if they were chairs, inanimate objects who couldn't understand a word he was saying. "I'll also act to show that I'm more of a friend to Killov, more in sympathy with his plans. It's time to bury the hatchet with the colonel—to save my own skin when Vassily kicks off. Yes! It's a good idea." He downed a shot of the brandy and reached for another. The liquor was working its way into his blood stream, making him feel woozy and powerful.

"But how to demonstrate strength? How to show I support Killov? How to combine the two?" The Negroes stood, still as statues, staring straight ahead at the opposite wall, their hands folded neatly at their waists. President Zhabnov paced back and forth, his eyes blinking madly, as he bit his upper lip, deep in thought. "I've got it," he suddenly yelled, throwing his brandy glass to the floor with a crash. "I'll do what Killov did—bomb a hidden American city with neutron bombs." He would do what the KGB Death's-Head leader had done on his own initiative. "Yes, in retaliation for the attack on Stalinville from within and without. Yes, and that will make it look as if I'm supporting the KGB who were so cowardly attacked in their flame-thrower mission." Oh, how clever he was. The others thought him not as sharp as Killov or the cagy Vassily, but they were wrong. Yes, that was absolutely the thing to do. His own intelligence reports had determined that a city called Union City by its inhabitants existed in the mountains of South Dakota—right in Killov's back yard. Why tell Killov and let him get all the glory? Why not use this opportunity to strengthen the morale of his United Socialist States Air Force. He could have their Sukoyov-97 bombers attack the Americans with the N-bombs.

He would call in his top officers that afternoon and give them two days to prepare to attack—all in the name of retaliation. But the attack had to succeed, as Killov's had. He had heard disquieting reports that his air force had been cannibalized by Moscow officials who needed the parts for the Eastern Front—the war with China that was growing rapidly in intensity, as the Chinese mounted their thirty-fifth attack in the last century against Red forces on the border. But surely he had enough functioning planes left to mount a small bomber attack.

He picked the phone up and called his top air force general, Lavkov. A weary-sounding Lavkov answered the phone. He claimed he had been on duty for forty-eight hours without rest, that there had been a number of rebel bands sighted throughout the country and reconnaisance flights had been going out in droves.

"I want to see you immediately," Zhabnov said brusquely. "Drop all that stuff. I'm calling a meeting of the Joint Chiefs of Staff for tonight—nine p.m. in my Oval Office—you will inform whichever of your staff must be in attendance. Make sure they're absolutely trustworthy. You know what I mean." He hung up.

That night at 9:00 exactly, the meeting began. The mood was uneasy, for there had been no meeting like this since the Black Rebellion in the Detroit fortress back in '82. Then the army had been called out to decimate twenty thousand rioters, resisting a thirty percent decrease in food rations.

Zhabnov gave a speech about the defense of the conquered territories. And just in case one of the officers assembled was KGB, he offered warm praise for Killov's recent actions.

"I think we can all be grateful for Colonel Killov's recent success with atomic weapons. He has been an inspiration to me. Now we will carry out our own attacks with atomic devices as well." A murmur of amazement went through the Oval Office as the twenty-seven assembled Red brass glanced at one another in confusion.

"The air force will carry out the attack using two neutron bombs, but I want the army as well to conduct massive maneuvers near Stalinville so that the civilians and the rebels in that sector will know of the president's determination to have order maintained."

"The air force will have ten bombers up within hours of receipt of the neutron weapons," General Lavkov said loudly, rising from a chair near Zhabnov.

"I was thinking more like fifty or a hundred," Zhabnov said right back. "As a show of strength. Fly over Little U.S.A., blacken the skies, the mountains around the area with aircraft—"

"But, Mr. President," Lavkov interrupted imploringly, knowing he was treading on thin ice. "With the equipment we have—the shortage of parts—orders from the premier to cooperate with Moscow Central's requests—we would be lucky to get twenty bombers up there. Besides we'll only need one if we're dropping two devices."

Zhabnov's face grew red. "I said fifty, Lavkov. Didn't you hear me? This is not just for the rebel's benefit, but for Killov and even Vassily. I want them to know that the damned army and air force are still powerful here in America. That we can move and move fast, that we can strike like one of these American rattlers and kill. Do you understand me?" The general staff were amazed. They had never seen Zhabnov like this. So there was something there after all. Perhaps they had all miscalculated the workings of Mr. President.

"Yes, Mr. President, but—"

"Well, get as many as you can up there, Lavkov—at least forty. Do you hear me? Send up fighters, anything. I want them all to feel the power and might of the Soviet forces. We need good press in *Pravda*. How long?"

"Seventy-two hours, Mr. President," Lavkov said glumly.

"Don't fail me on this one," Zhabnov said.

"Yes, Mr. President," the Red air force general replied. "I'll get them up there." He saluted and headed out. He'd have to get every damn air base on the East Coast on ready to pull it off. And he knew he'd better pull it off. His head was on the chopping block and he could feel the ax descending.

By Lenin, I'm getting to be a tough customer, Zhabnov thought later, after the generals had left with their orders. He called up his research-and-experimentation director and asked how Project Lincoln was going—the plan to turn American slave workers into fighters against their own countrymen, the Freefighters.

"We are making slow progress," Kaminski said, "but just a few more weeks and—"

218

"No weeks. I want a thousand Americans in two weeks, totally programmed to go in and attack the rebels in the mountains."

"But—"

"Do it." Zhabnov hung up the phone. He had never realized it was so simple. Command—that's what it was. You just had to command them with the proper authority. Make them obey your orders with veiled threats. Zhabnov suddenly saw himself in a changing light. Perhaps he was even cleverer than he realized. The black servant filled his brandy glass. He was feeling quite heady. He was becoming a power on this planet. Killov and Vassily would be surprised. Surprised—and frightened.

Admiral Kashkin was on the phone to Colonel Killov minutes after leaving the president's meeting. He was, in fact, one of five KGB agents that Killov had planted in the top echelon of Zhabnov's military structure. And none knew that the other was an agent. Killov liked it that way—confusion, of which only he knew the truth. The colonel thanked Kashkin and hung up.

What the hell was this action by Zhabnov? And why all the praise for me? Was the fat fool up to some sort of intrigue? Killov stared out at the black silhouette of the Rockies at four a.m. He stared and thought and finally decided that the president was scared of him—that was it. Zhabnov wanted to show his support now that Vassily had knuckled under to Killov's policies. Yes, Zhabnov was doing all of this to ingratiate himself with Killov. He knew that soon Vassily would be dead.

But Killov would not allow the insincere act of Zhabnov's to sway him. Once he was in power, Zhabnov would be banished to the gulag—or perhaps eliminated, as he appeared to be slightly more intelligent than Killov had given him credit for. Killov loved to dwell on the thought of himself being the premier of the world. He knew what he would do when that day came—how he would extend his power efficiently, ruthlessly until it was truly a world empire. He would be the first man in history to rule the entire world. *The entire world.* And he would not hold back when it came to fighting resistance. He would use whatever means were necessary. Of that the rebels could be sure.

He sent a message back to the admiral to keep him apprised of all developments.

Then he called his intelligence chief for the East Coast to find out why he hadn't known about this Union City that Zhabnov was going to take out. That was the one really disturbing thing about this whole scheme—it showed that Zhabnov's own separate intelligence net was working at least as well as Killov's. That could spell trouble. Perhaps the president even had his own agents inside the KGB. He had half a mind to attack Union City himself first. But why? Let Zhabnov succeed or fail. It would be useful to know Zhabnov's real strength—when and if it came to a power struggle once Vassily died. Yes, let the attack on Union City and the army maneuvers proceed. It would all be very interesting.

Twenty-Six

Ted Rockson took the lead as the Expedition Force left Century City. His nine-man team would be aided by Brady's crudely drawn map, but Rock knew that much of the land was unstable and that the landmarks would change. Also, they would push further, much further into the unknown land, following the directions of the little man. And there was no knowing if his directions were correct. But Rock was prepared for danger. His entire life had evolved in the center of the hurricane of death and disaster that was modern America. He was forged to an iron toughness and thrived on forces of destruction that existed everywhere, behind every tree, beneath every rock. Rockson always met danger head-on and, more times than not, it was the attacking force that fled.

The line of snorting horses, with their wary riders atop, rounded the base of Twill Mountain, the next tallest mountain after their own Carson's Peak, beneath which Century City was built. Soon they were out of sight of their base. The horses crossed a babbling brook, stomping up a spray of icy water which brought the force to attention as it slapped their groggy faces. Beneath them the mountain trout swam madly off avoiding the horses' powerful hoofs. With the moon settling down to some privacy behind the hiding walls of the Rockies, the night became black, inky with the moving eyes of the burning stars following the Freefighters as they slowly made their way through winding mountain trails and pebble-strewn passes. The Geiger counters that each man carried on his waist,

221

hardly bigger than a pack of cigarettes, courtesy of Dr. Shecter, were silent. The trees stood tall and healthy. Pine cones littered the ground. Owls hooted out their mournful song hidden amidst the gently blowing branches.

It sometimes looked in this part of the country as if there had never been a war, a cataclysm. After a hundred years these forests were coming back strong. But Rock knew that this was in some ways an illusion. The vast majority of the United States was still sick, hovering between life and death as it tried to cast off its shroud of radiation. And from Brady's account— much of what lay to the northwest was more lunar than terrestial terrain. This was the last they would see of the old Mother Earth for a while.

The next three days were fairly uneventful as they made their way through wooded, mountainous land that was fairly healthy and lush. On the fourth day, they left the higher ground and hit the plains. Here the change in weather conditions had had a catastrophic effect. The wide open country had turned into a virtual dust bowl. Parched, with only tumbleweed and an occasional struggling cactus growing, the Freefighters had to wrap bandanas around their faces and put protective eye coverings over the hybrids as the dust and sandstorms raged around them. They walked slowly, single file, tethered one to another by rope. If a man became separated out here in this bearingless desert, it would most likely mean his demise. Rock kept the column going for eighteen hours. The hybrids moving at slow speed were able to keep up the energy expenditure. At last they came to a changing terrain. Still dry, but with vegetation: palm trees, fields of purple and brown cacti stretching ten, twenty feet into the air.

"Whoa, Freefighters," Rock yelled out, holding up his right hand. "We camp here." They had been on the move now for nearly thirty hours. There was too huge a distance still to cover to get tired out now. Rock knew the importance of rest for the men and the steeds. Later, they might not be able to stop. The men bathed in a nearby bubbling, underwater spring and Erickson actually found some fruits and edible spinach-type leaves. They had a huge Special Salad as the Swedish cook called it and the men relaxed around a fire built from dead, dried out cactus.

"All we need is some damn marshmallows and I'd be in heaven," Detroit said, resting back on his pack.

"What the hell is a marshmallow?" Chen asked, sitting back in his black ninja outfit, the only clothing he felt comfortable in. His nunchakas hung loosely at his side. He carried a Liberator but no small arms. If he was in that close, his hands and his deadly feet, his nunchakas and star knives would be quicker than any gun.

"A marshmallow," Detroit said, still smiling, his white teeth glowing like pearls in the center of the coal-black face, "is a piece of heaven. Or so my mother told me. Now I must confess, being the honest man that I am, that I have never actually had a marshmallow. But my mother, who claimed to have had one when she was a child, told me the wonder of them. Americans used to roast them over fires like this. My mom used to say, 'Ain't no fire complete without no marshmallows.'" The men fell asleep wondering to themselves what this elusive marshmallow looked like and tasted like. One of the past foods of America that might never be known again.

The next day they made good time. The land was quite flat and easily traversed. They rode for a good eight hours before they reached the rim of the pink-misted lands that Brady had mentioned. The radiation picked up fiercely on their counters and Rock told the men to suit up in the anti-rad suits Shecter had given them. They rode into the mist which rapidly grew thicker. It had a sour taste to it, as if the very air were rotting. The 'brids kept spitting out gobs of saliva, as if trying to dislodge the taste from their long mouths. The Geigers went wild as they moved deeper into the pink fog. They could barely see ten feet in front of them as they traveled over loose dirt and gravel for hours. They kept heading downward at an increasing angle. Rock knew they must be far below sea level now. For men raised in the mountains the air felt positively thick down here at the lower altitudes.

Finally the mists thinned a bit and they came to the three volcanos that Brady had mentioned. The hot mineral baths too, which the men took instant advantage of to wash the grit and grime of days of travel from their greasy bodies. They camped on the base of one of the dormant volcanos and slept deep, their muscles relaxed as babies' from the heat-giving waters.

The next day they passed two huge H-Bomb craters, each some fourteen hundred meters wide. Still radioactive after a hundred years, although a black spikelike plant seemed to be growing around the edges of the crater, feeding from the hot soil. Once again they entered the pink mist, which became thicker for hours and then thinned out again as they came upon the expanse of jungle that Brady had described. Creeper Valley—creeper vines spawned by the mutated genes of the area's prewar vegetation. A dark dank jungle that should have been in Africa not the U.S.A. Another insane dislocation of the world's ecological balance. They headed into it, holding the reins of the hybrids tight as the animals seemed to be quite nervous about the terrain—and the squeals and croaks of a thousand hidden birds and arboreal creatures. They moved through the tangled world of beauty and death, through giant ferns climbing impossibly high, through huge multicolored orchids and flowers with petals as big as a man's hand. The going was slow and the men had to dismount and begin hacking their way through the dense growth with machetes and long knives.

A sudden stirring of the bushes to Rockson's right made him instinctively reach for his shotgun pistol. Not a second too soon. A huge, tusked wart hog dashed from the thicket right at Rock's palomino. The hog was only about three feet long but fierce as a tiger. The hybrid reared up in fear, pulling the front of its body out of the way of the charging tusker. Rock leaped out of its path like a bullfighter as the foot-long, razor-sharp tusks whizzed by, only inches from his stomach. The wart hog stopped on a dime and turned, preparing to charge again, but Rock wouldn't give it a second chance. Taking quick aim he pulled the trigger of the .12-gauge death-dealer and the right side of the hog's head disappeared in a splatter of blood and brains. It fell to the ground where it stood, strong, squat legs twitching and kicking for a few seconds.

"Saved us from certain death and bagged dinner," Detroit

said mockingly. Rock lifted the still-warm pig creature and put it on the back of his pack 'brid. Then they headed on, even more alert to danger than they had been. After another three hours of travel, with the jungle getting denser and denser, Rock stopped as they crossed a clearing. "Let's stay here for the night. I don't want any of these creepers for a bedmate tonight." And it was true. For, as the darkness descended like a blanket on the already murky jungle, the creepers, green and stringy, that were everywhere, seemed to begin moving, slowly, twining and reaching out for whatever they could grab.

Monkey creatures, lizards, large spiders—all became dinner for the carnivorous creepers which would slowly, without the animal realizing it, twine several of its long tendrils around the creature's legs and shoulders. When it tried to move it tangled itself deeper in this vegetable killer. It took hours to die, the vines slowly strangling the prey. Then, small needlelike hooks came out and attached themselves to the animals, sucking out blood until there was no more.

The men built several fires around the perimeter of their campsite to keep the creepers and other jungle stalkers away and settled down for the night. Erickson set up a whole little kitchen and roasted the tusker on a wooden skewer. The men usually made fun of his culinary abilities, until they tasted his latest concoction.

"How do you like the sauce?" Erickson asked Rock, as the team sat around the central fire eating huge slices of hog with a thick green sauce.

"As good as me mom's," Detroit shot out, his fingers greasy and teeth moving fast.

"What is it?" Rockson asked.

"Creeper juice," Erickson replied, ladling out seconds to Chen and Berger. The men all mock-gagged. But it was delicious. During the night, the creepers tried to creep into camp. They wove a path through the fires and began wrapping tendrils around Slade's and Lang's ankles poking out the bottom of their unzipped bags. "What the hell!" Slade screamed, bolting up suddenly at four in the morning. The two guards on duty, McCaughlin and Perkins, came rushing over, guns at the ready as the other Freefighters jumped up, reaching for their weapons. Slade jumped from his sack, and fell flat on his face as five creeper vines had him wrapped securely around both ankles. McCaughlin reached down and with a swipe of his foot-long Carter knife sliced the offending vines in half. The others had to suppress laughter at the way Slade looked going flat on his face.

"The old shoelace trick, eh?" McCaughlin said, helping the young doctor to his feet. Suddenly Lang jumped from his bag, kicking and stamping as if he had ants biting him.

"Goddamn things got me too," he yelled, pulling his own knife and cutting three of the tendrils that had wrapped several times around his left foot.

"Look, the packs," Rock yelled. They all turned to look in amazement as the creepers set about opening their packs, poking inside, searching for anything edible.

"Fucking things are like raccoons," Berger said. They ran over to their pile of supplies and began hacking away at the vines which pulled back into the jungle and the darkness. Rock posted more guards for the rest of the night and they kept a careful watch, patrolling the perimeter of the campsite with torches.

The men awoke groggily the next morning. They had nervously tossed and turned for the rest of the night, imagining green, leafy arms tightening around their throats. Rock let them have two cups of Erickson's Instacoffee before they broke camp. They continued to head at a slow angle of descent. The terrain grew less junglelike and suddenly, almost without warning, they were upon a long, flat volcanic plain. Rock checked the map Brady had drawn for them. It didn't check. He had been in the jungle for days and this land ahead looked like a dried sea bed. He hadn't mentioned that at all. He stopped the men for a minute and took out Dr. Shecter's navigation gizmo. He set it on the ground and adjusted the four thin plastic legs until the four bubbles on the top of the device inside a tiny plastic globe lined up into one. Shecter had said he had programmed in all of Brady's data so Rock pressed the Off Course readout. "Twelve degrees south," the device read out, "probable destination: eight hundred miles at course of three hundred degrees." Rock put the navigator away and noted the proper adjustment on his pocket compass.

They headed off across the absolutely flat, parched earth as hard as clay. The hybrid's prints hardly dented the surface. They had been going about four hours when Rock's senses suddenly went on full alert. He checked around him but there was nothing. No possibility of an attack when there wasn't a cactus, even a rock as far as the eye could see. He looked up. The air felt suddenly damper. There—storm clouds to the southwest. Far off, but dark black and purple, falling lower and lower to the earth. Lightning speared the sky again and again, breaking into streaks of slivered electricity, arcing across the entire horizon.

Rock hoped the storm didn't get too close. With that kind of electricity they would be sitting ducks for those lethal bolts out here on the flat plain. The rain traveled alongside them but far away for hours, dumping torrents of dark rain on the drought-striken region. It was the sound of the hybrid's hoofs slapping instead of cracking on the ground that made Rock look down. The cracked earth was seeping with running water. Within minutes the trickle became a stream of quick-running rain water shooting across the dry plains. They kept going. There was no turning back. Rock raised his right arm and swung it down quickly twice. "Let's move it, men," he yelled. The men slapped their hybrids wickedly on the sides and tore ass across the flatlands. They rode for nearly an hour as the slowly rising water grew to two, then three inches. The hybrids couldn't move at full gallop but with their powerful limbs were able to keep up a brisk run. Even they sensed the need for quick action.

Rockson's sixth sense picked it up first. Far away, a roaring sound like an approaching wall of—

"Men," he yelled, stopping them all suddenly in the midst of the wastelands. "We have to seek the highest ground we can find in, at most, three or four miles. There's a mudslide, a flood of wreckage and debris and mud coming at us. I've seen these before. They're—"

"Look, Rock, there!" Detroit yelled, standing high in the stirrups of his hybrid, scanning the plains ahead. "About thirty-five degrees to the right of our course—some kind of

227

boulder-strewn rise." Rock whipped out his field glasses and found the protrusion, breaking the horizon like a nipple.

They tore off toward the rise, watching back over their shoulders with dread at the thought of seeing the tidal wave of mud approach. They grew closer although the damned hill of whatever it was hardly seemed to grow. The water beneath the hybrids' hoofs grew dark brown, then black. Branches and several small drowned creatures floated by.

"It's coming," Rock yelled. "Keep it up, men. Keep it up." He stopped for a second and let them all ride by. McCaughlin seemed to be having trouble with the 'brids. He yelled at them over his shoulder as he tugged on the tether line that linked the four pack brids together. "Get on up, you dang mules."

"What the hell's wrong?" Rock screamed above the increasing din of the rushing water beneath them and the approaching storm above. He pulled alongside the rotund McCaughlin who looked exasperated, his face red and puffing.

"These fucking creatures don't know what the hell's wrong. They're just as stubborn as—well, as mules, which is to insult the mule. If Shecter can give us all these marvelous techno-wonders why can't he breed us a pack 'brid who works right?"

"We ain't got time to play," Rock said, pointing behind McCaughlin's head. The big man turned and looked out over the flood-swollen plain. He gulped, then gulped again. A wall of mud some sixty feet high took up the entire horizon. It came at them at twenty-five mph—and already looked a foot high. Rock pulled out his shotgun pistol. "Just keep a tight rein on 'em," he said and pulled the trigger about five feet from the lead 'brid's head. The thing took off like a bat out of hell, pulling its mates along with it. Instantly they combined in a stampede of fear. Holding on for dear life, wrapping the rope around the saddle horn, McCaughlin took off like a shot toward the other men ahead. Rock looked at the wall of blackness for a moment. They had maybe five more minutes. He turned the palomino around and urged it into a gallop through the slush, quickly catching up with the fleeing Freefighters.

They reached the base of the small mountain out in the middle of nowhere. It was about 300 feet wide and nearly 125 high. Hardened coral-like stone. The mud tidal wave was now only a mile away and coming at them like an advancing army. It roared with a deafening sound, the kinetic energy of ten atomic bombs contained within the rushing onslaught of debris. Pushing the hybrids ahead of them, the men quickly scampered up the side of the structure which was eaten away with countless little holes.

"I think this damn thing is an anthill of some kind," Rock yelled out to Harris, who knew almost as much about the wilderness as Rock, having been raised by mountain men before joining the city.

"Was, Rock, *was*. Definitely dead now. You'd see fresh dirt around the edges of the bigger entry holes, guards. No, this is dried out, old." They reached the top with no time to spare. The wall of thick, foul-smelling mud hit the dead ant hill with a smashing roar, rushing up the front of it. McCaughlin was still only two-thirds up—the damn mud was rising.

"Move," Rock yelled down. McCaughlin's rear 'brid was sliding in the mud. It slipped and fell in, instantly pulled to the side as the tidal wave of brown death flowed unceasingly forward past the structure and on, sweeping down everything in its path, enveloping the earth in thick, wet darkness. "Cut him loose," Rock yelled at McCaughlin as the other three 'brids were yanked backward, still tied to the flailing 'brid now totally submerged in mud. McCaughlin rushed forward and ripped out his Carver Woodsman. He slashed at the rope twice and it parted. The back 'brid, still struggling wildly for air and trying to right itself, was instantly sucked around the hill and off into the twisting lake of mud.

They watched from the flat rise of the hard structure as the mud crept higher and higher. They could see trees, animals, bushes and wreckage of every kind floating by, most of the once-living things now bloated corpses. An occasional monkey or field rat clung desperately to a piece of log or a floating square of peat.

Still the mud rose, threatening to engulf the entire hard dirt hill. "Turn the 'brids with their backs to the mud; sit them down in a circle," Rock commanded. They did as he ordered and got into the center. "Now fill the spaces between them with clothes filled with sand, pants, anything. It may not help much but it will give us another four or five feet which could mean the difference between life and death." The men complied, stuffing the space between the restless but lying hybrids with anything they could lay their hands on.

The mud slowed but still continued to ascend the hill. It touched the backs of the 'brids, who didn't like the idea at all but kept down at the repeated commands of their masters. Another minute would tell the truth. Some of the men prayed silently—surrounded by an ocean of blackness, of nothingness. Rock just looked out at the dark sea without expression. He watched it rise, acknowledged that it might take his life momentarily. He would rather have died fighting the Reds—but this would be good. The earth of the United States. Topsoil, rich material for growth in this dead part of the land. And he would join it. Part of his country forever.

As the dawn broke, shooting down streaks of purple and red rays onto the darkness, the mud began to subside. Slowly at first, as if reluctant to give up its recently held position of power, then quickly, the mud, stretched out to its limits, began crushing down on itself with its own weight. The sun came out brilliantly and baked the wet surface of the plain, now a good twenty feet higher than it had been the day before.

They waited two days on the peak before the mud had dried enough to walk across. The hybrids slipped and slid but managed to make their way across the rapidly hardening surface. Occasionally one would sink deep into the still-wet surface and would have to be dragged out by tying ropes to several of the other 'brids and pulling. They moved all day and into the night—a cold, clear night without a moon. At dawn they reached a plateau of shining mica, a good thousand feet above the plain. The Glowers' plateau, according to one legend.

Here, the sun again beat down on them like a furnace, the mica of the ground reflecting the sun's blistering rays back on them. They moved on slowly under the glare, for though the 'brids were tough, they too were susceptible to the temperature which hovered between 110 and 120 degrees. They saw dust devils spinning far ahead as the rock-surfaced land slowly changed back to a flat, lightly vegetated terrain. The rising heat off the ground created waves of rippling air and produced strange effects. Mirages would occasionally appear on the superheated horizon ahead of them. Trees, mountains, the far-off refractions of a herd of buffalo near a waterhole. Was it totally an illusion—or were these images somehow being transported wide distances through the reflecting light?

But the mirage that was most incredible was the one that occurred late in the day, after the intense heat faltered slightly and the men were happily able to take off their heat-radiation shields. The mirage danced enigmatically in front of them for over an hour as they plodded steadily on. They strained their eyes to make out the details in growing amazement. It was the mirage of a city—a city like none they had ever seen in their own lifetimes. There were buildings everywhere, tall spires with lights blinking on top—skyscrapers. There were hundreds of glass and steel structures reaching toward the sky. It seemed to be Salt Lake City if they remembered the pictures from their history books correctly. But they knew that all the population centers west of the Rockies were no more. How could something from the distant past be a mirage in 2089 A.D.? As the Freefighters watched in awe, they saw planes and helicopters circling the metropolis, the brilliant golden reflections of thousands of car windows and chromed bodies sending out dazzling sparks of light like a million fireflies in the gathering darkness.

The phantasmagoric image shimmered, sometimes faded and then came back as strong as ever. The Freefighters discussed what it could be, each offering his own interpretation of the unique phenomenon. Rockson remembered some of the basic physics courses he had taken as a teenager in Century City. He remembered reference to such an occurrence—only theoretical of course. As far as he could remember there had never been an actual witness of such an event. A time warp! An image from over a hundred years ago, trapped by the spatial interference created in the center of one of the hydrogen bombs that had demolished this region of the country. In another dimension, these people were driving home from work, typing in their offices, eating the evening meal, watching television, perhaps talking about the peace conferences that were taking place and how World War III would, thank God, never occur now, because both sides were negotiating so earnestly. They were locked forever in that day, the people of Salt Lake City, cast out of normal space, placed in the fourth dimension, forever. They relived one day in their peaceful existence, eating the same breakfast cereal, watching the same rerun on TV, laughing, loving, dreaming, in the fourth dimension. Forever.

Finally, as Rock's team plodded on, the image winked out. The men, who had sat transfixed on their rocking mounts, looked at each other, eyes wide, somehow wanting to share the moment. They felt sorry that they could see it no more. And each wondered in his inner heart would it not be better to be in that city in the old world, be in that forever-the-same-day land, forever, forever, forever.

Twenty-Seven

Premier Vassily turned the last page of the old book and put it down. *Notes from Underground*—a most profound and odd book. Dostoyevsky—in Vassily's opinion, Russia's most gifted writer of all time. But no one out there in Red Square could carry this book, no one could possess it. Such speculations on esoteric non-materialist subjects were forbidden. The state atheism would not allow itself to be challenged by such radical religious doctrines.

After the Great War, the peoples of the world, reeling under the blow of atomic destruction, turned to religion. In Russia, the survivors clung fiercely to the old Russian Orthodox Church. They disobeyed orders to work on Sunday and prayed in secret masses together, spreading not only God but underground propaganda. The KGB—at that time merely the security arm of the Kremlin, a spy network no longer needed after the war—went ruthlessly after all dissenters and religions, purging all views that the war was a failure. There were mass executions in the Politburo as well. The ruthless KGB Blackshirts kept the empire together through the reorganization period. They maintained the premier as a mere figurehead while they swept through the Soviet Socialist Republics killing all who doubted the party line. The KGB virtually ran the Soviet Empire for thirty-five years after the war, but when the great famines hit in the Thirties and Forties the rioting masses brought a revival of the traditional Russian leadership—the premiership—which again became the most powerful position of authority. With his new powers and the army firmly behind him, the then-premier, Aleandri Druznhy, was able to push the KGB down into relative obedience, their powers greatly stripped.

And so it had been until now, Vassily mused. Now Killov, the cleverest and most ambitious KGB leader for over half a century wanted the premiership. Already, rumors were spreading, with Killov as the source, that Vassily was a failure, was losing his grip of control. There were intrigues, spies—how many of his closest "friends" were Killov's men? Vassily rose on shaky legs and walked to the window. It was dusk—the changing of the guards was taking place, far below the Kremlin walls in front of the Lenin-Drabkin Tomb. What had been a foot of snow the week before was now, in August, a wet, muddy mess outside the Kremlin. The goose-stepping guards splashed but somehow didn't slip as they changed posts. The ever-present lines of heavily clad women, peasants and stooped laborers waited patiently in endless lines to see the only icons left in Mother Russia.

We have taken their religion and substituted dead bodies to worship. Vassily saw it all now—he was forced to see it from his daily reports of starvation, rioting and rebellion. The whole planet was ready to explode again. The war had all been for nothing. The cultures, the great religions of the worlds, the beautiful wonders—the Eiffel Tower, the Roman Palaces, the Acropolis, Paris, Venice, London, Leningrad, Tokyo—all were gone, all were now leveled, radioactive plains, swept to this day by deadly winds. And all for nothing.

The world was sliding slowly back into primitives times. Technology had stagnated in most areas for the past hundred years. Each year, the ability to build machines, electrical generators and weaponry regressed. As was the ability to service those machines still functioning. Even the Russians had let their technology stagnate, preferring to use what was left over after the war. They continued to produce tanks and rifles, but all R&D had ceased. Only the huge control station outside of Moscow was kept up to date as it still kept the forty spy satellites aloft—the killers that had shot down the American retaliatory strike with laser and particle beams. It wasn't really needed anymore as no other country possessed nuclear weapons. All were within the Red Empire now anyway—still the central control station was furnished with all the money it needed. It was almost a ritual offering to the past and the weapons that had won the war for the Reds. But otherwise, the entire planet was sinking back into the Middle Ages.

The empire Vassily had inherited in the bloody power struggles twenty-two years before had diminished in size. Half the south Asian peninsula was no longer firmly in control. The war lords there—some ex-Russian army officers—had carved out their own little empires. Nothing came back to Mother Russia from those places. China was nearly a third under the control of the fanatical Muabir, the Flame of Allah. His hordes of horse-riding crazed soldiers were attacking Russian convoys more and more frequently. Half of Indochina was immersed in mystical Buddhism as more and more monks burned themselves in protest. The Red troops were powerless to gain control of people who would kill themselves rather than submit. Everywhere, there was resistance—even Killov couldn't stop the American rebels. Stalinville had even been attacked by what the officials there had said was a five-hundred-man force, and a munitions dump had been blown up. These pesky mosquitos were turning into tarantulas, Vassily thought uncomfortably.

I am only trying to keep the world together under one power so there will be no divisions that will again become nations— nations that will eventually have another world war and finish off our tottering ecology. I am on the Earth's side. I swear it, Vassily said silently to that little bit of belief in God inside him.

Ruwanda appeared, holding the silver tray with his now twice-daily hypodermic injection on it. A hypo instead of his customary golden brandy. Everyone was plotting against him. Why were the lesions on his body getting bigger, the welts under his blue-green skin more numerous? Why were his legs more unsteady each day? Were the doctors in league with Killov?

Perhaps the doctors were giving him cancer not curing it. How was it that they couldn't cure him as they had cured so

235

many other cancers with the Tibetan drug—the Chi Gompo—a powerfully effective anti-cancer agent ignored for centuries by the "civilized world" which scoffed at the simple combination of herbs and minerals dug out of the Tibetan Mountains by red-clad monks. Finally, after the cataclysm—the Great War—when millions were dying of cancer every month, the doctors, ready to try anything, experimented with the ancient brew of the shamans of Tibet, discovering to their astonishment that the cure for most cancers had been created by Gompo Rinpoche in the Sixteenth Century.

Why didn't they get me the goddamn stuff, Vassily fumed. What was in those injections? Live cancer cells? A slow poison? Perhaps arsenic—something, yes. Killov couldn't wait for the premier to die a natural death. No, he won't leave me in peace. He's too eager to destroy the world. He's the one. He prayed again to his secret God. God, let me stop him—grant a dying man one request. Let me do this for mankind. Let Killov die before me; help me defeat him.

"Is something the matter, your excellency?" It was Ruwanda's concerned voice. He had put down the tray, come over and caught the premier as he began sagging toward the floor.

"Yes, Ruwanda, help me to my desk." He looked at the big broad nose, the ebony skin so flawless. "You, Ruwanda," he said, slurring his words, "you are my only friend."

"Not so, your excellency! The whole world loves you."

"The truth, Ruwanda, is I am despised. But I am a good man, in relation to history. I will die and I will go wherever animate things go and I will have little to be ashamed of. I am the victim of my circumstances. It was my destiny to rule the world."

"Your karma, your excellency," Ruwanda said soothingly. "You are doing the best you can. You are trying to save the world." Vassily sat heavily back into the chair; the African released his grip under the frail arm. The premier stared up at Ruwanda. "I'll let you know a secret, Ruwanda—the doctors are poisoning me. Killov controls them."

"You are imagining things, your excellency," the black slave said. "No one wants you to die. It would be too great

236

a loss."

"Ruwanda?"

"Yes, excellency?"

"I don't want my injection. Get me—get me some brandy. And then get me a priest."

"But there are no priests; your excellency knows that. All religion is against the law. Your excellency is tired. He needs some rest. His mind is cloudy."

"Then—then get me some sort of holy man. Call someone with *feelings,* Ruwanda. Feelings like me. I'm sick of all these cold, calculating assassins around me. Murdering doctors, ice-cold functionaries and statisticians. Get me a holy man!"

Ruwanda just stared at the frail old man. The premier ran his fingers through his hair—for a long time. He just sat, stroking the thinning, dark black, lightly greased hair. Then he said, "No, Ruwanda, you are right. I am foolish. There are no holy men in Russia. But there is something I must do. Tell my phone operator to adjust the transmitter to Top Secret Ultra Scramble. I want Zhabnov. President Zhabnov in Washington. I will save the world as the Earth wants me to. The only way I know how."

"Yes, sir," Ruwanda replied, heading off to notify the phone personnel. Vassily waited a few seconds for the circuits to be made and then lifted the red receiver from the desk. The satellite scramble disk turned on the roof as the radio waves were bounced off Satellite Communications Relay Five some ten thousand miles up and then back down to Washington, D.C.

It was five a.m. in Washington as the phone rang next to Zhabnov. He stirred restlessly as the young girls on either side of him poked him awake. Bleary eyed, the president picked it up, his heart pounding. Only one person would be calling him now. The little drugged girl stirred and smiled wanly from beneath the wet sheets.

"This is Vassily. Are you awake? Listen to me! Code Potemkin. You hear that? It's in your personal code book. Do you understand me? This is a direct order from the premier. I know you will carry out your command. Code Potemkin." He

237

hung up, without waiting for a reply.

What the hell was Vassily talking about? What was going on? Zhabnov stumbled over to his bedroom safe and took out the Top Ultra Secret—for the eyes of the premier only—sealed, leather-bound command book. He stood naked by the night table, his huge stomach and small organ casting shadows from the table lamp. The president opened the book to Potemkin and read, "ELIMINATE KILLOV—HE IS A TRAITOR. IMMEDIATE TERMINATION WITH EXTREME PREJUDICE."

Zhabnov slammed the book shut. Grandfather, he screamed silently. Thank you. Code Potemkin. Kill Killov. So now Vassily was directly allying himself with Zhabnov. That meant that not only was his presidency safe, but that the premier was grooming Zhabnov to take over. Yes, and between the two of them, surely they would be able to eliminate the Blackshirt leader. He was clever. But he was mortal!

At precisely 10:30 a.m. the next day, Killov was walking in KGB Central, Denver with his omnipresent elite bodyguards—with their head-to-toe black leather uniforms, knee-high boots and submachine guns over their shoulders—on his way to a meeting on the Mind Breaker's effectiveness. He saw Yablonski, one of his most trusted officers, walking toward him, smiling. Yablonski extended his hand, something he normally didn't do. Killov saw it as Yablonski's hand reached for his—a small, pointed object concealed in the palm of his hand. Yablonski's smile turned into a grimace as he leaped forward. Killov lunged to the side at the last second and the dart plunged into a guard's shoulder. Shellfish toxin. The guard slumped to the floor twitching, hands on his stomach as a thin trickle of blood seeped from his mouth and eyes. Killov's guards surrounded Yablonski and knocked him to the ground.

"Don't kill him!" Killov screamed. "Take him to the Mind Breaker." Killov was shaken. He had thought he was in total control. Yet his own man had tried to kill him. That meant an organization at work to destroy him. Something that he knew nothing of. But Yablonski would talk when the white-hot

238

needles plunged into his skull cavity. Yes, he would reveal everything. Killov glanced down at the corpse turning blue on the floor. He turned to another guard.

"Get rid of it," he said, motioning to the body. The KGB colonel headed into the demonstration. Now they would have a very interesting subject indeed. And he had thought the day was going to be boring.

Twenty-Eight

The Expeditionary Force headed across burning plains for days. Only an occasional black-spiked cactus or a strange multicolored lizard would show itself from time to time. At last they reached the foothills of the next range of mountains. Groves of trees, cool shade and underground springs bubbling lusciously to the surface awaited them. They ran to the water holes, men and hybrids alike pushing aggressively for space to lap some of the precious liquid up. Then they lay back in the shade with a breeze coming down from the mountain ridges ahead of them.

"The one good thing about heat," Chen said, lying flat on his back, his ninja suit sopping with cool spring water, "is that it feels so good when you hit the shade."

"Is that the same as the thing about Red bullets is that they feel so good when you pry them out of you?" Detroit asked. Erickson began to set up a small kitchen for the approaching night. They would eat good this evening.

Rock got up early the next morning, refreshed from the first good night of sleep for days and left word with one of the guards, Slade, that the men should rest up and clean out their supplies. "Just take it easy," he said with a grin, patting Slade on the shoulder. "I might not be back for up to a day. I'm scouting ahead. So just pull out the cards and rest."

Rock headed through the thick woods up into the foothills of the looming range of mountains, some of which poked into the clouds. He was looking for a passage to the West. According to the old Esso map he carried with him wherever he went, they were in what had been eastern Utah and the range ahead was the Uinta Mountains. He pulled out his binoculars and sighted the sheer rock walls ahead. No way would the 'brids be able to traverse those.

Rock walked through the meadows and larger and larger hills as he approached the Uintas. The land was thick with trees, birds chirping, small creatures rustling through bushes. It was alive, Rock thought, breathing the afternoon fragrances of the bursting flowers as they opened their petals to the sun and the passing insect, offering draughts of nectar. It always brought a warm feeling to his gut to see life slowly building its way back from the pitted wasteland. In the middle of nothing, life fought back. Maybe it was stronger than death after all.

He finally reached the lower slopes of the closest mountain. From back a ways, it had appeared that there was a very narrow passageway between this and the next towering monument of dirt and rock. If there was a pass it would save them days. He climbed the mountain, which quickly became much steeper than it looked. After an ascent of nearly three hours, Rock reached the peak. The sun was just setting and it was spectacularly beautiful. Rock could see in every direction at once. The plains they had just crossed were an enormous emptiness, flat and dead. Then he swung his head 180 degrees to what lay ahead of them—more mists obscuring the terrain, thick and impenetrable, a blanket of pink and purple and yellowish fogs writhing and covering the land for hundreds of miles. What the hell was in there? Rock wondered. It wasn't on Brady's map. The sight of the hot zone into which Rock and his men would have to travel gave him a chill. It looked dead and cursed.

He headed south along the ridge of the long mountain until he reached its southern drop. There, far below, there was a way through. A narrow gully, probably once a river bed, had sliced through the base joining the two mountains. He took out his binoculars. A stone pathway, smooth, a good four feet wide— perfect. He couldn't see a trace of lichen or any river life. The gully must have been carved long, long ago, perhaps in prehistoric times. He wondered if any of the American pioneers he had read about, in their treks to reach the West, had ever come across this same passage.

Rock started leisurely down the mountain, swinging back north. He knew he wouldn't make camp until late, but he had traveled many times at night. The darkness was not an enemy. Not to Ted Rockson. Deer, startled, ran as he approached. A herd of them, thirty or forty. Rock wished he had his rifle.

They were running low on fresh food. He reached the base of the mountain around midnight. The crescent moon was rising over the pine-tipped hills, making them look furry, covered with a hide of needles and cones. Rock passed a large swamp. Frogs croaked madly as insect life filled the air with fleets of stinging, biting mosquitos, dragonflies, water bugs and other assorted life of the lower strata of the food chain.

Suddenly Rockson heard a noise, different from the croakings and creakings of the night life. A sucking sound, like something being pulled down a drain. He moved to the edge of the murky green water and came upon an expanse of quicksand. A bearded man, only his arms, shoulders and head still free, was being pulled down into the quicksand pit. He waved his hands wildly, reaching vainly for the shore, trying to grab hold of a branch, tantalizingly close to his reach.

Rock ran to the very edge of the quicksand, testing it carefully with his foot before he advanced. He got to within about six yards of the wild-eyed trapped man. Rock reached into a back pocket of his utility belt and pulled out a fifty-foot piece of half-inch nylon rope. He quickly tied one end to a tree and threw the other to the struggling stranger. The bearded man lunged for the rope and, after missing it on his first two tries, managed to just touch the end with his fingers. He quickly wrapped two ham-hock-sized fists around the rope and began trying to pull himself out. On the other end Rock pulled the cord end over end, his arm muscles straining and bulging as he slowly dragged the man out of the iron-clad grasp of the quicksand. The going was tough; the stranger emerged only an inch at a time. The swamp would not readily release its quarry. But at last the man was free from his hips up. He began slithering across the slimy surface of the sand as Rock pulled. With a huge slurping and sucking sound, the man's legs and

242

feet came free. His terrified face at last relaxed into a smile as he realized he was out of the muck. Rock continued pulling and minutes later the man was pulling himself onto solid ground. He stood up, dripping thick, dark, foul-smelling swamp mud, and looked Rock in the eyes. Rockson was big, six-foot-three, but this fellow towered over him. Must have been at least six-eight going on seven feet, and 250 pounds. The man moved his mouth to speak, but no words came out. Just grunts. The man couldn't make a word. No wonder he hadn't yelled. The stranger, clad in buckskin clothes and boots, laid a big hand on Rock's shoulder and looked at him with a deep, sincere expression.

"I'm Rock," Rockson said, pointing to himself. He pointed at the mute. "You?"

"Archer!" the big man said with a proud smile. He walked several steps to a tree and lifted up a strange weapon that Rock had but a vague memory from childhood of having seen before. It was made of wood and had a stock with a large, curved bow at the other end. The man bent down again and picked up a quiver of steel-tipped arrows. Rock whistled. Lethal-looking toys. The big man took one of the arrows out and mounted it in the center of the device along a narrow shaft. He pulled a steel wire back, making the bow bend, and attached it to a hook just behind the arrow. The man pointed to a tree across the swamp, a good hundred yards away. He took graceful aim and pulled the trigger. With a *thwack* the arrow shot forward as fast as a bullet and instantly embedded itself dead center of the thick tree.

"Archer," the mud-dripping specimen of humanity said again, pointing at the tree.

"I see why," Rock said. "I'm glad you're a friend not an enemy." The man appeared to be trying to read Rock's lips as he spoke but Rock couldn't be sure if he could understand him or not. "If I ask you a question, could you nod yes or no to answer?" Rock asked the question slowly, letting the big man look closely at his lips. The bearded bear of a man looked at Rock and nodded vigorously up and down.

"Good," Rock said, smiling back. It was hard to tell if the man was mentally retarded in some way or just hard to communicate with because he knew no language. "From these parts?" Rock asked. The man shook his head, no, and pointed with his finger beyond the mountains. Then he held up both hands spreading his fingers, and opened and closed them three times.

"Thirty days. You came from there thirty days ago?" The man nodded yes. "You have others?" Rock asked, the man's face a foot from his studiously reading Rock's lips on every question. The man shook his head sadly. He held up a hand with five fingers and then grabbed it with the other fist and squeezed it. Then he pulled open his buckskin jacket and showed a huge scar that ran from his chest down to his belly button. The others had been killed and he escaped with that wound. Rock hoped he wouldn't meet the thing that got this guy.

"And now, where do you go?" Rock asked. The man pointed due west, the direction the expedition was heading, but wouldn't explain further. "That's where we're going," Rock said, "and you're welcome to come along." The man nodded vigorously and smiled, slapping Rock on the back. He uncocked his bow weapon and slung it over his shoulder.

"I'll call you Archer," Rock said, turning to the man as they walked down the mountain together. "Archer," Rock said again, pointing to the man's chest.

"Archer!" the big guy said, his voice sounding twisted, slurred. "Archer." He said it again and began laughing, pointing to himself. For some reason he found it amusing and said the name over and over again, laughing and slapping Rock on the back with the force of a bull elephant. Rock found the laughter infectious and soon he was chuckling too as they walked through the maze of pines and hickories that lined the lower hills.

Twenty-Nine

It took them another hour and a half to reach the edge of the campsite. Rock knew something was wrong immediately. The fire was too low; anyway, there should have been two fires going. He put his fingers to his lips in a gesture to Archer, and together the men moved forward in a crouch as silent as snakes. Rock's heart was beating faster. Whatever had happened was bad. Very bad! He pushed aside a large bush and looked down the hillside at the wrecked camp. Rock knew there was no one there, alive anyway. No voices, no breathing. He rushed forward, shotgun pistol in hand, with Archer close behind, an immense Carter knife, nearly eighteen inches long and glistening like the silver eyes of death itself, in his hand.

Rock looked around. Blood on the ground. Their packs had been ripped open; the hybrids were gone. Suddenly he saw a shape behind a tree. He felt sick. It was Harris, his throat slashed from ear to ear. Good God, what had happened? How could all his men have been taken? They were such good fighters. Chen . . . Whatever had taken them off was human—of that he was certain. Bandits, maybe. The mountain ranges of the West were said to be filled with cutthroat killers who preyed on anyone who passed. Rock looked around the site. Everything of value was gone. But no blood, other than around Harris. Maybe the others hadn't been hurt—yet. He saw a glinting in the dirt and reached down to pick up a knife. Primitive. Bone handle. Whoever these killers were, they had regressed tremendously. Maybe they were nearby. Rock hadn't been gone that long—the fire, although down to the coals, had been stoked at least two hours before.

Rock motioned to Archer, who on his own had pretty much sized up the situation. "Ban-dats," he said in that whiny guttural voice. Rock nodded.

"We've got to save them." Archer looked back and reached up for an arrow. He loaded it into his crossbow and nodded yes at Rockson. The two men took off at a brisk pace.

The trail the bandits had left was easy to follow. Obviously, they hadn't expected anyone else to be around to follow so they had made no effort to conceal their tracks. Bent branches and the hoofs of the hybrids spelled out the direction as plain as day. They had only gone about two miles when Rock smelled smoke from a nearby fire and heard voices, drunken and laughing.

Rock and Archer edged up to some bushes on a ridge just forty feet away from the bandits' hideout. In front of a small run-down farmhouse, about twenty men, filthy, teeth missing, half without shoes, sat around screaming and drinking deep swigs from cider jugs filled with home-brew. Rock scanned the entire scene. There—to the right, his men, tied to stakes. All still alive. They looked a bit worked over but Rock didn't see any deep wounds or blood flowing out of severed arteries. Several of the Freefighters were unconscious; the rest nervously eyed their captors. Chen stared impassively, waiting.

"Let's shoot 'em now," a drunken bandit suddenly yelled, jumping up from the porch and pulling out an old, rusted Western six-gun. He walked to the leader, Garvin, a huge man with a face full of scars and sores. "Now, kill 'em now," he yelled again. "I'm hungry!" The other men yelled out their agreement. "Kill 'em, Garvin, kill 'em now. We ain't et meat for days!"

The swine were cannibals. He suddenly noted the stack of bones behind the woodpile that fed their cooking fire. So they ate people and used the bones for weapons. Great, Rock thought. We've sunk this far. He looked at Archer who stared back. Unafraid. Rock knew he could trust this man implicitly. Whatever happened now, he had a good fighter by his side.

246

Archer pointed at his arrows and then at Rock's gun. Rock said "When I fire!" Archer nodded, he pulled out eight arrows and placed them in a little wire contraption beneath the stock so that each time he fired, an arrow would release into his firing hand so he could instantly reload. Rock pulled out his second pistol—a snub-nosed, nickel-plated .38. He had decided to carry an extra gun on the expedition just in case.

The leader of the bandits walked toward the prisoners with the second one, waving his pistol, screaming for blood. The rest of the motley crew rose to their feet and, licking their lips, started toward the imprisoned Freefighters. Rock gripped both pistols tightly in his hands. The scum would be upon his men in seconds. It was now or never.

He and Archer leaped over the crumbling edge of the rise, and rushed down a steep embankment about ten feet to the ground, firing as they moved. Rock got off two shots from each pistol before he reached the ground. Two of the killers fell, their chests ripped open, spurting blood. The bandits looked around in confusion. Then they saw the two men coming at them, a crazy-looking man with a white streak of hair across the middle of his head and a huge, hulking one firing some kind of wooden bow. They reached for their own archaic weapons as the two intruders came forward, still firing.

Surprise, Rock knew, was their only chance. They had to down as many of these slime in the next few seconds as they could—before they were armed and realized what was happening. Rock split to the left and Archer to the right, to avoid giving them too simple a target. Rock's shotgun pistol spoke death again and again. At this range, he was taking out two, sometimes three with a shot. Bodies flew backward as the heavy shot entered their soft flesh from less than twenty feet. Hands and eyes, shattered bones, and spilled guts sprinkled the already-bloody ground.

To his right, Rock could see Archer shooting away with the crossbow. He took out three of them, firing, jumping to the side and then reloading. But they were upon him. The huge man disappeared beneath a pile of bodies, only to reemerge a moment later like a giant from the seas, literally heaving the bandits into the air. He reached for his huge knife and began

247

slicing at anything that came near. Necks poured blood, chests were opened like sides of beef as the huge razor-sharp knife made target contact again and again.

Rock was in the midst of the screaming, confused bandits now. He fired at a mass of charging bodies. Fired at anything that moved. The shotgun pistol sent out hail after hail of death, finding faces and stomachs to bury itself in. Bodies fell around Rock like trees in a hurricane. He saw a knife coming at him and twisted around, smashing his gun butt down on the murderous hand—then he fired at the body attached to the hand and it flew backwards in a spray of red, knocking down two other bandits behind it. His shotgun pistol empty, Rock used it as a club, hitting at anything to his right while he began firing the .38 at the murderers who had tried to ply their trade on the wrong man.

The bandits, never used to a fair fight, their usual policy being twenty to one, were in a state of terror. They didn't understand what was happening. They were the toughest. They were the ones to be feared. Everyone in these mountains had stayed away from these parts as if it were hell itself. And now . . . They reached for rusty pistols and broken knives and charged. But who was attacking? It seemed like an army! The white-haired mutant was unreachable. Whenever they charged him he spun out of their path and blasted out of the whirl, taking out two or three of them at a time. The huge one was felling their number with smashes of his wooden bow, knocking in heads and breaking necks with each thunderous smash of his weapon. Brown, cavity-ridden bandit teeth littered the dirt.

The leader of the cutthroats, Garvin, saw Rockson in the middle of the barrage of death and saw his own men flying out of it, blood spurting from their dying bodies. Already half his men were on the ground feeding their guts to the earth. His kingdom was crumbling. In a rage, Garvin pulled his own bone-handled knife and ran at the white-haired killer, pushing his way through his own stumbling men. He came from behind, saw the spinning back of the stranger and lunged forward.

Rock felt the wind of the attack, a thousandth of a second before it reached him. He spun his hips around as the knife entered his shoulder, instead of his back where it had been aimed. Rock held his .38 to the attacker's face, the muzzle an inch from the man's nose and pulled the trigger. The face dissolved into a flurry of red as blood poured out the greasy mouth. The bandit leader tried to scream but only gargled death coughs. He sank to his knees as his brains began running like undercooked pudding down the back of his head. Then he fell forward, flat on what had been his face and never moved again.

Rock turned quickly and fired again as two of the thugs came at him, one firing a luger of some sort, the other swiping down with a two-foot machete. Rock caught the gunman square in the groin with his last .38 slug. The bandit fell screaming, slamming his hands over his missing balls. The second one brought the machete down in a screaming arc toward Rock's head. Rockson dropped both pistols on the ground and caught the machete handle as it reached him. He bent down and continued the motion of the attack, flipping the bandit over his shoulder. He ripped the machete free from the attacker's hand as he flew over. As the man spun round and started to rise, reaching in his belt for a second knife, Rock came down on his head with the machete. The dark-haired skull split in two, like a coconut. The soft, gray brain matter splattered down onto the ground as the dead bandit hit the dirt like a stone.

Rock waded into the remaining group, only eight now, swinging the machete like a sword. Two more stomachs were sliced open, their contents spewing out onto the bloody, charnel ground: a mixture of yesterday's food and quarts of precious blood from their dying bodies. A hand came out of nowhere, holding its own machete, lunging for Rock's heart. Rock stepped instantly to the right and swung down with his weapon. The hand, still clutching its weapon, fell to the earth, veins and tendons hanging out from the parted flesh.

Rock glanced to Archer who seemed to be doing fine, as he slammed another would-be killer to the ground, his crossbow turned club now covered with a sheen of red. Rock let his vision dart over to the Freefighters who watched the struggle from fifty feet away, screaming encouragement to Rock and his unknown assistant. Suddenly Rock saw two of the bandits running toward the Freefighters, machetes in hand. So they wanted to take out the ones who couldn't fight. Ducking from the pitchfork one of the remaining bandits lunged at him, Rock ignored his own little group of attackers and ran as fast as his strong legs could carry him toward the prisoners.

The bigger of the two bandits intent on finishing off their captives picked Chen for his first butchering job. He walked up to the diminutive Chinese and, with a twisted grin, raised the machete to deal the death blow. First mistake—never try to kill a martial arts expert. Chen's untied foot came flying up in the air with the speed of a ground-to-air missile. It caught the pimple-faced murderer square under the jaw, lifting him a foot off the ground. The man came down in a crumpled heap, his windpipe crushed. He gasped desperately for air, his hands around his throat, but could find none. The second of the finisher-offers had walked to the other end of the row of tied-up prisoners. He looked at Lang, the kid, who stared back and spat in the bastard's face. He raised his machete. "At least you will die," he sneered, bringing the two-and-a-half-foot jungle trimmer down toward the center of Lang's neck.

Suddenly, he was being twisted to the side. The machete buried itself in the ground. He spun around and saw the white-haired killing machine that had taken out half the clan. Rockson looked at the bandit with certain death in his eyes. Then he moved forward. The bandit kicked for Rock's groin, but his feeble strike was slapped aside with a laugh. The bandit reached for his hook, his personal weapon—a curved loading hook, with a dagger point on the end. He waved it in little circles at Rockson. "Come on, come and get it, white hair," the bandit chortled, his eyes wide and insane with blood lust.

Rock stepped forward suddenly and the bandit lunged, swinging the hook and ripping back. Rock swung his hips 180 degrees right around the killer, reaching over with his left hand and grabbing the grip of the hook. He jerked back, flipping the bandit through the air, and ripped the hook from the crazed killer as he flew past. The greasy faced, stinking cutthroat screamed and lunged at Rockson with his bare hands to strangle him. Rock moved like a flash, swinging his arm. The hook sank deep into the bandit's throat, exiting the other side of the stubble-covered neck. The bandit's eyes grew wide as if in surprise. Rock pulled his hand sharply back and the bandit's throat ripped out, trailing on the tip of the hook: tendons, windpipe and larynx, followed by a flood of blood. Rock threw the hook from his hand as the bandit gurgled his way to a writhing death on the bloody dirt.

He swung his vision back over to Archer who still battled three of the remaining mountain savages. Rock started forward but Archer slammed another into his kingdom come and the last two fell to their knees, screaming and begging for mercy. Rock quickly untied the Freefighters. They rubbed their wrists and their bumps and bruises from the bandits' brutal treatment, but they were OK.

"Thanks, Rock," Detroit said. "What can I say?"

"Say thanks," Rock said mockingly.

He got to Chen and cut through the leather thongs that bound the Chinese man's arms behind the six-foot-high post. "What the hell happened?" Rock asked. "How were they able to take you?"

"Rock, they snuck up on the guards. Somehow got 'em. I started in on them, but they held guns to Slade's and Perkins's heads and I just couldn't do my thing. Then they tied us up. Harris made a jump for his Liberator and—"

"Yeah, I saw Harris," Rock said softly. One of his oldest friends in Century City. A man who had befriended Rock when still a teen, who had taught him much of his wood's lore and shown him many of his survival techniques. He had seen Harris.

The Freefighters walked over to Archer who was holding the two remaining bandits on the ground as they pleaded for mercy. Everywhere were bodies and severed limbs. Blood covered the scene as if the banks of the River Hell had overflowed.

"Who's that?" Detroit asked, pointing to the huge, bearded man Rock had rescued.

"Just call him Archer," Rock said. "I found him stuck in a quicksand bog around the mountain. He's a super fighter and a good man."

"We saw that," McCaughlin said. "Goddamn guy's a

251

whirlwind." Archer smiled at the Freefighters and then looked sternly down at the whimpering savages.

"Look over here," Chen said, his face growing a slightly pale shade of yellow. They walked around to a long metal trough. It was filled with bones and the still-rotting flesh of recent dinners of Homo sapiens.

"It's incredible," said Perkins, the archaeologist and anthropologist. "Here in America. I wish we could study this phenomenon more. It's really quite unusual for an advanced Western society."

"Yeah, right, Doc," Rock said drily. They walked back to the two cowering cannibals.

"What the hell are we going to do with them?" Detroit asked. "Can't take 'em with us. They'll eat someone else if we leave them."

"Only one thing to do, fellows," Rock said, reloading his shotgun pistol. "By the authority vested in me as commander of official United States forces, I hereby sentence these men to death." Rock motioned for Archer to step back. The big man did so, spitting in disgust on the two wailing and begging bandits.

"Please, mister," one of them said, his nose twisted and broken, half his front teeth knocked out in some long-ago bandit brawl. "We wasn't going to eat your friends—just play with 'em a little."

"That's right," the other chimed in in a stuttering high-pitched voice. "We d-d-don't eat Americans—just Russians."

Rock walked over till he was about eight feet away. "Sorry about this," he said. "I'd rather not have to do it. But—" He pulled the trigger and the two bandits, minus their faces, tumbled to the slaughterhouse ground with slopping thuds.

"Should we bury them?" Green asked, sweeping his hands around the blood-soaked yard.

"No, let the mountain have them," Rock said, his eyes narrow and cold. "They'll be better fertilizer than they were people."

Thirty

Ullman sat in a stupor in the hard plastic chair he called home these days. He could barely move. The others were just as listless in their spots around the computer room. They slept and stared at each other. No one talked. There was nothing to say any longer.

Watching a species becoming extinct, Ullman thought bitterly, how exciting. Should be taping it all down for future scientists to study. Unfortunately for the leader of the Technicians, though his body was as weak as a dying blade of grass, his mind, the mind of the scientist, the analyst, was still crystal clear. The curse of consciousness, he thought to himself, to see everything. No possibility of self-deceit. It was so goddamn clear!

They were dying, were eating their own tissue away. Death wouldn't even have to expend any energy when it came to take them, their stomachs would have predigested them. So? So what? He looked around at the zombielike faces of the thirty-one. Why should we survive? Only those fittest—and all that. We are not fit enough in this postwar America. An interesting experiment by Mother Nature, her claws glowing slightly, that went awry. Nothing ventured, nothing gained. Countless races, species and branches in the Earth's evolutionary history had gone down for the long count. The dinosaurs, the saber-toothed tigers, the Neanderthal man. Really, the Technicians should have gone down in some eternal record book as the shortest-lived creature since the dawn of time. One hundred years. Almost to the day. Surely the Technicians had only two, at the most three days left.

They had used the rest of the paste, a foul-tasting decomposition of flour that had been stored a century earlier. They had gone down in crews of four—and then the murderous struggle back, hoisting the huge barrel. Two of them had been killed in that endeavor. And now even that is gone, Ullman mused bitterly, biting his lips. He felt like he was going slowly mad, witnessing the demise of his people. Death stalked the window of the room, glowing blue and wearing a long, black robe. He stared in at the failing Technicians. Ullman could feel him, could nearly see those hydrogen-bomb red and white eyes glowing in the darkness of the outer room. Mad, he was going mad listening to the sound of his own stomach growl.

Thirty-One

The Russian masons built the wall around Little U.S.A. higher and higher. Behind it they could hear the inhabitants gathered, singing:

> O beautiful for spacious skies
> and amber waves of grain
> O purple mountains majesty
> above the fruited plain
> America, America God shed his grace on thee
> And crown thy good with brotherhood
> From sea to shining sea

The wall-builders paused in their work and listened to the cacophony of voices, the contrasting, rising choruses of the walled-in Americans who would soon starve to death inside those walls. The masons continued to work. This was a rush job, order of the KGB—and after they were done with the thirty-foot wall, they had to lay the barbed wire atop it.

None of the Americans some hundred feet away in the tire-rutted road tried to stop the masons. If anyone did, the KGB machine gun squad that strode back and forth atop the slowly rising brick cage would turn them into flopping, bloody dead men. But the Americans were quiescent, not resisting. Just singing and singing. They shifted to another song.

> Oh say can you see
> by the dawn's early light

The wall went up inexorably, unstoppable, at the rate of six inches an hour. The fifty-man crew who worked at this end of Little U.S.A. had been on the job two days and were behind schedule. They worked into the night, floodlights lighting up the area as bright as day. At every road, highway and alley into Little U.S.A. similar Red building teams were walling the inhabitants in.

Killov himself had directed the punitive measures. "Since they delight in dying in combat, let's take that away from them. Let them die without purpose—let them starve, let them die of thirst. The word will go out to the occupied workers—resist and die. I vow this," he had said to his gathered Death's-Head officers, "no more KGB Blackshirts will die. For every one who dies, ten thousand Americans must perish. Make them understand those numbers.

"My loyal officers," Killov had continued, addressing his top thirty men in America. "These are times of change. Great changes will sweep the face of the Earth in the coming decade. Premier Vassily is old. Soon he will be dead. I will be his successor. It is destined. You, my most trusted men, will accompany me to the very peaks of power. We shall rule the world." Killov went on, growing excited. His eyes strained heavenward, his hands clenched in fists. The officers looked nervously at one another. Colonel Killov rarely betrayed more than the iciest of exteriors. "But there will be much blood and destruction before our leadership will take over. This is necessary. I will call upon you all to make sacrifices and carry out suicidal orders. But I know," Killov said, "you will carry them out for me. Whatever you are called upon to do."

"Yes!"

"Of course, your excellency."

"Our lives are yours."

The voices bounced back at him, each louder than the other. Killov watched the eyes of every man. Who was the spy? Who was the assassin? He would find out.

At last the wall was thirty feet high, six feet wide and topped with its cherry of razor-sharp wire. Killov himself flew in from

Denver to Stalinville to make sure that the demonstration for the whole country would not fail. The senior KGB commandant of the Russian fort, Major Gorky, met Killov at the airport and accompanied him back to the main entrance of Little U.S.A..

The guards on the death-wall saw the official vehicle pull up. Everyone stopped as the honor guard below saluted and snapped their elite guard Kalashnikov Specials to their chests. Killov alighted from the black limo and perfunctorily saluted. He looked up at the ugly, gray brick-and-mortar construction. The KGB colonel ascended the wooden plank stairs and addressed Gorky who stood nervously behind him. "I trust that the wall is this high all the way around the three-square-mile area—with no gaps whatsoever?"

Gorky shook his head quickly no. "See for yourself, Colonel, with these excellent binoculars," he offered, handing the KGB commander the sixteen-by-sixties. Killov slowly scanned the wall and the crowd of ragged Americans gathered several hundred yards inside the Little U.S.A. compound. The buildings in Little U.S.A. were, at the most, four stories high, so with little obstruction Killov could see that indeed the wall reached around the entire ghetto.

"So," he said, handing back the binoculars and letting a razor-thin smile etch across his hawkish face, "they think they can do without us. Well, let them do without our food and water. Without our supplying them with any basics, their pilfering and murdering bands will be stopped now."

"There is one thing, commander," Gorky began nervously.

"What's that?" the KGB leader snapped.

"Well, traffic is snarled—some of our convoys used to go through the center of—"

"Ah, yes. Demolish part of the sector, build a roadway through with a wall on each side. Call it Premier Vassily Highway." Killov watched a group of scraggly Americans gather and begin singing again. If we fire, Killov thought, they will die singing their patriotic songs, like martyrs. He barked out orders to bring up water cannons and mount them on the wall. "Let them be pushed back if they try to assault the wall. But don't waste the bullets. Let them die starving, not as martyrs. Let them be contained like animals and die like animals. Animals in the pound." He gave strict orders to mix poison in with the water they sprayed. That would make it undrinkable, of course. He smiled. They wouldn't know until they started vomiting their guts out if they tried to save any of the water. The wall reminded him of some ancient history— before the Great War. He couldn't remember exactly where but a wall had been successful then too in keeping order—for a while.

Killov's lean figure descended the makeshift scaffold stairs from atop the wall. He glanced up at the sky. The damned clouds were moving in. If it rained, there was no way the KGB could poison the rain. The Americans could build catch basins and last a long time. Well, so much the better. To starve is just as good as dying of thirst—and slower. A better lesson.

Killov had other things to do. "Keep up the good work, Gorky," he said stiffly. The KGB commandant of Stalinville saluted.

"So good to have you pay us a visit, Colonel," Gorky said. Killov smiled wanly.

"Yes, yes. Well, keep me informed of their deaths. I want a weekly report of the proceedings on my desk each Monday morning." The KGB leader turned and entered the staff car. "Back to the airport," he commanded the driver. A motorcade of six motorcycles in front and two armored vehicles tore off to the outskirts of the fortress city. Killov had other things to do, other plans to make. Events were unfolding rapidly. The streets and shops of Russian Stalinville slipped past like phantoms. Tobacco, meat shop, a nightclub—he felt weary. What was wrong? He was forty-three. Perhaps that's what it was. But at forty-five he would be premier of the world. And then these walls would go up all over the country. Because as far as Colonel Killov was concerned it would be just as good to wipe out all the Americans and start from scratch. They had only been trouble from the start. If they used neutron bombs they could effectively dispose of the remaining twenty-three million population—and then bring in more docile laborers from Africa and South America. The country, what fertile soil remained, could be turned into one vast agricultural field to supply the kitchens of Russia. Yes, he had it all planned out. On paper. When the right moment came, he would run things his way.

At the wall, the masons continued their work as the water cannons were drawn up by pulleys and placed on top of the still-setting wall. Long water hoses led back down to fire hydrants, their connections spitting out little geysers of water as the hoses filled with liquid, waiting to explode.

The senior construction engineer, a KGB architect, watched as the water cannons were adjusted and secured. Then he gave the guards the order to fire the water on the milling American crowd on the other side. Killov was right. Let them suffer in their own filth. Let this be the lesson that the American workers needed. Once this lot had died, this whole part of town could be redeveloped into a new series of dormitories for American prisoner-workers. They would be imported from other cities, apprised of the fate of their predecessors and locked up carefully at night, to be released in the daylight hours only.

He walked up and down the wall, yelling out orders to the KGB guards who manned the water cannons. "Fire at will! Make them feel the Soviet brand of justice." He couldn't stand all that infernal singing any longer. His scarred face—from acid thrown by one of those street children as he had ridden through Little U.S.A. the year before—was still red. It wasn't responding to the plastic surgery. He had had no way of finding the one responsible for the attack. But now they would all die—including his youthful defacer.

The hoses were turned on full and aimed down at the crowds of ragged Americans below. They fell off balance and ran screaming as the water blasted into them with the power of a mule's kick, smashing them in the faces, knocking the wind out of their chests and stomachs. As they fell, the powerful stream followed them across the intersection, pushing them ever-backward, rolling them around like twigs in a stream. The construction manager watched the water push the crowd back, ramming them across the mud, against the walls of buildings, back and back into the rotting innards of the ruins they lived in.

Good, it was all working so well. Killov would be proud.

Several hundred yards away, in the basement of a four-story burned-out tenement, Sally was making a speech. Sally—the bagwoman—now the heroine of Little U.S.A., basked in her new-found status. She constantly displayed the ax with the bloodstains still on the steel head from killing the leader of the KGB flamethrower team.

A few of the rabble grumbled that her action had put them behind the wall—that they were beaten now. No food, no water. She had about fifty of them gathered about her.

"I am the smart one," she said. "I have a plan. Listen, folks, we gonna die. No matter what—we die. But let's die like the Black Dukes did—free, as Americans. We do something that makes the Reds know we not just sit and starve."

"What we do?" someone asked angrily from the crowd.

"Let's storm the walls," someone yelled. A rotund man with a patch over one eye and a scar down the right side of his face. "Build a battering ram or ladders and attack."

"You think they let us get ladders close?" Sally asked. "No, it all over for us but we take some of them with us. I say we burn the whole city."

"Burn it? What good that?" a voice screamed out.

"Fool, we burn yes, but fire spread to other parts of city. Wall no stop sparks, heat, flames—they die like us. All die in flames."

"I say ladders," the persistent voice yelled out. "Ladders try first."

"OK, OK, but you be fools," Sally screamed out.

They made crude, wooden ladders from scraps of wood in the ruins. As they had no nails, the twisted, uneven pieces of wood were held together with ropes and belts. "We make many ladders," the man with the plan said. "Give to fast runners. At night sneak up, put ladders up. Then we all come."

There were no lights on the wall except in the middle and on each side. The weapons the garbage people had stolen from the flamethrower squads would take them out when the moment was right. They would tear along the street. They would be slaughtered, of course, atop the wall, but some Reds would die too, and if they could gain control of the wall itself . . .

Five of the fastest, legs still firm, not wounded, took the ladders and waited behind a crumbling brick wall. The moon went behind a cloud and the garbagemen opened fire with their captured Russian rifles and pistols. Two of the floodlights went dead, their glass coverings exploding down the front of the thirty-foot-high brick wall. "Now, now," the crowd yelled behind them. The ladder runners tore across the open intersection of the once-bustling main highway. They made it to the wall though Red gunners opened fire with the water hoses and machine guns. All five ladders reached up, just short of the top. The maddened crowd of subhumans ran from the alleys, from the doorways, from the manholes and stormed the walls, scampering up the ladders. Half of them fell from the gunfire but some made it over the top. The first wave of assaulters became tangled in the razor wire, their faces and bodies cut to shreds. The others climbed over them, oblivious to their screams, and dove at Russian throats, slicing with their long knives.

Suddenly a whirring sound rose from the other side of the wall. Choppers—one, two, three of them, rising into the air just above the wall. Their powerful searchlights went on and instantly the scene of battle became brilliantly lit. The choppers began firing 50mm rounds, peppering the entire top of the wall with a deadly barrage of white-hot slugs. Their own Red troops on the wall screamed up, begging for mercy, but the chopper pilots had orders to take out everything, to stop any spillover into the Russian sector. The three choppers hovered for minutes, spraying their twin guns up and down, turning the already-dead bodies of Americans and Russians alike into bloody hamburger, shreds of flesh floating along rivers of blood, filling the walkway atop the wall and rushing over the side to create a waterfall of blood down onto both the Russian and the American sectors. The few survivors on the ground, who had been rushing the wall, screamed in horror at the instant carnage and turned, fleeing back to the cover of the nearby basements.

That night, Sally held another meeting in a huge,

underground storage warehouse. Hundreds of the dregs of humanity showed up to hear her.

"Now, now, you fool, you listen to Sally. Not be ants squashed by Red foot. They got many today but they not be able to stop Sally's plan. We burn city. Burn whole city. We die yes. But everyone come with us. Everyone." She laughed maniacally. And some in the crowd of tattered creatures joined in.

"Everybody die," they chanted. "Everybody die." They sang and laughed. The ultimate joke.

"We send sparks to Russian side. They wooden like us. Anyway they not have enough water to stop such a big fire. It kill them."

"I not want die by flame," a filthy, nearly naked creature said through his food-encrusted beard. Sally thought a moment, then said, "We build catapults. Throw fire, like Romans." The crowd cheered. "Yes catapults," they chanted back. "Like Romans. We kill. We throw death on Reds. They burn. If they come get us, we shoot with weapons from hiding place." Murmurs, shouts of agreement.

"That good idea," a woman screamed out.

"Yes good, good idea," they echoed around the dusty basement floor lit only by torches. They broke up into groups—each one responsible for making a catapult, though some of them had only the vaguest idea of what one looked like or how it worked. They spent the next day constructing the devices out of everything they could lay their hands on. Somehow the things were built, huge wooden contraptions using everything from immense truck springs to thick sheets of rubber, stolen from a Red truck convoy, to create the thrust for the catapult. They made six, twenty people working on each one.

That night the sky was filled with clouds. Thank God. They moved the catapults up to the crumbling wall some 150 feet from the Red barricade, carrying the torches that would light the ammo. Sally was with the catapult on the far left. They would light the world with their fiery deed, she thought, as the torches touched the huge balls of greasy rags wrapped around concrete chunks that they had piled in huge bunches next to each catapult.

"Go," Sally screamed. The men on her catapult pushed the lever and the metal springs released the eight-foot-long wooden shaft with a huge, bent-in garbage-can cover at the end serving as a throwing bowl. Five of the fiery balls shot through the night like comets burning through the heavens, landing inside the Russian lines. One of the fire bombs landed atop the wall, instantly igniting a guard's uniform. He ran screaming over the side. The others hit, variously, a truck, a wood-roofed supply store, the street, and a guards' barracks. Because they had been doused with some sort of fuel—kerosene, gas, oil, whatever the garbage people had been able to scrounge up—they quickly spread the flames to whatever they landed on, squeezing out a fiery juice that oozed in every direction. They fired again and again; the night became a storm of flaming death. The balls of fire landed on building after building, some crashing through roofs and walls. The catapults were amazingly effective. And the bag people cheered each time they sent another barrage over the wall.

For a while the Reds didn't know what was going on. Fire alarms and smoke detectors went off all over the eastern edge of the Russian sector. Then they got their choppers up and back came the incredible news: "The bastards have built some sort of catapults and are hurling the flame balls over the wall." They began firing down, but in the smoky darkness it was hard to see. On the ground, the assembled masses, now numbering close to a thousand, having crawled out from every little hole in this part of Little U.S.A., fired up at the Red choppers with pistols and rifles, with slings and bow and arrows.

"Keep firing," they screamed at the catapult teams. "Get as many as you can."

Commandant Gorky was awakened at 12:30. He had dimly heard the sirens, but as his quarters were on the side of the Russian section as far as possible from the stench of the American quarters, he hadn't heard them well. He was on the phone screaming orders in seconds. "Call out the air force. I want the area, the entire American sector bombed. Saturated with bombs. I want the place blasted to the ground. Do you hear me?" He screamed into the phone.

"Yes, Commandant," the air force major on duty said. "Yes, immediately." He pulled the switch that set off the airport siren. The Full Alert code. Pilots rushed over from their barracks and were suited up in minutes, their oxygen masks dangling over their faces. They were quickly loaded with high-explosive bombs and sent up in MiG 21s, armed to the teeth.

Sally urged her people on. The fireballs continued to arc through the night onto Russian buildings on the other side. The top of the wall was now enveloped in flame, the bodies of the Red guards and the exploding ammunition adding to the fuel. On the other side, the Russian sector was burning up. The wind was picking up, and blowing to the west, quickly spreading the flames. It was better than Sally had dared hope— the entire city might well go up. Every damn Red a flaming pyre.

"Everyone die," she screamed with joy. "Everyone die!"

The others joined in. "Everyone die. We all die." They laughed and pointed at the rapidly expanding curtain of yellow and red flame in the center of Stalinville. "Everyone die! Everyone!"

The jets suddenly screamed overhead, falling from the smoke-filled sky like hawks of death. The concussion of their blockbuster bombs could be heard all over the city. Black dive bombers dealt out death to the rebellion inside the walls. Sally watched the bombs fall closer and closer. She looked back at the dancing flames on the far side of the wall. She raised her fist at the closing jets. "We won! Not you! We won!" She screamed her throat hoarse as a five-hundred-pound H.E. detonated two feet from her scrawny body.

The sky was aglow all night. The Little U.S.A. sector was bombed for four hours straight, using nearly fifty thousand tons of explosives. When it was over, it was little but a rubble-strewn plain. Not a trace of life. But the Reds hadn't fared well at all. Fires still raged out of control. Seventy percent of the fort had been destroyed. The records buildings, most barracks, virtually all their armaments, tanks and cannons had gone up in a tremendous roar at three in the morning. There was little left to save.

In the morning, Colonel Killov drove slowly through the

sooty streets of the Red fortress. One of the biggest in America. Now in smoldering ruins. He couldn't believe it. It was impossible that the rabble of the American sector had done this by themselves. They were barely capable of excretion, let alone the construction of these insane catapults that Gorky had told him were the cause of the fires. Not one was left on the American side. Nothing remained but ashes. No, the underground, the rebels must have had a hand in this. Maybe that Rockson.

Killov surveyed the ruins in disgust. The great example he wished to set had turned topsy-turvy. It was the Russians who had been taught a lesson. They had been defeated again! A whole Soviet fortress. This was the first time this had happened, as far as he knew, in the whole history of the occupation. Was it all just terrible bad luck or were the Reds much more vulnerable than they could have imagined? Was this the beginning of a series of attacks in fortresses all over America? There were so many unanswered questions. What was wrong with his intelligence? He had thought it was in total control. But that was not the case. And even worse, his standing had been eroded by this escapade, just as Zhabnov was strengthening his hand. Killov felt his body tremble with a violent rage. His rise had been meteoric. He had never faltered. Never made a mistake. Until now. Others would question his power. It had been his plan and now it was his disaster.

Thirty-Two

Leaving the charnel ground, the Freefighters retrieved theire supplies and hybrids from the bandits' barn. Their bruises and lacerations were beyond tallying. They ignored all but the punctures and open cuts for these had to be sealed. The radioactive sands had a way of digging into wounds. The smallest cut left uncovered could be fatal in a high-rad zone. The men took out the medikits and used the plastisalve—cleanser, healer and sealer all in one—and rubbed it on every wound. Detroit had a gash, one he hadn't mentioned, that you could put a finger into. A gift from one of the bandits on the way to their hideout. He put salve on it and then spray-bandage, leaving a thick plastic seal over it.

"Hey, you need better medical treatment than that," Slade said, his doctor instincts acting up.

"Hey, relax, man. I'm A-OK. Sure as hell I am," Detroit shouted back. "Besides, when we get to these Technicians, I'm sure they have some computer-operated infirmary that will heal me instantly with some kind of purple ray." The men smiled weakly and tended to their own wounds from the bandits' pushing knives and slamming gun butts.

With the red sun starting to rise over the trees, they resaddled their hybrids and gathered what supplies they could find back into their packs. Some of their stolen weapons had to be pried from the bandits' hardening fingers, and then the blood had to be wiped off. Most of their things were retrieved.

Rock gave Archer the largest of his pack 'brids. The big man seemed confused at first, not quite sure just where to put his legs and butt. But after mounting several times he got the idea. He pulled the reins of the horse and it responded jerkily, not sure what he meant. It reared and then came down, running in quick little circles. The Freefighters laughed aloud at the exasperated Archer, who finally fell, thrown by the bucking hybrid. He got up and tried again. And again. By the fourth time the hybrid seemed to tire of the game and grudgingly began to follow Archer's brusque commands. Rock looked over at the big man. Archer had been an incredible help in the fight. It renewed his faith in providence. Luck had been on their side all along—despite their losses. And Archer, by God, could fight. And that crossbow weapon of his—such tremendous accuracy. The bearded giant of a man seemed to enjoy the company of the Freefighters and made quick friends among them with direct, albeit slightly strange, gestures and stutterings.

Soon, they were all mounted again and off over the mountain ridge toward the pass Rock had discovered earlier. Already, small forest mice were eating the cooling bodies that lay in piles around the blood-filled yard behind the Expeditionary Force. Buzzards circled lower and lower, eyeing the motionless bodies beneath their clawed feet.

It took Rock and his team a good two hours just to reach the opening of the long-dried stream bed Rock had discovered. The men entered it single-file, slightly apprehensive. If there was another cloudburst, they'd be trapped inside the cutaway, sheer rock walls on each side, climbing hundreds of feet into the air. But there was no choice. With Rock in the lead, they moved slowly through the pass, the hard hoofs of the hybrids echoing like gunshots on the close walls. They came to what must have been an avalanche fairly recently, with rocks and small boulders piled ten feet high. But using the muscle power of the hybrids and throwing some ropes around the biggest obstacles, they soon cleared enough of a path for the 'brids to stumble over.

They moved through the rocky passage for nearly four hours—the stream had been a long one. At last they saw the opening at the other side of the mountain. They came out on the pine-covered hillside and looked ahead at their destination. The fog-enshrouded plains that Rock had seen from the mountain top. They didn't look any more appetizing up close. Several of the men looked over at their commander. He just nodded wordlessly. It was the leader's duty to pull the men forward—even when they didn't want to go. They headed quietly down the hillside, then rode through several miles of brush and cactus-filled field before reaching the outer wispy fingers of the dense, pink and purple fog banks that lay ahead. Fortunately the fog wasn't particularly high rad. God knew what it was made of, but taking a deep breath, they rode into the mists.

They rode for hours, not able to see more than ten feet ahead. Keeping careful eye on the hybrid in front of them, and calling out from time to time to make sure they hadn't gone and gotten themselves lost, the Freefighters made their way across the sour-smelling, fog-encrusted plain. Rock kept checking his compass. It seemed stable enough, not rocking or spinning madly on end as it sometimes did amidst highly magnetized, radioactive rocks or stretches of land. They went on for seven, nine, eleven hours. Rockson didn't want to stop in the middle of nowhere. Besides, though the fog wasn't high rad, who knew what else it might be, though he didn't notice any horrendously painful effects taking place inside his lungs.

"I've got a weird feeling, Rock," Detroit said, riding up alongside the head man.

"What?" Rock asked.

"I've just been feeling that something is watching us from out of the fog. Had it for about ten minutes."

"Me, too," McCaughlin piped up from the horse behind Rock's. "Been seeing shadows out of the corner of my eye." The other men spoke out. Half the troop had been twisting and turning in their saddles, anxiously scanning the impenetrable mists.

They moved ahead slowly, Rock's senses radaring out into the blankness ahead. There—in the fog—running figures. Were they human? "Let's ride, men!" Rock yelled. "This way." They tore off after the fleeing figures, the hybrids pulling up alongside them. They looked primitive, like cave

268

men. They screamed and scattered again into the mist. Rock
kneed the palomino sharply in the left side. It turned and sped
into the mist. There! The creatures were disappearing into
some sort of huge structure covered with cracked asphalt. He
shouted to the others.

"Over here, men. They've gone into some sort of building."
The Force pulled up around Rock, and stared at the immense
squat structure. It was but two stories high but spread off in
every direction, apparently going on for hundreds of feet.
Broken windows, huge, nearly ten-by-fifteen-feet square,
stood every few yards along the wall nearest the Freefighters.

"My God, Rock," Perkins, the archaeologist said, "I know
what it is, I think. If my memory serves me correctly, from my
twentieth century American buildings, it's a shopping mall. A
goddamn shopping mall."

"A what?" McCaughlin asked, dismounting.

"Americans used to come to these structures to buy all their
goods—shoes, cars, food, clothes. Everything in one place.
The car was king then. And so, people drove to do their
shopping. The mall was the peak of the evolutionary scale of
the American shopping center. This looks like a classic."

They walked inside, through one of the large, now-empty
picture windows. Vast corridors stretched off in every
direction, filled with clothes, torn and eaten away, appliances,
dishware—all the goods America had coveted one century ago.
It was dark inside. The sun was falling low on the horizon and
the fog bank grew rapidly denser and blacker.

"I think it's worth exploring, Rock. In fact, we could hole up
here for the night." Perkins looked at Rockson hopefully.

"Got them primitives lurking around in here somewhere,"
Rock commented. But it was true. They had to stop. They'd be
blind out there with no light at all. Easier to fight off cave men
inside than get swallowed up by a pitch-black fog. They all
dismounted, tied their horses to the sides of counters, and
looked around. The men spread out, in pairs, their pistols
ready, safeties off. The Freefighters were fascinated by the
stock of the shopping mall. They had never seen so many items
in one place and all of them from the old America. They
prowled through the rows of dresses, shirts, lingerie, socks and

hats, picking things up, trying them on in the cracked mirrors that dotted the walls. It was like being in a dream. A dream of childhood when they had often had nighttime visits to the old America brought on by reading their history books in Century City's classrooms. Archer was just as fascinated, trying on jackets and hats and finding them all on the small side.

Rock walked along with Perkins, who kept explicating the importance of such a find. "Really, Rock, it should be turned into a museum. This is all most exciting. Why, look over here. Televisions, radios. I bet a lot of these still work." He picked up a transistor radio and turned it on. After a century, the batteries inside still managed to put out a tiny current. No music came through the Sony Walkman but static filled the little speaker. Even Rock had to admit, it was all quite amazing.

Rock suddenly saw figures by the far wall. Crouching, skulking along. Rock shined his flashlight up and the beam hit the three primitives, who covered their faces and uttered little high-pitched screams. They scrambled off, swinging their long arms.

"They never saw an artificial light before," Rock said, running toward them. The Freefighters rushed from different aisles of the main floor—women's clothing, lingerie, men's shirts and jackets—toward the fleeing creatures. They passed a large, open artificial courtyardlike structure with a fake fire and benches. The plastic flowers that had ringed the display still made their attempts at beauty but had become black with dust over the hundred years—ever since business had experienced a rather quick shutdown.

The Freefighters passed a dead campfire built in the middle of a marble lobby. "They can make fire," Rock yelled out to the others. "Careful, they might make spears or traps."

As if listening to this warning, a spear landed right next to Rock, clumsily bouncing off a pillar to his right. The Freefighters flattened out on the fancy-tiled court that separated the two main sections of the first floor. They aimed their pistols into the darkness. Several yells of primitive glee or fear, Rock wasn't sure which, burst forth from the shadows. Three more spears came flying out, bouncing across the floor.

"At least their aim is bad," Rock said.

"Rock, I know this sounds crazy," Perkins, the archaeologist said, "but I don't think we should try to hurt them. After all, look at it from their point of view. These crazy, pink-skinned creatures come smashing into their home, riding atop hairy monsters and begin taking over the place. You see?"

"I get the drift," Rock said. "All right, let's give it a try the other way. Hold your fire men," he yelled out.

"Why don't I have a go at it?" Perkins said, poking his head over the top of a long glass case filled with earrings and bracelets.

"OK," Rock said, lowering his gun, but keeping it at the ready in case of a sudden attack.

"Hello," Perkins began, yelling out across the darkened innards of the mall. "We are friends. We are Americans like you. We're here to help you, not to hurt. To help, not to hurt."

"You go way," a guttural voice screamed out. "You hurt. You go way. We no want!"

"But we must talk with you. We are friends. If you're hurt, we can help you. We don't want to hurt you. Help you. We help you." Rock looked over at Perkins skeptically.

There was silence at the other end, then frantic whispering between what sounded like at least ten of the creatures.

"How we know you good?" a querulous voice asked. "How we know you not Reds?" Perkins stood up suddenly, ignoring Rock's hand motion to get down.

"Here, do I look like a Red?" Perkins asked. He stepped on top of the glass counter, spreading his weight at the edges so the thing wouldn't collapse. His baseball cap, big, oversized mountain boots, khaki uniform that somehow resembled a duck-hunting outfit, and sandy-haired freckled youthful face gave him an unmistakable appearance of Americana.

Hairy heads appeared about forty feet away, rising ever so slowly above a wooden display of children's toys. They edged forward nervously and the Freefighters could see that they were primitive indeed. Their bodies had growths of dark hair everywhere, covering their shoulders and backs, their legs and arms. Their faces looked somehow apelike with wide, square jaws, pushed-in, flattened noses and a narrowing of the skull at the back. The leader of the primitives stood in front of his clan, nearly naked, clad only in what looked like a loincloth, but on closer examination turned out to be a pair of blue boxer shorts.

"You no hurt?" he said, trying to put up a brave front, raising his shoulders high, filling his lungs with air.

The Freefighters all slowly rose until they were standing. They put their guns away, moving easily so as not to frighten the store creatures.

"We no hurt," Perkins said, jumping down on the aisle floor as Rock leaped over the counter and joined him. "Who are you?" the archaeologist went on. "Do you live here?"

"We are the shop people. Yes, live here. Always live here," the leader, the tallest of the creatures, said. "We thought you be Reds. They come here years ago and kill. You carry rifle sticks like them. We thought you kill."

"No," Perkins continued, walking closer to the tribe of huddling savages. "We fight the Reds too, like you. We are all Americans."

"Americans," the lead savage said strangely. "I am Floorwalker."

"Floorwalker?" Rock asked.

"Yes, that be my name. Son of great-great-grandfather named Floorwalker Macy. That be my name. That be all our name. We Floorwalker." Again, he raised his head high, obviously proud of the family title.

"Can you make sense out of that, Perkins?" Rock asked.

"Archaic expression. I think it's a title of a store employee in ancient times. Probably someone who literally walked the floor. Some sort of security perhaps. And Macy's, if I'm not mistaken, was a chain of large stores that sold general merchandise."

One of the savages in the crowd suddenly fell forward, hitting the floor with a thud. The others pulled away, leaving their fallen comrade in the aisle.

"Him hurt," Floorwalker Macy said. "Rip flesh and now red and blood." Slade walked over to the fallen primitive and looked at the young man's leg which was swollen purple from a nasty slash the week before.

"Grab me my medikit would you, Detroit?" Slade yelled over to the Freefighter. Detroit high-tailed several hundred yards over to the hybrids and came back with the kit. Slade quickly stuck a painkilling hypo in three spots around the infected spot, as the savage grimaced on the floor.

"Him hurt! Him hurt!" the leader of the primitives started up again.

"Calm down," Rock said softly. "He's helping. He's fixing the hurt." The leader looked suspicious, but folded his arms across his hairy chest and looked on curiously. Slade waited a minute or two until the local anesthetic had a chance to work and then sliced the wound open. Green and white pus oozed out of the infected area and dripped onto the ground. Slade wiped the inside of the wound down with alcohol and then rubbed in antibiotic cream. He sealed the wound with plastisalve and stood up.

"Good as new, Chief," the young doctor said. "Just keep him off his feet for two days and he'll be throwing spears like the rest of them."

"Good. That be good," the chief said eloquently. "We be friends now." He walked over to Slade and grabbed him in a bear hug. "Friend!" Slade's face turned red as the bear hug squeezed half the wind out of him. The other Floorwalkers ran over to their new hero and, one by one, grabbed Slade around the shoulders and pulled him close to their hearts.

"I think that's their form of payment," Chen said, watching with amusement. After all the profuse thanks were given, Perkins questioned the store creatures who sat on the floor grouped around the Freefighters.

"Are there any firesticks here or food?" Perkins asked, notebook in hand, as he took notes on the fascinating offshoot of the human race. The war had led to the evolution of man in thousands of isolated little communities. Adapting to their special needs and situations and helped along by the genetic engineering rearrangements of atomic radiation, countless new forms of Homo sapiens had sprung up throughout the world.

"Food all gone in store here, but there be more cans in Price Chopper Store."

"Price Chopper?" asked Rockson.

"Probably another food chain store. Don't forget, Rockson,

273

America was a huge, vast society with chain stores that sold every kind of goods throughout America. There was A&P, Associated, Grand Union—"

"My God, do you know everything about Americana?" Rock asked, smiling. "When do you get the time to learn all this stuff?"

"I'm fascinated by history. Someday there'll be a unified America again and we'll need to know her history. A country without a history is like a man without a heart, no soul, no spirit. We need every precise bit of our history that we can find and reassemble. Someday, Rock, this mall should be a museum that our children and their children's children can come to and learn of their nation's past."

"And those spears," Perkins continued, questioning the Macy's creatures. "You made these?"

"Yes, from pots and pans in Kitchenwares, sharpened over fire, beaten into points. Use kitchen knives too—tie to mop handles. We kill. Kill death dogs and cat beasts out in fog. Sharp!" he said, holding one up, handing it over to Rockson. Rock hefted the homemade weapon. It was actually very well balanced. He pulled it back and swung his arm forward, flinging the four-foot spear through the air. It flew a good eighty feet and twanged to a stop in the center of a pillar, still adorned with ribbons and paper garnishes of a century before, now yellowed and turned to dust from the relentless grinding down of time.

"We live here," the chief said, sweeping his hands across the vast, shadowed expanses of the mall. "I am Chief Floorwalker. It be that way since our fathers' fathers' fathers' fathers' time. We stay here, hunt and trap creatures that come near. We eat food from Food and Delicacies on second floor. We wear clothes from racks—" He pointed down at his new blue boxer shorts. "You like? There be more—" the creature said benignly to Slade. The Freefighters all laughed.

"Go ahead, Slade," McCaughlin said through guffaws, "take a dozen. You could sell them back in C.C. Underwear like that is hard to find." The Freefighters, even Rock, cracked up. The Macy's creatures looked on, confused at first, and then joined in. Laughter filled the darkened aisles, echoed up the

274

rusting escalators.

"Any Russians nearby?" Rock asked.

"Last time come—two, three years ago. We killed with spears. Many. We kill all. We have. Want to see?"

"What the hell is he talking about?" Rock asked Perkins.

"I think I have an idea," the archaeologist said nervously.

"Come! You come with us!" the leader of the Macy's people said, pulling Rock and Slade with his two huge, hairy hands. They went through a long aisle of gloves, mufflers and ear warmers and then through two swinging doors to a back room. Here, hundreds of mannequins, naked, waiting eternally to be clothed and displayed, stood silently. Floorwalker led them to the center and, pointing proudly, said, "Russians."

Rock and Slade and the other Freefighters gathered tightly behind, looked up and gasped. There, in full uniform, were thirty Russian troops. They had been partially preserved but had still decomposed over the years. Their faces were dripping, rotting monstrosities, held together with glue; their bony hands, flesh curdled down to a thin leather, clutched the pistols or weapons they had been holding when the end came. They were posed in positions of action—one Red with his leg lifted as if running, another holding up a Kalashnikov to take aim.

"Good? Yes?" Floorwalker said, looking at Rockson. The other creatures looked on anxiously, listening to his response.

"Careful, Rock," Perkins said. "I think this corpse museum has some sort of religious significance to them. Be complimentary."

"It's beautiful. Truly beautiful." Rock walked over and hugged the beaming savage, who grabbed him back. The people all cheered. Rock stepped back and surveyed the sculpture of dead flesh more closely.

"I think you've got a friend for life, Rock," Perkins said, examining the creation.

"I like their rifles," McCaughlin said. "Looks like they're still serviceable. Freshly oiled. These Macy's folk must take good care of their merchandise."

The Floorwalker clan seemed overjoyed by the enthusiastic reaction to their display of Russians. They exited the main lobby and walked out into the fog bank and then quickly back into another building some hundred feet away. The Price Chopper. They walked through the ruins of the supermarket. Cans, cans everywhere—mostly rusted to bits, some opened and eaten long ago. But not the prize that Erickson went looking for and found.

"Look men, Maxwell House coffee—two containers of it. We can have old-fashioned American coffee." They wasted no time, this being a treat of extraordinary dimension, and made a fire on the floor, brewing the coffee in a big pot that one of the primitives ran and got from Kitchenwares. They poured the bubbling, gritty brew through a strainer and into orange-and-blue designer cups.

"Goddamn delicious!" Berger said, starting a second cup. The men all savored the brew. The coffee beans that were grown in hydroponics back in C.C. somehow didn't have enough richness. These, on the other hand. Rock offered a cup to Archer and then to the Macy's creatures, who hesitantly took the steaming coffee and, after burning their lips several times, got big smiles on their hairy faces.

"This good," the leader said. "All this time we no know."

"Tell me," Perkins continued with his questions, trying to gather as much data about the Macy's people as possible. "Where are the women? Children?"

"We keep in other building, way in back. Pet Supplies—big building. Thick walls. Safe there. No come out. Many dangers here." He swept his hand across the outside window. What strange creatures were breeding out in that fog bank, Rock wondered, that put such fear into these people.

"Tell me," Perkins asked, leaning closer, "what do you all believe in? I mean, why are you here, what is your god?"

The Macy's man looked at him incredulously. "What our god? Macy's is God. We here to serve Macy's and Mr. Macy. This his temple on Earth. That why we keep displays neat. Take what we need but everything ready for business." The Freefighters listened in fascination.

"We keep store clean for when Mr. Macy come down from the fog and open store. Then he take us in giant Buicks and Toyotas down the highway to the home of the gods—New York

Macy's. There we live happy, no danger." He smiled as all around him, the Macy's creatures, sighed in appreciation of their myth they lived for and would die to protect.

"Mr. Macy be very proud when he come here and see store so neat. That why we kill Russians. They mess up place. No one can mess up store." He looked fiercely at Rock and Slade.

"It is very well kept," Perkins said dubiously, looking down at the leader who sat, his long, hairy arms hanging to the floor, in front of his people.

"We decorate store every Christmas—have plastic tree with stars we put up. Hold special sale on all goods. But no one comes. Never. You want buy anything?" he suddenly asked, looking hopefully at the Freefighters. "On sale, everything, plus ten percent discount for Americans."

"I think you might have a few sales," Rock said, looking around at the amused Freefighters. "But God knows what we'll pay you with."

Thirty-Three

The Expeditionary Force headed out the next morning after stocking up on several hard or even impossible things to obtain in 2089 A.D., courtesy of the Floorwalkers. Perkins had stayed up nearly half the night questioning them about their society. He had taken pages of notes and begged Rock to let them stay another day.

"Sorry, pal," Rockson said as they loaded up their 'brids. "We're already behind schedule and off course and I'm sure there are loads more surprises ahead, so—"

"But, Rock, it's so . . . so fascinating. These people have evolved a unique society in a hundred years, using just the materials at hand. It demonstrates the infinite adaptability of the human species. The isolated tribes that have sprung up around the country must be studied. As scientists it's our obligation to—"

"I agree, Perkins. But we also have a mission to obtain weapons that will help return America to us. That will have to have priority over all other scientific experiments for the moment. Sorry. Anyway, you can come back. They ain't going nowhere."

The mist seemed slightly thinner as they rode northwest from the mall. After several hours it began to dissipate altogether and they found themselves back on one of the many almost-dead plains that seemed to fill the midsection of the country. The sun was strong once they came fully out of the mist, but a constant wind blew across the flatlands keeping the men and the 'brids relatively cool.

They began passing ruins of towerlike structures. Spires forty feet tall, twisted red metal, arches in doorways, entrances twice the height of any human.

"Ever see anything like 'em, Rock?" Perkins asked, taking pictures with his 35mm camera.

"Not me," the man who had crossed nearly half the country in his days of trekking, replied. "They look functional somehow. Perhaps astronomical tools, or timekeepers, using the sun." Rock had seen pictures of the ancient Druid Stonehenge and the sundials of the pre-technological world. Perhaps these were part of America's distant past as well, though he couldn't remember reading about them.

"I've never heard of anything like this, Rock," Perkins continued. "There's something strange about them, though I can't quite put my finger on it."

They passed more of the slightly tilted metal towers, every nine-and-a-half miles, all pointing directly northwest, the tops of the towers just visible to one another. Perkins got Rockson to agree to a rest stop next to one of the structures and quickly shot up the ladder, snapping shots of everything. He reached the top, a kind of oval room, and yelled down from one of the ten large windows evenly spaced around the egg-shaped chamber, "Nothing in here. Just metal, but I can see back and forwards, just the tops of the towers. With mirrors you could easily signal messages." He poked around some more, trying to figure out how the structure had been built, finding no seams, rivets or screws. It was as if the entire tower was one piece. Impossible.

They headed slowly forward, keeping a steady pace that the 'brids could keep up indefinitely, provided they had their daily water and grass or wheat or whatever. Hybrids were extremely versatile—one of their major strong points being the ability to eat almost everything and anything, which they continually tried to do.

The sun crept like a wounded creature searching for safety beneath the horizon, as the sky turned green then ocher. As the beet-red orb fell lower and lower to the cracked, parched surface of the endless flatlands ahead, the stars grew brighter.

The northern lights came on like a kaleidoscopic light show of the skies, flashing, splashing, dancing across the purple-tinged sky. Curtains of super-accelerated electrons, caught in the magnetic intensity of the Van Allen Belt high above the Earth, poured explosions of rainbow shrapnel across the northern sky.

The edge of the sun touched the desert floor, then something happened. A noise—coming at them. High overhead but dropping. Something they had missed entirely thus far on their expedition—a Red drone flying reconnaissance. The drone, its sensors picking up movement below, zeroed in on them. There was nowhere to hide, nowhere to run. The ground was flat for miles with scarcely more than a few dwarf cactuses to hide behind.

The drone, veering sharply downward had detected their presence. The robot rocketplane emitted white thick smoke as it accelerated in their direction, its built-in scanners already transmitting information a thousand miles back. It was a big one, a ramjet model, equipped for long, long journeys, sweeping back and forth across America, searching for clandestine activities. And this time it had hit pay dirt. It soared in closer, gyros coming into play, setting the spydrone into a slow roll to keep it stable at its slowing speed as its cameras tried to focus on the "unusual presence" below. Somewhere in Pavlov City or New Lenin or Denver, some bored console watcher was growing excited. He had found something. He would get a medal.

The Freefighters drew their Liberators, put them on full auto and sprayed the craft as it circled above them a hundred feet away, trying to get a clear picture in the gathering darkness of the targets. But bullets wouldn't stop it—it was nearly two inches thick, alumnatungsten alloy. Even the exploding 9mm shells of the Liberators just dented it, making little pockmarks around the surface of the craft.

Detroit reached for two grenades from the crisscrossed bandoliers that covered his broad black chest, preparing to make a throw. Rockson put a hand over one of Detroit's throwing hands and motioned for him to put them back.

"It's not worth a try," Rock said, lowering his Liberator to scream at Detroit through the din of the rifle fire and the drone's loud engine. The Reds, in building the drones so defensively, with two-inch armoring, had had to put tremendous engines into them which burned up liquid and solid fuel by the ton. But then Soviet technology frequently preferred brawn over brain in such matters—and then had to strip the rest of the world to fuel its dinosaur-sized creations.

"You might hit one of us," Rock said, and Detroit lowered his arms. With the Freefighters spread out over several feet, firing from atop their 'brids, frag from the grenade could easily wound someone. Besides, the goddamn drone had probably already sent back its pictures.

Archer dismounted calmly from his horse, not really noticed by the Freefighters as they continued to fire. He took out a short arrow from his quiver, with some sort of small explosive device glued to the front and a spiral-shaped feather on the tail. Moving carefully, he placed the arrow in the groove of his crossbow and pulled a lever that caught behind the bow's thick wire and stretched it back. The metal bow creaked and locked back in place. Archer lay down on his back as the Red drone flew slowly lower, circling in a five hundred-foot orbit around the Expeditionary Force. He rested the crossbow atop his high knees and got the orbit of the screaming drone in his sights. He let it go around twice, pretending to fire and counting as he estimated the arrow's time to striking. On the third orbit, he pulled the trigger. The metal shaft shot out of the steel crossbow like a bolt of blue lightning. It shot toward an emptiness in the sky that was suddenly filled by the ten foot long, forty-five hundred pound spydrone. The arrow hit the unmanned craft at the very tip, where its guidance antenna and laser navigational transmitter and receptor were located. The explosive device on the arrow, made by Archer himself by pouring powder from twenty 50mm machine gun shells into a small, metal Band-Aid canister, was designed to create explosive power rather than shrapnel. It did its job. The arrow nearly tore through the entire cone, embedding itself deeply in the guts of the craft. As the explosive pack hit the outer armor it went off with a loud boom, startling the Freefighters below who hadn't realized what Archer was up to.

The drone seemed to hesitate for a second as if surprised, then it lurched wildly, its control mechanisms shattered by the blast. It spun end over end, completely out of control, and fell to the ground some twelve feet from Lang, who dove madly from his rearing animal, hitting the ground with his shoulder. The drone exploded on contact with the earth, its liquid fuel tank igniting into a wall of brilliant flame. Five Freefighters were blown from their steeds, crashing down onto the cooling earth. Lang scrambled away like a fish out of water as the pool of flaming hell spread rapidly out in all directions for twenty-five feet. Lang's hybrid screamed in mortal agony as the burning liquid oxygen mixture consumed it. The smell of burnt hair and meat filled the air.

Rock ran over to Lang who kept just ahead of the advancing wall of fire. He was almost free. The flames surged ahead and caught his pants leg. It burst into flame, quickly covering the whole lower part of his body. Rock grabbed a blanket from Berger's hybrid's saddlebag and threw it on top of the screaming Lang, pulling him back from the sea of twisting flames, as the drone exploded again, sending out a shower of white-hot shrapnel into the air. Rock dove to the ground on top of Lang, continuing to smother the flames on him with the blanket. He quickly extinguished them and dragged Lang, who seemed to have fallen unconscious, back to safety some hundred feet from the bonfire created by the crashing spycraft. The other Freefighters dusted themselves off and rose from the dirt. No one else had been severely injured. Blood was streaming from McCaughlin's forehead from falling on a rock. Lang's screaming hybrid mercifully stopped its death cries as the flames consumed it completely, eating away the layers of thick hide and chewing on the bones of the creature, blackening them with its fiery teeth.

The Freefighters gathered together around Lang as the drone continued to burn, like a torch in the now-dark night, sending up a glowing funnel of sparks and bursts of intense heat.

"He all right?" Detroit asked, looking with concern at Lang who lay sprawled out on his back on the hard ground. Archer came over and looked downcast. His shot, which had seemed so

282

remarkable just moments before, suddenly seemed like a mistake. His face was white, as if he had done the damage to Lang himself.

"Relax," Rock said, looking up and seeing the frozen expression on the bear of a man. "You did the right thing. It was an accident. Anyway, he's going to live." Rock cut open the pants leg with his bowie knife and ripped it apart, revealing the entire leg. It had been burnt worst on the upper thigh, where the liquid oxygen had actually made contact with his clothing. The skin wasn't blackened but was bright red and blistered badly. Huge, white bubbles covered Lang's leg as the limb began swelling from the damage. Lang moaned and tried to raise his head. Then he grimaced as the pain hit into him like a knife.

"Damn, that hurts!" he said, looking up at Rock.

"You're going to be all right, kid. Just relax. Breathe deep and keep your energy going. The worst thing you could do now is go into shock. Then your body really would be in danger. You've got to keep calm, keep control. Feel the pain but don't let it numb you." Rock stared down, his purple and blue eyes piercing into Lang's, trying to make him understand.

"I got you, Rock," Lang said, letting his body untense slightly. The pain was unbearable, yet he was bearing it. He let his mind go down to his stomach and breathed deeply. He would live. His leg would heal. The pain was just a meditation.

Slade quickly opened the medikit and cleaned the edges of the burn. He rubbed the plastisalve mixed with the antibio cream over the upper leg. Lang gritted his teeth from time to time, but seemed to be dealing with it much better after Rock's words. Slade sprayed the sealant over the burn then pulled out a disposable hypo with twenty grains of morphine. He injected the painkiller into the artery on the back of the leg and stood up.

"Should be good as new in a few days. Infection is the main problem now. But if anything can keep it away it's these." He held up the medicines that had been created by Dr. Shecter's staff, and packed them carefully away.

Lang rose to his feet, the ripped pants leg whipping slightly in the night wind. "Feels about a million times better," he said, his eyes a little blurred from the morphine.

"I can give you another shot or two of this stuff," Slade said. "But after that you're on your own. The stuff's incredibly addicting."

"Can he ride?" Rockson asked.

"He should be able to. He'll just have to keep the wound from rubbing against anything. Should be raised up. If you could rig up some sort of contraption," Slade suggested. Rock quickly gave commands for a rigging to be built using tent poles and rope and they hooked up a kind of raised sling device which kept Lang's right leg in the air. He was twisted around in his saddle backwards, but using a frame from a backpack they managed to rig up a metal and canvas backrest. The entire structure looked somewhat odd, but it functioned. The Freefighters headed out slowly, single file, Green holding tightly onto the reins of Lang's new 'brid, which plodded along lazily behind him. Lang was looking backwards. Through his pain and drug-hazed eyes he saw the charred remains of what had been his hybrid. Shackles! He had had the 'brid nearly three years. It would be missed. The flames of the burning fuel still sprouted orange and blue fingers but had burned down to a much lower intensity. The heat and the smell of charred horseflesh headed up, up to the stars twinkling madly in the clear black night, a million billion crystal clear eyes, looking down on the desert, on the planet, on the death that was occurring everywhere.

In Denver, the console monitor went dead. The soldier manning the twenty drone transmissions of the Far West Flight Group smashed his hand down on the video monitor. The damn thing was always blinking out. The drone had seen something—what, he couldn't be sure. He replayed the video transmission from the master recording tape. There—it was at normal altitude. He spotted a thin line of—were they animals? The sun was going down so the video image was very dark, and marred by the high-rad soil. The drone circled closer. There! He saw them suddenly. Men, firing from atop the wild hybrids that roamed the American countryside. Yes, at least three or four. The image suddenly went haywire, spinning around. He saw the sky, then the ground twist by and then . . . it went dead. So it wasn't the screen. Rebels. And somehow they had shot down the "impenetrable" Heavy Drone Soyuz II. He picked up the phone, keeping an eye on the huge display of screens relaying images from all over the ruined lands of America—deserts, dried-out lake beds, volcanos, cratered regions—the video recording of the destruction the Reds had caused across the American landscape. The recording was transmitted to central records for future viewing.

"Comrade, comrade," the second lieutenant, video corps, said into the cigarette-burned mouthpiece of the telephone. "I think you'd better notify the commandant. There's definite rebel activity far deeper than anything we've picked up before. The coordinates? Let's see." He went through the digital readout that accompanied the video imagery. "Make that Sector K, fifty-five degrees, twelve minutes west, north thirty-six degrees, forty-two minutes. They were moving in a northwesterly direction."

Thirty-Four

The Freefighters moved ahead through the night. Rock had to assume that the images had been transmitted before the drone had been blasted to whatever technological hell machines are sent when they die. Lang, looking bleary-eyed but out of the numbing pain of the first few hours, seemed to be handling his burns well. His strong, young body should be able to fight off infection with the help of Shecter's potions. The land remained flat—with occasional volcanos popping up like tumors from the ground every thirty or forty miles. The area had been saturated with Red missiles to take out the huge U.S. MX system—a network of highways through three western states, with trucks carrying the missiles, patrolling at least twenty miles apart. The Reds had seen those MX bombs as their biggest threat and had targeted nearly one thousand of their own five megatonners into the five hundred mile square system. Much of the land looked like the dark side of the moon. Nothing grew or lived. Bones sticking up from the now-dried ground were testament to the fate of creatures that wandered into this Godforsaken land.

The sun dragged itself out of the coffin of night with orange hands. The landscape once again lit up, showing its ugliness in full panorama—shades of gray and black. It looked as if someone had held a barbecue using a thousand miles of American soil as the charcoal. Rockson kept them going, twenty degrees further west than before, in case the computers of the Red control center tried to establish a bearing for them.

He rode back to see how Lang was doing and the kid was sitting up, eyes bright, talking with Detroit who held onto the kid's hybrid, the reins wrapped around his saddle horn. He was telling Lang war stories about other battles he and Rockson had fought together.

"Hey, Rock," Detroit said with a huge smile as the commander of the Expeditionary Force rode up. "Remember that time when we were both taken prisoner and they had us in that basement prison waiting for transportation and—"

"Yeah, Detroit, I remember," Rock said, raising his eyes skyward. "How could I forget it after hearing you remind me twelve thousand times." He looked over at Lang. "How you doing?"

"Just bring 'em on, Rock," Lang said, raising his Liberator from across his stomach. He lay back on the rest they had built, looking quite happy about the whole turn of events. "Like riding in bed," he continued with a grin. "Used to have dreams about this kind of thing. Just get me a better pillow and a good-looking woman and I'll live up here."

Rock grinned back. "Since you're feeling so good, we'll keep on going. I want to get as much space between us and that damn drone as possible."

"Hey, don't stop on account of me," Lang said. "Unless you see a diner. I could use a hamburger and a Coke." Detroit and Lang laughed.

"What the hell you been teaching this boy?" Rock asked Detroit as he turned his hybrid around to head back to the front of the line.

"Just the truth, Rock. Just the truth," Detroit yelled after him.

Rockson took the lead and fell into pace. But he couldn't get rid of the feeling that something was wrong. The sky was a sick indigo. Precognition they might call it. Something about the sky. He searched the indigo, laced with small, green strontium clouds that floated overhead like dead lillies in a swamp. He wanted this mission to succeed. Other missions had been important, but now they were tantalizingly close to the greatest success America had ever had in its postwar fight against the Reds. To fail to bring the knowledge of the Technicians back would be too much.

His senses went on full alert as his heartbeat quickened, preparing for danger. They had gone about a mile further on the never-changing flat terrain when Rock heard it: the dim whine of a jet. From the grinding sound of the whine, it was a big one. Within a minute they could see the big Soyuz II transport craft. The huge loading doors of the plane opened up from the front and figures leaped out. As they hit the air, parakites popped open above them and they streamed down, dozens of Blackshirts from one of the elite special forces team. Figure after figure jumped from the slowly moving jet until the sky seemed to be filled with the quickly falling parakites.

"Let's move it," Rock yelled, raising his arm and quickly bringing it down. Lang would have to hang on. They tore across the plain, the hybrids quickly picking up to a good speed as there were virtually no obstacles to watch for. They gave it all they had as the Freefighters kept hitting them on the sides with the ends of the reins and whispering in their ears to move it.

But the parakite force easily kept up; their curving orbits brought them ahead of the Americans. They were going to be cut off, Rock could see that. It would be better to be in a good position defensively than to be picked off the hybrids' backs. Rockson held up his hand—the stop signal—and the troop came to a whinnying, hoof-stomping, dusty stop. "Let's fight it out, men. We're not going to be able to outrun them so let's get our defenses as strong as possible." They quickly dismounted and broke down into their defense squads. Four men got out two machine guns and quickly set them up, using the pack 'brids, lying flat around the Freefighters, as shields. Berger and Perkins worked the small mortar and quickly set up range of 150 feet. Rock and the others set up their Liberators on the fold-out bipods that were built-in underneath the barrel. Detroit took out ten grenades and laid them carefully down in front of him. Five concussion and five fraggers. Each man did his job calmly and swiftly as the parakites came zigzagging down at steep angles. The Reds didn't want to waste time either. They circled ever lower, nearly forty of them in black leather gear, oxygen masks and goggles to keep out the dreaded radioactive air and soil. Some of them began firing their 9mm submachine guns from the armrests of their nylon paragliders. Slugs bit into the parched earth just twenty feet from the Americans' defensive circle.

"Let's get them, men," Rock yelled. He began firing his Liberator on full auto at the descending flying force. "And watch your backs—they're swinging around." He had hardly gotten the words out when a Red paraglider came swooping in from the back, barely ten feet off the ground and moving a good 150 mph. Rockson could see the leering face of the Blackshirt as he let loose with a burst of fire that cut right through the center of the defensive circle. One of the 'brids in the middle let loose with an ear-splitting bay of pain and began flopping around out of control. Rock opened up with his Liberator before the parakite had reached the other side of the circle. The bullets arced up, making target just as the skyrider zipped by. Rock's hail of death pounded through the nylon of the kite and into the Red's stomach and chest, slicing the man in half. His body, spitting blood like a fountain statue, fell from the parakite and into a lifeless lump about thirty yards past the Freefighters.

"That's one down," Rock yelled out to the Freefighters who were cutting loose with their own weapons. But the zigzagging patterns of the highly skilled Blackshirt parakite squad made them extremely difficult targets. Archer aimed carefully, shooting four arrows in ten seconds. Two found their marks, a hundred yards up and two hundred yards away, piercing the bodies of two of the elite squad troops. Their parakites wavered out of control and then plunged to the earth. The Freefighters cheered every time a Red went down.

But the first Blackshirt had landed. They quickly set up their assault-team equipment: light machine guns, a bazooka-type rocket launcher and other sundry Soviet field weaponry. Not waiting for the rest of their comrades to land, they opened up with the machine guns, hitting two of the pack 'brids in the side of the circle facing the Red gunners. They were ripped apart, dead before they had time to scream. It was a shame that the 'brids had to be sacrificed like this, Erickson thought. Lang, his foot resting up on a pack, handled the belt to the 9mm machine gun, guiding it up to Erickson. But their deaths meant our lives, Erickson rationalized. 'Brids had often saved the lives of their parties by affording protection where there otherwise was none.

With the machine gun resting securely on one of the dead 'brid's haunches, Erickson opened fire, cutting a trail through the rippled dry earth straight toward the Red gunners. If the Americans had hardly any cover, the Reds had none. The seam of death swept through the machine gun nest, tearing it apart with the force of a whirlwind. The big slugs tore through two of the Red gunners, chewing up their faces and necks into pulpy hamburger. The two flew backwards and lay motionless on the shell-cluttered ground. The machine gun, smacked by two slugs, exploded in the chamber, blowing apart and into a third Blackshirt, the barrel of the long machine gun ripping into the belt-handler's skull, piercing him like a lance. Dead eyes rolled up, staring up at a godless sky.

Two more of the KGB Death Squad, still gliding down, came in for another try on the Americans. They soared in from two sides, firing their subs from atop their hang bars. Rock saw the stream of lead coming a second before it slammed into the ground where he had been standing, making little clouds of dust spurt into the air. He dove to the side in the nick of time then, lying on his back, fired at the two crisscrossing Blackshirts. His shots hit one of them in the neck, severing his spinal cord. He fell face-forward onto the glide stick as the parakite glided slowly down. The second Red pulled a grenade and droped it as he flew overhead. He soared past and headed for his comrades several hundred yards away who were setting up a steady stream of fire on the trapped Americans. An arrow shot from forward side of the defensive circle and, spinning ever so slightly, slammed into the fleeing Red's buttocks at three hundred miles an hour, piercing the KGB elite's intestines and then lungs. He let out a bloodcurdling scream and fell thirty feet, landing directly in front of his own men. They turned their heads in disgust at the still-lanced, bloody corpse and set up their lines of fire. Within five minutes all thirty-six survivors of the drop were organized into strike teams. One advanced slowly, crawling on their bellies, sending out a blizzard of fire from three machine guns, while the other two worked their way around to either flank. They would soon have the Americans cut off on three sides. Then they'd close in.

Rockson surveyed the scene. It was apparent what their plan was. He glanced around at his own men inside the defensive circle of hybrids. Three of the 'brids were already dead, on the edge of the circle facing the guns, their bodies riddled with bullets. But the thick hides and four foot width of the creatures made them good cover. He hoped no more would have to die.

"Anyone hurt?" Rock yelled out.

"I'm winged, Rock," a voice yelled out. It was Slade, with his hand over his shoulder. "I guess it's only appropriate that the doctor on this expedition get a dose of the real thing," he said, wincing slightly as he shifted his body. "But my instant diagnosis, additional fee, of course, for visiting the patient, is that I'll live. Could you hand me the medipack, Perkins?" Slade asked, sitting himself straight up against the back of the 'brid behind him. With Slade's direction, Perkins cleaned and sealed the wound with the instant plastic sealant that even held the edges of the wound together, stopping the bleeding almost instantly.

The Russian firing continued, coming in from three sides as the Reds slowly moved their flanking forces forward. "This is the story men," Rock said decisively. "They've got our asses cooked in about five minutes. There's no way to outfight them from this position. So we'll have to outflank them. Detroit! Chen! I want you both to go straight back, away from the Reds, and then circle around them, coming in from behind. You're both exceptional runners so I know you can cover the ground in good time. You'll have to be at least three or four hundred yards away from them or you'll be spotted. Then come in on them while their attention's on us. Detroit, you've got your grenades. Chen, do you want to carry grenades?"

"I've got something new I've been working on for the last few months with Dr. Shecter's help. Here, Rock, I haven't shown you these as I wanted to wait for the right moment to use them." The Chinese martial arts master pulled out two five-pointed star knives. The blades were round in the center with five razor-sharp points coming out like a starfish. "Made them myself—well, with Shecter's help. They're lined with explosives, Rock. High explosives. Go off on contact, with the explosive force of about half of one of our standard grenades. I've been working with them—they're quite efficient. I've got ten of them in the back of my belt," Chen said, lifting the back edge of his long, black jacket to reveal a row of knives, each in its own small, leather pocket.

Rock looked at the master of death, then said, "I'm glad I'm not a Russian today. Good luck to both of you." The two headed out from the back of the defensive circle of 'brids, jumping quickly over the backs of the neighing animals and running as fast as their pumping legs could carry them in a line straight away from the advancing Red forces. They went about two hundred yards and stopped.

"Take it slow," Detroit said, glancing over at Chen, who took two of the lethal star knives from his hidden belt pouch.

"I'll take it fast, if you don't mind," Chen retorted. They headed off in opposite directions, moving like blurs, bent over as far forward as they could without falling over. They circled far around the action, watching the Reds send out curtains of flesh-seeking slugs. Then they heard the sound of rockets. Good God, they were shooting goddamn rockets at the trapped men. The sounds of battle pushed the two Americans on, faster and faster, as they raced against time to save their fellow warriors.

Inside the circle of hybrids, Rockson directed the return fire. He had wanted to go out against the Reds but felt that he should stay with his men, just in case.

"Try to cut that right flank off with a steady line of fire right along that slight rise there," Rock directed Erickson who shifted the machine gun over several feet.

"Will do, Rock," he said, sending out a line of screaming slugs that tore up the dirt just ahead of the Red Blackshirts. They returned the fire and Erickson ducked as the Red bullets dug deep into the hide of the dead hybrid in front of the machine gun. The corpse of the animal shuddered violently and then was still. Erickson returned the fire, with Lang, now sitting wide-eyed, handing him the heavy belt of ammo.

Perkins and McCaughlin got the mortar going, slowly

zeroing in on the Red squad directly ahead of them, less than two hundred feet away. Their first two shots fell behind the crawling soldiers but the third hit the outermost group of men and blew two bodies into the air like rag dolls. The two Free-fighters looked at each other and patted one another on the back.

"A few more like that," McCaughlin said cheerfully, "and it's time for dinner." But the Reds had gotten their own bigger stuff going as well. A Blackshirt jumped up from the left flanking group, the legs of his leather uniform covered with blood from some already wounded comrade. He aimed a long, tubular weapon at the Freefighters. It whooshed fire from the back and a rocket tore at them, forcing Perkins and McCaughlin to jump away from the mortar as both knew instinctively it had their names written on it. The shell landed nearly square on the mortar, blowing it into a rain of red-hot scraps. Shrapnel tore into Perkins's back and McCaughlin's legs. They both let out yelps of pain and then checked out the wounds. They'd live. The mortar gone, they raised their Liberators and began firing on auto at the constantly advancing lines of black-leather-uniformed troops.

As if on signal, three Reds suddenly jumped up, one from each of the three advancing squads and pulled their arms back, obviously to throw grenades. Every one of the Freefighters opened up and two of the Death Squad fell dead. The third got off his grenade before he too was cut down by the whizzing wall of death. The grenade spun gracefully through the air like a well-thrown football and plopped in the dirt dead center of the Freefighters' circle. Lang, who was nearest the shrapnel cocktail, leaped forward without a moment's hesitation and grabbed the grenade. Without stopping his motion, he lifted his arm and heaved the explosive device back out over the body of one of the dead 'brids. It went off just as it slipped behind the corpse. A burst of metal fragments tore into the hybrid's cold side, just barely protecting Lang from the blast. He rolled back over to Erickson and, as if nothing had happened, said, "Hey, man, keep firing. We still got at least two dozen to go." Erickson stared in amazement at Lang, who put his burnt leg back up on the pack and, smiling, resumed feeding the belt of

9mm slugs to the machine gun.

Erickson aimed the machine gun at the rushing troops, pulled his trigger finger back, and didn't let go for twenty seconds, spraying the entire area to the right of them, creating a dust bowl of sand, metal and blood. Like hornets, the bullets tore into ten Red troops who had made a break for it, stinging, slashing, ripping at their flesh. The very air turned red with the spray of hot blood, shooting out from countless holes in the jerking, screaming bodies. When the smoke cleared after Erickson finally released the trigger, nothing moved in that direction. Nothing.

The other side of the perimeter was not doing as well. Slade, Perkins and Berger fired away at the advancing left flank. Rock and McCaughlin also slammed clip after clip into their smoking Liberators. Thank God the damn things hadn't jammed, Rock thought as he pushed what must have been his twelfth clip of 9mm shells into the Liberator, clicking the catch into place. He raised the rifle and saw two targets. Two Reds, seventy-five feet ahead, with grenades in their hands. He knew they were about to stand. He waited until he saw the upward rise of their bodies and pulled the trigger, emptying the clip as he moved the rifle from side to side. The two Blackshirt uniforms of the grenade-throwers turned bright red where the slugs tore through them and exited out their backs, rivulets of thick blood gushing down onto the dry earth. Their grenades fell back with them. The surrounding Red troops crawling on their bellies saw the devices fall. One Red soldier reached forward and threw one out to the side. The other Blackshirts, about fifteen feet away, tried to run from the second grenade which lay ominously on the ground. As they rose, Rockson and McCaughlin unleashed a hurricane of lead into them. Five more fell to the earth just before the second grenade went off. Two more Reds screamed in agony, the side of their uniforms facing the grenade staining a deep red.

Still they advanced. McCaughlin took a shot through the upper arm and fell back, gasping. Perkins got a slug right in the chest. He dropped to his side, straining for air with a horrified look in his eyes.

"Air, air, I can't breathe," the wounded archaeologist

groaned. Rock ran the ten feet separating him from the gasping Perkins and sat him upright. He looked at the hole. It had gone cleanly through, puncturing the lung but not the heart. He had to stop the bleeding.

"Perkins, listen to me," Rock said, catching the coughing man's attention. "You'll live. I promise you. But you've got to stay absolutely still and keep your hand over the wound. Understand me? If you calm down you'll be able to breathe, even if just through one lung."

"Understand," Perkins groaned out, trying to slow his heaving chest so he could catch a breath of air. Rock ran back to McCaughlin. "You all right, man?"

"Buzz off, Rock," McCaughlin said gruffly, already lifting his Liberator again to fire. "It's just a nick." Rockson could see that it was more than that but there wasn't time to stitch everybody up. If they lived they could tend to their wounds. He raised up and let go with a burst, blasting two Reds who had taken advantage of the momentary lull from the American side to rush forward. They stumbled backward, their stomachs hanging from their dripping red uniforms and collapsed. Rock turned to the left flank where he could see them setting up some kind of rocket again. He raised his rifle to fire and a slug tore into his face, knocking the side of his head around. Damn, hit! He slapped his hand up. Blood, but the wound wasn't deep. Must have sliced along the outside of his cheek. He raised up again and fired, letting off a full clip before ducking down.

Rock looked around the inside of the defensive circle. They weren't doing too good. Almost everyone had been hit in some way. Their fire was somehow grinding down. The Reds had at least half their force left and were continuing a steady barrage of fire that would lay waste their small circle of hybrids if it kept up much longer.

Detroit and Chen had made their full circles, sweeping deep behind the Russian lines. Now they came forward toward the backs of the firing Reds. Detroit pulled out two grenades and aimed at two groups of Reds in the center squad. He threw one and, a second later, the other. The grenades, short-fused so the Reds couldn't throw them back, went off, blasting the two groups of Blackshirts into bloody silence. A third group turned

295

to fire but Detroit had already dove to the ground. The Reds couldn't even see where the frags had come from. Rock started up again from the front and the Death Squad spun around to return the fire. Detroit pulled two more pins and jumped to his feet, heaving the grenades. They fell into the largest group of the central Red squad, six black-suited men, firing as they crawled forward. One grenade went off about three feet to the right of the group, the other detonated just above them. The one to the right took a Red's shoulder clear apart, severing the arm which flopped down onto the ground, trailing a spume of red. The second grenade did more damage, sending out a blast of razor-sharp shrapnel that tore into the Soviet troops' spinal cords and backs, making three of them instant paraplegics. Two more twitched silently their hearts ripped apart by metal splinters coming in through their backs. The sixth Blackshirt continued to fire, in shock from the sight of his blasted comrades.

Two hundred feet to the left, the left flanking squad, the least damaged of the three Red units, moved in for the kill. They could see that the Americans behind the circle of mutant horses were weakening. Now was the time. They rose and began forward. Suddenly two small explosions rang out. Two of the Blackshirts fell to the ground, half their backs blown away. The Red squad of twelve turned to find their attacker. A man ran crouched over, spinning small, glinting, metal weapons at them. Two at a time, he flung them with incredible speed, running a broken pattern toward them. Two more star knives whistled through the air, seeking Red flesh. One snapped into a Blackshirt throat, the explosive charge cutting through the neck, severing the head which toppled from the body before it could fall. The second slammed into a Russian stomach, blasting a hole clear through to the other side. The Red officer behind the man could see daylight through the opening until a geyser of blood filled the space and the mortally wounded soldier fell over in a messy heap.

They tried to get a bead on the running man, who would go twenty or thirty feet, stop for the merest instant, throw two of the weapons and then take off again. He was impossible to sight up. They fired but their ripping slugs found only emptiness.

Chen continued his ravaging of the Russian squad. He reached behind him and flung the star knives, snapping his wrist back at the last second to spin them into the proper death trajectory. His hundreds of hours with the things in the woods around Century City hadn't been in vain. Two more star knives whizzed out from the Chinese death-dealer, finding contact in a chest and a thigh, both instantly blasted to pieces. From far on the other side, the Freefighters were concentrating their fire on the last remaining group of Reds. It was they who were caught in a crossfire now.

Chen flung two more of the lethal star knives at two Reds who had begun rushing at him. Both fell, blasted apart from the whirring bombs of death. Detroit rushed over to join Chen. They dove to the dirt as the last of eight Blackshirts rose as a unit, guns blazing, and charged. Retreat was their only chance now. The two Freefighters each pulled out two more of their exploding weapons and jumped up, flinging them. The second the death devices were in the air they hit the dirt again as a scythe of slugs sliced the air above them. The Reds had no time to avoid the spinning grenades and star knives. The star knives hit first, burying themselves in Red flesh—one landing right in a Blackshirt's eye, exploding the screaming man's forehead into bloody powder. The second star knife sliced into the groin of a charging Red, blowing his balls into stew. He flew to the hard dirt screaming a sound that could be heard over the gunfire and explosions. His six comrades kept moving forward, spinning in every direction as they poured out a covering fire. Detroit's two grenades landed right in the midst of them, going off with a fiery roar. Bodies flew into the air trailing plumes of misty blood. Then, there was silence, but for the groans and screams of the dying Red troops.

Detroit and Chen walked slowly back to their fellow warriors some hundred yards away in the circle of hybrids. They had to step over Russian bodies everywhere. Bodies without heads, arms and legs. Bodies with gaping holes in them as if they had been drilled through with jackhammers. Pools of blood, ever-thickening as the corpses drained themselves of the precious red fluid. But it was no longer needed by the Russians. The dry ground lapped up the blood like rain. Something would grow

297

from the nourishment. Something would arise from out of all this death.

They reached the circle and jumped over the four dead hybrids who had given the lifesaving cover to the Americans. Rock and the other men were tending to their wounds. Almost everyone had been hit somewhere. They had won the battle but it had been costly. Slade, McCaughlin, even Rock had been hit. Rock's face was smeared with blood from the bullet that had gouged a neat little path along his cheek. But it was Perkins who had been most severely injured. His lung punctured, the Freefighter sat propped up against the back of a hybrid. He gasped for breath, his face pale and clammy. The men cleaned up the mess, letting the hybrids rise. Four were dead. Slade worked on Perkins. The bullet had gone clear through so he didn't have to operate. He closed the wound, cleaning and sealing it. The problem was what the hell to do about the puncture. Sometimes they healed themselves, sometimes not.

In two hours they had gotten the 'brids reloaded, and tended to their wounds. The men were all somewhat depressed. They had won but were all in pain. Perkins, still looking very shaky, gave Rock the thumbs-up when asked if he could ride. He mounted, grimacing from the pain of the motion, and the Freefighters left the slaughterhouse around them. They headed off deeper into the vast, flat wasteland of the West as buzzards began circling overhead in larger and larger numbers. They were going to feast tonight.

Thirty-Five

The forces of the People's army and air force were finally ready to carry out their sweeping attacks across the country. Already the planned attack was several days late—but the reality of having to find the planes that Zhabnov wanted and of getting the forces together to conduct sweeps in the American sectors of Russian fortresses across the country had taken more time than anyone had bargained for. When Zhabnov's top officers had gone out and commanded their underlings to get things in preparation, they found that there wasn't a hell of a lot to get together. Between Vassily's priority requests for parts—jet, helicopter, ammunition and large field equipment to fight the growing war on Russia's eastern and southern front—and Killov's gradual commandeering of supplies over the last several years, eighty percent of Zhabnov's military materials were gone. The president's advisers were unsure whether to relay the startling information to their supreme commander or let it all lie buried in a storm of bureaucratic dust where it had been hidden. They opted for the latter— better to let sleeping dogs lie than awaken raging killers. Who knew what the wrong revelations would mean to each one of them—a confrontation between Killov and Zhabnov? Heads would roll no matter what, of that they were sure. Silence was the order of the day. Let others rake the muck. For Zhabnov's men the choice was clear—silence!

They were able to scrape together a facsimile of the forces the president had requested by pulling in other units from around the country. At last they had assembled the strike force—twenty jets, fifty helicopters, and nearly two hundred thousand troops—who would be conducting sweeps for undesirables in and around the United States. The entire event was to be kicked off with the command of the president, himself, from his military headquarters in Washington. Around the United States, the Red officers and troops waited impatiently, looking at their watches. They had been standing for nearly an hour and a half. Where was the great general?

At 11:07, nearly two hours late, Zhabnov's limo slid into the space between his honor guard and his top generals. They waited at one end of the Trotsky Airport and jumped to their feet as the president's official car, festooned with banners and flags, came to a screeching stop. The president alighted with a big smile on his jowly face and the band behind the podium began playing the Soviet national anthem.

"Yes, yes, everything is going just fine, I presume?" he said with a raised eyebrow to his top general of field operations, General Myovsky.

"Absolutely, Mr. President," Myovsky loudly reassured him. "Our units are standing by all over the country waiting for your command to begin their assault on the bandit forces. Operation Neutralization is on all burners, Mr. President."

"Good, good, excellent. Well, let's get on then with the official ceremonies," Zhabnov said, beaming, looking down at the rows of medals that nearly covered the front of his crisp, green uniform. It was so seldom that he got to wear his full military regalia.

"But, Mr. President," Myovsky protested quietly. "The troops are waiting to begin. The jets are standing by with their engines on. We—"

"In due time, Myovsky," Zhabnov said coolly. "This is a public display of force for all to see. Both American bandits and our own superiors in Moscow. There must be a certain amount of display for the media. Therefore . . ." He walked off to review the pink-cheeked honor guard, standing crisply at attention as reporters and TV crews filmed everything. Official staff publicity personnel followed closely behind Zhabnov, taking down his every word. After Zhabnov was satisfied that he had been photographed sufficiently, the president, surrounded by forty of his top staff, headed over to the viewing station from which he would see the bombing force take off.

"The best place to watch from is the control tower, Mr. President," Major Dobrynin, head of airport security, said.

"Well, lead the way," Zhabnov muttered irritably. Suddenly he was terribly impatient to see the plan carried off. The Killov assassination had failed miserably. The colonel surely knew that Zhabnov was behind it. When would he strike? Zhabnov had to be on full alert at all times. His ten personal bodyguards, with submachine guns under their long coats, formed a semicircle around him as he walked toward the tower. This neutron bomb attack on Union City had to succeed. Killov had to see that Zhabnov had power and could use it.

They walked up a wide ramp and took the elevator six stories up in the slim tower. The view of the flat terrain of Washington, D.C. was pretty fogged in.

"No problem for our planes, Mr. President," Myovsky said, standing directly to the right of Zhabnov. "And our reconnaissance advance teams tell us there's no fog over Union City."

"Excellent, excellent," Zhabnov boomed. "Now, let's get, as the Americans like to say, this show on the road. Where do I give the command so that all forces will begin their attacks?"

"Right here, Mr. President." Myovsky leaned forward and pointed to a table mike, shined and polished, waiting for Zhabnov's three words. He stepped to the table and turned around to the phalanx of photographers.

"Ready? I'm about to give the command."

"Yes, Mr. President. Yes, go ahead," the chorus of official White House reporters clucked.

"Begin the attack!" Zhabnov declared. The command tore across communications lines around the country and over 250 thousand Soviet personnel around the country began to carry out their plans of official murder.

Zhabnov watched with satisfaction as the cockpits slammed shut on the waiting lines of jets. Sleek, rapier-nosed, magnalloy MiG 112s: two with N-bombs under their wings; ten more

301

flying shotgun, although exactly who would attack the attackers was not clear since the rebels possessed no air force at all. The first set of three roared down the field, the scream of the big ramjet engines shaking even the heavily insulated tower. Zhabnov felt a thrill. This is what he had been missing—command, action.

"Now, here on this viewer, Mr. President," Myovsky said, pointing to a large video screen, "you will be able to see the attack just as the pilots see it from the air. A camera has been mounted in the nose of one of the jets carrying the bomb."

"Wonderful," Zhabnov said. "How innovative of you, Myovsky." He'd have to remember this man. Myovsky, smiling broadly, turned the viewer on and an image of the landscape from ten thousand feet burst onto the screen. Zhabnov watched in fascination as the rolling hills, the mosaics of fields, of green and then black, passed the watchful eye of the camera. The jets found their target and dived, the angle of the camera banking sharply to the right. Zhabnov saw the bombs fall and then the camera turned sharply away as the jets tore ass.

In Union City, one of the largest Free Cities, the shotgun-pistol factories were chugging away, as over sixty thousand people went about their daily business. Suddenly the air-raid sirens went off. The women and children hit the shelters as the men ran to their anti-aircraft stations. They had never been attacked before but they were prepared. They hit one of the jets, but then two more dropped gleaming bombs. How large they wouldn't know until . . .

Blinding light, vaporization, atoms in acceleration stripped down to their mesotrons. Then nothing. Nothing at all. No city, no life, no survivors. And more radiation filling the poisoned skys.

Zhabnov watched the bombs falling. The screen suddenly burst into blinding white overexposure. He threw his hands over his eyes, cursing. Frantic aids came running with cold compresses as a doctor was called from the security station. Myovsky stood as white as a ghost several feet away.

"Mr. President, I-I had no idea it would be so bright. I—"

"Fool!" Zhabnov shouted, seeing a bright red dot in front of each eye. The doctor came rushing in and quickly examined Zhabnov.

"It should be all right, Mr. President. Radiation can't pass through a television screen. Still, perhaps you should come into the hospital for some tests.

Zhabnov stamped out, furious, his hands over his eyes. Myovsky stared, frozen, at the departing president. He wondered if he would survive the next twenty-four hours.

Thirty-Six

The Freefighters marched wearily on. The memory of the costly encounter with the Reds was still fresh in their minds, the wounds were still fresh on their bodies. Most of the men were back in form from the attack, except Perkins whose lung didn't seem to be healing well at all. He coughed a lot and tried to feign health. But his ghastly pallor and extreme fatigue were too obvious to ignore. Lang, too, was having problems from his burnt leg resulting from the fiery crash of the drone. It had seemed to be healing at first but now, on the fifth day, the leg was showing signs of deep infection, turning a ghastly purple color. Slade had done everything he could for the badly hurt men. Now it was up to God. They couldn't turn back, so Rock moved forward, the injuries weighing heavily on his mind.

They passed more of the forty foot towers every few miles, the structures mysterious and haunting and totally inexplicable. The ground grew increasingly dark, moving from gray to charcoal black. Nothing lived here. Not a weed. Not a thorny cactus. Not a bird flew overhead. The place was what had been called in the old days overkilled.

"Must have dropped ten or twenty of the big boys right in this one area," Detroit said, riding up alongside Rockson, "to make it so black like this. Not that I have anything against the color black," Detroit said, smirking. "It's just that I think it's a better color for skin than dirt."

"I doubt anything will ever grow here again," Rock said, shaking his head in disgust. "The very atoms of the ground look like they've been burnt." He took a counter reading. The rads were rising rapidly. Rock stopped the force.

"Men, it's getting super hot in this dirt here. Goddamn needle's off the meter. We'll have to suit up in Shecter's anti-rad outfits, and this time let's put those leadsynth shields around the hybrids' hoofs." They attached the odd-looking, hoof-shaped shoes that Shecter had created for the 'brids when it became too radioactive even for them. The men tied the shiny coverings around their 'brids' feet and then donned their own lightweight suits. They remounted, taking out their gamma-reflector blankets and wrapped themselves in the silver-foil plastic. Not bad, Rock thought, as they rode forward. He already felt cooler as the blanket reflected the sun's blistering rays as well as the rads from below.

They rode for hours in single file, the hybrids keeping up a slow, plodding pace. Even their powerful bodies were beginning to tire from the endless journey. And they had seen the deaths of their fellow 'brids. Heard their death screams. It didn't set well in them at all. They knew that something terrible had happened and now felt a trembling anxiety inside their dim animal minds that something even more horrendous was about to occur. The men sensed the skittishness of the 'brids and treated them with kid gloves, speaking quietly and hardly using the reins at all.

Rock knew they couldn't go on much longer like this. But there wasn't a drop of shade or cover in sight. They were down to extremely low water rations as it was. He scanned the horizon with his binoculars. Black, black, gnarled twisted terrain as if the moon had fallen onto the earth.

"Wait!" Rock threw his arm up. The Freefighters pulled in on their reins as the hybrids came to a slightly confused stop. Rock focused the binocs in on some—what was it? It appeared to be some sort of bunker house about two miles off. The expedition veered to the left and made for the artificial structure. Rock's senses went on full alert, his ears picking up, his eyes narrowing. He felt something ahead. Very close. He loosened his shotgun pistol in its holster, not taking it out but leaving his hand resting lightly on top. Detroit, directly behind Rock, recognized the motion from years of missions with

Rockson and loosened his own gun, looking reflexively at his grenade belt to see what was readly available.

There was a flurry of motion just ahead of them. A hatch seemed to open out of the very earth; a round segment of blackness falling open. A small, totally bald humanoid-looking creature jumped in front of them, holding a weapon.

"Stop! I command you to cease motion," the pasty-faced, midget-sized man yelled out in a squeaky voice.

"What the . . . ?" Detroit exclaimed, going for his .45. The strange man, dressed in a white lab coat, now stained and gray, his head as smooth and shiny as an egg, raised his weapon to chest height and fired. A broad black beam shot from the pistol and instantaneously enveloped Detroit and his reddish colored brid. The hybrid fell over onto its side as if dead and Detroit rolled off as the 'brid hit the ground in a motionless heap. The other Freefighters reached for their pistols.

"Wait!" Rock threw his hands in the air. "We are friends," he yelled down at the little man who again raised his weapon which Rock realized was similar to the particle beam Brady had brought back. "We are Americans like you. One of our men found one of your people about a month ago. He was hurt pretty bad and—"

"Vorn? The quantity you speak of," the bald-headed creature asked, "was that his designation? Vorn?"

"Yes, I think that's what Brady said," Rock answered, trying to remember the details of Brady's tale. He glanced over at Detroit, who seemed to be stirring slightly and then immediately back at the pint-sized stranger who grew nervous and fingered his weapon. "Yes, Vorn!" Rock said firmly. "He told my man he'd been attacked and then died. He gave our first expedition his weapon. A particle-beam disintegrator. We've come nearly a thousand miles to find you and to have you share what knowledge you have of such weapons with us so we can kick the goddamned Russians out of America," Rock said in one long breath, wanting the creature to hear their story before it started firing again. It seemed extremely agitated, trembling bug-eyed as it listened to them suspiciously.

The Technician lowered his pistol slowly until it was pointing at the ground. "Americans," it muttered to itself.

"We are Americans, yes. We . . ." it tried to remember just who it was and why. "We are the Technicians," it said suddenly, looking up at Rockson, who sat still on his hybrid, not wanting to frighten the man. He glanced around at the Freefighters and motioned with his eyes to move their hands away from their pistols, which they reluctantly did. Detroit groaned and sat up, rubbing his head. The hybrid, too, shook its hind legs and tried to rise. Whatever level of force the Technician had fired with had been extremely low. The creature continued, "We are, were descended from the original crews that manned these silos." It swept its arm across the nearly flat plain around them. Small, circular grooves could be seen everywhere. It had been a missile base—and a big one. "A number of ten megaton Soviet missiles hit this area, turning it into . . . this." It looked around at the black nothingness.

"I've seen," Rock said dryly. He let his hands fall back to the saddle. The little man looked up again, its eyes suddenly bright as if taking in Rockson and his band for the first time.

"Americans. Yes, we are all Americans. Come, please, all of you must subtract yourselves from your riding animals and accompany me. Down—into the silos. I am Ullman." It raised itself up to the height of its three-and-a-half foot tall shoulders and looked at them through nervous eyes. "It is much more comfortable down there, although, I'm afraid we can't provide sustenance."

"Sustenance?" Rock asked, looking over at Slade, who as well as being the expedition's doctor had been chosen for his abilities as a linguist.

"I think he means food, Rock," Slade said.

"Well, then, please share some of ours," Rock said, pointing to the pack 'brids. "We shot three boar several days ago and have enough for a feast. If you have water."

The creature's eyes lit up wildly at the mention of food. "Yes, water." It smiled weakly. "Follow me!" It led them forward down a slowly sloping ramp hidden from view by the black, sooty ground until they were right on top of it. At the bottom stood a corrugated steel door. The creature pressed a button barely a quarter inch in diameter, built specially for its

307

long, narrow fingers, and the rigid gate raised itself, silently disappearing into the cement ceiling. They entered, single-file, down the four foot wide and about eight foot high cinder-block tunnel, the 'brids' big bodies barely able to squeeze through.

"May need some Vaseline on this one," Detroit yelled up to Rock, who led his palomino just ahead.

"Yes, that was Vorn, your people found," the Technician said, walking about five paces ahead of Rock in the dimly lit tunnel. Some sort of built-in fluorescent shone down every forty feet or so. The things looked ancient. They had been burning dimmer and dimmer for a century. The large-headed Technician was dwarfed by Rock who stood nearly three feet taller than it. He felt like he was walking behind a four-year-old child. Yet the creature exuded a tremendous intelligence, a controlled mind.

"Vorn was our best hunter. I should say our only hunter. We are, if you'll pardon the equation, $E = mass \times food$ factor, divided by $age \times .4367$."

"What was that?" Rock asked, grinning ever so slightly. Ullman stopped suddenly and stared at Rockson as if he were mad. Then he laughed out loud.

"Ah yes, I see, of course, you can't know our terms. We speak English, but we've probably elaborated on it over the years. We're all mathematicians and physicists and have spent so many years together—our whole lives—that we've developed a kind of mathematical slang. I'll have to recalculate my grammar. We haven't had many guests around here. Not one in a hundred years. We've been alone out here in the middle of this wasteland, developing our science—and dying."

"Dying?" Rock asked as the Technician led them to a much larger open bunker, walls of cinder blocks piled a good twenty feet high. An old American flag still hung on one of the dusty walls, twenty shades grayer than it had begun but still the U.S. flag.

"Here. Attach your animals here," Ullman said, pointing to a long, metal railing that nearly surrounded the room, separating it from a three-foot walkway that a century ago must have been patrolled by some sort of guard. "My people await upstairs in the Computer Analysis Chamber. That's where we sustain life." Ullman looked up at Rockson. "Yes, dying. We have not reproduced in this generation. And now we are reduced down to thirty-one of us, and our last food. It is a pitiful state to be in. We were sitting up there together, watching the end of our race in slow motion when your presence set off some of our alarms."

"Well, I don't know about the end," Rock said, "but I don't think you'll die while we're here. We've got enough grub to feed a small army and one of the best cooks this side of the Rockies. By the way, I'm Ted Rockson, representative of Century City." He proffered his hand to the small man, who reached up and took it. Rockson introduced each of the Freefighters, who waved and smiled. Even Detroit managed a lopsided grin as he rubbed his head from the slightly painful effects of the black ray.

"I am apologetic for using the Particle Beam on you," he said, looking over at Detroit, who lashed his hybrid to the three-tiered metal fence that circumnavigated the chamber.

"My fault, pal," Detroit said. "I shouldn't have gone for my gun so fast. Thing packs a nasty hangover," he added, rubbing the back of his head.

"Yes, but at that frequency no permanent damage is done. I assure you." Rock glanced down at the Black beam pistol that hung like a child's toy on the Technician's hip. Shecter hadn't even discovered that function. How many levels of operation were on the damn thing anyway. The Technician led them all forward. He was taken with Rockson's ways. The man was obviously a hardened warrior, yet gentle too. Ullman trusted Rockson instantly. He and his people would share every bit of their knowledge to help this man.

Ullman led the Freefighters into the silo complex and started toward a rung ladder that disappeared straight down into the ground. Rock whistled as he looked down the silo shaft. It was some thirty feet in diameter and stretched from the concrete base two hundred feet below to the steel hatch one hundred fifty feet above. Piping and electrical circuits ran like spider webs along the edges of the cylindrical, metal tube.

"This is where the missiles were?" Rockson asked.

"Yes, that is a positive theorization," Ullman said, stopping and stepping back from the ladder. He walked over to the Americans who stared in awe at the home of one of America's missile fleet from a century before. They had never seen the actual launching mechanism for one of the big ICBMs and were somehow bizarrely fascinated.

"You haven't got a few old spares lying around, do you?" McCaughlin asked. "Can you imagine, Rock? If we could get our hands on ten or twenty of these babies, the Reds wouldn't know what hit 'em. Probably ain't got no more defenses against missile attack. We could take out Moscow, Leningrad. . . ." His voice trailed off in wishful tones.

"Unfortunately, I must reply in the negative," Ullman replied. "All the missiles were shot in the first hour of war. And from our information, which you are welcome to assimilate, the Soviets were able to shoot most of the U.S. strike from the skies, using technology similar to this." The Technician pointed to his pistol.

"So that's how they were able to survive the attack," Rock said softly. "All our data indicated that they shot down the missiles with some sort of super-elaborate anti-missile system." Shecter would be fascinated. It seemed to be extremely important information though Rockson wasn't quite sure why.

Ullman again started down the long silo ladder. Rock had McCaughlin and a few of the other men carry big sacks of food from their kitchen supplies in backpacks. They came shakily down the metal ladder, hanging on for dear life as the big loads of food, including two boar, shifted unnervingly on their backs. It would be the height of absurdity to have traveled a thousand miles, to have fought off mutants, Reds and everything else in this Godforsaken part of America, and then be killed falling off a ladder. The sheer possibility of having gravestones with epitaphs that read, "He died missing a rung" made them move with unusual caution.

They came to the bottom of the long, black metal track of rungs and started across a vast underground warehouse, filled with electronics and equipment of long ago.

"As you can see, Ted Rockson," Ullman said, pointing around as they walked across the immense concrete floor filled with every kind of furniture, lamp, wire and fuse, "we've let the place deteriorate. Factors have gotten quite bad over the last ten years." Ullman opened the Computer Room door and the others of his people shrank back in horror when they saw the large, dirty creatures that followed closely behind their leader.

"It is all right," Ullman said reassuringly. "These are not negative quantities. They have food." Whatever misgivings or childhood fears the Technicians had of the other beings quickly vanished when they heard the word food. They stirred in their plastic chairs and moved in their blankets spread out on the floor of one of the most advanced computer rooms in the world.

"Here, men, put the chow down here," Rock said, pointing to an unoccupied corner of the room. "McCaughlin, why don't you and Erickson get a fire going out there in the big storage room. Got to be all kinds of old wood furniture you could use to get something started."

"I can just use the stoves, Rock," Erickson interjected.

"To barbecue a whole hog on a spit?" Rock asked with a grin. "These people need some livening, not to mention fattening up," Rock said, sweeping his hand around the roomful of lethargic Technicians who did indeed look as if they were at death's door.

"Oh, you want *that* kind of dinner?" Erickson said, opening his eyes wide. "I got you, Rock. Archer," he yelled out, "you're needed on work detail." The huge bowman rose and accompanied the other two to gather wood for the bonfire that Erickson already had visualized. As the three men were the largest Freefighters in the expedition, they made quite a sight; their 250 to 300 pound bodies, over six and a half feet tall, barely fit through the Technicians' small entrance.

"Here, while we're waiting," Rock said, "we have some canned juices and bread. Please, help yourselves." He opened a sack and spread the victuals out on a work table. The Technicians eyed the presence of the precious sustenance as a criminal eyes a gold necklace. Moving slowly at first, so as not to appear desperate, they headed slowly over to the tableful of bounty. But by the time they reached it they couldn't contain

311

themselves. They reached down greedily and ripped chunks of bread, stuffing them in their mouths in huge pieces that they were barely able to swallow. They took tremendous gulps of the apple and orange juice. Rock looked on, remembering his own childhood days of hunger and how wonderful it had been to come into a Free City and be given all that his growling stomach could hold.

Ullman seemed embarrassed by the manners of his people and looked at Rockson disapprovingly. "We're usually not like this, I assure you. There aren't more well-mannered people on this planet than the Technicians. We—"

"It's all right," Rock said, smiling down warmly, repressing an urge to pat the childlike creature on the head. "I've been hungry myself, believe me. Very hungry! And I don't remember waiting politely when food was offered."

"You are $x = x$," said Ullman, his huge black eyes looking directly into Rockson's. "You are a straight equation, Rockson." Rock wasn't sure of the mathematics but he understood the emotion.

In no time at all, Erickson had a big fire going outside in the ten-football-fields sized, concrete underground complex. Two autostoves burned sharp blue flames alongside the wood fire, which had a whole boar on a spit, turning slowly. Food sizzled away and the smell of all the rich juices positively saturated the stale air of the underground silos. Rock led Ullman, with his people tightly grouped together behind him, out to the waiting victuals.

Some of the other Freefighters had gathered tables and chairs from the piles of junk that lined the walls and dusted the spider webs and dirt from them. The entire area around the cooking fires was ringed with eating tables, like a picnic ground.

"Everybody just sit down now," Erickson bellowed out. "Me and my staff—that's you," he said, pointing to Green, "and you, Archer, will help me serve. So just sit down, twiddle your thumbs or some appendage and get ready for a feast." The Technicians sat down around the tables that were too high for them, on chairs from which their legs dangled loosely. But their faces were shining, their hearts beating with vigor for the first time in years. Rock sat next to Ullman at the head of one of the three long tables. Soon the food was being piled out in steaming, delicious helpings.

The Technicians gobbled it all down and asked for more. Rock knew they would regret it later but didn't say a word. They had to gorge themselves, to fill that acid-grinding emptiness in their stomachs. They ate and they ate and then they ate some more. Two hours later, all thirty-eight of the Technicians were lying on the floor groaning in painful happiness.

Rockson sat and talked with Ullman who still chewed on some of the artifruit pudding that McCaughlin had whipped up out of powders mixed with the Technicians' water.

"I can't thank you enough, Ted Rockson," the leader said. "We were at our breath's end. You have given us a respite. Now you must tell me what it is like on the outside. None of us has ever been beyond a few miles surrounding these silos. Vorn told us of lands beyond the blackness, but even he had just gone out to the edges where there was some hunting. Animals would stray there to roll in the black dust. Vorn thought it helped them alleviate bugs and insects that had attached to their hides. What is out there, Rock? Is it all black? Are there more Americans like you? Have the Russians—"

"One question at a time," Rock said, laughing, leaning back in his folding wooden chair. "First, there *is* a huge world out there. Although much damage was done by the war, large parts of the United States are healthy, and damaged parts, at least many of them, are starting to come back as well. This blackness that surrounds you, Ullman, is the worst of it. You had the insane luck to have your people evolve in the center of possibly the worst concentration of hits in the country. So, no, it's not all black. Not at all. It's green and blue—there are forests, lakes, birds and flowers. Many parts of our country are still as beautiful as the day before the bombs went off. As for there being more Americans out there, why there are over—" Rock looked across at the Technician. Ullman was sound asleep, his small mouth open and breathing deeply. Rock glanced around the floor. All the Technicians had fallen asleep. They lay with little smiles on their white faces. Rock grinned. He felt a

313

strange tenderness for the peculiar race. Across the vast storage depot, the Freefighters sat around, finishing up the remains of dinner and playing cards. A serious poker game was in progress with the clothing and goods they had received from the Macy's creatures as bets. Lang was sitting upright, though Rock knew his leg hadn't been healing too well. Perkins sat off to the side, breathing raspily. Rock was worried about him. The man just didn't look well at all. Tomorrow he would have to ask the Technicians if they had any medical devices that might be of help.

But for now he would let them sleep. Let them dream pleasurable dreams for the first time in years instead of the nightmares they were used to. Tomorrow, he would learn some of the secrets of the Technicians.

Thirty-Seven

Colonel Killov sat in his eightieth-floor office in the monolith watching the Olympic Games from Crete via satellite TV. Twenty years after the war the Olympics had been promoted by the Russians as a tool for getting the peoples of the occupied countries to take their minds off the realities of their harsh, everyday lives. The Reds now did gala publicity worldwide for the games, making the different nationalities root for their country—as if it mattered. The satellite hook-up was lined and fuzzy—perhaps because the Reds were using a 110-year-old American Telsat. Technology connected with space development had gradually deteriorated over the last century, with maintenance of existing ground controls to the Russians' own killer satellite force still orbiting around the planet being the only thing kept up to date. Several of the Russian premiers had wanted to do away with the ground stations, the main one located in Moscow, as being too costly. But each had been voted down by the entire Presidium. The killer sats were the Reds' ace in the hole. They ruled now, but their country's own volatile history made them collectively aware that anything could happen. If, somehow, one of the captive nations got hold of a missile—none were capable of building one—and launched it, the Reds would still be able to knock it from the sky. Thousands of technicians manned radar and other defensive early-warning control systems around the world, waiting to detect the missile or plane that never came.

Killov banged the twenty-six-inch color TV with the side of

his hand. There! A little better. The fact that the American satellite could continue to transmit television signals around the world was a testament to their technology at the time of the war. Somehow, it always slightly amazed Killov, when he had read of the past, that the Russians had been able to defeat the Americans, who he had to confess, to himself only, had been quite intelligent and ingenius when it came to technological breakthroughs and long-lasting equipment. The stuff the Russians sent out of their factories was lucky if it made it off the assembly line without cracking or dropping into a hundred useless pieces.

Killov sat back in his velveteen armchair and watched as the pole vaulter from the Soviet Union easily beat the Malawi pole vaulter. Once again, the Russians were winning nine out of ten medals. Guess we're all just better athletes, Killov thought cynically. He reached over to the bar bureau next to his chair, opened it and mixed himself a martini, dry. The sour taste poured down his throat with an easy pleasure. He took another swig and watched the Olympic games continue.

The Reds won the next three events—long jump, hurdle and tumbling—gold, silver, and bronze. They'd better let someone win, Killov thought, or there'll be riots around the world. The boys back in the Athletics Committee in Moscow were getting a little greedy.

The phone on his desk rang. A report of strange occurrences in the Far West region—sector five, vector three.

"An entire Blackshirt parakite commando squad was wiped out, sir," the KGB major in charge of coordinating incoming data from the western regions told Killov.

"What?" the commander of all the Blackshirts in America screamed into the phone. "What the hell do you mean was wiped out? You mean crashed? What?"

"No, sir, I wish I did," the officer on duty, just forty-five floors below Killov, said meekly. "The report just reached me, Colonel, and I felt you would want to hear it. Three days ago, one of our drone watchers saw what looked like a line of rebels in that region. The drone suddenly went dead and the officer in charge felt that there was enough information to warrant sending out a search-and-destroy team. Parakite commandos

316

—the best, sir, elite corps. They were dropped right over the target area according to the pilot of the Soyuz transport. He saw the rebels himself. The men headed down, seemed to be getting the best of the bandits and the plane headed off. The commandos were to be picked up by helicopter within the next hour with whatever prisoners they had taken." The officer stopped suddenly, as if afraid to go on.

"And?" Killov said brusquely.

"And—they were all dead when the chopper force arrived. Every last one of them, Colonel. Cut to bits. The crew found four dead mutant horses that the bandits had apparently used as cover but no dead. I just now received the message, sir, and called the officer in charge to confirm the story in its entirety. It's all true."

"Damn!" Killov exploded, slamming down the phone. This, he would have to see for himself. He called his service officer and had him arrange a flight of four choppers, the big jet-powered Minsk IIs, armed to the teeth, for immediate flight to sector five, vector three.

The screaming fleet of helicopters hovered over the battle zone, settling down just off to one side, sending up waves of black soot from the scorched earth. Killov, attired in full Blackshirt strike uniform, black leather, full plastasteel face mask, carrying a sub himself in case of attack, stepped out of the lead chopper and walked quickly over to the bodies, still lying where they had fallen. Buzzards had congregated around some of the more rapidly festering corpses, picking out eyeballs and tongues and other tasty morsels. Killov fired a full burst from his submachine gun, beheading five of the long-necked, ugly birds as the rest flew off, wings flapping like sheets, screeching shrilly.

He looked over the slaughter. They'd been killed by bullets and what looked like grenades, judging by the amputations that lay around the dark ground in their own little display backdrops of blood. And . . . what was that? Killov bent down and picked up a sharp, five-pointed throwing device. One of Chen's that had failed to detonate. It had stuck halfway through the throat of a Red lieutenant, whose hands were still around his throat in a frozen grip of death. What the hell was it? Killov wondered. He had never seen the bandits use this sort of weapon. Could there be armed tribes far out in these unknown regions who are beginning to attack? Was there more to the picture than he had realized? That was the one thing the Russian KGB leader hated, not knowing.

He walked among the rotting bodies, looking at the wounds on each, poking around the dirt under the bodies, looking for he knew not what. Around him, his officers, nearly twenty-five of them, scouted around the black dirt, following the lead of their commander. They too had no idea what they were searching for, but imitated Killov. The colonel spent an hour walking around the field, examining every thing, every bloodstain, every splattered gut, every shell casing for a clue. At last Killov walked across the dirt to where the bandits had made their defense. It still seemed incredible. More than forty of the KGB's top men wiped out by what couldn't have been more than a small force. He walked around the dead hybrids, holding his nose from the stench of the swollen, decomposing animals, their guts already strewn like moldering garbage from their bloated stomachs. He again examined the shell casings, the empty boxes of ammo. It was the Freefighters, he was suddenly sure of it. He had seen too many of these defensive encampments in the past not to recognize one now. Blood here too. Some of their men had been hit, he thought with at least a little satisfaction. And possibly killed as well. The bandits never left their dead.

"Sir, over here," one of Killov's officers yelled out. The colonel quickly walked over to the man who was kneeling down next to one of the dead mutant horses. "A locket of some kind." The officer stood up, handing Killov a small, gold pocket watch on the end of a long, brass chain. The colonel flicked the little dial on the top and the front piece popped open. Inside was a watch, still ticking, and on the inside of the shiny cover was the inscription, "To my darling Peter Slade. May he be the best doctor Century City ever had."

"Century City, I've heard that name before," Killov said out loud to Petrovsky and Vorshnev, two of his top officers.

"Yes, sir," the gaunt-faced Vorshnev replied, nearly a carbon copy of Killov himself, with eyes as cold as an arctic glacier. "The name has been linked by our analysis computers as being the most probable base of operations of Ted Rockson."

Killov's eyes lit up like an exploding phosphorous bomb. "Rockson, what the hell would he be doing all the way out here? Something's going on and I want to find out what." The KGB leader strode back to his chopper in long, angry steps, yelling all the while to his note-taking underlings around him. "I want this whole area, from this point all the way back to the Rockies to be filled with drones. I want four Special Squads made ready for this mission only, to be on full alert at all times until I take them off. Two parakite teams and two helicopter assault squads. He's going to have to come back this way sometime, whatever the hell he's doing out there," Killov said, looking out into the black wasteland which stretched off to the horizon. The chopper took off, again raising a tornado of soot. "And when he does, we'll be ready for him."

Thirty-Eight

The next morning Rockson greeted Ullman, the first Technician to awaken. "You ate your fill last night," Rock said. "That's for sure."

"Hunger = emptiness × caloric needs divided by time lapse since last sustenance." Rock grinned back, somehow deciphering the message. "We haven't eaten like that since Vorn dragged back an entire elk-type creature nearly three hundred day cycles ago. That was before he began losing his strength. At the end he was capable of carrying only small game—rabbits, several birds. We are not big, Ted Rockson, I know, but we have lost nearly thirty percent of our body mass in the last year. You see us at our lowest bodyfat-to-muscle ratio."

"McCaughlin, up and at 'em," Rockson yelled over to the grumbling Scotsman who turned uncomfortably on the hard concrete floor of the cavernous silo complex. Slowly, he began rousing himself, scratching his red beard, cursing his joints which felt like hell warmed over after a night on this extra-firm rock mattress.

"But, Rockson, you must relay your information about the world to me. Our conversation last night was terminated by my descent into biological satiation. What is it like out there?" Ullman's black eyes glimmered, a dull golden streak in the middle like a light at the end of a long tunnel. His face seemed much pinker after the feast of the previous evening.

"It's beautiful, and ugly, out there, Ullman," Rock said, sitting in one of the old wooden chairs that men of the missile crews must have used in the twentieth century. "Parts of America are lush and green but much of it is still terribly damaged. But this is the worst, by far, that we've seen. You'd be wise to leave this area."

"Leave?" Ullman snorted. "We've lived the past five generations here. This is our entire world. It is too late for that, I'm afraid. But tell me, Ted Rockson, where do you and your people live? Are there more like you?"

"We're the Freefighters of the hidden cities," Rock said, his nostrils flaring at the sudden scent of the eggs and boar bacon breakfast that McCaughlin and Erickson were preparing nearby on the small autostoves. Rock continued as the leader of the Technicians listened, fascinated. "The Reds invaded right after their first strike, sending in millions of troops. And now." Rock looked down at the flat, gray floor. He hated to say the words. "And now, they rule America from their fortress cities."

"The Russians are here? In America?" Ullman seemed genuinely surprised and disturbed. "We had known, of course, from records that our original ancestors kept, of the attack. Then all the missiles here were launched and the entire base was sealed up tight as a tomb. The original Technicians had tons of food and oxygen down here. When the bombs went off all over this area, they were untouched. They didn't come up for nearly five years—and then, seeing the blackened condition of the land, submerged again and began working on their own pure science. Doing what they knew best.

"We've caught transmissions from time to time but always garbled. The radiation in the surrounding environment inhibits the transmission of nearly all frequencies of radio or television."

"Well, they are out there. The Reds still have armies of men here and they think they run things. But times are changing, Ullman. We undertook this journey to find out more about these Black Beam weapons of yours. Such devices could make us superior to the Reds' armor and their field artillery."

"Ted Rockson, all that is ours shall be yours. I—we—are all Americans. We have kept working decade after decade, developing weapons and medical equipment from our discoveries, in several fields of research. We have kept the machinery, the laboratories functional here, made as many devices as we could, preparing for the day when we would be called on. For what purpose we have never known for sure. But now, it becomes clear. We developed our technology for the day when you arrived. And now our function can be fulfilled. Yes! Yes!" Ullman grew more and more excited, his big eyes nearly bulging out of the egg-shaped head. He and his people had been so empty, both nutritionally and spiritually for so long. Now there was meaning again. That was the deepest hunger of all.

The other Technicians awoke and were again fed huge, steaming portions of good American food. They took to it like beavers to trees and seemed to want to eat more and more, as if they would start growing before the Freefighters' eyes. Already their pale, thin stalks of arms seemed to be filling out, their walk was steadier, their heads held higher.

"You mentioned medical equipment," Rock said, looking at Ullman. "Two of my men were recently hurt and aren't responding well to our treatment. What sort of medical devices are you equipped with?"

"Well, a side discovery, quite accidental, of the Particle Beam was made by one of my illustrious ancestors, Drior the Quantuum Mechanic. He noticed that cultures of bacteria placed under an extremely low level Particle Accelerator destroyed said culture in under twenty seconds. Much experimentation with this fact led to the development of what we call the Neutron Accelerator and Micro-Biological Extermination Unit. The MB, for abbreviation. It destroys all bacteria and viruses within an organism without harming the organism itself."

Rock looked at Ullman intently. "Do you mean the thing destroys all germs?"

"Yes, I guess you could enumerate that," Ullman replied. Rockson whistled.

"Then you never get sick?"

"No, never. We are given a dose of the ray once a year and none of us ever contracts sickness. But for genetic reasons our lifespan seems to be quite short. Few of us live over the age of

322

forty-five, dying as if by command of some preprogrammed force. We know when we will die weeks ahead."

"Can we use it on my injured men?" Rockson asked.

"Come," Ullman said, jumping down from the chair he was sitting in. Rockson had several of the Freefighters help him carry Perkins and Lang up the two levels of ladder and into the medical section of the Technician research laboratories. Perkins was looking worse all the time, his breath coming in quick little gasps, his eyes hardly open. They had had to feed him by hand for two days. Lang acted in good spirits but his entire leg had turned bright purple and was threatening to evolve into gangrene. Ullman gave directions to the Freefighters in how to use the equipment. Both men were strapped down on long tables and three cylindrical, cone-shaped objects were placed over each of the bodies. Ullman told the Americans to step back behind the shielding at one end of the apparatus-cluttered medical chamber. He turned numerous dials on a large control board, clicked a Power On button and waited a moment for the black crystal diodes inside the cones to warm up.

"Just lay there and don't move," Ullman yelled to the two fully conscious Americans who lay flat on their backs in the center of the room on two high, plastic meditables. "It won't hurt. You'll just see a little bit of light, feel a hum go through your body and maybe a little bit of heat. But my people and I go through this each year on our birthdates."

"Go to it," both Americans said vigorously. Ullman pressed the Activation switch and the Americans were bathed in a shimmering black light. It seemed to dance across their bodies before entering them. The rays lasted for twenty seconds and then Ullman pressed the Disengage switch and turned the rest of the machinery off. The two wounded Freefighters were helped to their feet.

"Can't say I feel much better," Perkins said, smiling with the slightest lift of his pale lips.

"No, it's not an anesthetic," Ullman said. "Your pain will be with you for a little while longer anyway. But all the bacteria inside you that were causing the infections are dead. Now your own body can heal itself." The other Freefighters helped the two somewhat-skeptical Americans back down the long rung ladder to the floor they were camped on.

After the men were set back to rest, Ullman came to Rock's side. "Come with me, Rockson, and bring whoever you deem technologically comprehensive in relation to weapons mathematics," Ullman said. Rock called for Green and Slade to accompany him.

"You men, straighten up around here, will you?" Rock yelled out to the others. The campsite was already looking filthy, littered with broken chairs that had collapsed under the Freefighters' weight and plates of uneaten food from the previous night's pig bash.

Ullman took the three Freefighters through long, winding corridors and down two levels by the ladders. They entered a large assembly plant, filled with machine tools, torches and plastic molding presses, all the equipment of what looked like an ultra-modern factory, covering the floors of the parking-lot-sized weapons plant.

"This is where my people spent most of their lives over the last eighty years," Ullman said, leading Rockson to a pile of what were clearly weapons, stacked neatly on steel racks along one of the center walls. "The correct enumeration is actually Particle Beam Dispersal Disintegrator," Ullman said, lifting one of the plastic pistols. It was much like the one Brady had brought back to Century City only this model seemed slightly longer and narrower and came equipped with a long, green lens scope on top.

"The technology is simple, really, once you understand it," Ullman said, handing the weapon to Rockson. "A question of Energy = Mass × atomic disintegration factor × constant .99998812 + the energy charge of the weapon squared. In this case the energy charge is solar-collected and battery-stored in the handle of the weapon. One charging of two hours' duration will power the pistol for approximately one thousand firings."

"And the capability of the weapons?" Rock asked.

"Of the small pistols like this, a range of about one hundred yards," Ullman said, lifting another one and handing it to Detroit. "It can be kept in a tight beam, approximately one half inch in diameter, with the destructive force of D = Energy

× mass × charge acceleration. One of these pistols would destroy any object with a steel-type density up to two tons. It actually knocks out the neutron/proton balance within the individual atoms and causes the solidity to implode."

"And these?" Rock asked, lifting a much longer, rifle-sized weapon. Again, smooth, made from some sort of shiny black plastic with fibers of green embedded in it. It seemed absolutely impervious to scratches or damage of any kind just by the hardness of the material. Yet it was as light as a feather, as it would have to be for the Technicians to be able to lift it.

"These are the most powerful of the Particle Beam weaponry except for two much larger ones over there, which have the destructive capability of small atomic bombs." The Freefighters glanced over at two cannon-sized weapons a good ten feet long.

"One of these is capable of sending a beam up into space. It is similar in design, we believe, to the Russian Particle Beams mounted on their satellites. Of course, to fire to that high a target—ten thousand miles up—requires extremely complex sighting gear which, I am slightly embarrassed to confess, my people have not yet perfected. It was one of the priority projects we were working on when things started going at an accelerating negative slope over a year ago." Ullman turned back to the rifle that Rockson held in his hand.

"But to get back to the Long Beam rifle—it has an accuracy of ninety-three percent up to five miles. The beam can be adjusted from a half-inch kill beam to a wide-spectrum ray that spreads out ten feet per five hundred feet per second. The additional acceleration of the rifle enables it to—"

"Tell you what," Rockson said, rubbing his head. "All these numbers and equations are making my brain do flips. The only way to really understand a weapon, I think, is to use it. Why don't we go up top and try some out?"

"Up top?" Ullman gulped, growing pale again. His last journey up, when he had found Vorn or what was left of him, had been one of the most terrifying experiences of his life. Still, he couldn't appear a coward in front of these fellow Americans. "Of course, yes, let's go up. Why don't you each take a smaller and a larger accelerator for testing." Ullman handed them each a weapon from one of the many piles of the Particle Beams. The Technicians had been making the devices for so long that they had nearly run out of storage space. Pistols and rifles filled every recess, sat stacked on steel shelves from the floor to the twenty-foot ceiling above, filled drawers and bureaus. A weapons plant with no one to use its product. Until now.

Rock, Green and Slade took one of each size weapon apiece and followed Ullman around to another ladder. "It's a long climb," he breathed out wearily before even taking a step.

"We're ready, and after all that food last night," Rock said, "I think you'll be pretty strong." Ullman started up the ladder which disappeared in the gathering darkness far above. He waited for his usual fatigue to set in after any exertion and was surprised to find that he suddenly felt quite strong. He found himself growing more and more confident of his body as he easily stepped up the three hundred-foot metal-runged ladder to the surface. Ullman pushed at the heavily oiled and filthy hatchway that opened up onto the surface. He grunted, pushed again with his shoulder and the hatch flew open. A pile of black dust flew into the air on the surface, creating a throat-sticking cloud around the exit. Ullman pulled himself up and put his feet on the ground, a place he had been only ten times in his life. Rock and the Freefighters followed right behind, grateful for a little light and air even if it was in the middle of this hideous terrain. They walked several hundred feet and then stopped. "There, that black rocklike formation over there," Ullman said, pointing to a wall of almost coal-density atomic rock formation some three hundred feet away. "We've used that for testing a few times. It used to be about three times larger. Now watch," he said, obviously pleased to be giving something to the Freefighters. "You flip the activation lever here on the right side and then just sight up your target. I'll start with the lowest energy release. This dial, with the number 00 on the top, goes, as you can see if you look at your Particle Beam pistols, up to 10.00. This means from narrowest and most lethal beam to widest, most expansive ray but with the least power. Here, like this."

He aimed the pistol, raising his small, slightly trembling

hand, and sighted down the strangely-shaped, triangular tube on the top. Then he lightly pulled the trigger. A beam of black light shot out—silent, perfect. Three hundred feet away, a hole the size of a watermelon appeared in the wall of rock followed by a loud explosion as the surrounding rock blew out for another four feet in each direction. When the dust cleared, a hole had been sheared through five feet of solid rock that a man could walk through. Detroit whistled.

"And this is the lowest power of the smallest one. I want to see the big stuff."

They all tried their pistols one after another, leaving the shiny black wall like a piece of Swiss cheese, smoking and filled with holes.

"Now, the rifle Particle Accelerator works much the same way but its range and destructive capabilities are greater," Ullman said. He set one of the three-foot-long, smooth, plastic weapons down on a rock and pulled out a tripod of thin alumasynth legs from the front. "It's important to stabilize this as a movement when it is activated could have disastrous results. Control! Absolute control is important with these weapons."

He flipped up two sights on top of the rifle and said, "Look through your scopes, Freefighters. There is a tall, conelike structure forty feet high about two miles away." They found it readily through their high-power scopes. Ullman lay down, getting his gray smock even blacker from the ground dust. He sighted up and again pulled the trigger every so slightly. The cone was there, then it was gone. The beam of blackness hung in the air like a wire the entire two miles to the object. The disintegration was total and instantaneous. The sound of a powerful explosion hit their ears some seven seconds later.

"Yes, there is quite a loud explosion," Ullman explained, "but not from the conventional explosive power of dynamite or gunpowder. Here, the nuclei of the molecular structure, as they collapse, cause a roar as the atoms smash together."

"The enemy has to know something hit him," Rock said, fingering his rifle. He sighted up a similar natural formation about a mile and a half away and fired. Again, nothing. It was there, then it wasn't. The Freefighters tested the weapons for

327

over two hours, getting Ullman to explain every detail of firing, maintenance and repair. The Technician leader was proud to be of such service. The Technicians for so long had had no function. Now, their function could save America. He suddenly saw his people's complete history so differently than he ever had before. What had seemed like a wasted century, a futile attempt at meaning in an absurd world by a dying, diseased race had suddenly become a unique act of heroism. He and his people were heroes. Dedicating their lives to a weapon that could defeat the Russian invader.

Finally, as a dark, crackling storm grew overhead, Rock, his men and Ullman headed back to the underground silos. Ullman's gait was becoming strong, almost cocky. They again ate like hogs, talking and laughing with the Technicians, who were slowly and shyly opening up to the Americans. It felt both frightening and exhilarating to make contact with outsiders. As if they were speaking with aliens from outer space. They had had only their own faces to stare at.

Even Perkins and Lang seemed to be faring a little better. "Look, Rock," Lang said, as the commander of the Expedition Force strode by. "My leg. Can you believe it? In just four hours."

He pulled open the split trouser leg. The leg, which had been swollen to double its normal size and purple as a rotting piece of meat, was now shrunken nearly back to normal. The discoloration had faded to a musky red.

"It's amazing," Rock said, looking down.

"I don't feel feverish for the first time in days. It's a goddamn miracle, Rock. I'll be honest with you, I thought maybe—"

"I know, Lang, me too." He walked over to Perkins lying six feet away on his blanket mattress.

"How's it going, my man?" Rockson asked. Perkins's eyes looked more alert than they had since the ambush.

"Rock, I can't believe it but I think I'm actually starting to feel a little better. I can breathe slightly in my right lung now. And the pain is subsiding. We should get one of these for every damn Free City in America. It's incredible—with these kinds of devices, man's lifespan could be doubled, even—"

"He's right, Rock," Slade cut in, walking over to the two men. "How's the patient coming?" he asked with a twinkle. "As if I had anything to do with it. It's amazing Rock, five thousand years of medical evolution come to this—this ten-second ray. Push a button and, zap, no more illness. I can't get over it. My mind keeps looking for the loophole."

"If there's a loophole, don't tell my lung about it," Perkins said, shifting himself to an upright sitting position.

"In many ways, Rock, I think this medical discovery of the Technicians could prove to be far more important than their weaponry."

"Well, I respect your opinion, Slade, and I'm sure ultimately that will prove to be true, when we can throw away all these goddamn weapons once and for all. But until then, it's these Black Beam weapons that are going to make the Reds sit up and take notice."

Rock sat up against the concrete wall watching his men sleep on the hard floor. They snored and turned from time to time, mumbling unintelligible murmurings in their sleep. Finally Rock drifted off himself. Dreaming. Dreaming of every Free City supplied with the Particle Beam. Squads of Freefighters armed with them. He dreamed of the giant space cannons the Technicians had invented and what would happen if one were aimed at the side of a Russian military fortress. He dreamed on into the night—the most beautiful sights he had ever seen.

Thirty-Nine

The next day, Rock took Ullman aside. "I want you to pick four of your strongest men. Get some of those Particle Beam pistols and come with me. I think it's time you learned how to live as free men." Ullman gulped nervously, but he trusted Rockson enough to heed his words. Within an hour they were back up on the crusted black surface. With Rock in the lead and Ullman right beside him, the other four Technicians kept spinning around, expecting something to attack. They kept their hands on their holsters, ready to draw at any second.

"If you are to survive, Ullman, you must learn to fend for yourselves. To hunt like men."

"But Vorn was the hunter," Ullman protested. "He had been trained to—"

"Vorn is dead. Soon my people and I will have to leave. We can leave you food but it will be gone before long. You *must* learn the ways of survival. When I was young I was forced to survive on my own. I know it's not easy. But I learned then that only what each man does will keep him alive. We are born into this world alone and go out of it alone. No one can be counted on other than yourself." Ullman listened to Rockson's words, trying to digest it all. So much was changing so fast for him and his people.

"All right, Ted Rockson, we will learn from you. But don't expect us to enjoy this knowledge acquisition." Rock smiled.

"Of course not. You're not supposed to. Now tell me. Where did Vorn go when he hunted?" Rock asked.

"He said he had gone north. About twenty miles—there was some sort of fairly untouched brushland that extended for a hundred miles."

"North it is then," Rock said. "Come on, let's move out." He kept a slow pace, knowing the Technicians couldn't keep up with his long stride, but kept it going. He was going to work them as hard as he could. When he left they had to be able to survive on their own—both for their sakes and for America's. Rock couldn't afford to let anything happen to them. He led them for hours through the black land as it very slowly grew grayish. After about three hours they took a rest stop and Rock gave them each two sips of water. They waited five minutes, then moved out. Rock could feel their eyes burning into the back of his head, but he had discovered long ago that there was no man on earth who liked training missions.

"The first thing, Ullman," Rock said, turning to the other Technicians, their eyes still darting around the absolutely flat terrain wildly, looking for whatever might attack them. They had all been raised on stories of monsters that roamed the surface, had been put to bed with their mothers promising to send the "boogyman from the surface" to get them if they didn't quiet down. "And this goes for all of you," Rock continued, facing around to the other four, who started slightly when he addressed them. "Ullman is not the only one learning today. What if he dies—you will all be back where you started." The others seemed angered by Rock's commands, but listened. "You must learn to take control, each of you, to be responsible for yourselves. That way no one man will mean the life or death of your community. Do you understand?"

"We are feeding your data into our cerebellums," one of the Technicians said to Rockson.

"All right then," Rock said sharply. He wanted them to observe his every move, listen to his every word. "There is no game here on the blackness." As they walked further on, Rock picked up the pace slightly without the Technicians realizing it. "Nothing that lives would be foolish enough to venture out on this—except humans, of course. You must go beyond it, as Vorn did, to the edges where game will come." He pointed out bones in the gray dirt. "A large-horned elk. See the antlers

331

here. A male. Must have weighed three hundred pounds. God knows how it got this far." They walked on for hours, the Technicians beginning to complain.

"We should start heading back," Ullman said softly, noticing the sun beginning to fall rather rapidly toward the waiting black jaws of the horizon.

"Oh, we're not going back. We're out for days now. Didn't I mention that?" The Technicians stared at each other in horror.

"But there's no food, no blankets, no anything," one of them practically screamed.

"I know," Rockson said with a grin. "I know." They marched until dark, the air growing steadily colder. Rock had them go another hour or so into darkness. The western sky was alive with a billion flashing stars, like neon signs advertising the beauty of the night. The half moon, tinged with greenish strontium clouds rose across the vastness, slicing the sky with its sworded edge.

"Here, this is a good place to camp," Rock said as they came to a little valley in the gray sand that they could rest their backs against. "Now, I like to find a nice cozy spot—like right here," Rock said, diving down onto the dirt. "Lean up against a nice slope and make a little dirt blanket." The Technicians stared at the mad American, their eyes popping from their heads as he covered his legs and stomach with handfuls of the soil. "It's quite warm really," Rock said. "When you get cold, give it a try."

They looked at each other and then the four who had been picked to come glared at Ullman. "You entered us as factors in this ill-fated exploration," Napr the Trigonometric said. They spoke in whispers as they watched the Freefighter fall slowly asleep beneath his dirt blanket. But as the night wore on and the plains air grew chillier and chillier they imitated their survivor mentor and shoveled handfuls of dirt onto their lower bodies. It was still quite warm. Amazing. Soon, they felt warm again, their shivering and shaking melted under the heat of the sun-soaked sands. They grinned at each other.

"Maybe this Rockson really does have some overriding factors in his equation," Napr said to Ullman, who had covered himself in sand up to the neck and was staring with wonder at the flashing sky above. He had never really looked at it before.

The next morning they rose as the sun slowly edged up into the jagged pink sky. Rockson gave them each two sips of water from one of the canteens he had brought and they moved on. The terrain changed over the next few hours, growing lighter and lighter, until brownish grasses and small cactuses began appearing. The land grew rich quickly then and before they knew it they were walking through fields of brush and flowers, and small trees stood in cool groves, beckoning. The Technicians stared around in total fascination. The world outside wasn't all black.

"Shh," Rock suddenly said, putting his finger to his lips. "Now do what I do," he whispered to the others. He dropped down on one knee. "You mustn't let your prey see you. You must stay down wind of it too."

"Down what?" Ullman asked. Rock explained.

"But what is it you see out there?" Ullman asked, scanning the land ahead of them. "I see nothing."

"There!" Rock said, pointing. "By that thorned bush, about five hundred yards away. Just at the base. Some sort of small mammallike creature. Raccoon, maybe." The others sighted through their pistols and found the animal. They whispered enthusiastically.

"Yes, I see it. Yes, there it is." They were almost like children as they got into the game of hunting that Rockson was demonstrating.

"Your weapons are almost too powerful. We want to kill the game animal, not destroy it. Is there any way to set a pencil-thin beam without creating an implosion in the target?"

"Yes," Ullman answered. "This power transformer switch on the base. It reduces the charge down to just its own energy. Works more like a laser, cutting through objects, but not creating the imploding reaction."

"Good," Rock said. He carefully knelt down and took the rifle in his arms, laying down flat on the dirt. He rested both elbows on the ground, after having opened the tripod on the front end of the barrel, and sighted along the long scope. The Technicians laid down alongside Rock, spaced about five feet apart and set their rifles like him. Rockson squeezed off a shot and the light beam shot through the air, leaving the barest trace of a sizzling sound as the molecules of oxygen and hydrogen in the air were vaporized. Rock took his finger off the trigger and the dark beam instantly disappeared.

"Let's see!" Rockson said, jumping to his feet and moving at a half run to the animal he had aimed at. The Technicians followed along, racing on their much smaller legs. But they were catching the enthusiasm of the hunt and wanted to see if Rock had bagged the creature. He was the first to reach the dark, thorn-covered bush and reached down, proudly holding up some sort of half-skunk, half-raccoon creature, with thick, gray fur, black and white stripes and fangs the size of a Doberman's. The shot had penetrated its chest and the sizzling fur released a small trickle of blood through the penny-sized hole.

"Excellent shot, Ted Rockson," Ullman said, reaching over to touch the still-warm flesh of the downed game. Suddenly, he saw a whole new world opening up for the Technicians. Why, if they could go out on their own and be self-sufficient . . .

"I must try," he said, gripping the gun and sighting slowly around at the thick vegetation and brush that filled the terrain ahead. He looked and looked, straining his eyes to catch sight of anything.

"Look for movement, for something—a branch moving against the wind. Let your instinct guide you," Rock said. "You'll see. It's inside you all. The hunter, just let it come out."

Ullman breathed out and tried to feel what Rockson was saying. He let the sight lazily drift amongst the small trees. There! He suddenly saw motion. Some sort of spotted deer creature. He sat down in the position Rock had shown and fired. He sighted quickly again. Damn, the thing was gone. He had missed.

"Let's check it," Rock said. They all rushed forward; this time the Technicians nearly kept up with Rockson on their thin legs. Ullman looked around the spot at which he had fired.

"Nothing," he whispered.

"Oh no?" Rock said. "I guess this thing just died of natural causes while we were walking by." Ullman walked over to where Rock stood. There, behind a rock, the creature lay, a bloody gash in its side. "You've got to go after them," Rock said. "Often an animal won't die immediately unless it's a kill shot. They'll run, anywhere from feet to miles. And that's also when they're at their meanest. That's the other most important knowledge in hunting—tracking." The deer animal, much smaller than twentieth century deer, with black spots randomly marking its brown hide, still twitched feebly, not quite dead. "Also, if an animal is still alive—don't let it suffer." He dialed the pistol to its pencil-beam setting and fired a shot through the mammal's skull. It stopped moving instantly.

"Now, we can't take this with us but we can . . ." He showed them how to gut the animal, bleed it and then hang it high in a tree branch to avoid the clutches of other predators. "We'll get it on the way back. But in this way, you don't have to carry extra meat with you. Multiply your possible kills on a single outing." They headed off across the green and brown, slightly-more-hilly terrain, the other Technicians bagging a kill apiece, which they gutted and hung on their own, Rockson standing by but not helping.

They spent the night under the stars. This time, Rock showed them how to build a fire in the hills, to keep warm and keep nightly fanged visitors away. They stayed up until the moon had visited the sky and then gone home again, talking with Rockson about the world, about survival. Rockson knew that their very lives depended on learning these lessons well. And on becoming tough. They had to be a hundred times tougher than they were now.

The Technicians began to actually enjoy the harsh life. Their bodies ached, they could feel all their childhood fears surfacing as all beings must that have led a sheltered existence. But they also felt something new. The stirrings of pride, of manhood. They sat and talked and shared their common heritage with Rockson. Rock told them how Americans were working together to free the United States. Slowly, a warm friendship grew between Ullman and Rockson. Different as they were, they shared something in common—they were both leaders. Inside each man burned brighter than the average flame. Something pulsing, daring to reach up and out. Something that led man into new avenues, not just trampling the old.

As small as Ullman and the others were, Rock could see that they were growing—inside. They had been led down the wrong road. Now, the neurosis, the self-doubt of the entire race was wearing off—through the hardships of the real world. There was just one more lesson that Ullman must learn before the race could truly begin to change.

The next day they were on the hunt again. The land now was almost bountiful. They had come nearly forty miles from the silos and marched through rounded hills covered with a dark orange grass and low, purple bushes covered with long, prickly thorns. Animal life was plentiful, even birds could be heard calling from time to time. The Technicians were in awe. They had never seen so much life before.

"It is amazing, Rockson," Ullman said, walking in step alongside the American Freefighter. "We honestly believed that the entire world had been made black. But to see so much life, I—" They were just stepping into a grove of trees when a shape dashed from within and, with one swipe of its immense paw, slashed one of the Technicians, Napr, into a bloody corpse. He fell to the dirt, throat severed, blood pouring out across his small body. The predator, as large as a tiger but black, black as coal with one large white spot on each side, grabbed Napr by the neck and lifted him as if he were a doll, immediately running off into the woods.

The others hadn't had time to respond. Even Rock had just raised his pistol when the three hundred-pound monster was gone. The other Technicians stared after the fleeing beast with shock on their thin mouths. "It got Napr. It killed Napr," they mumbled over and over. Even Ullman seemed to have gone catatonic.

"Snap out of it," Rock yelled, ripping them from their stupor. "This is the reality of life out here. There are many things that will try to kill you, eat you. It's not a question of just going out with your beams and gathering dinner as if you were in what the ancients called a supermarket. If you hunt, others will hunt you. That is the way. You must be prepared at all times to kill or die." Ullman straightened up at the words.

"Yes, you are right, Ted Rockson. We cannot fall into the old ways of self-pity. We must become fighters. I am going to get it!" He marched forward with his pistol held hip-high, not even looking back to see if the others were following. Rock moved closely behind, then the others, following in back of him, huddled together, searching the terrain—the trees and bushes, with their terror-stricken eyes, waiting for the next attack.

With Ullman in the lead they walked through thickening woods for an hour, following the blood drops from Napr's body. The bark on the trees grew thick and turned almost reddish, the ground became covered with some sort of toadstool fungus, as big as pumpkins and twisted into gnarled black and brown shapes.

"Here," Ullman said, kneeling down to look closer at flecks of blood on some five-pointed leaves. Rock watched approvingly. Someone was learning something. With his own Particle Beam pistol at the ready, Rockson let Ullman continue. There was only one way to become a man. The hard way. Ullman pushed the bushes ahead of him carefully aside, walking as quietly as he could. Somehow, his ancient instincts, instincts of hunting and stalking that were buried in his memory cells from tens of thousands of years earlier, were opening up, giving him an internal knowledge that he didn't know he had.

They heard low ripping and growling sounds. Ullman walked forward toward the sound, and stepped into a clearing surrounded by rotting logs. There it was. The black-furred cat, its ivory-white fangs tearing into Napr's guts. Its black face was red with the blood of the prey. The victim's entire throat, chest and stomach had been torn out and eaten. Ullman felt sick to his stomach for a moment and instantly realized that he had seconds to live. He raised the pistol just as the beast, its red eyes wide as suns, jumped up and rushed toward him. He aimed the pistol in his trembling hands as the carnivore bared its dripping fangs and, growling loudly, advanced in a direct line toward Ullman. His hands froze. He felt his muscles stiffen

337

with fear. The creature had already killed Napr—how could *he* stop it? He was not brave. Why didn't Rockson kill it? He looked around quickly but somehow Rockson wasn't there. The creature speeded up, snarling, its big body breaking into a run. It reared back on its powerful haunches and leaped from twelve feet away. Ullman saw its front claws reaching— reaching for him. Somehow, without even quite realizing it, he raised his beam pistol and fired. A medium energy ray of black death hit the killer's chest. The scream of the huge cat was the only sound that filled the clearing. It fell to the earth, dead. Smoke sizzled from the two-inch hole that neatly pierced its body. Its big eyes were wide open, staring up at Ullman who stood only feet away.

Trembling, the Technician leader let the pistol fall to his side. He stood there in a daze. He had killed it. He, Ullman, had destroyed the monster.

"Good shot," Rock said, walking around in front of the Technician leader. He stared at the dead cat.

"Rockson, where were you? I almost was negated by the creature!"

"Almost," Rockson replied. "I was right behind you, Ullman. I couldn't shoot it. You had to. So you could learn something about yourself. That you are strong. That you have power. Now you are a man."

Ullman heard the words strangely in his mind. He said them silently in the back of his throat, where all silent discourse takes place.

A man! He was a man! The words sounded unfamiliar. But powerful. He *was* a man. A man who had dominance over the beasts, over his environment. The Technicians had thought themselves weaklings—so they were. But now Ullman saw them, saw himself as something different—something to be reckoned with. A thrill of pride rippled along the small man's backbone. The others would be in awe of him now, as they had been of Vorn. Of the hunter. But he would not let himself be the only one. It was as Rockson said, they all must learn to become powerful. They must all become *men*.

"I thank you, Ted Rockson," Ullman said, bending down and touching the claws of the fallen man-eater. "Suddenly I

338

begin to understand you. You are a far deeper and wiser man than I had realized."

"No, Ullman, I was you when I was a young man. I know what you are going through—the tests of courage and cowardice that each man must experience and pass or fail in life. I know that you and all your people have it in you—it's just been suppressed for so long, while you worked in your subterranean machine shops. It is good to create and build inventions for mankind, but you must live *in* the world."

"Yes, Rockson, you are accurate," Ullman said, nodding his bald head. "Courage = death challenge divided by depth of experience × constant .3278885."

Rock grinned. "Something like that." They found a large pole to carry the man-eater on and tied it up so that it hung upside-down. Two of the Technicians took turns at the back while Rockson held up the front of the beast. Slowly, they headed back to the silos with their prize catch. And more. A changed Ullman. A man who would really be able to lead his people for the first time.

Forty

Ullman and ten of the Technicians came to the surface to see Rockson and his party off. The rest stayed below. They were still frightened but they were learning, learning the truths of survival that Rockson had taught to Ullman.

"Goodbye," Ullman said, looking up at Rockson and the others who were all mounted and ready to ride. The two remaining pack 'brids were loaded with Particle Beam pistols and rifles—fifty of each. It was just a start.

"We'll be back to get more weapons," Rockson said. "Once the other Freefighters of America get wind of these, they'll be banging down your doors."

"We'll be ready for them," Ullman said. "It is time my people had intercourse with the outside world. We can remain moles, hidden deep underground no longer. Life = sensitivity of sensory receptors × new experience + pleasure/pain factor of .3332."

"We'll meet again," Rock said, smiling.

"Again, Ted Rockson." Ullman let his ever-serious, pencil mark of a mouth bend open into a smile. The Freefighters rode off into the falling night.

The next few days were good. The men were all in excellent moods from their successful mission. They had gone out to get something and had done it. A mission that might well someday go down in the history books, equal in importance to the ride of Paul Revere or the crossing of the Delaware. The Freefighters were filled with a bursting pride to have contributed so much to their country.

They rode single-file almost due east, retracing their steps. It took nearly a day and a half to get out of the black soot that surrounded the silos, and both the men and the 'brids were glad to see it go, as the fine-particled dirt got into every pore, every mucus membrane of the body. But the black turned to gray and then to an orange-green as they reached some flatlands, dry but covered with a fuzz of vegetation, an occasional prairie cactus with its dark violet flowers on the top. Rock was much more relaxed than he had been on the outward journey. And thank God he didn't have to worry about Perkins and Lang. Both were regaining their strength daily. Lang's leg was nearly back to normal, though it was slightly scarred. Plastic surgery back in C.C. would take care of that. Perkins's lung was functioning almost perfectly. Slade took daily stethoscope checks and reported that the rasping sound of air being drawn through a punctured lung was gone. "Should be good as new," he told the patient. Rockson wished they could have taken one of the medical machines, but the things weighed nearly half a ton when they were all hooked up. That would have to wait.

It was the weapons that were the priority. Just the feel of the Particle Beam pistol on his left hip brought a smile to his face. Rockson knew what it could do. The knowledge was awesome. He still carried the shotgun pistol on his right side. It was too familiar to discard. Besides you never knew when one of these new-fangled weapons was going to go haywire. No, he'd keep both.

All the man were now armed with the beam weapons but were unable to get rid of their lifelong pistols and rifles. They rode along with their double sets of weaponry. Only Archer and Chen stuck to their tried and true ways, and refused the new devices—Archer preferring his crossbow and hands, and Chen his martial arts, nunchakas and the exploding star knives which had proved their worth in the parakite attack.

As they reached the outer edges of the blasted terrain Rock realized the place was familiar. There—ahead. Bones. A field of bleached bones, looking like a dinosaur graveyard. Only the fossils were Russians. The Freefighters rode past, looking down on the huge carcasses of their pack 'brids. The rib cages of the animals were enormous. No wonder they were so strong, their bones were thick as small trees. Then past the dead squad of commandos. They lay right where they had fallen, each one posed in some bizarre frozen moment of death. Only there was not a trace of flesh on them. The buzzards and rodents and trillions of bacteria in the air had licked their bodies down to gleaming white skeletons, grinning the eternal smile of death. Their empty eye sockets, an occasional worm crawling through, stared up at the Freefighters as they rode past. The dead and the living taking each other in. But it was the living that Rockson watched for. The dead hadn't hurt him yet.

"We have them now, sir," Major Chernik said to Colonel Killov. "It's air reconnaissance reporting in from thirty thousand feet above the graveyard of our parakite commandos. They've picked up a line of men atop mutant horses, heading directly past the spot. Heading east, sir."

"That's them." Killov's eyes burned with murderous fire. Rockson—he had a chance to get Rockson now. Somehow he knew that the man was in that group. "Excellent. Let's go." The two men headed out to Killov's staff car, waiting directly outside the Center, and were whisked to the Denver KGB airport. Killov had insisted that he have his own airfield as KGB maneuvers occurred at odd times of the day and night. Zhabnov had acquiesced. And now Mr. President had tried to have him eliminated. Killov smirked. He had to hand it to Zhabnov for guts. He hadn't thought the fool had it in him. The only question was whether Vassily was in on it too. If that was the case, it would call for drastic countermeasures. Actions Killov had hoped he wouldn't have to carry out.

But, all that was for later—after this Ted Rockson was captured. That would break the back of the American resistance. He could put Rockson behind bars and televise it every night. Show them what power their "hero" had now.

The staff car screeched to a stop just behind the fence that ran the perimeter of the KGB runways. Killov was greeted by the commander of the helicopter Death Squad, Captain Potavka.

"We're ready, sir. The helicopters are warmed up and ready to go."

Killov looked at the ten waiting Soyuz II jet attack helicopters, part of the Death Squad's fleet. "Are they equipped with everything I asked for—? The gas—everything?"

"Down to the finest detail, sir," Potavka reassured him. He led Killov to the lead helicopter, its blades trembling slightly, waiting for activation. The KGB colonel slid into the seat next to the pilot and waved his hand in an upward motion.

"Go! Go!" The pilot spoke into his chin mike and started the engines. The rotors above spun faster and faster until they were a blur in the night air. The other nine attack craft roared into life, gunners already at their posts in large, plastic bubbles on each side, dual machine guns poking out.

Clearance was given from the control tower for takeoff and the lead chopper tilted up into the air, joined by the other nine helicopters, right behind it. They reached a speed of 200 mph and then threw on the jet engines in the rear. The craft lurched forward and tore into the clear, purple-tinged night at 425 mph. They flew in a V-formation with Killov's helicopter in the lead, about one hundred feet apart, a flock of black hawks with red stars on the side.

Killov looked down over the countryside, the vast dead stretches of land mute testimony to the damage the Russians had done. And there would be more, much more to come. They flew for two hours, the pilot at last announcing to Killov that they were within thirty miles of the reconnaissance sighting. The KGB colonel pulled the mike down from the black helmet over his head and spoke. "This is your leader, Colonel Killov," he announced to the other craft. His voice boomed out from speakers on each helicopter. "You've all been trained for this mission. You are elite troops so I know that you are ready. But let me stress once again that this Ted Rockson must be taken alive. Try to take the others prisoner, but if you can't—. But Rockson must not be hurt. That's why we have the gas and the netting. The man that takes him alive will get one hundred thousand rubles and the Medal of the Supreme Soviet Hero. The man who kills him will die the most excruciatingly painful death ever experienced on this Earth. That is all." He lifted the mike from his lips and stared out through a polarized blue visor at the rapidly brightening land below as the sun began its trillionth climb into the terrestrial sky.

The Freefighters rode past the dead KGB commandos and on toward the fogbanks ahead. "We'll get to the edge of the fog and then rest for the morning. The 'brids have been going for nearly fourteen hours," Rock told the men as they marched toward the rising sun, strangely twisted into a flattened pancake shape by the thick, radioactive mists on the far horizon.

Suddenly Rock's senses went on full alert. Something was wrong. Something was going to happen at any moment. He threw his hand up, and the party came to an abrupt stop. Rockson looked around the land ahead for a possible ambush. No, not there. From the sky.

"Dismount! Quickly, men, and get out your Particle Beam rifles." Although they saw nothing, the men followed Rock's command instantly. They had been through too much with him not to totally trust his instincts. They had just hit the ground and were unwrapping their plastic Black Beam weapons when the unmistakable deep rumble of a jet engine reached through the morning air. More than one—many. In seconds the sound grew louder and off in the distance Rock could see, through the scope on his Particle Beam rifle, the fleet of helicopters coming at them.

"Got a fight coming. Big one," Rock said to the others. "But they're in for a big surprise. Now we've all been working with these but they're still new. Just remember not to fire ahead of the choppers as you would with a machine gun. These babies are instantaneous." The Freefighters found what cover they could in the low bushes and got into good firing positions, lying on their stomachs, setting the rifles on their front tripods as they had practiced. Even Chen grudgingly took a rifle and set it up.

The helicopters came in fast, shutting their jet engines only

344

when about a mile away. They spread out from a V to a straight-line formation, headed down to an altitude of a hundred feet and came in for the kill.

Three of the Freefighters fired at the closest two choppers. The black beams hung in the air for the merest second and then were gone. Both helicopters exploded in midair, sending out balls of fire in every direction, nearly igniting the craft to each side of them. They plummeted to the earth like meteors, crashing in flaming wreckage. The radios of the helicopters blared, screaming at one another, "What the hell is going on?"

Rockson and Berger sighted up the helicopters on each end of the advancing line of KGB jetcraft. They gently squeezed the triggers and the Particle Beams shot out as silent as a ray of light, finding their targets some two thousand feet away. Both choppers disintegrated into a screaming, burning metal high in the air. They fell in a shower of glowing parts to the orange-lit ground, growing ever brighter from the now-full sun.

Panic set in among the Russian helicopter crews. Nearly half their number had been blasted out of the sky in a matter of seconds.

Killov looked over at his pilot and motioned with his eyes to turn and move back. The chopper pilot wordlessly responded, taking the lead craft into a sudden dive and turning at a sharp angle around and underneath the still-advancing attack force. Then he tore off straight back, out of range of whatever weapon was being fired.

The pilot of the second command ship screamed out orders over the mike. "Fuck taking anybody alive. Fire. Fire those damned missiles. Whatever's shooting at us is in that grove of trees right ahead." In each ship the men prepared to fire the air-to-ground missiles as the helicopters rushed forward drawn like moths to a flame.

On the ground, the Freefighters took careful aim and squeezed off another series of shots. Eight beams of the blackest light ever seen on Earth shot out in an absolutely straight line at the helicopter fleet. Four craft were hit. They exploded as one, sending a wave of white-hot shrapnel into the air and to the ground. The crews of the disintegrated helicopters barely had time to scream before their bodies were melted into the atoms of steel walls and rotors in the burning hell that consumed them.

The pilot of the sole remaining craft opened his eyes wide in horror. He was the last. The rest were all gone. Every one. What in his mother's name was going on? It was survival time. He tilted the control stick full forward and the chopper broke into a steep dive. He pulled the rear gyro as hard as he could to the right, whipping the craft into a full circle. Keeping just feet above the ground and pulling the control shaft of the chopper madly from side to side to avoid being a clear target, the sole surviving helicopter of the elite KGB attack squadron fled for its life. The pilot threw the jet engine of the craft on, knowing that he might lose control. The helicopter shot forward, barely skimming little copses of trees. Yes, they would make it, they—

The Freefighters fired at the fleeing Red chopper, this time four black beams finding the target at once. The craft evaporated into gas from the combined energy of the shots. Not even wreckage—just a flaming vapor that quickly burned itself into nothingness.

Killov watched with long-range binoculars from some eight miles off where he had had the helicopter pilot stop and hover for a minute. His face was livid, his body shaking uncontrollably. The pilot looked at the KGB leader with terror. Every one of the fleet was gone, smoking ruins on the ground. He had almost lost his life. That Ted Rockson was among the bandits who had fired on them—of that he was sure. But what weapon could do damage like that? The Russians had nothing in their arsenals to match it. Killov had never even heard of such a weapon. A black beam that destroyed anything.

"Denver, Denver!" he yelled at the pilot and the craft tore off toward the East and thickening clouds. He was shaken to his core. Things were worse, much worse than he could have imagined. If the rebels had weapons like that, it could change the entire balance of power in the world. Could mean the end of the Soviet Empire. He and Zhabnov and Vassily would have to stop their bickering and ally themselves together to fight this common threat. Or else they'd all go down in the blast of the black beam.

The Freefighters rose from their firing positions and looked at the piles of smoking debris that littered the hills ahead of them. Rockson clicked the safety on his Particle Beam rifle and turned to Detroit.

"The thing works. The goddamned thing really works."

THE BLACK EAGLES
by Jon Lansing

#1: HANOI HELLGROUND   (1249, $2.95)
They're the best jungle fighters the United States has to offer, and
no matter where Charlie is hiding, they'll find him. They're the
greatest unsung heroes of the dirtiest, most challenging war of all
time. They're THE BLACK EAGLES.

#2: MEKONG MASSACRE   (1294, $2.50)
Falconi and his Black Eagle combat team are about to stake a claim
on Colonel Nguyen Chi Roi—and give the Commie his due. But
American intelligence wants the colonel alive, making this the
Black Eagles' toughest assignment ever!

#3: NIGHTMARE IN LAOS   (1341, $2.50)
There's a hot rumor that the Russians are secretly building a
nuclear reactor in Laos. And the Black Eagles are going to have to
move fast—to prevent the nuclear fallout from hitting the fan!

McLEANE'S RANGERS
by John Darby

#1: BOUGAINVILLE BREAKOUT   (1207, $2.50)
Even the Marines call on McLeane's Rangers, the toughest,
meanest, and best fighting unit in the Pacific. Their first adventure
pits the Rangers against the entire Japanese garrison in Bougainville. The target—an ammo depot invulnerable to American air
attack . . . and the release of a spy.

#2: TARGET RABAUL   (1271, $2.50)
Rabaul—it was one of the keys to the control of the Pacific and the
Japanese had a lock on it. When nothing else worked, the Allies
called on their most formidable weapon—McLeane's Rangers, the
fearless jungle fighters who didn't know the meaning of the word
quit!

#3: HELL ON HILL 457   (1343, $2.50)
McLeane and his men make a daring parachute drop in the middle
of a heavily fortified Jap position. And the Japs are dug in so deep
in a mountain pass fortress that McLeane may have to blow the
entire pass to rubble—and his men in the bargain!

Available wherever paperbacks are sold, or order direct from the
Publisher. Send cover price plus 50¢ per copy for mailing and
handling to Zebra Books, 475 Park Avenue South, New York, N.Y.
10016. DO NOT SEND CASH.

OTHER BOOKS ON THE WORLD AT WAR
by Lawrence Cortesi

D-DAY MINUS 1	(1318, $3.25)
THE DEADLY SKIES	(1132, $3.25)
PACIFIC HELLFIRE	(1179, $3.25)
PACIFIC STRIKE	(1041, $2.95)
TARGET: TOKYO	(1256, $3.25)
VALOR AT LEYTE	(1213, $3.25)
VALOR AT SAMAR	(1226, $2.75)
THE BATTLE FOR MANILA	(1334, $3.25)

Available wherever paperbacks are sold, or order direct from the Publisher. Send cover price plus 50¢ per copy for mailing and handling to Zebra Books, 475 Park Avenue South, New York, N.Y. 10016. DO NOT SEND CASH.